PRAISE FOR *THE SHANGHAI WIFE*

'A superb debut, conjuring all the mayhem of pre-revolutionary China through the eyes of a young Australian woman. I hope Emma Harcourt writes many more!'

Paul Ham, historian, author and journalist

'With extraordinary historical and sensory detail, Emma Harcourt brings the world of early twentieth century Shanghai to contemporary readers. Into this lush and complex setting comes a young woman straining against convention. In Annie, Harcourt has created a dynamic and vivid character, a woman both conflicted and courageous, a woman readers will fall in love with.'

Kathryn Heyman, author of *Storm and Grace*

'Emma's book is lyrical and beautiful . . . she has written a love story as dangerous and exotic as the worlds she describes.'

Caroline Overington, author and journalist

'An immersive tale of illicit love set in Shanghai during the Chinese anti-Imperialist movement of 1925. Propels you straight to the streets of 1920s Shanghai.'

Nicole Alexander, author

'It's got it all, romance, politics, mystery, controversy, forbidden love and death. A great read, travel back to Shanghai in the 1920s and enjoy!'

Beauty & Lace

'Emma Harcourt's . . . writing style is beautiful; riddled with descriptive prose and glorious snapshots of the exotic richness of China's elegant 1920s, along with the dangers lying on Shanghai's rabbit-warren of streets . . . excellently researched.'

Starts at Sixty

'*The Shanghai Wife* will delight fans of historical fiction who like to be taken places and told terrific stories, as well as anyone who enjoys experiencing a life lived to the full in one of the world's most fabulous cities at a very interesting time.'

Better Reading

Photo: Noel Mclaughlin

Emma Harcourt is an author, researcher and journalist. She began writing historical fiction while completing the Faber Academy Writing a Novel course and now spends all her available hours either researching history or writing about it. As a young adult she travelled to Florence to learn Italian and fell in love with the place. From there she moved to London where she lived for ten years before eventually returning to Australia to raise her son. She's now based in Sydney with her teenage daughters. When she's not writing or researching history, you'll find her reading in her garden. Emma is the author of critically lauded, internationally published bestseller *The Shanghai Wife*. Her second book, *The Brightest Star*, is set in Renaissance Florence.

Also by Emma Harcourt

The Shanghai Wife

The Brightest Star

EMMA HARCOURT

First Published 2022
First Australian Paperback Edition 2022
ISBN 9781489249166

Published by
HQ Fiction
An imprint of Harlequin Enterprises (Australia) Pty Limited (ABN 47 001 180 918),
a subsidiary of HarperCollins Publishers Australia Pty Limited (ABN 36 009 913 517)
Level 13, 201 Elizabeth St
SYDNEY NSW 2000
AUSTRALIA

A catalogue record for this book is available from the National Library of Australia
www.librariesaustralia.nla.gov.au

Printed and bound in Australia by McPherson's Printing Group

For Mum

PROLOGUE

Villa Careggi, 1479

It was the wet nurse who sealed Luna's fate. So powerless a figure and yet her small act of defiance changed the path of the Fusili family history forever. None could have foreseen the turn of events she would initiate by letting the baby cry. Such an innocent sound and so loud.

*

'Deliver her to the nuns; I do not want this curse upon my family. Quickly, before my husband arrives.' Giulia Fusili fell back against the bed. It had taken more energy than she realised to speak.

'Hold her, signora, just for a moment, and you will surely feel her goodness. She needs her mamma.' The wet nurse, Livia, thrust the swaddled newborn at her mother but Giulia turned her head away and dug under the coverlet, refusing to touch her baby daughter, for she knew once she had the warm, sleeping bundle in her arms, she would not be able to give her up. The baby's smell was already more familiar than any other in the room.

'She's waking, mistress. Look at her little smudge of a nose and see how she searches for your milk.' The baby had indeed begun to squirm and she let out a gentle whimper, no louder than the puff of air escaping from the pillow Giulia pressed against.

'You will be her milk mother now, not I. Take her away.' Giulia exhaled sharply at another wave of pain as the midwife pressed a cloth to her temple. Giving birth was a pitiable task when there was no reward. She'd thought the birthing pains would stop once the babe was out but her belly was pierced by the same excruciating tightenings as in labour. This was some trickery of the female form, kept secret from young women.

She fixed her gaze on the midwife beside her. The woman dabbed at her brow, squeezed the cloth into the rose-infused water and dabbed again, her expression unreadable. Not for the first time, Giulia wished she'd been born a man. She pushed the woman's hand away and tried to raise herself more comfortably against the goose-feather pillows. She was not even in her own home and longed for the familiarity of her marriage bed. This room was too grand for a clothmaker's wife but her husband had been right to insist she leave the city with so much plague about; il segno was like the Devil's breath, dropping innocents where they stood. So many good families in Florence were suffering, but she was protected here in the hills of Careggi, within the walls of the

Medici country estate. Even so, she felt ill at ease to be in this imposing home where Lorenzo de' Medici and his wife, Clarice, spent much of their time. The open loggia on the first floor was superior to any she'd stood in and the decorated corridors were constantly busy with servants. The lady of the house had been gracious in her welcome, but Clarice was preoccupied by her own baby boy, Giuliano, still a whelp, who she was determined not to lose to an infant death like the twins.

At that moment, he struck up a wailing somewhere in the house and his healthy cries carried all the way through to the birthing chamber. When she'd first arrived, Giulia had found comfort in knowing she would be delivered of her firstborn in a house of children, but now she heard the sound of the newest Medici baby with a jealous ear.

The midwife raised the cloth to her brow once more and Giulia lifted her head proudly. This woman had helped birth ten babies in nine years, none of them touched by the Devil as hers had been. She would stare down her judgement.

There was a noise from the side of the room and she saw her friend Elisabetta had not left as she'd asked. Instead she hovered with the cloth bundle in her arms. The cotton had begun to discolour.

'I thought you had already gone to do my bidding,' Giulia said. Only hours earlier she'd kissed Elisabetta's hands as she placed a soothing poultice on her belly; now Giulia eyed her friend wearily.

'I could not leave till I heard sense from your lips once more.' The young lady held firm to the bundle which had begun to mark her dress with its seeping fluid. 'I beg you not to abandon your own child.'

Giulia considered her friend, so sure of herself and still fresh-cheeked despite the hours spent assisting through the birth. Elisabetta had always spoken her mind more freely than any amongst their circle of friends and whilst her forthright nature did not endear her to many, it was one of the things Giulia admired about her. She couldn't imagine being in this big, strange house without Elisabetta but her well-meaning talk was simply too much right now.

'Don't make this harder than it already is. I need you to do my bidding.'

Giulia saw her friend's brow crease. She steadied herself, preparing to defend her decision, but a flood of warm liquid surged from between her legs and with it another wave of agonising pain gripped her. It was all she could do to stay sitting upright. She shifted in the damp bedsheets and saw how Elisabetta looked at her, how everyone would look at her now—with pity.

'All I suggest is that you sleep first, regain your sensibilities and then consider your choices. You may feel very differently in the morn.'

'And give my husband time to blame me for this thing that I did birth? No, I most certainly will not wait for that!' Giulia was annoyed now; she had little enough energy without wasting it on this argument. 'Did I not ask you to take the filthy cord for burning? It must go into the fire downstairs without delay, else our sin will fester like maggots feeding.' She didn't bother to keep the sharpness from her tone.

'I am worried for you, Giulia, and for your baby. There are some, myself amongst them, who do not believe the act of conceiving a child is sinful. You and handsome Vincenzio have created a beautiful baby in the image of our Virgin Mother. Can anything be more pure?' Elisabetta shifted her hold on the cloth parcel as she spoke, her fingers pressing into the soft bulge.

'Have you looked upon the broken thing?' Giulia's voice was fearful. 'What do you know of motherhood, anyway? You're lucky to still be whole and as yet free.' She sighed deeply. 'This day was to be my glory and it has ended most monstrously.'

As though she'd heard her mother's words, the baby cried again and so intimate was the sound, it made Giulia's heart contract with a pain more fierce than that which racked her body. 'I am spent. Go and do my bidding, I beg you.'

Elisabetta left the room. The wet nurse still waited with the newborn in her arms. Giulia silently cursed the exhaustion that threatened to drag her down with its intensity but she could not rest until the pair was gone. She considered the woman standing by the bed, no more than a girl, heavy breasted after the plague had taken her own babe, and now about to lose her chance at mothering the broken thing she held. The woman's son had died swiftly, between dawn and dusk of the same day. A flicker of compassion stirred in Giulia but she took a deep breath; this was no time for weakness.

'Take her away now. Do as I say, Livia. She will be well cared for at the convent and I will still pay you until the end of the month.'

'Please, mistress, every whelp deserves a mother's love. The foot can be hidden and her face is pretty enough.'

'Quieten your tongue else I'll cast you out at the same time. Foolish chit of a girl. You are too young to understand.' Giulia turned to the window where the daylight was beginning to fade. 'So much damage will come.' Her voice was pained. 'All because of this deformed babe. I have no doubt the good people of Florence will blame me. I would do ever so myself. They will paint me as a wretch who bore a demon in her womb. My husband's eye will begin to wander and I will be turned out, the Fusili name lost to me ...' Her voice dropped to a whisper as she fumbled with her hair and rolled it into a knot. 'Vincenzio has been working diligently to build his business so that we may enjoy a better life. What would this do to him ... to our future?' She clutched her hands together to still their shaking.

The baby snuffled and squirmed and Livia rocked the small bundle, shaking her head as she watched her mistress, but she said no more. The door closed quietly behind her as she left.

Giulia lay back. She would bear other children for her husband, of this she was sure, and the firstborn must be strong and healthy: a son and heir whose looks would rival those of the Medici princes. She must pray.

In the next room, the baby squirmed with longing for her mother's familiar feel and smell. The wet nurse, believing there was no immediate urgency to depart for the convent, settled herself comfortably against the bolster of her bed and opened her blouse. 'Eat, little one, hush now,' she crooned softly, rocking herself back and forth as she pressed the baby's face into her bosom. It was a relief to feel the pressure of her milk ease and she sang a lullaby as the baby drank. The tune was one she'd sung to her own darling babe. Had it already been one moon? This baby girl sucked much more strongly and Livia cursed the heartlessness of her mistress. Still, her husband would be angry as the Devil himself if she came home without a wage and she would need this lady's good word if she was to find another position.

In her chamber, Giulia crossed the floor on all fours to kneel in front of the image of the Virgin and Child that rested in a gilded frame atop the wooden dresser. She supposed that most women suffered this crippling tiredness after the birthing and sucked in another lungful of air. The hard floor pressed uncomfortably into her knees, a poor distraction from the belt of pain that tightened in her belly again and again.

'Hail Mary, full of grace, our Lord is with thee. Blessed art thou amongst women, and blessed is the fruit of thy womb, Jesus. Holy Mary, Mother of God, pray for us sinners, now and at the hour of our death.' Then she added her own prayer: 'Heavenly Mother, forgive me my sins, so that I may bear children in your perfect image. I ask this not out of pride, but for my most cherished husband.' She sat back on her haunches and cradled the weight of her empty belly. Blood droplets filled the cracks in the wood. 'I ask this in the name of the Father, the Son and the Holy Spirit. Amen.' She did not rise until the final supplication was fulfilled then crept back to her bed, whispering incantations. 'May God give me a child without fatigue or danger, a baby boy who makes urine of silver and gold.'

It had been three days since her labour began under a waxing Moon after two sennights confined to her chamber in this vast country villa. Vincenzio had been due to join her, but the arrival of a shipment of English wool had been delayed and so he'd remained in the city to negotiate a fair price; he trusted no one else. The business was doing well and Giulia was proud of his ambition. Still, was it not a husband's place to be with his wife at a time like this? His journey north through the contado would not be long, yet the country road was poor and uneven, dipping into valleys and along dangerous ridges. She'd heard talk of brazen attacks on travellers too since the return of il segno. Her heart raced. What if Vincenzio had been attacked? She could not do this without him. She whispered an entreaty to St Christopher and crossed herself three times, listening hopefully for the sound of horses' hooves, a rare occurrence these days since her host had shut the estate to all except the most essential suppliers and expected guests like Vincenzio Fusili. Despite Giulia's protestations, even the local doctor had been denied entry, for fear his ministrations to the sick of the village would put them all in jeopardy.

So it was that Clarice Medici's woman had assisted at Giulia's birthing. The midwife said that a baby born under the eye of a full Moon carried dangerous possibilities of godless dark magic and a lifetime of ill health. The portent in her words had scared Giulia so she'd pushed as hard as she could to get her baby out before that ominous Moon glowed whole. But her baby did not come quickly. She ignored the woman's entreaties to stop pushing; this was what she'd been born to do and her absolute conviction of bearing a son and heir for her master kept her focused through the increasingly frequent bouts of agony. Still she could not force her son into the daylight, and when the dusk closed in on the night of the Moon's fullness, Giulia felt an overpowering dread. She cried out unremittingly as the pain consumed her mind and body, and when her daughter was born malformed and small, she cried out again with disappointment and horror at the thing that slipped from between her legs.

The candles lit to help the midwife through the final stage of birthing gave off a cloying heat. Giulia's fresh nightgown was already wet with sweat and blood. She called for assistance but the midwife was yet to return from emptying the pail of dirty water. Giulia tugged the linen sheet up around her throbbing breasts, recoiling at the fetid smell; how fast the sheets had soiled again. She pulled her nightshirt over her head, letting it drop to the floor. Then she reached for one of the folded lengths of linen on the table beside her bed and slowly wrapped it around her chest. She pulled another length of linen to her and stuffed it between her legs. There was one more clean nightshirt hanging from a hook on her bedhead. She managed to tug on it till it fell into her hands and was grateful to the generosity of her hosts for such fine cotton. At last she could lie back again, exhausted but infinitely more comfortable.

The last of the dusk light slipped away in the square of sky Giulia could see through the window. Hurrying to make space for the impatient Moon, she thought, so that its glow might bewitch them all. She shifted onto her side and watched the door instead. Vincenzio must surely arrive soon.

From somewhere outside, there was a whistle and the rumble of barrels rolling across the courtyard. She thought of her own empty house and wondered how her husband had managed without her housekeeping skills. For a moment her mind turned to the horrible possibility that Vincenzio had another woman in her place. She shook her head; her husband loved her, of that she was sure, though would any man wait for a sickly wife who bore him crippled offspring? She must get back to Florence as soon as she could.

Yet here she lay, exhausted and weak, which she would not mind if she had a son to nurture as her body recovered. She looked over to the empty crib. Bedridden, she would be vulnerable to rumour and blame. Only her husband could stop such vicious talk.

Giulia called for her servant Camilla, an older widow who had been her companion since before she was married. Camilla must wait on Vincenzio; Giulia could not trust any of the household servants. The woman stood in the doorway staring at her mistress whilst fingering a string of wooden rosary beads. Usually, the rhythmic click soothed Giulia, but not this evening.

'Come in, come in.' Giulia tried to keep the tiredness from her voice. 'I am not dying.' Even though the bloodied cloths and pails of pinkish water had been cleared away, Giulia supposed Camilla still saw a room of evil. She sighed and continued in a gentler tone, 'Is everything laid out for the master's arrival?'

Camilla nodded.

'Make sure they serve him the wine we received from the Lana Guild. It arrived last week. The vintage is ready to drink. Don't let his cup run empty.'

'Is that not the wine set aside for the baptismal celebration?'

The question was innocent but Giulia was in no mood to be challenged. 'What if it is? Do not question me today of all days; I have barely the wit to speak.'

The rosary beads clicked loudly in Camilla's hands.

'Forgive me, Camilla.' Giulia wiped her brow and breathed deeply. 'I did not mean to sound harsh, only this day has drained the very marrow from my bones. Tonight the wine is needed.'

Giulia blew out the candle closest to her, but still the room felt unbearably warm. The air caught in her nostrils. Another rush of hot liquid seeped from between her legs.

'Did you finish sorting the linen? I will need more before the night sets in. The birth has left my body in a pitiable state.'

'I will fetch clean sheets,' Camilla answered but she did not move.

The first star shone beyond the glass-panelled window. Giulia took a deep breath and silently offered a prayer to the heavens that tonight there would be stars in the sky to balance out the full Moon's wanton light. She felt an urge for the sting of cold air upon her cheek.

'Come, come, Camilla, I am not contagious! Must I even ask you to open the window?'

The woman skirted round the bed, crossing herself discreetly as she went. Giulia saw herself as the maid must: a pale-faced, weakened mistress. She breathed through the stab of pain in her abdomen as she raised herself to sit again and frowned. From her maid's demeanour she guessed the household was already talking and any further frailty now from her would be taken as a sign she was most assuredly to blame for the baby's deformity.

'Get rid of all these candles so that I may breathe clean air. And pass me the stone. I will flush this curse out myself.'

Giulia clutched the cold, waxen rock in her hand and rubbed it across her belly until another wave of pain overtook her. She would take on whatever challenges the Heavenly Mother saw fit to send her way, as long as Mary kept her in Vincenzio's favour.

Camilla curtseyed and crossed herself, stopping by the window momentarily to acknowledge the full Moon. Giulia heard her soft incantation, 'Benvenuta Luna che mi porti fortuna', but did not chastise her servant, for surely they could all do with some luck this night.

The evening's cool breeze so longed for by the mistress rattled the window of the baby's chamber. A candle burned and the flame flickered and grew large in the draught, dancing across images of naked, fat-cheeked baby boys that adorned the four walls of the small room. The smell of beeswax was strong. Within the linen cloth that bound her, the baby girl had settled into the rhythm of suckling. The wet nurse stroked her tiny, wrinkled fingers, which very occasionally flexed and kneaded at the bosom where she drank. A few tufts of downy hair clung to the nape of her neck but otherwise the baby was bald. The lace cap intricately embroidered in anticipation of the birth of an heir still rested in the empty crib so beautifully decorated with images of a baby Hercules strangling Juno's serpents.

With a heavy sigh, Livia stroked the newborn's cheek and gently eased her off her breast. It was time; she must take the child to the convent. She shook her head with pity at the almost perfect infant now lying on the bed before her, mouth open and still softly shaped as though around her nipple. Then she wrapped a length of plain linen around the baby's head, tucking the end in amongst the folds before deftly swaddling her once more. She could at least protect her from the night air that would meet them on the road.

'Are we blessed with a son?' Vincenzio Fusili's booming voice carried up the staircase.

The wet nurse closed her door and hurriedly gathered her belongings. She had lingered too long.

Giulia listened to her husband's fast step on the flagstones as he made his way to her bed chamber. She just had time to pluck some colour into her cheeks before he appeared. With a strength she did not feel, she raised herself to greet him.

'My love, you are here at last. I am honoured by your visit.'

'God be praised in all His wisdom for this day.' Vincenzio fell to his knees at his wife's bedside, kissing her belly tenderly. His thick, dark hair fell forward and Giulia pressed her hands into the rich curls. When next he spoke, there was pride in his tone. 'Lay back, mistress, you have earned your rest this day. Where is my firstborn? I would see him.'

Giulia stroked his cheek. 'Your presence gives me strength.'

Vincenzio kissed her forehead as he stood. A finger of light crept across the floor from where he'd left the door open in his haste. There was a rustling in the next room.

'Do you have him with the wet nurse already?' he asked.

Giulia felt her heart contract at the smiling satisfaction in his words. 'Come, sit with me.' She patted the spot beside her on the bed and felt her husband's weight press into the mattress. Her heart beat fast as she tried to form the words to disappoint him. A stabbing pain cut into her belly and made her gasp.

'My love!' Vincenzio pressed the covers around her with concern. 'There is such wonder in a woman's strength at this time. Now you must rest.'

Giulia smiled; many a husband would not show such kindness. She chose her next words carefully. 'It was a long and painful birth but I saved spirit enough to speak with you.' She paused, a half-formed wisp of hope on her lips. 'My heart weeps for the sweetness of new life.' Her voice caught in her throat and her eyes prickled with tears. Vincenzio leant in and cupped her face in his hands. She saw the worry in his eyes but there was such peace in the stillness of his hold she did not want to speak and nudged her chin against his soft palm.

Another sudden pain tugged at her insides and brought her back to the present task. She must tell him the truth before tiredness overtook her completely. Raising herself to face him, she took her husband's hands. 'Forgive me, my master, for what I tell you. There is no baby.'

'Come now, do not tease me with riddles, I hear him crying even as you speak.' He laughed again.

'I pray you, do not listen to that noise.' Giulia let her tears flow then. 'For I have failed in my duty as a wife.'

'You are befuddled, my love. I hear it can happen when the birthing is long and arduous. Rest and I will call for Camilla.'

'No!' Giulia grasped his arm tightly as he rose to leave. 'No, I must speak to you now.'

'Hush, mistress, and let me at least call for some wine to soothe your agitation.' He stroked her brow and the concern in his eyes made Giulia's heart contract again.

'Please hear me, Vincenzio, this cannot wait.'

'Very well, I will stay and you may speak, but then I order you to rest, for I begin to worry.' He sat back again.

'I will rest willingly once I have said what must be said, God knows I could sleep for eternity, so heavy are my limbs.' Giulia shifted in the bed, but it was impossible to find relief. 'You are my only salvation, dearest husband, and I thank God every day for the blessings of your love. The baby is not dead but worse, for there is a part of her which is the Devil's work, malformed and stunted so she will not walk nor ever bear the grace of God's image.'

Vincenzio's grip tightened on Giulia's small hands. 'What is this you tell me? The Devil's work ...?' He would not meet her gaze and his eyes swept across the bed as though looking for something. 'What happened?'

'There will be another seed soon and I will not fail you a second time. We cannot blame ourselves. It is God's will.' Giulia spoke quickly and crossed herself in confirmation of their loss, hoping this would be enough to end the conversation.

'What of the baby I hear crying? It sounds healthy as an ox. I do not understand?' He stood and turned towards the door.

A great sadness swelled in Giulia as she watched him. It flooded through her like a drowning wave so that her breaths came short and swift and she gasped for air. Vincenzio swung round and stood over her, so close she could see the throb of his pulse in the side of his neck. She instinctively shrank back but he did not raise his hand and his silent judgement was more oppressive than any previous punishment she'd endured.

'I will bear sons pure of body and heart, many Fusili to honour you, but this one was born under a cursed full Moon.'

She glanced towards the open window and the dark of night beyond, where the Moon she feared was rising. 'Behold and you will see la maledetta luna, taunting us with her fulsome glow even as this horrible, cursed day ends.' Giulia took a deep breath. 'You do not need to see the child. I have dealt with it.'

'What have you done?' Vincenzo's voice was low.

She knew better than to answer. They may only have seen one winter as a married couple but the signs of her husband's dark mood were clear and the chance to appeal to his affection was over.

Giulia watched Vincenzio stagger to the framed image of the Virgin Mary and fall to his knees, spreading his arms wide. Minutes passed in which all she heard were his mumbled prayers. Then he cried out and it sent a jolt of shock through her.

'Why have I lost your favour thus?' His arms, raised up momentarily in adoration, dropped again to the floor.

Giulia shrank against the bedhead, more terrified of this strange and melancholic outburst than of her husband's anger.

'This is my doing and it is I who must repent,' she said as firmly as she could. 'I will pray every hour for God's forgiveness, until you tell me to stop.'

He did not seem to hear her. 'Am I no longer the head of this family?'

'Most assuredly you are.' She paused to find the strength to continue. 'There are none who command the respect of the wool guild as you do, my husband.'

'Then who are you to decide the fate of my child?'

She closed her eyes so as not to see his fiery judgement. The sheet was sodden now, with what fluids, she did not know or care. She had misjudged things terribly.

'I have done what no mother ever desired; I have abandoned my babe to keep your family name unsullied and pure. But my sorrow is as nothing compared to yours, sire, as truly you have suffered the loss of none more precious than an heir.'

He walked to the door.

'Do not turn away from me, I beg you,' Giulia cried out in desperation, but the soft cry of his baby in the room next door had distracted Vincenzio again.

'There is a babe under this roof still, and you, mistress, seek to keep him from me. Most assuredly am I dishonoured by this.'

'I did what I thought best, for us and for the child. She will be spurned by everyone, but the nuns will take care of her.'

'You would cast my offspring out?'

'Please, my love, this was not easy for me. I am suffering too.'

Beyond the door, Livia listened, horrified. The night was dark; she must leave now to avoid her mistress's fury. Yet the words of Signore Fusili kept her in the nursery. She lifted the baby gently against her shoulder and whispered soothing sounds into the small ear pressed against her cheek. 'Cry, little one, let him hear your voice.'

Soft sucking began, rising to a jerky wail.

Thus was the future of Giulia and Vincenzio's daughter sealed. Her cries travelled through the corridors of the

Careggi villa like a longed-for breeze. A sound full of hope. The kitchen servants stopped their tasks and crossed themselves in thanks at the healthy cry of new life. The hunting dogs in the yard pricked up their ears, sniffed the air and howled.

Vincenzio went to find his child.

Giulia made to stop her husband, gasping as she rose to grab at him. 'Vincenzio, don't! Stay here, I beg you, stay here with me.'

But her pleading fell on deaf ears. She watched him rush from the room and only when she heard his muffled voice next door did she fall back against the bolster.

Then Vincenzio was at her door again, the bundle in his arms.

'Here is my firstborn, mistress. Look on her. A girl, I grant you that disappointment, but still a Fusili.' He laid the bundle on the bed and unwrapped the swaddling. For the first time, Giulia saw the rounded belly and smudged nose of her daughter. She was as perfect as Livia had described.

Vincenzio paused, hand in the air as though about to stroke the baby's head. Soft, muffled noises came from the squirming infant. Instead, he crossed himself. 'We must embrace the path our Lord Jesus Christ, in His divine mercy, has chosen for us. Did He not say blessed are the meek for they shall inherit the Earth? This is my daughter and she will be raised as a Fusili.'

An immense tiredness swamped Giulia. Another flood of warm fluid gushed from her and she reached for a fresh piece of linen to push between her legs. But her body felt heavy and she struggled to move at all. The bursts of pain had solidified into an agonising, tight band that left no space for air. The baby cooed and squirmed where she lay exposed, so near that Giulia could almost touch her.

The spark of mother's love she'd suppressed ignited once again; her daughter was to stay with her after all. She felt a prickling in her breasts and realised that now she had permission to mother, her milk would come soon enough. She reached out for her baby, but a prodigious weight pressed on her arms. Vincenzio picked up the newborn and walked to the window. Only when he was ready would Giulia be allowed to hold her babe. This was her punishment and she was as powerless as her baby. In truth, she could not lift her arms; a new lethargy had swamped her and it was as much as she could manage to stay awake.

The wind had dropped so that all was silent. The sky beyond the window was as dark as the winter's soil and spotted with a million stars. The Moon hung high above them all. A small hand flapped helplessly from the swaddling and Giulia sighed at the healthy bracelets of skin that rolled around her baby's wrist. How cold her little fingers must feel. But her baby had stopped crying. Her husband's mood had settled too; Giulia could tell from the steady way he swayed from side to side, rocking the baby. He bowed his head to speak into the smallest, softest of ears.

'Rejoice, lunetta del mio cuore, on this most magnificent night of your birth in the year of our Lord 1479, under a Moon as innocent as you are pure. Beyond those hills is your home, Florence. You are a Fusili and I will protect you, little moon of my heart. We will explore this world together.'

Giulia smiled and tried to speak but only a thin gasp escaped. She shivered in the damp sheets. She could not call out or lift an arm. The pain was now pressing on her like a thick blanket, so she lay still and watched her husband and daughter silhouetted against the window as the pain smothered all she could see.

When Vincenzio eventually turned to pass the baby to his wife, she was already dead, one arm hanging loosely from the covers and a pool of blood spreading on the floor beneath.

CHAPTER ONE

City State of Florence
June 1496

The young woman sat as still as she could, but a tickle had started in the small of her back. It moved up her spine with the swiftness of the kitchen mouse she'd seen darting across the flagstones that morning and just when she felt some relief, it began again. She had a fierce desire to scratch the spot, but she was determined not to give the master painter any further reason to think Vincenzio Fusili's daughter immodest. Instead, she clasped her hands together and fixed her mind on dislodging the piece of apple that was caught in her teeth. She pressed her tongue against the gap between her molars where the bit of apple was stuck and felt it move. It didn't take much more to free the morsel and she swallowed it.

The fruit monger in the piazza had given her the apple as she passed his stall earlier that morn and she'd enjoyed its juicy sweetness as she walked on to the monastery, not thinking anything of it till she'd seen the painter's reaction. She'd stepped into the room with the apple to her lips and halted, still as one of his painted likenesses, under the critical gaze of his artist's eye. Her good humour had withered at the sight of his prickly brows rising. How could something that tasted so good have evoked such judgement? Of course, it wasn't the apple—fruit of man's downfall such as it was—that the painter had frowned upon, it was the provocation of her eating it in front of him. She'd briefly considered her options before settling on the simplest and most satisfying, and taken another bite. She ate the remainder of the apple after the painter had retreated outside to wait in the cloister whilst she changed behind the curtain. When she'd called to him to re-enter and had taken her seat in the high-fashion dress, they'd both nodded as if it were their first welcome of the day, and thereafter she'd adopted so obliging a demeanour that not even the brow of the Pope himself would have raised. The terce bells had sounded shortly thereafter and she'd not moved since.

So here she still sat, hands clasped together, body uncomfortably constrained by this fine woollen gown, and with a devilish tickle about to undo her. She set her mind to another distraction and recalled the path she'd walked to the monastery, having left home when the sun was already risen and any chance of taking note of her beloved stars had passed. She would make up for that another night; the pages of her small notebook would soon be full of descriptions of the positions of the stars she spied. It was simple astronomy but she'd not the skill to do more. If she was a student of the subject, she'd have access to books such as that of Ptolemy or Sacrobosco, with valuable tables that gave instructions for predicting the positions of celestial bodies. She hoped to be in possession of such a text soon.

Yet that morn was not made for decrying the fading of the night sky but for delighting in the wakening of a new day. It had been a perfectly crisp spring morning when she'd set out, blanched of the icy chill of winter, just warm enough to hint at the season's change. A streak of glorious colour shot over a rooftop as she walked, then hid again till she came round the next corner, when it appeared anew as glittering particles that dappled the cobblestones. She thought of the sweet smells that had enticed her towards the baker's shop along Via dei Neri and the curiosities she'd seen on the table outside the apothecary's before she'd turned down her secret, quicker path through the tiny alley with no name, overhung with bricked arches at either end. In the quiet of the alley she'd shaken off her hood and let the first breeze of the day twist in the curls at her neck. She'd looked up to where the roofs of the crooked buildings almost touched, like lovers leaning for each other. The thought had made her smile. Before long she'd come out into the Piazza dei Peruzzi where a group of foreign men in strange hats waited for admittance into the palazzo. But none of it was any help; her back still tickled and the notion of a persnickety little mouse, whiskers twitching and tail flicking back and forth betwixt her shoulder blades, filled her with such an urge to jump up and shake about that she clasped her hands so firmly together her knuckles turned white.

Luna took a deep breath and blew out slowly. Then she shuffled back on the hard chair. There were creases in the drop of her dress! How did the other young ladies of

Florence keep their skirts smooth? She stretched her small hands as wide as she could across the embroidery and decorative pearls. The hard balls bumped against her palm. Beneath the beautiful detail was a complicated structure of layering. But the overskirt looked like a constellation of delicate and perfectly round baby moons had landed in her lap. The pearl was her favourite jewel. The paleness of the stone belied the warmth it gave to her skin and this contrary coupling appealed to Luna's nature. Other young ladies coveted the spectacle of the emerald or the dramatics of the ruby, but she was charmed by the simple beauty of these luminous little balls. She knew it took great skill to sew each pearl onto the fabric. She herself had not been gifted a seamstress's dexterity, even though her step-mamma made her sew, as was the duty of every respectable daughter of Florence. Mamma Lucrezia gossiped that the dressmaker earned more in a year even than Signore Brunelleschi, such was the importance of looking fashionable. But whilst Luna admired the style of her dress, she couldn't agree that the value of this material was greater than the designs of a mind such as Brunelleschi's; his innovation for the dome of the city cathedral was a wonder.

She smiled, for she recognised the finish of embroidery as from the needle of Mistress Baldovinetti, one of her father's most loyal menders. Luna had sat beside the old lady on many an afternoon in her father's first cloth shop, mesmerised by the swift dip and tug of her needle. All that industry used to be so much a part of her life when her father had still been involved in the daily operations of his cloth-producing business. Now his business was one of Florence's most successful and a manager oversaw the three Fusili shops. She was pleased for her father's good fortune but she also missed the community of workers she'd known.

Luna looked at the screen behind which her shift and day skirt hung. At least she didn't often have to dress so grandly. Today it was necessary for the painting; the gown was a mark of her father's status and wealth. The thick slew of her dark hair had been styled into a tight knot and covered with a finely webbed net sprinkled with small pearls. A single curl dropped lightly from either side of her central parting and drew the eye towards the heavy gold and garnet cross hanging at her neck. The hairpins pinched her scalp. Luna breathed through the discomfort and the twist of hair that rested against her cheekbone wobbled. Every element of her portrait must reflect the Fusilis' position in Florence society. Her father moved in influential circles now amongst those learned men steeped in Greek and Latin, who kept company with his patron, the banker Lorenzo de' Medici. These were the humanist scholars who spanned Florentine intellectual life.

So the morning inched forward. Noises drifted in on the breeze off the Arno: the flap of sails and the distant sound of boatmen's voices. Luna recognised them as Pisan natives by the hard bite at the end of their shouted words. She wanted to turn to the window and watch their progress. They'd be pushing their barges to reach the docks swiftly and offload their sacks of English wool before nightfall, when the city gates closed. It was only a few hundred yards through the marshland to the eastern wall and the bend of river where the last of the season's trading barges made their way towards the docks, yet she was as good as a world away.

Candles marked the four corners of the monk's cell, a luxury approved by the prior so the painter could use the golden hues to best effect in Luna's image. The candlelight traced the line of her long and aquiline nose and the downward angle of her face accentuated her smooth, high forehead. The tall wicks flickered and twisted. She lifted her nose to the familiar smell of mire on the air and knew it as a sign of warmer weather and receding waters. Her father's factory manager would be anxiously watching the tidal flow and pushing the workers hard, for washing, fulling and dyeing cloth all needed a plentiful water supply and each week's dropping tides brought the threat of drought and lost earnings.

The arrival of a new shipment of wool used to make Luna clap with excitement because it meant a visit to the factory for the inspection and weighing. That was when her father still selected the raw fleeces before entrusting them to his broker, whose job it was to deliver the wool to the spinners, then collect the yarn to take to the weavers, who in turn transformed it into the finely woven cloth that her father sold for premium prices. She'd spend hours with her father as he graded the fleeces and watch as he took a small amount of raw wool between his fingers, rubbing it for texture and grittiness. Even now as a young woman, Luna could still conjure up the musty animal smell of the factory floor. Her job was to mark the price in the ledger, for even as a child she was good with her letters. He'd lean down and hand a tuft of the greasy wool to her and she'd pocket it and secret it in her treasure box at home till there was such a pile it came to resemble an exotic plant. Once the wool had been graded, she sat by her father's side as he negotiated the price, ready to note it down. Believing in the expediency of clarity in all business transactions, her father would only relay the figure to her once, and so she learnt to listen with focus and intent. The wool traders admired the respect they saw between father and child and stood back to let the girl with her ledger pass; no one made comment on her limp.

A shadow crept across the coarse rug and as it did, the wind dropped and the distant thrum of river noises faded. The room turned close and hot. The acrid smell of tallow from the burning candles intensified. Even the birds in the garden of the cloister no longer chirped, preferring to roost in the branches of the orange tree through the hottest part of the day. No footsteps sounded on the arched walkway; the quadrangle was quiet. Luna wondered if her father was somewhere close by. She'd been in this room for so long he might have spent a goodly time praying in the church or reading in the monastery library without suspecting she was nearby. God rewarded him for such passion. They had a fine home and luxuries far beyond his humble beginnings, as he liked to remind his family. Florence was a city where anyone could rise without family or fortune, if you had courage enough and a good head for finance, and he'd both. Enough to convince the wealthy banker, Lorenzo de' Medici, to give him his first loan.

But things had changed since those exciting days of her papa's early prosperity. Lorenzo had been dead four years now and his son Piero exiled from Florence for two. Luna sighed. Since the Medici family had been banished, her papa no longer held evening forums and poetry recitals in their home. Now the most common talk was all about the latest sermon of the preacher of San Marco, Friar Girolamo

Savonarola. Only last night, Papa had brought home news that the preacher's congregation grew so fast he was moving to the cathedral. Her step-mamma shared snippets too, of how Friar Savonarola had predicted the French king's attack. She said he must be as close to God as the Pope and that when he'd preached that the city's decadence would be punished and the wealthiest family, the Medici, was exiled soon after, it showed he was even closer.

The whole city embraced the friar's fresh passion for the word of God. No one dared defy him. Even the stable boys talked about which of them would join his followers and wear the white robes of his band of boys, the fanciulli. Luna listened with interest and a little trepidation, because the preacher commanded his flock to read only the Bible and said that to engage in discussion of ideas other than the word of the Lord was to entertain the Devil. She couldn't imagine choosing not to read.

The tickle in her back began again so, keeping a watchful eye on the painter, she shuffled her good leg ever so slightly, enough for the scratchy wool of her gamurra to rub against the irritating spot. Her relief was immediate and she sighed happily, aware a moment too late how loud she sounded. Not for the first time, Luna wondered where the sense was in having her sit for a painted likeness to give to her father when they celebrated his saint's day. Better it had been her sister Maria sitting before the painter's gaze these past months; a portrait of her youth and beauty would give their father much more pleasure.

The painter did not seem to have noticed Luna's fidgeting.

She told herself to remember to pass by the small chapel when she'd finished with the painter, the one off the central nave with the fresco by Giotto that her father so loved. If he was here, that's where he'd be praying.

She liked to know her father's whereabouts; it had been this way since she'd lost her mother so young. He had told her the story many times: how they'd been summering at the Medici country estate in Careggi—her beautiful mamma, Giulia, with her precious firstborn, Leonarda Lunetta, by then three years old, helped by Livia her wet nurse, who was still with them to this day, and Papa, so proud to be a father. Only that year he was called away on business and whilst he was absent, her mamma was struck down by the Naples flu so that it was many moons before news of his wife's death reached her father and he hurried back to his daughter's side. Livia, who'd been widowed shortly after, had stayed on with them as companion and servant to the toddler.

Luna wasn't sure if her memories of that time were truly her own or moulded from the stories her father had since shared. The details of her birth and first three years differed with each retelling, but she knew her mother had loved her—of this there could be no doubt. She asked Livia to tell her about those years, but, dear to her as she was, Luna had to admit Livia was terrible at recalling details and would usually end up purse-lipped and leave Luna feeling guilty for haranguing her, so she'd stopped asking. When she thought about those early years, a gentle warmth would flood through her chest; that feeling was real enough.

Her father told her that losing her mamma so young made it easier to bear, for she'd not been old enough to comprehend the greatness of her loss, and Luna knew this to be true, for how else could she take such pleasure in the close bond she shared with him? He'd ignored the whispers of the Florentine ladies who said his daughter would grow to be independent and wilful from spending so much time in the company of menfolk; rather he took great pride in her mental agility and enlisted the help of the librarian at the monastery of Santa Croce, Friar Bartolomeo, to develop her learnings. Under the friar's tutelage, Luna's mind flourished and from a young age her quick wit drew the attention of the Medici circle of humanist philosophers and poets whom her father courted. When he was not tending to his business, her papa would retreat to the monastery library and read the texts recommended by the humanists. He was determined to attain their acceptance and revelled in their commendations of his daughter as though it were he who stood before them and debated. When the invitation he so coveted to join their Platonic Academy was finally sent to him, Signore Fusili had hosted a lavish dinner and Luna had entertained the guests by reciting Plato. Her father had been a member of the Academy now for years, a singular honour for the son of a weaver. She was so proud of Papa.

By the time Luna was eight, her reputation as a child prodigy was spreading; she could read Greek and Latin, and used the classical authors to understand grammar and acquire vocabulary. She read aloud to her father to develop her elocution so that she would be at her most articulate when he wanted her to perform for his friends. Friar Bartolomeo continued to tutor her in history, philosophy and poetry.

Luna's eighth year was also when her father took another wife. She was excited and grateful that Lucrezia Bartoletti, the widow of a statesman from Bologna, accepted her without complaint, for Livia had warned her there was a chance the new lady of the house would not want a crippled daughter underfoot. Best they stick together, she'd advised, quiet as mice and give no one any reason to cast them out. Luna saw through Livia's insecurity and hugged her hard. Yet secretly she couldn't wait to finally feel a mother's love once more.

Soon after the wedding, the Fusilis left Via dei Spiago for a grander palazzo. Luna liked the trees that lined the piazza in front of their new home, an abandoned palace her father had bought for a pitiable price from Signore Amieri after that family went bankrupt. He spent lavishly on improvements for greater comfort and luxury until the Fusili palazzo matched all the other great houses of Florence. Then Papa began inviting distinguished Florentines to sup with him.

Lorenzo de' Medici and his sons Piero, Giovanni and Giuliano visited and Luna could tell from her father's enthusiastic reception that this was a good thing. She couldn't remember her time in the Medicis' country estate but she understood their two families were bonded by the great tragedy that had left her in their care and that her father carried an obligation to his patron. Luna loved the evening soirees. Mamma Lucrezia would go to great trouble, preparing her most renowned dishes with the kitchen girls and Luna would linger at the door into the main hall listening to the men's conversation, shivering with anticipation of an invitation to entertain them as she spied faces she recognised: Lorenzo de' Medici, liked by everyone; his brother-in-law Bernardo Rucellai with the potato nose; Marsilio Ficino—whenever he attended her father seemed particularly pleased. Signore Ficino was working on a new set of writings about a healthy life, which Luna was curious to read, as it seemed so different a topic from his Latin translations of Plato.

Every few weeks, Luna's wish came true and her father would ask her to join them. She would enter confidently to stand in front of the men and answer their challenge, whether it be to recite her father's favourite Petrarch or, when her father was feeling generous, to argue her right to a liberal education. She'd carry the thrill of those gatherings in her heart for weeks afterwards. Of course, there was usually one man who'd rise and offer an argument against her. This always delighted her, for to have an adversary in debate was a sign of her acceptance. She'd stand dutifully beside her father and watch her challenger strut about vaingloriously before the assembly. Tommaso Palagio, a businessman from Bologna who, gossip said, was on the rise, often sat arrogantly in judgement of her. He clearly thought his arguments were nuanced but Luna found his lengthy, convoluted retorts quite boring. Once finished, he was prone to turning full circle with such self-aggrandising that Luna had to stop from laughing. Ofttimes she saw, by glancing around the audience, that she wasn't alone in her assessment of his intellect, though none of the gentlemen spoke up against him. Signore Palagio especially liked to challenge her when she spoke in support of educating girls. The foolish man never realised that even as he praised her intelligence, he insulted her by suggesting she was unique amongst her sex. Yet, Signore Palagio was a friend of her step-mamma's from her Bologna life and her father insisted she treat him leniently, so she would eventually let him think he'd bested her.

Luna scrunched her hands into the softness of her skirts. She was no longer that child, free to speak her mind. She was one and seven and unmarried; a dangerous state for a young woman, Mamma Lucrezia reminded her often. Luna hated it. She was the same person, only now her self-assured tone of voice was heard as immodesty. The spectre of her unresolved future grew stronger with each year. The acceptable path to marriage, should she even wish to become some man's wife, would never be hers to tread because no family wanted the curse of her deformity on their lineage. Papa never mentioned marriage to her anyway and she'd made this right in her mind by believing he would not waste their time on such a pointless topic. Yet he alone would decide her fate.

Luna's insides churned as tightly as the twist of wool she held to. She wanted to remain living with her father and have his permission to study astronomy. Why could this not be her path? She thought of her sister Maria at home, and of all the girls sent forth in this complicated world, believing themselves inferior creatures purely because of their sex and the foolish pride of men such as Tommaso Palagio. Yet their sex had a long history of greatness. Zenobia, the Egyptian woman who became so well versed in Egyptian, Greek and Latin literature that she wrote the histories of barbarian and foreign peoples. And the Greek woman, Semiramis, who spoke her mind in a court of law and in the senate so that the Romans deemed her praiseworthy. Compared to these women's abilities, Luna knew she was but a mouse, yet when challenged, she felt a passion as fierce as any lion.

In her own beloved land there were cultivated women like Nicolosa of Bologna, Isotta of Verona and Cassandra of Venice, for whom knowledge was not a novelty but earned through hard work. These scholars were her example and, just like them, Luna knew she'd always have to defend herself against the envy of men such as Tommaso Palagio. Her father had cultivated her skill in rhetoric so she could do just that. Now, she must use that talent to convince him to allow her to study astronomy. She rested her hands in her lap, cupping her palms one atop the other. She'd remind Papa of his past as the son of a weaver and how he'd changed his future. Now it was her turn.

Her father rarely spoke of his childhood except when he took Luna star gazing. She'd been very young the first time they'd stood on the bridge near their old home and turned their faces to the sky but she remembered it vividly. He'd pointed to the planets where she saw bright dots and then to stars, which she thought appeared exactly the same except for their size, though he knew where to find the red eye of Taurus, the star Aldebaran. She'd followed the line of his finger as he drew the shape of the bull, moving from one bright star to the next, telling her how his father—the grandfather she had never the chance to meet—had drawn the constellations for him. The night sky had filled her vision and the bright stars looked like holes pricked in a cloth of her father's blackest dye. So immense was the view it had overwhelmed her and she'd lost her balance and fallen, scraping her knees. After that her papa stood behind her and she'd leant into his shape whilst he pointed out the planets and stars and explained how his father had read the night sky for portents, though he'd never been able to change his own fate. She hadn't known what that meant but she'd listened without questions because she'd not wanted Papa to stop talking and turn for home. Other times he'd taken her out to witness the full Moon's rise and it had seemed so big and close she'd expected it never to climb beyond the line of the trees, yet it always did and then they'd marvel at where it hung like an untethered orb. Once she'd seen a shower of stars cross the night sky and they'd hurried home for fear of what disaster it heralded. She'd not seen portents of her own future in the stars, not yet at least.

Her natural ability to read the night sky was a gift she'd inherited from her grandfather, but it did not satisfy her curiosity. She wanted to master the theory of astronomy and understand the mathematics of the science. This was how she would bring virtue and glory to the family name.

Her father already believed her worthy of reading the works of the great thinkers and poets and of expressing her views within his eminent circles. It seemed a logical progression that she'd approach further study with the same dedication and respect. She'd talk to him about it when she got home.

Luna spoke a silent prayer to St Sebastian for strength and courage and added a prayer of gratitude for the library in Santa Croce and for Friar Bartolomeo, her teacher and friend. Without his tutelage, she'd never have discovered the thrill of knowledge. She'd spent many happy hours here with him. Luna knew the private passage that allowed the monks to move between the baptistry and their chapter house and she coveted the little bench beneath the orange tree in the garden of the small cloister as though it were hers exclusively. Yet for today, she must sit in this room where there was only bare wall.

The painter's back was bent to the easel and the stroke of his brush against wood was calming. With each beat of her heart, Luna felt the accompanying flush of blood that moved through her veins. Here was her boldness, her intent. When she talked to her father her voice must be as strong as the beat of her blood.

For a moment she forgot where she was and nodded in agreement with her thoughts; she would seek out a time to raise the subject of her future with Papa forthwith.

The painter dropped his brush to the palette he held and spread his free arm in a pleading arc. 'Signorina Fusili, you must sit still.'

'Forgive me, Master Lippi.' She busied herself with smoothing her skirts. 'I find this unexpectedly challenging. Your painter's eye sears me.'

'It is understandable, mistress. I must replicate you perfectly if I am to produce a speaking likeness and for a lady of good family, such scrutiny is, of course, confronting.'

Luna tugged at her belt. 'I will try harder,' she said and glanced up as the smell of fresh lime-wash prickled her nostrils. The painter was opening a bottle of varnish. She lifted her head to better watch him mix the tangy liquid with the oil; she'd read about this new medium and was curious to understand the process.

'I read that adding more varnish and oil stops the paint from cracking,' she offered in the hope of a reply, but the painter was silent. Luna shrugged. He wasn't going to talk to her about his art. She watched him spill a few more drops of varnish into the mixture. How she wished for some conversation, even the sound of the monks hurrying to Mass would be welcome, and she strained her ears for the tolling of the sacramental bells, but all was quiet.

She pulled a book from the pocket of her skirts. It was small and square and the parchment pages were enclosed within hard board covered in tightly stretched goatskin. The size balanced perfectly in her hands. She pushed back the brass fasteners at the head and tail of the book and opened it gently. The binding creaked and the painter scowled at her.

'This will not do. My letter of commission demands I capture your virtue and modesty.'

Yet Luna opened the book and began reading. Despite the discomfort and constriction of her skirts, Luna now sat quite still. She marked a line on the page with her finger as she mouthed the words silently. The gold rings on her fingers stood out like bejewelled clasps.

The painter straightened in his chair and tilted his head to one side, viewing the image before him. Then, dipping his brush into a pot once more, he smeared some paint across the board. 'So, we continue,' he said.

Luna remained in the same position. She was no longer aware of the man staring at her in order to capture the smallest detail of her features. Her mind was absorbed in the words of Isotta Nogarola, the Veronese child prodigy who'd chosen the cloth of God over marriage and gone on to engage in an astonishing eight-year correspondence with the Veronese governor Ludovico Foscarini. That famous dialogue was held within the pages of the small book in Luna's hands; her greatest treasure, for the conversation captured within showed that a woman could meet a man in debate and even best him. Oh, how she admired this lady! Isotta Nogarola had been alive in a less enlightened age, more than thirty years ago, and still she'd found a way to freely express her ideas and engage in debate with men, even to have her dialogue reproduced in a book such as this. That was true acceptance of her intellect. If this lady's words could be published later in her life then there was hope for Luna's own desire to further her education in astronomy now she was a woman.

Luna opened the book to her favourite passage, where the author so cleverly defended Eve as the lesser sinner in the Garden of Eden. Her command of the argument was masterful, for how could her opponent disagree with a woman who acknowledged it was the innate weakness of her own sex that led Eve to sin and so she could not be held responsible, when all of Christendom agreed that women were inferior to men? Woman could not be held both to be weaker in nature and to be more culpable in original sin. The lady Nogarola had turned man's judgement to her advantage and in the process proved she was the more intelligent of the two. It was bold and exciting thinking. Luna wished she could have met Isotta Nogarola.

There was no shame in wanting to use your mind; Isotta Nogarola had proved it and so Luna must prove to her father that she deserved to tread a different path from other daughters and be allowed to keep studying. There was so much to explore in astronomy. The planets were lonely and majestic things, each carried by an elusive force in the sphere in which it was embedded, unable to move beyond its orbit in the infinite space of the heavens. She felt a symmetry with her own fate. She was yet to see an eclipse of the Sun or Moon but she imagined, as the Moon slipped into the Earth's shadow, that the one shivered in close proximity to the other. It would be wonderful and utterly shocking to see something so distant with her own eyes and she prayed her father would gift her such a moment.

Luna stretched her neck to one side and then the other to loosen her collar. There would always be limitations put upon her by God and her sex, such was her life, but Isotta Nogarola had found a way to express herself despite these challenges, and so would she.

She picked up the book once more. The corner of the page was soft as velvet as she pinched it between her fingers. That her father made time for his crippled daughter at all was a blessing, and his tolerance of her reading was indulgent. She'd heard the words so often from her step-mamma's lips they'd become as familiar as lines from her Book of Hours. Mamma Lucrezia was especially inclined to remind Luna of her good fortune after Papa came home tired and hungry and shouted for his wine. Perhaps Mamma Lucrezia was jealous of their bond. Luna lifted the cover to her lips and kissed the soft leather; it still carried the aroma of lavender from the poultice of crushed skullcap seeds Papa used to ease his headaches. He'd listen to her, she was sure of it.

'Again, I entreat your patience and stillness, signorina.' The painter could barely contain his frustration.

'Forgive me, master painter.'

'I require only a little more from you, otherwise I will not finish the portrait in time, and then I will not be paid and my children will go hungry. You do not wish such a turn of events upon my family, do you?'

'No, most certainly not. I promise to remain still.'

'Let us pray your father is happy with this scene,' the painter mumbled.

'As I am the one who commissioned the work, I believe your prayers should be directed for my benefit.' Friar

Bartolomeo had slipped into the room quietly. Luna sat a little straighter. 'How fares my student?' he asked with an approving nod as he took in her fine dress.

'I'd much rather be in the library with you.'

'You've done well to sit for this long.'

Luna nodded and waited. He stood behind the painter with his arms crossed in a serious manner, his belly rising and falling with short, wheezy breaths. This past year the friar had begun to move more slowly and the draped robes of his order did little to hide the crook that curved his back. Luna feared that old age was overtaking him.

Their friendship had grown over the years since he'd first taken pity on the crippled girl sitting bored and alone in the garden of the small cloister whilst her father read in the monastery library. He'd distracted her, initially with a game of rolling the oranges he picked from the tree and then, as the cooler winter months closed in, with books he'd choose from the library. She'd been mesmerised by their vibrant painted images. Her command of language had impressed him so much that he'd talked to her father and the two men had devised a schedule of learning for Luna around the hours of her father's visits. Each month, the friar found himself looking through the monastery collection for a new volume to interest his young pupil and then, as her proficiency increased, each week.

The sight of the odd couple had long ago become unremarkable within the cloistered walls: the little girl hobbling behind the industrious friar as he shelved manuscripts in the library. Back then, Luna thought the steep curve of the wooden library shelves seemed as tall as the tower of the Palazzo Vecchio. Ofttimes she'd lose her balance as she stared up at the friar on his ladder and he would scold her in jest, commenting, 'If I had wanted a frog for an assistant, I would have become a gardener.' But he would scoop her up and carry her a while after that, saying, 'Now we move as one, and the silence is ours.'

The painter waited and Luna saw how he picked at his nails and watched the friar anxiously. She knew her friend enjoyed the theatre of his silent, grey-robed contemplation.

Then the friar nodded and murmured, 'Good, good,' with hands pressed to his chin and the painter clapped him on the back with relief.

'You could not leave the book at home for a day, my dear girl?' The friar raised his eyebrows in amusement as he came to stand beside Luna. Of course he would comment on the text she held, rather than let her know if the painter had caught her likeness. Luna should have known better than to expect any such vainglory. She shot him a conciliatory smile.

'It is the only thing that has kept me sane these past hours of boredom. Sitting for this portrait is a form of torture.' She slipped the book back into her pocket.

'A very expensive and beautiful torture. You've done well, Luna.'

She stood and dropped into a curtsey, but had to clutch at his arm for support as she rose. She didn't quite manage to suppress the hiss that escaped her lips.

'Sit, sit,' he entreated softly, before turning to the painter. 'What say you, Master Lippi?'

'Yes, indeed, friar, a very pretty face and you will notice how I have painted the skirts to hide everything beneath.'

Luna felt the painter's critical gaze lingering on her sturdy boots.

'Such a shame,' he said, as if she wasn't in the room.

Friar Bartolomeo placed a hand on her shoulder and squeezed gently but she shrugged it off, for she'd heard herself described far worse. Hiding her boot in a painting did not change who or what she was.

'That will do for today, Master Lippi.' Friar Bartolomeo ushered the painter from the room and, turning to Luna, gestured for her to change. She did not need encouragement and disappeared behind the screen, tugging off the gamurra and underskirts with relief. For a moment she stood in only her shift, enjoying the rise and fall of her unconstrained belly. There was a woman's shape about her body now; her waist dipped inwards and her hips balanced out the roundness of her bosom. When she lifted her arms there were dark patches of hair like the curled fur on a kitten's belly. Luna released the clasp of her necklace and felt the heaviness of the garnet cross in her palm before replacing it in the jewellery box along with the rings from her fingers. Friar Bartolomeo would arrange for the box to be returned to her home. There was only the pearl netting to remove. Her temple had begun to throb because her hair was so tightly pulled back from her face. She tugged on the knot and felt it loosen and the two front curls dropped a little. She looked forward to taking out all the pins when she got home and running her fingers through her hair till it felt free and loose.

Friar Bartolomeo coughed discreetly and so she hurried along, pulling on the long-sleeved shirt and slipping the woollen skirt over her head before tying it around her waist. Then she hooked together her bodice before draping her cloak around her shoulders.

'Let us get you home.' He held out her walking stick. 'There's no need to pretend any more.'

'If that was pretending, I've done a poor job of it.' Luna lifted her chin defiantly but she took the wooden stick without further protestation and, after a few steps, rested her other arm on his shoulder for support. Her leg throbbed from lack of movement and with each step, she felt her stump press and pinch within the boot.

Outside, Luna waited on the grassy verge whilst the friar went to saddle the mule. She shifted about to avoid sinking into the mud that lay beneath the top cover of grass and straw. The Franciscans complained to the city officials about the uninhabitable bog that stretched behind the church to the city walls but nothing could be done to counter nature's wilfulness. Her quiet contemplation was broken by the church bells, ringing in the nones prayers. Luna looked in the direction of Porta alla Croce. Before long the streets would be busy with the butchers and tanners who traded beyond the walls and others who worked on the river and in the fields, making their way home before the nightly hour of curfew. Luna didn't like being amongst so many strangers; they were not kind to cripples.

She moved to the stepping stones the monks had laid and cast around for Friar Bartolomeo. A group of young men, barely older than she, approached. They talked and bumped against one another and laughed when one managed to up-end another. It was a confidence Luna might admire under different circumstances but she knew only too well what it meant: bold young men in fashionably tight hose looking to impress one another with tomfoolery. She moved back against the wall of the monastery, but they had spied her and did not miss the chance, meandering closer. She heard their jeering bravado and started to turn away, pretending not to notice them. The stone hit her cheek with a sting. It was the same naive cruelty her little brother, Filippo, showed when he tried to scare the birds who landed on the young grapes in their family vineyard. Luna picked up a handful of gravel and threw it angrily but they were already scooting out of sight.

'God will judge you!' she shouted after them, breathing heavily. The spot on her cheek smarted and she touched it gently, thankful that her skin was not broken. At least the friar had not witnessed her humiliation.

When she was very young, Luna would sit by herself watching the children in neighbouring houses playing freely. It took her much longer than most to learn to walk and she would always hobble on the painful stub of puckered muscle that replaced her right foot. She didn't give up through the pain and humiliation of stumbling and falling and eventually she mastered a lopsided, awkward gait using a stick for balance. She excitedly joined the other children playing in the street, but soon discovered that her abilities were limited and someone only had to bump her to make her fall, which happened often and rarely by accident. Her tears would darken the dirt as she lay with a cheek pressed to the gravel but then she'd pull herself up and loudly condemn their retreating backs. At night in her bed, she'd pray for strength and balance, even though she knew there was only so much God could do.

She returned to the open path where Friar Bartolomeo would see her and waited on the stepping stones. Her stump ached and the supportive padding inside her boot was damp. Her very first pair of boots had been a present from her father, fashioned to add length to her right leg and provide balance. They were made of thick leather, the right boot broader than the left with a firm paddle that extended up the back of her calf. The sole was raised with extra strips of thicker leather. It had hurt when she pushed her stump into the unyielding material but she'd clenched her teeth—a Fusili never complained—and soon discovered that putting the boots on quickly was the best approach. Papa had patiently taught her how to lace them up using the eyelets and how to stuff lengths of linen into the heel and toe end of the bigger right boot to support her stump. She knew tugging on the paddle didn't offer any relief but it had become a habit, and she pulled on it now.

On her twelfth birthday her papa had given her a sturdy walking stick with a rounded top encased in beaten gold and embedded with a lustrous pearl. She'd viewed the stick dismissively, seeing a cripple's crutch. Then he told her the stone was linked to the heavens and attracted the spirits of purity and good health. When she inspected it more closely she saw the Moon reflected in the pearl. He showed her where he'd had rings of tiny words engraved into the gold casing:

> *O Lord, rebuke me not in thine anger, neither chasten me in thy hot displeasure. Have mercy upon me, O Lord; for I am weak: O Lord, heal me; for my bones are vexed.*

'Take comfort from the pearl when you hear the laughter of scorn,' he told her in his deep, confident voice, 'and be reminded that you walk in the Lord's shadow, whose sacrifice teaches that beauty is not always visible to the eye. You are a Fusili, lunetta del mio cuore, and you must never show your weakness.'

One morning, shortly after she'd been given the walking stick, Luna was in the square in front of their palazzo, testing the extra balance it gave her, when a girl stuck out her foot just far enough for Luna to trip. Quick as a whip, Luna brought her walking stick down upon the girl's ankle with a mighty smack. There followed many minutes of shocked silence amongst the girl's friends, during which Luna stood her ground though her heart pounded loudly. Her father's words rang in her ears. No one spoke as they helped their friend away but Luna never left the house without her cane after that.

Luna leant heavily on her stick as the sound of the mule's slow plod grew louder. The afternoon sun beat down and she wished she didn't have to wear her cloak, but her stepmamma insisted. Friar Bartolomeo brought the mule to a standstill beside Luna. She grabbed hold of its coarse mane and the sweet smell of trampled barn hay caught in her nostrils as she clambered into the saddle.

'Stop your fretting. I'll get you home well before curfew,' the friar said reassuringly as he kicked the footstool away to rest against the monastery wall and took hold of the mule's lead, clicking his tongue in encouragement to start the animal walking.

There was naught Luna could do to speed up their progress so she settled as comfortably as she could into the side saddle, both legs bumping against the mule's warm side. They moved apace through the dirty streets of cloth dyers and weavers, and even though her father had left this quarter before she was born, Luna felt a kinship with the locals. The houses were high and narrow with shopfronts at street level and private apartments above. Some were no wider than a wagon, but rising three or four storeys so they always cast a shadow and trapped the sewer stench in the air below. Owners were closing the shutters across the botteghe and tired shop assistants sidestepped the mule in their haste to get home.

The silversmith sat on his doorstep sharing conversation with the baker next door. Luna turned her gaze from the two old men, noisily conversing, and ahead to the view she loved as they turned into Via dei Neri. Brunelleschi's domed roof of the cathedral rose in the distance like a rich man's belly. Nearby, in stark contrast, the cathedral campanile pricked the sky with its thin, tall tower. Friar Savonarola preached from that pulpit now; his sermons were the most popular in all of Florence, though Luna had not attended yet. Papa did not like Friar Savonarola. He thought him arrogant for professing to hear the Lord, Jesus Christ, directly in his ear, as though the Pope in Rome was not the chosen one.

Luna breathed in fresh air as they passed beneath a brief patch of open sky. Banners in the colours of Friar Savonarola flapped overhead. All the districts flew the Dominican's colours these days alongside their own.

'So tell me, my student, did you discover anything new in your readings today?' Friar Bartolomeo patted the mule's neck and dropped back in line with Luna.

Luna felt the mule's hide shiver at his master's touch and she too relaxed. 'More admiration for Isotta Nogarola, if that's possible. I think I could recite her entire dialogue to you.'

'I am constantly astonished by you, a young woman who encounters infinitely more obstacles than men in familiarising yourself with knotty problems, and yet ...' here he sighed, 'I must warn that your vanity will be your undoing.'

'Why should I pretend to be humble when I could win an argument with any of these shopkeepers we pass?' She straightened in the saddle.

'Hush, Leonarda!' he hissed. 'Those are dangerous words!'

The mule whinnied and stamped its feet in objection to the firm pull on its reins. Luna had to grab a handful of its mane to stop from slipping as Friar Bartolomeo hauled the beast into a side alley.

'Papa allows me to speak in public thus and he would not put me in the path of danger.'

The friar shook his head. 'Indeed we have all indulged you but how could it have been otherwise, with a voice so young and yet so assured? But Florence has changed. Friar Savonarola is clever, do not forget that.' He looked to the busy street corner and his voice dropped to a whisper. 'No one charged him with conspiracy to take power when he helped to drive the Medici out of our city. Friar Savonarola made sure his pious hands were clean. Rather, he would have us believe that plot was the work of the Medicis' unknown enemies, nothing to do with the preacher. But I know the truth, for though my name may not be Medici, my mother's sister is married into that family.'

His lips curled as he spoke. 'Now we are ruled by one man alone, who claims to take instruction directly from the mouth of Jesus Christ our Lord no less, and who has beguiled the city into believing his is the only truth. I am a man of God, I dedicate my soul to His work on this Earth, and I do not question another's private contract with the Lord, but this preacher goes too far.'

Luna frowned. It seemed he'd forgotten she was there. Her friend was breathing heavily. His cheeks were red and his eyes flicked about. She'd not meant to cause this dark humour. It worried her. 'No one is listening, friar,' she said.

'Hush, now! Your loose tongue will be your downfall. You are no longer a child and the city is a changed place. You may match any man in argument, yes, but your sex discredits anything you say. We must tread carefully; the preacher Savonarola looks harshly upon any woman who, by using her mind as you do, questions the very essence of her purpose. For God created woman for procreation. Friar Savonarola preached this only yesterday. You are an aberration in his eyes.'

'What of the book I carry with me? The work of Isotta Nogarola is held in high esteem.'

'Isotta Nogarola lived a life of seclusion devoted entirely to God. That is why she was allowed to write such books, and she did not boast about her intellect.' He looked at Luna pointedly. 'She overcame her own nature and embraced a book-lined cell, a praiseworthy resolution, to be sure.'

'I wonder if you use this argument merely as an excuse to silence me because you know I am right.'

The friar shook his head. 'I do not jest. Your woman's body is as clear as the Sun's roundness in the sky; no longer can age protect you.' He slapped the mule's hide and whistled it into step once more. They re-joined the busy thoroughfare.

After a while, Luna spoke again. 'Isotta Nogarola needed a father like mine.'

'I advise you to read further on the life of this lady you so admire.'

'Do you not think she was the model of a good citizen?'

'Be quiet, Leonarda. Must I remind you that Friar Savonarola's followers loiter in the shadows to root out just such womanly pride? Is there no common sense amongst all that knowledge in your head?' He cast his eyes about and muttered to himself, 'I scarcely recognise these streets where now I must pay a toll to Savonarola's boys to pass from one district to the next, disguised as alms for the poor. No one can stop them ransacking homes. The arts have no patron, the city's liberal thinkers flounder—Botticelli has stopped painting altogether! I have myself witnessed a group of these righteous boys bear down on a pretty woman for nothing more than a rouged cheek, practically stripping her naked. The shame! Perhaps my teachings have only served to make you more laughable. At least all this will come to an end soon enough. I pray it will not be hard on you.'

Luna was momentarily confused but then shook her head. 'Do not fret. I will never forget what I am. How could I, when everywhere I go I am mocked?' She lifted her chin. 'There is little chance the city's preacher would bother with a cripple anyway.'

'Perhaps I do overreact. These times are hard enough, with Friar Savonarola accusing many of heresy who only seek to debate and not to disavow. Your father says the Signoria did not reckon with the preacher usurping their power, yet here we are, governed by his magistracies and a Great Council made up of the preacher's devoted partisans. Meanwhile, Piero de' Medici squeals in exile like a stuck pig and our city becomes more dangerous with each passing moon. Savonarola promised us a new Jerusalem, instead we must resign ourselves to the thought "Lord, in thy hands are all things." I fear what the preacher would do with a girl of such a mind as yours. Please God, your father keeps you close.'

Luna crossed herself automatically and the movement allowed her to discreetly wipe away the tear of frustration that slipped down her cheek.

'I am sorry to have upset you.' Friar Bartolomeo sighed and the heat went out of his voice. 'I'm just an old man who worries too much.'

Luna hated to see him troubled. 'I know you only mean to protect me and I will try to be more careful. I feel the injustice of my sex so keenly, it's hard to be silent.'

'You are used to hardship.' He patted her leg. 'This is the price you must pay for knowledge. I think we both agree it is worth it.'

'Yes ...' She paused and an image of Isotta Nogarola flashed in her mind. 'Have you heard that a printer in Venice has finally published the *Epitome of Ptolemy's Almagest*, the one Joannes de Monte Regio started with his teacher Georg von Peuerbach and finished after that great man's death? Even their names sound inspiring. Of course, Papa has a complete set of the work.'

'Yes, he brought the first volume to the monastery to show us, or to show it off, I should say!'

'I would very much like to read it.'

The friar raised his eyebrows. 'There is your overconfidence again. This *Almagest* is much different than reading Petrarch's poetry. What's more, there are very few copies of this text in circulation, not enough to share amongst the educated men, let alone a girl,' he said. 'But for now, we must hurry.'

Luna nodded and kicked the mule's flank with her boot. She wanted to get home too.

*

'Will you come in? I'm sure my step-mamma has some of the sweetmeats you so love.' They had arrived at Palazzo Fusili. Luna stood by the central door, her slight figure dwarfed by the huge arches. Only the one door was still open as the day's business came to an end. Inside, the horses were being moved into their stables and the sound of their stubbornness rang out into the square.

'I cannot tarry, for tonight Friar Savonarola preaches in the robes of a poor man and our abbot has commanded us to attend, such is Savonarola's power, even though we Franciscans do not break bread with the Dominicans. I cannot be absent. Mind you tell your stepmother it is my fault you're late. Sleep well, my child.'

He laid a hand on her head a moment and Luna kissed the wooden cross that hung from his belt as he dismissed her with a prayer. The mule snorted loudly. Luna took her walking stick and retreated inside.

CHAPTER TWO

The Fusili household was busy with evening preparations. Luna hurried through the entrance hall to the loggia of the courtyard, ignoring the two gentlemen putting on their cloaks to depart. Business transactions took place here every day. In the courtyard, two servants grappled with the lead reins as they tried to cajole the horses into the stables. Her father's mount, Apollonius, had fouled the paving stones and a stable boy was scooping up the manure. Alessandro, the household's manager, watched. Luna balanced against a stone pillar as she sidestepped the stinking pile.

She mounted the staircase and was glad to sit when she reached her bench on the gallery of the first floor. Luna ran her hand along the uneven wood, feeling for the natural imperfections of the once great tree trunk before reaching down to unlace her boots. Her father had commissioned the seat and its use had become so much a part of her routine that it was only here, once she'd sat, that the tightness in her back unravelled and she let down the guard she kept up when in public.

The door to her father's studiolo was closed; he must not be home yet. Luna wondered if he'd have the book of astronomy with him. She heard the servants in the main hall preparing the table for their meal. A flicker of candlelight danced on the stonework. It would be dark before long.

Her step-mamma's lively voice echoed down to the courtyard. Luna looked up, expecting to see her leaning over the gallery from the floor above with a tongue-lashing ready to burst from her lips. Only that morning, Mamma Lucrezia had reminded Luna it was her brother's bath day and here she was, too late to help. The speed of the painter's brush paid no heed to her waiting chores but that would not appease her step-mamma's temper; she must hurry up now.

The wood beneath her shuddered as, downstairs, the last door was bolted for the night. Her father must be home. He'd be hungry and calling them all to the table before long, which meant Mamma Lucrezia would be even more impatient with her. The family ate together at least three times a week, never the same days. Papa would usually mention in the morning that he'd sup with them as though giving his family a wonderful honour, leaving her poor step-mamma in a whirl of preparations. Mamma Lucrezia was busier than ever on days such as this. But she was proud of her table and skills in the kitchen. Luna could not disagree; her step-mamma's mutton stewed with wines and spices was the tastiest she'd ever tried.

She grabbed a single house slipper from the basket beneath the bench and slid her left foot into it, then placed her boots into the basket and pushed it back. Next she reached for the wooden contraption she strapped to her right leg when she was indoors. It was a simple peg-leg made of two lengths of smooth wood attached at right angles. She rested her right knee on a small pillow on the horizontal length of wood and tied the straps around her calf. When she stood, the peg-leg gave her instant relief. Then she reached across for the crutch that supported her under her armpit. The peg-leg was much easier to bear than the boot, but it slowed her down and it was an unsubtle thing to look at. She readied herself to see her step-mamma, angling the support under her arm till it felt comfortable and hovering briefly at the staircase for any sound of her brother or sister, before continuing up to the top floor.

She hurried into the kitchen. Freshly laundered clothes were drying by the hearth and she heard the spit of delicious juices from that night's birds roasting in the oven. The room was hot and sweet and savoury all at once. Luna breathed in the mix of spice and fat with pleasure. Her step-mamma was loudly praising two girls who stood at either side of the thick wooden work table, pummelling portions of bread dough. They energetically pushed the heels of their hands into the sticky mounds. Luna watched and waited.

'Brava, that is much better!'

The servant girls nodded at their mistress's instructions. Luna's step-mamma hung her head over a copper bowl being held by another servant. 'More salt; it needs flavour,' she instructed, licking her fingers clean of the sticky mixture. 'You know, before I was married, I had to help in my mother's kitchen, which is why I'm so particular.' She addressed them all equally. 'My mother did not employ anyone else, for she believed her daughter should learn the skill of cooking and what better way than to put me to work? Else it was that my free service gave her more coin to spend on dresses!' She laughed and Luna saw how the girls responded to being taken into their mistress's confidence, turning back to their tasks with added vigour.

Lucrezia Fusili was a sensible, well-rounded woman, with light hair that she swept up in a plaited knot. The pink of her cheek was marked by its curve, the colour heightened by the heat of the kitchen, and her slender nose had just the slightest dusting of flour. Her lips were red with the lustre of an exotic pomegranate and flecked with tiny salt crystals that she licked off as she turned to where Luna stood by the door.

'Leonarda Lunetta, here you are at last!' She beckoned Luna to her, cocking her head to one side and raising her brows pointedly. 'Come, stand by me.'

Luna went to kiss her, bowing her head at the sound of her formal name. She angled herself around the table, which took up most of the space in the middle of the room. The kitchen was large, but it was congested with furniture and utensils; nothing was small save for the numerous little drawers in the spice cabinet that took up most of one wall. Oval serving dishes had been placed on the top of the cabinet in readiness. The hearth glowed with coals and two large terracotta pots were strung across the heat. To one side lay an array of unused pots and pans. Ladles, carving knives and other utensils were hung from large hooks in the stone beside the hearth. Dried grease coated the bricks within the hearth making them look like mangled, disfigured creatures.

'You are late,' Mamma Lucrezia said as she kissed Luna's forehead. She smelt sweet as dough. 'I expected you in time to bathe Filippo. You know how he loves those games you play with him. I had to ask Livia to bathe him, though Lord knows how that went.' She shook her head and gave Luna a scowl as if to say her brother's state of cleanliness would be her fault.

Luna pictured Livia trying to get Pippo to wash, and that made her feel even worse, for Livia had not the patience to chase Pippo, nor to entice him towards the wash room. She was still his favourite, though, when it came time to be put to bed, and Livia kept his room in order and managed his mealtimes. Luna couldn't imagine the household without her.

'Forgive me. I always think I will be faster than I am.'

'Did I not tell you to take the litter?'

'It's too big for me alone.' Luna didn't reveal that she'd ridden a mule home.

'It's my choice to shield you from ridicule, daughter. My words may chafe at your pride, but they are plain and true; when you are in the litter, you are hidden. I may not be able to stop you from roaming the streets like a boy—your father lets it be so—but I can and will insist on modesty whenever possible.' The kitchen had fallen silent. 'Now, wash your hands and find your sister for me. She frolics somewhere outdoors and ignores my calls to come inside. Her antics age me ten moons in a day.'

Luna nodded and moved to the basin of water set aside for the kitchen girls to wash, where she splashed her hands about briefly. Her step-mamma had already turned away to the fireplace to check the bubbling pots so she left the kitchen, happy to have escaped without a harsher chiding.

She knew Maria would be in the garden and made her way to the courtyard, stopping a moment to catch her breath when she reached the ground floor. She turned down the corridor to the rear of the house where a door led out into an enclosed garden of grass and paving stones surrounding a low-walled pond. A breeze brushed against her cheek but it hadn't made any difference to the temperature; it felt as hot as it had been all day. The petal heads on the rose bushes fought the droop of heat valiantly.

Luna walked around the pond to where her sister sat hunched over something. Maria had come into the world less than a year after their father married Lucrezia—a fat, creamy-skinned baby. Everyone said she was perfect, and Luna knew it too. She'd had a covering of blonde curls that stood up from the crown of her head like a quiff and made her seem constantly surprised, which was generally considered to be charming. As soon as she could make a sound, she cooed and gurgled with happy delight. Luna loved her little sister with a pureness she had not thought possible.

Sitting was not easy so Luna perched on the wall beside Maria and watched her sister's skill—she had a dexterity far beyond her nine years—as she scratched lines into the shell of a hard-boiled egg with one of her sewing needles.

'Didn't you hear Mamma calling you in?' Luna asked, wondering at her sister's concentration. When she got no response she tried a different tack. 'Explain to me the pattern you are making.'

'I've made a mess of it,' Maria said without looking up or stopping. She methodically flicked the tip of the needle at the end of each slow etch. 'I try to do what Mamma says, and concentrate on the task, but I keep making mistakes.' She stopped abruptly and crushed the egg into the stone wall.

Luna knew it was the black bile. Maria's young body had never been in balance and her soul was burdened by an excess of melancholic humour.

Luna touched Maria's forehead. It was cold and where she had expected a sheen of moisture, she felt dry skin. Her sister's expression had the same weariness as the roses fighting the effect of the heat on their delicate petals. Often, Maria was dramatic and loud and took up the space of any room she was in, preferring to dance than to stand still, flinging her long, gangly arms this way and that, her unpinned hair swooping in a thick, flaxen mass. She minded not who was watching and her confidence both enthralled and tested Luna. Yet Maria had been born beneath the eye of Saturn, and her misfortune came in the form of a demon spirit who reared up and overtook her person when she was most out of balance. She would become madly, excitedly, unhappy with herself, her insults harsher and louder, and her temperament illogically cruel. To Luna it was like an eruption, as though Maria were full of bubbling, hot lava that had to be expelled. There was no reaching Maria when she was in one of these episodes. Mamma Lucrezia would banish her to her room. Eventually Maria would reappear, abashed and apologetic. It was exhausting and it disrupted the house entirely.

Luna saw now that Maria was pressing the tip of the needle against the delicate underside of her wrist.

'There now,' she whispered as she tucked a loose strand of hair behind Maria's ear. 'What cruel game is this?'

Maria seemed not to hear. Her skin was white where the needle's point marked it. A bubble of blood appeared.

Luna placed a hand over her sister's and gently took the needle. 'Stop it, my little dove.'

Maria's breath had quickened. Luna grasped both her hands and pulled her round.

'Hush.' She slowed her own breath until she saw Maria copying her. She was still just a child. Then she held out Maria's arm and turned it over and kissed the angry veins. 'All better.'

The two sisters sat in silence. Luna gathered the needles into the basket and was content to wait beside Maria in the calm shadows of the garden. After a while, she stood.

'Come inside now. Mamma is waiting.'

'I'm sorry, Luna.'

'I know you are, silly. We don't need to mention it to Mamma.'

Maria nodded and Luna saw with relief that the storm had passed—her eyes were clear. As they walked, Maria snuck one arm around Luna's waist and smiled. It was as if the last few minutes had never happened.

'Why don't you ever take me on your adventures?' Maria asked.

'Indeed I believe I did ask you once to come with me to the monastery and if I remember correctly you groaned and made a face like a chicken laying one of those eggs.' Luna popped her eyes open wide and filled her cheeks with air. Maria giggled.

'How I wish I had agreed to go with you, for now it seems I'm only ever to see the streets of Florence when we go to

Mass. Papa keeps me inside so much of late. Tell me about your day.'

'It was dull as you'd expect at a monastery.' Luna nudged her in the ribs. She wished Papa had not stopped including Maria in their outings. His invitation to his daughters to stroll with him to the Piazza della Signoria alongside other families had always been one of their shared excitements. They would each hold one of his hands as they made their way up the broad paved street, ambling amongst the crowds. Luna found this especially thrilling because it gave her a chance to listen in to her father's conversations. He was often detained on their path and when this happened the girls would take the chance to watch the activity surrounding them, Luna only half concentrating as she tried to hear the gentlemen, though setting a lady's stylish dress or a hawker's basket of trinkets to memory, so that later when she lay in bed beside Maria they'd recall what they'd seen in whispered giggles of made-up stories. They knew Papa was in a good mood when he'd treat them to a cantuccini to share from one of the street stalls. She couldn't think of anything terrible that had happened to warrant the change, just that Papa had put a stop to it. When she asked him why, he told her that Maria had reached the age when she must be protected. Luna was glad then for her crippled stump, for it meant she was freed from the social restrictions of other young ladies of Florence.

Luna took Maria's hand. Her sister's grip was strong. She'd surely grown over the past year, but her cheeks still wobbled when she laughed and the gap in her teeth had not closed. She was just a little girl. Luna knew Mamma

Lucrezia had grand plans for Maria's future, but that would have to wait till she was grown. She watched Maria's hair ruffle and fly in the breeze as they walked. It was as long as the length of her back and as deep as the yellow of a duck egg's yolk. She had her mother's beauty.

'Friar Bartolomeo made me sit for the master painter Lippi again,' she told Maria. 'I do not find it easy, but at least it will be a good surprise for Papa. Friar Bartolomeo says the painter is a fine man of his craft and I should be much admired in the form he paints.'

'I am curious to see you in a portrait.'

'I would rather it were you in the painting. I'm sure Papa would better prize your painted image. I wish Mamma had listened when I told her I was an odd choice of subject for this gift. Then I could have spent all these wasted hours in the monastery library instead. Friar Bartolomeo told me Papa shared with him his new book of astronomy. If I'd been there, I would have seen it.'

'I think that sounds very dull.'

'Then it is just as well it is I who has a curiosity for learning.' Luna stroked her sister's blonde tresses. 'Your soft beauty will see you through this life well enough, whereas I must find some other talent to recommend me.'

'It does not matter, for we all know Papa will keep you close. How lucky you are, Luna.'

'You will have handsome young men falling at your feet and Papa will find the perfect match for you when it is time. You will marry and live in a fine palace and have lots of little Marias who will fill your heart and your days and I will visit often. I should be excited if I were you!' Luna made her voice sound bright. Maria's future was set; her mamma talked about the fine match Papa would be able to make on account of his daughter's looks, so it was as well she was prepared. Luna, on the other hand, would never marry.

The girls went through to the main room where their parents and brother were already seated at the table. Luna lay her crutch beneath her chair. Steam rose off the roasted pheasant and her mouth watered at the smell. Other dishes were placed along the centre of the table, though the children and Mamma Lucrezia waited for Papa's permission before reaching for any food. Luna watched him dig his hands under the thick body of the bird and tear off a thigh joint, snapping the leg bone easily. Even though he was a man of books now, he'd never lost his shop-floor appetite.

'How much did this fine bird cost me?' he asked as he spat a mouthful of gristle into the basket.

Mamma Lucrezia pushed the platter closer to his reach and ignored his pointed question. 'Have you begun on the dyed cloth for Margherita Palagio?' she asked. 'I'm curious to see how the crimson colour comes out. I do so want to ensure she is pleased, for it is my reputation at stake as much as that of the business.'

'It is a time-consuming and costly process and I'm sure your friend would not wish my dyers to rush, else a remnant of insect wing remain in her bolt of cloth.'

'Good grief, husband, I do not wish to know such details. I merely inquire when the cloth will be delivered. It was, after all, on my recommendation that the order was placed. This could be very profitable for us if she is pleased. My dear, departed husband Signore Bartoletti,' here she crossed herself and muttered a penance to the dead, 'always said the Palagio family would outgrow Bologna, and he was right. The brother is a papal envoy in Rome now and I hear Tommaso commands the ear of the preacher Savonarola.'

'Business is good, the factories are at capacity. The lady Palagio's cloth will be ready when it is finished,' Vincenzio answered drolly. 'Your reputation will remain untarnished.'

He broke off the other leg. Luna watched him shake his head back to avoid the dripping fat. His wild curls were caught beneath the velvet cap he always wore, though he had not managed to contain all of his charcoal hair. He finished the leg, giving Mamma Lucrezia a nod of approval. Luna hoped the food would make its way across to where she sat beside Maria but her step-mamma did not move it from Papa's reach just yet.

'What of that other matter?' Mamma Lucrezia asked.

'It is arranged,' Papa answered.

Luna saw the broad smile that lit up her step-mamma's eyes but her father's near enough mirrored little Filippo's, who was becoming increasingly frustrated, sitting in front of an empty plate.

'Are we any closer to knowing when the contract will be signed?'

'What contract?' Luna asked.

'Nothing has been decided,' Papa said.

'But you just said it was arranged?' Mamma Lucrezia crossed her arms tightly.

'I have agreed to meet with Tommaso next week, nothing more, and mark me, mistress, I have no intention of seriously entertaining his offer. I do this to humour you, my dear, though even on that front I may yet change my mind.'

'You wouldn't be so rude.'

'I may yet if you do not stop haranguing me.' He picked up a wing and bit into the roasted skin.

'Do you not want a good match for your daughter?'

Papa dropped the bone to his plate.

Luna sat quite still, listening now with ears attuned. A thud began in her chest.

'Indeed I do, though my sights are set much higher than young Guido Palagio. The boy's father is no patrician. He voted in favour of exiling Piero de' Medici from our city and he now follows the ways of the preacher. He would have me destroy the work of young Sandro Botticelli hanging there,' he pointed to the wall behind him, 'and my books. You begin to see my reluctance, I hope?' He licked his fingers, adding as an afterthought, 'How much did you spend this month?'

'Only a little over budget. Do you enjoy the pheasant?' Luna saw her step-mamma rest a hand over the yellowish bruise on her upper arm.

Papa grunted approval.

'Then I must beg an increase in the household coin. I stretched it this month but only because I charmed the butcher into giving me five birds for the price of four.' Mamma Lucrezia took up her wine and sipped. Luna watched her father. 'Would it be such a bad thing to side with those in power?' Mamma Lucrezia shrugged.

'Do I now take political advice from my wife?'

'Of course not. I wait for your direction.'

'I would finish my meal in peace,' Papa said.

Luna noticed her step-mamma rub the fading bruise then she nodded and turned to where Filippo was making a noise beside her. She ripped off small portions of the bird's white flesh to feed to her son.

'May we learn of what you speak?' Luna asked her father.

Mamma Lucrezia cocked her head towards Papa. She had a flush of colour in her cheeks.

Papa took some time wiping his hands clean. Luna shuffled in her seat.

'I have received an offer of marriage,' he said eventually and waved Maria to stand. 'Though I warn you all against an outbreak of women's nerves, especially since I have not accepted it.'

Maria exclaimed softly and cast a dismayed eye at Luna before she pushed back her chair and went to stand by their father. Luna felt her heart begin to race.

Papa kissed Maria's forehead and smiled. 'I will petition other offers now the first has been received. The game is afoot.'

'We will not need any other offers, husband, for I can tell you now that none will outrank the Palagio family in wealth and honour. I have known them since I was married in my younger years, and my dear departed Marco always admired the pious nature of Signore Palagio.'

Papa made a noise like a snorting bull and Mamma Lucrezia was forced to sit back in silence. He took Maria's delicate hand and kissed it.

'How long till I am wed?' she asked him, and Luna marvelled at her sister's composure even as her question belied her childish ignorance, for she must bleed before her marriage bed could be laid in. Maria viewed the world through a child's eyes and why should it be any other way, for she was still a child and deserved to trust.

'Your betrothal will be settled as soon as your papa sees sense and accepts Signore Palagio's offer,' Mamma Lucrezia answered hurriedly.

They all looked to Papa. There was a long moment of silence then he took up his wine, ignoring his wife, which Luna could see from her step-mamma's fiery expression infuriated her even more. 'You will be promised when I receive an acceptable offer, though the marriage must wait until your womanhood.'

Luna smiled at Maria as she came back to her seat, though she knew it was a weak attempt at reassurance. At least Maria would not be wed for years.

A servant delivered a dish of leeks baked with onions to the table and Papa piled a piece of bread with the mixture. Mamma Lucrezia pushed the pheasant over to the girls, though Luna only stared at the platter. Her appetite had vanished.

'Eat, eat! We cannot have you become scrawny as a chicken!' Mamma Lucrezia chided Maria.

Luna took a sip of wine. She reached under the table and squeezed Maria's hand. It was cold and so she squeezed again in sympathy. Her brother was bored with his food and was grumbling loudly. Luna waved her handkerchief at him and was rewarded with a laugh as he tried to grab it. Her step-mamma shoved a handful of white flesh into his mouth, nodding with satisfaction at Luna. In the four short years of Filippo's life, the girls' had been turned upside down. Luna and Maria were moved to the smaller bedroom on the top floor beside the kitchen so that Filippo could occupy the larger room with enough space for his mother to sleep with him, and Papa had already commissioned a marble statue in his son's likeness to be placed in the forecourt of their house for all to see. A line of grease smeared down Pippo's chin as he chewed on the meat with an expression of concentrated pleasure. Luna prayed they could stay like this forever, messy and happy around the family table. Papa set down his wine glass and pushed back his chair with a satisfied grunt.

'It seems very early to begin seeking a husband for Maria,' Luna commented. Papa did not speak so she continued. 'Cannot it wait till she is at least old enough to fully understand what a marriage contract means?'

'What a suggestion!' Mamma Lucrezia said, looking to her husband. 'You do tease us, Leonarda.'

Luna fixed her eyes on her father. 'You are not like other fathers, Papa. You indulge me with a benevolence that most daughters never know. Can your kindness not extend to Maria also?'

'Don't be naive,' said Mamma Lucrezia.

'I know Maria must marry,' Luna answered with a pointed nod to her step-mamma, 'but she is very sensitive and still so young. Once it is known that you are accepting marriage offers, it will change the way our friends and society see her. She will be pored over by men as if their mouths are watering over a ripening fig. We girls are not without feelings.'

'It has nothing to do with feelings, child,' Mamma Lucrezia said more gently, turning to her husband expectantly. When he remained silent she continued, 'Marriage is the reason we women are born, and Maria will be wed with your father's blessing—and God's. The earlier Papa can secure a betrothal contract, the better, for the most sought-after families will already be eyeing their choice of bride for any marriageable sons. The younger the bride, the more assured is her groom that she is untarnished. I would have Maria's future settled well before she becomes a woman.'

'I trust Papa,' Maria said quietly, though her lips quivered as she spoke.

Papa sipped his wine as calmly as if it were only bolts of cloth he was selling and not his daughter. A wave of frustration engulfed Luna. 'What of her family here? Do we count for nothing?' Luna felt like she might burst. 'Maria is too young to wed. The betrothal must last years and what if a better offer comes along? How do you manage that, Papa?'

'You go too far, Leonarda,' Mamma Lucrezia warned, but Luna could only hear the pounding in her head.

'Perhaps none of us goes far enough,' she retorted.

'Dio Mio,' she heard her step-mamma exclaim just as Papa's fist hit the table. His wine glass crashed to the floor. Mamma Lucrezia cried out in surprise then shut her mouth and watched her husband in nervous silence. Luna froze.

'Am I no longer the head of this household?' His voice was low and menacing.

Luna nodded. She knew better than to speak again. Mamma Lucrezia grabbed the pitcher of wine and a fresh cup. Luna saw her eyes fire up then quickly cloud over. She placed another full glass before Papa.

Filippo alone was unperturbed and set up again with wailing.

'Sire, could you distract your son?' Mamma Lucrezia lifted the child out of his seat and placed him in his father's lap without waiting for a response. Filippo stopped crying and stared at his papa, who seemed equally shocked and held his son stiffly. Then a bemused smile broke across his face and he bounced the boy up and down. Filippo giggled and Papa spun him round deftly to face the table. Mamma Lucrezia clapped with exaggerated swings of her arms and Pippo laughed. The danger had passed.

'You look just like a jelly,' Maria said to Pippo and Luna's heart went out to her dear, trusting sister.

'He enjoys the game and I enjoy the peace it delivers. Thank you, my love.' Mamma Lucrezia leant over and filled her husband's cup again. Pippo squirmed with delight at his father's tickles. He had the long Fusili face and his blond colouring mirrored that of his mother and sister. Luna alone of the children resembled her dark-haired father, though she didn't feel very close to him at this moment.

The family were spared any further conversation by the appearance of Livia. 'Say good night to the master.' She spoke directly to Filippo in a voice that had deepened with the press of years and loss. Neither of her sons had lived past infancy and she'd been widowed just after she'd first joined the household to care for Luna as a newborn. She was devoted to the Fusili children. 'I should get him settled, mistress.' She bobbed into a curtsey and took Pippo's hand as they turned to go.

Once they'd left the room, Mamma Lucrezia gently placed a hand on her husband's arm. 'Leonarda Lunetta has finished the lace trim on the handkerchiefs you requested.' She nodded at Luna. This was her step-mamma's way of moving the conversation to safer ground.

'My clever daughter, I am most humbled by your diligence.'

'If it pleases you, then I am happy, Papa. I took my time with the trim to ensure it was properly finished and so as not to waste any of the most beautiful lace that Mamma made for me. Could I use the remaining to make a collar for Maria?'

'Maria will not want for fine lace where she is going, of that you can be sure,' Mamma Lucrezia said with pride and went on to describe a long list of other advantages of marrying into the Palagio family. Luna's gaze alternated between her step-mamma and her sister, and she worried at the way Maria had begun to sway back and forth in her chair. She reached beneath the table once more for her sister's hand.

'Do not be afeared,' she whispered.

Maria leant towards her. A bubble of spittle was caught in the corner of her mouth. 'I cannot leave home. I think I will scream.'

Luna sat back in alarm. Mamma Lucrezia continued to speak excitedly about the Palagio family's great wealth and the potential for Maria's happiness, and without thinking, Luna cut across her. 'I spent time reading Isotta Nogarola's dialogue on Adam and Eve again today, Papa,' she said loudly, ignoring Mamma Lucrezia's frown. At least her abrupt change in subject seemed to surprise Maria out of her distress; she'd settled in her seat. 'I know her writings extremely well and I do adore her.'

'Must we have such talk at the table?' said Mamma Lucrezia.

Luna kept her eyes trained on her father.

'Do you indeed?' he said eventually. 'Then impress me with something of this lady's rhetoric.'

She hesitated a moment, trying to gauge his mood. 'What would you like to hear?'

Mamma Lucrezia snapped. 'Enough of your badgering, Luna! Your father has more important things to deal with.'

'I would rather listen to Luna than the two of you arguing,' he answered and Luna edged forward on her seat.

'I do have something to ask you,' she said, a rush of bravado overtaking her common sense. 'I would like to resume my studies and focus on astronomy.' She paused, breathing quickly, and passed her father the plate of sweetmeats. At least Maria seemed to be calmer, for Luna heard her whisper, 'What are you doing?' and felt her prod her thigh.

Her father crossed his arms and smiled. She saw, by the slight rise in his eyebrows, that she'd piqued his interest.

'Astronomy?' he said with a mixture of curiosity and pride.

'Yes, Papa. Let me learn what makes the Sun turn about us.'

'Truly, husband, you must know this is unacceptable.' Mamma Lucrezia sounded aggrieved.

'You used to take me star gazing,' Luna added, 'as your father took you. I want to understand the science of the heavens.'

He smiled at her indulgently. 'To stand in the stillness of a dark night and turn your eyes to the heavens is to honour our Lord.'

'As we were wont to do.' She willed her father to remember his pleasure at their outings. 'You instilled this curiosity in me, Papa, and now I want to grow it.'

'My dear, she has become incorrigible.' Mamma Lucrezia grabbed her husband's arm and dropped her voice to a whisper. 'We have all humoured your prodigy and I see how it inflates your ego, but she is that child no longer and it does no service to indulge her any further.' She leant in closer. 'Especially now.'

'Sacrobosco explains the Ptolemaic model so thoroughly, but he's been overtaken by the new work from Peuerbach and Joannes de Monte Regio. It is their *Epitome of the Almagest* I want to read.'

'So you have heard about my latest acquisition? I suppose the whole of Florence is talking about this book—why not my own clever daughter?' He seemed pleased.

Mamma Lucrezia stood abruptly. 'It is the betrothal of your younger daughter that rightfully demands attention.'

'Will you take me star gazing again?' Luna asked, ignoring her step-mamma. Their night-time excursions had dwindled in the past years as her father became more occupied with his burgeoning cloth business and with impressing the Academy. Now, with all this talk of marriage, Luna felt a sudden longing for that closeness with him again. 'Will you?'

'Enough, Leonarda Lunetta. This must stop! Your own future will be here soon enough,' snapped Mamma Lucrezia.

Luna didn't get the chance to challenge her step-mamma, for a servant appeared in the doorway and close behind him was Friar Bartolomeo, red-faced and out of breath. Papa stood at the sight of his friend.

'Sire, my nephew, Roberto, is arrived in the city under cover of night. I'm a man of God, not a politician. What am I to do?'

Luna saw surprise in her father's expression as he went to his friend and took him by the arm. She sat quite still, trying to hear what was said, and once again held Maria's hand beneath the table.

'We will take wine in my studiolo,' Papa instructed Mamma Lucrezia, and Luna thought he was trying hard to keep his voice level, though she couldn't be sure. He guided Friar Bartolomeo out of the room.

Mamma Lucrezia pushed back her chair and hurried away to the kitchen, leaving Luna and Maria alone.

CHAPTER THREE

The Moon was high by the time Luna undressed and dropped her clothes onto the trunk beneath the window in the bedchamber she shared with her sister. She'd sat for a long time, stroking Maria's hair until she fell asleep. It was no surprise her sister had not settled easily, with her future suddenly so real. Once they'd reached the privacy of their bedchamber, Maria had clambered under the covers and squirrelled into the corner as though she were safer there. Anxiety flashed in her eyes as she whispered, 'I don't want to leave home. I've never been anywhere, save this house. I won't know where anything is, nor any of the servants. What if my husband expects me to cook like Mamma?'

Luna was as ignorant as Maria when it came to any real knowledge of what married life entailed, save for the example of her papa and step-mamma. She steeled herself against her own unease and prayed fervently that the man who would take her place in her sister's bed would be good and honourable. She told Maria that Papa would not agree to anyone less.

After Maria had fallen asleep, Luna stood by the open window, pushing the shutters wide and stretching out over the drop to the garden. At least there was now a breeze and she felt it caress her cheek. The night was cloudy but the celestial bodies were still there, buried in the deep blanket of sky. Luna thought of Papa's reaction when she'd spoken to him about resuming her studies; he'd not been angry at her boldness nor had he dismissed her curiosity for astronomy. She looked for the three stars of Orion's belt as he'd taught her to do, wondering as she so often did at the physics that kept the planets turning whilst the Earth stood still. She was determined to understand the mathematics of astronomy. As if in encouragement, the clouds gave way and the Moon shivered into sight. The stars once again showed themselves and in the crisp darkness, Luna found the points of lights that marked the great hunter's belt.

'Next I discerned huge Orion, driving wild beasts together over the field of asphodel,' she whispered—lines from Homer's tale. Odysseus had come upon Orion in the underworld and Luna saw him now too. 'Who grasped in his hands a mace of bronze,' she recited as her eyes found his shape in the stars. There was so much beauty to be found in the study of astronomy, not just the mathematics but poetry and tales of the mythical gods. Luna left the shutters open as she prepared for bed.

Maria's breathing had settled into a soft pulse that told Luna she was deeply asleep. Even after the distress and trepidation of learning a husband was already being chosen for her, she dreamt easily and Luna hoped for the same restful slumber as she snuggled in beside her.

*

Luna woke with a jolt at the creak of the door. Her father was standing there and she only just managed to stifle a cry as he pressed two fingers to his lips in conspiratorial silence. It was past the midnight hour, in the second sleep of the night, and only the mice scuttled through the scullery nearby. Luna sat up and blinked at the ghostly vision, imagining for a moment she was still dreaming, but Papa's heavy breathing was of flesh and blood.

'Follow me. Hurry now,' he whispered and Luna nodded. She gently eased the covers down and dropped to the floor, tucking the blankets back around Maria's warm body before turning to the door. She shivered in the silvery light, confused by her father's request.

'I'm coming,' she mouthed silently, pushing through the familiar stab and prickle of pain. She did not stop to attach her peg-leg but hobbled carefully to the door, passing the pile of clothes she'd dropped on the trunk earlier, avoiding the creaky section of floor she knew only too well. When she was close enough she held on to the doorframe to steady her weight. 'What's the matter, Papa?' she hissed.

'Hush, Luna, don't wake your sister. I'll explain outside.'

She followed him to the landing, stopping to close the bedroom door gently. It was as dark as the depths of a well in the corridor and quiet as the still water waiting at the bottom. Luna paused a moment in case the noise had woken Maria, but there was silence. The smell of roast pheasant still lingered and Luna's stomach twisted with hunger. Her father stood impatiently tapping a toe against the top stair; there'd be no sneaking something to eat from the kitchen this night. She bundled her hair into a knot then felt for the firmness of the staircase.

'For goodness' sake, Papa, what on Earth are you up to?'

In answer he chuckled softly and disappeared down the stairs. She followed, copying his light tread as carefully as she could. This was not easy, and she half hopped, half jumped from one step to the next, making sure she landed as evenly as she could on her good foot as she tried to keep up with him.

'Papa, slow down. What is this all about?'

He was sitting on her bench, holding up her boots with an expectant glint in his eyes. 'I'm taking you to see the stars. I could not sleep, and then I thought of our star-gazing adventures, as you reminded me at dinner.' He sighed. 'It gave me such pleasure back when you were small …'

Luna saw hesitation press upon his closed lips. Her father seemed lost for words. She sat and rested a hand on his shoulder, fearing ill health. 'Papa? What ails you?'

'Is it so strange that I want to spend time with my little moon?' He was smiling at her.

She flushed with pleasure. He'd heard her request and now here they were, about to go star gazing. 'Of course not, Papa, thank you.' She took the boots. 'I'll get these on as quickly as I can.'

Beside the bench was a wicker basket and from within she took out a linen cloth, breathing in the heady smell of lavender and sweet rosemary before the witch hazel stung her nostrils. The unctions Livia rubbed into the linen cloths eased the throbbing and disguised the smell of her stump;

it sweated profusely when she walked in her boots for a lengthy time and it would rub and sometimes blister. That was agony. Her father was gathering their cloaks and stood above her, waiting. She wrapped her stump in the infused cloth before pushing it into the boot till she felt the padding towards the heel end. Then she added more padding into the toe end of the shoe until it was firm enough to stand and walk on. She worked quickly but she did not know where they were going or how long they must walk, so it was important to be prepared. The left boot was laced and done in no time.

'These cloaks will do the job against the night's cold.' He held one out and Luna pushed her arms through the sleeves and tied the cord about her waist, enjoying the snug protection; she wore only her night shift beneath. She didn't want to say or do anything that might change her father's mind, so she grabbed her cane from its spot beside the bench and followed him down the stairs where he turned into the corridor that led to the back of the house and the garden.

Her father pushed open the door. She paused. If he had told her they were only going as far as the house garden, she would have used her peg-leg instead. She sighed; Papa would always be fastidious with his business but never took the time to see the details in his home. Still, he'd interrupted his night's rest to take her out, and when he turned and beckoned her to follow, she felt the delight of being his little girl again.

Without daylight to see the boundary walls the garden seemed to stretch endlessly and the inky shapes of the fruit trees made it feel intimate. Luna stumbled a little in the pebbles scattered along the path but she righted herself before her father saw and followed him to where the low stone wall ran around the perimeter of the central pond. They stood in silence for so long her leg began to prickle. Then she felt him grasp her shoulders and manoeuvre her so that he was standing behind her.

'Cast your eyes up, Luna. What do you see?'

She craned her neck back and her head swam as she looked into the vast, anchorless dark. It took a moment to find her balance then she saw one star and another and then another in an endless and intricately laced pattern of tiny silvery specks.

'Sometimes our Heavenly Father rewards us with a perfect night,' her father whispered, pointing into the dark sky. 'This is all God's work. Can you see the three stars of Orion's belt, in that line there?'

Luna strained to see where he pointed. 'Yes, I see them!'

'Now, if you keep looking along that line do you see another bright star?'

Luna followed the line of his outstretched arm. She eased back into his warm shape for support. 'A little red dot, there, I see it—Aldebaran.'

'The red eye of the bull in the constellation Taurus. You know the stars almost as well as your grandfather.'

Luna tucked the compliment into her mind to savour later.

'Aldebaran portends of riches and honour. I saw that star the night you were born.' She felt herself move gently with each rise and fall of his chest. 'So I knew you would be blessed. The Fusili name is made for grand things.' He kissed the top of her cold head. Luna blinked and for a second lost sight of where she was looking.

'What of the Moon, Papa?' Luna pointed. She hoped to tease another retelling of the story of her birth from his memory.

'When I see a Moon such as the one above us tonight, I think of your mother in God's illuminated house.'

'I wish she were here.' Luna's voice was a whisper. Even without a history to bind them, she'd fashioned the love of her mother into a cloak that warmed her.

'Yes, my child, as do I. I still remember how your mother held you with such adoration that first night under a full Moon and you a tiny whelp of new life that so awed us. She only stopped holding you in death. Hers was a soul too pure for this Earth.' He turned to the left and pointed again to a spot in the night sky. Luna felt her body lift with the movement of his arm, like the young girl she once was. She followed his line of sight again and saw the Moon, high and glowing white as marble.

'I hope Maria weds a man as good as you.'

'Do you think I would choose poorly?'

Luna shook her head.

'Maria will look to you for guidance, so you must speak well of marriage. She is fulfilling her duty, which is something of which to be proud.'

'Yes, Papa.'

'You don't sound persuaded, Luna, but you must remember that a betrothal brings good fortune to our family. There is much to be happy about.'

Luna nodded slowly as she wrapped her cloak more closely about her. She thought about her sister's fate, but knew no way to change it. They stood together and watched the sky in companionable silence. A cat shrieked from the alley beyond the wall and it was a lonely sound in the night's stillness. She thought about the planets so far away as to be unreachable, and yet there they shone, ever-present markers in the sky.

'Sit,' he instructed. 'I will return shortly.'

Luna dropped onto the wall gladly. Her foot had begun to ache. Dew dampened her cloak and she shuffled on the hard stone in search of a drier patch. She watched as her father's cloaked figure weaved behind one of the potted fruit trees and then reappeared near the high wall at the back of the garden, overgrown with vines. He leant into the old gate that led into the alley and Luna wondered what tomfoolery had overtaken him. Then she heard the gate creak and saw him stumble as it swung wide and the vines sheared apart. He dipped his head and slipped through.

Luna shifted round. It was terribly quiet. She strained to make out her father's figure returning from amongst the dark shadows but instead saw a bear crouching by a bush and a boy hovering near the wall but it was only a trick of the moonlight, teasing her with its shapeshifting. She would not let her nerves best her. Papa would return presently. So she gazed up again and focused on finding Aldebaran in the constellation of Taurus. First she must seek out the three stars of Orion's belt. She tilted her head and circled around till she had them in her line of sight, only their repeated blinking made her feel even more uneasy. She looked to the gate again. It was hanging open but she could hear no sound of her father's return. There was nothing else to be done except to go and find him. Despite herself, she shivered.

CHAPTER FOUR

Vincenzio Fusili stood resolute and angry. He did not want to be in the filthy alley behind his palazzo at this late hour, yet he knew it was the safest place to meet the messenger. Piero de' Medici would be impatient for news of his spy's safe arrival. Just as well Friar Bartolomeo had alerted him to the appearance of this agent, Roberto di' Rivaldo de' Medici—his nephew as it turned out. The Medicis had not even forewarned him. Roberto's purpose, too, was a mystery, though Vincenzio was sure it would be dangerous to them all. How was he to act as private emissary for the Medicis if he was not included in their communications? Every day that he stayed loyal to the exiled family he risked his own safety and that of his family. God's teeth, he struggled with Piero's ineptitude.

Still, he must do whatever was asked of him—and he must do it with great discretion so there would be no chance of those in power uncovering his allegiance. His fortune was tied to the Medicis as tightly as a new grape bud grafted to the trunk of one of his vines. He was proud of the steadfastness of his loyalty to them but he must be clever and careful meeting with this Roberto, lest he be exposed as a traitor. The Great Council would show no mercy. His head pounded at the thought of discovery. He could not afford the disgrace this would bring to his name nor the inevitable ruin to his business. He thought of his bolts of cloth: plain wool one moment then dyed dark as night the next. Gossip could spread as swiftly; whispered secrets could change a man's fortunes in an instant. Why had Piero chosen this moment to resurrect his family's return to Florence? The timing was reckless. The preacher Savonarola was still favoured by the city and the Medicis didn't have the numbers yet to change that.

He'd meet with this agent and get the answers he needed but for now, he must dispatch this note to Piero. Vincenzio's fingers closed firmly across the seal on the rolled parchment that told of Roberto's safe arrival. He looked one way and then the other; no sign of the messenger. Beyond the garden wall, his daughter sat. He'd brought Luna out to view the stars thinking he'd only be gone briefly but still he waited. A cat skittered across his path and he kicked out at it, muttering under his breath. He hung back in the shadows against the wall. He must not be seen. The minutes passed and he paced back and forth. How long must he wait? He glanced briefly towards the gate, thinking of Luna sitting by the pond. She would be worrying, or worse, about to appear; she did have an unusual need to know his whereabouts. When Giulia birthed a crippled girl-child, he'd accepted it as God's punishment, though he questioned what sin he'd committed graver than any other young man to deserve such a blow. He supposed he'd find out when his day of reckoning came, though he hoped his benevolence towards Luna would right whatever were his sins in the eyes of the Lord. He stamped his feet. If he'd been blessed with a son seventeen years ago, it would be him waiting in the dark right now. His mind turned momentarily to Filippo. The Lord had eventually answered his prayers with a healthy, robust son who would grow to be a capable and strong heir to the Fusili name. He frowned; Filippo was to sing with Savonarola's choir at Mass in two months' time. Vincenzio had not been able to say no when all the good families of Florence had embraced the preacher's request, though it made him nervous. Another reason to be especially cautious in his dealings with this Medici agent.

Another cat slunk from the shadows and perched nearby, looking up at him expectantly. He kicked out again and felt the reward of its softness against his boot. Where on Earth was the man? He peered left and right once more. He knew Luna's curiosity would get the better of her soon enough. At least she'd be slow. Luna was clever, though he had to admit Lucrezia was right: his daughter had passed the age where being precocious was acceptable. He felt a stirring of compassion for his little moon, but there was no cause for pity. He had her future in mind and it would come down to patience and diplomacy, both of which he understood.

He heard footsteps and a figure came into view. Vincenzio hurried to greet him and the two moved to a doorway that hid them beneath its eaves.

'Here is the letter.' He thrust the rolled parchment into the man's hand.

The stranger slipped it into his satchel and nodded. They froze at the sound of movement, till two cats shot out from the opposite doorway.

'Godspeed.' Signore Fusili grasped the man's arm then turned towards the gate. He did not wait to see the messenger retreat into the shadows for he thought he heard footsteps and wanted to get back to the safety of his garden. He hurried, pulling the hood of his cloak down so that his face was shielded. At the gate he stopped and scanned down the alley one last time. That moment of hesitation was enough for his assailant's weapon to find its mark.

CHAPTER FIVE

When she woke the next morning, the first thing Luna heard was the sound of banging. She went to the window and saw that workmen were already replacing the old garden gate, clearly on her father's orders after last night's misadventure. When she had gone to investigate why he was taking so long out in the alley, she had found him unconscious, his face covered in blood, and had revived him enough that she could help him stumble back into the safety of their garden, locking the flimsy gate behind them. He had said that it seemed to be a robber who had attacked him but fortunately he had been carrying nothing of value. She hoped it wouldn't mean an end to their re-established star-gazing endeavours.

Now, she shielded her eyes from the morning brightness. It was late to still be abed so she dressed hurriedly. Filippo's voice echoed and, by the sound of it, he was in the courtyard. She rubbed her throbbing shoulder—still sore from supporting her father back through the gate—as she went downstairs.

It was cool in the courtyard, though light spilt along the corridor from the outer street doors, already opened wide in anticipation of the day's business. The central well around which the home's three floors were built would not brighten until the middle of the day, when a waterfall of sunlight dropped down into the cavity. Then it would become busy, as merchants and visitors held conversations in the pleasing space.

Luna found her brother playing with his knucklebones. Alessandro was directing one of the stable boys to clean out Apollonius's empty stall. Her father must be riding this morning. The stable boy stopped what he was doing and leant his back against the wall, timing it just as Luna walked past. She felt his eyes on her as she went to where her step-mamma sat on a bench against one of the pillars.

'I slept late.' She kissed Mamma Lucrezia in greeting as she sat beside her. The scrape and rustle of the stable boy's pitchfork turning over the hay resumed.

'You needed the rest—Papa told me what happened.' Mamma Lucrezia spoke quietly so Pippo couldn't hear. 'God will forgive you for missing morning prayers.'

'How is he?'

'Well enough, though the bruising is nasty. He was cross as the Devil when he woke. I managed to rub some tincture into his cheek before he went out.'

'I knew you'd have something to help. I see the gate is being replaced. That's good.'

'This house must be safe; you all play in the garden. I can't have my children in danger.'

'Does Papa know any more about who it was?'

Mamma Lucrezia shrugged. 'Let us just be grateful neither of you was hurt. Your father said he would inform the Council so tonight the patrols will walk the alleys around us. I told him no more adventures.'

Luna nodded, though she hoped Papa would ignore her step-mamma's request. She wanted him to take her star gazing again.

'I want you to stay home today, Leonarda.'

'But I go to the monastery shortly to sit for the painter again.'

'Not today, my dear.'

It was comforting to feel her step-mamma's hand warm upon her arm and Luna's expression softened as she realised Mamma Lucrezia was worried.

'Mamma, I will be safe. We both know robbers hide in the daylight and the painter must finish on time otherwise Papa's surprise will be late.'

Mamma Lucrezia patted Luna's knee. 'Do not be wilful.'

Luna was touched by her concern but she had no intention of prolonging the torture of sitting for the painter. 'I will ride in the covered litter. Will that appease you?'

Mamma Lucrezia lay her hands in her lap and frowned. Her poise belied an indecision that Luna rarely saw. It softened the edges of her usual fortitude.

'Very well, Leonarda, do as you wish.' Mamma Lucrezia stood up. 'Now I must get your brother to his tutor.' She called to him with such impatience Pippo jumped up in shock.

When the pair had disappeared up the stairs, Luna went in search of Alessandro.

He was in the stables. She stood and watched him a moment.

'I won't ride in the litter today. You do not need to ready the horses.'

She went to put on her boots and gather her cloak.

*

Luna enjoyed the walk. She knew the streets so well it felt like passing through a village rather than the grand city of Florence. Mamma Lucrezia didn't understand her need to walk; it was an ability that able-bodied citizens took for granted but every time Luna chose to use the legs God gave her, even the one in its half-formed state, she felt capable and not weak. The baker's boy swept the dust and grime from the square patch in front of his father's business. Luna waved to him as she passed and he smiled and waved back before turning again to his task. The broomstick's rushes sounded like the wind in the pine trees down by the Arno. To one side of the bakery was the apothecary, Matteo Palmieri's shopfront, who sold all sorts of interesting medicinal remedies, and beside him, the most excellent glove maker of Florence. Luna had accompanied Mamma Lucrezia to purchase a pair of the softest leather gloves only the previous week. The floor below the workbench had been scattered with offcuts and Luna had wanted to gather them to make a fine set of play materials for Pippo but her stepmamma would not let her take dirty shreds of leather home. Through the door she'd seen a table of neatly stacked gloves, the fingers fanning in shiny, scalloped layers. She loved the smell of the shop, like the sweetness of freshly turned soil in the rose beds at home. One day she'd visit as a respectable lady of Florence and buy her own pair of gloves.

A warm breeze rose unexpectedly, flying along the thin laneway and skimming round the corners. Luna was glad of her cane's support as she took the longer route so she could walk through the grace and grandeur of the city's main piazza where the Palazzo della Signoria kept watch on all who passed beneath its tower. Two officials stood in discussion by the Loggia dei Signori. Luna stopped to admire the marble sculptures, virtues of the free republic her father held dear. She'd stood before the stone men often, listening to her father describe the values of prudence, temperance, justice and fortitude. When she was little, their cold marble expressions and height had frightened her, but now she understood their significance. Her father had been furious when enemies of the Medici family had convinced the priors that their system of governance was tainted by Medici bribes and had Piero and the rest of the family swiftly exiled. It was Piero's father, Lorenzo, who had brought peace and prosperity to this dear city, along with the statues. Luna vaguely remembered the old man in singular images of his nose up close and the sound of his shouting at the table in Villa Careggi, but she'd been too young to remember more.

A group of men walked by and stopped in front of the statues. Luna moved along politely to the edge of the loggia. They were young and bright and they wore the white robes that the preacher Savonarola insisted his devoted followers adopt. Luna watched them discreetly. They were not afraid to attract attention as they spoke loudly and took up space with their gesticulating. There was something familiar about the group, and she realised they had the same wild camaraderie as the boys who'd accosted her outside the monastery the day before. She turned to go, but glanced back at the sound of one of their voices and saw it was indeed one of the same mischievous louts. It surprised her that the preacher should accept these boys as followers. They showed no sign of God's spirit within them, at least in her experience.

She moved on before the group noticed her presence and hurried down Via dei Neri, turning into one of the tiny alleys that linked through to the Borgo dei Greci. She stopped at a tabernacle to pray for her father's swift recovery. The chubby cheeks of the baby Jesus in Mother Mary's arms reminded her of Pippo as a baby. An offering of fresh flowers had been placed against the terracotta base. Luna crossed herself; this would make up for missing morning prayers at home.

The laneway snaked between uneven shopfronts overhung by apartments. In the open space above, a tablecloth had been hung out to dry on a length of twine strung from one window across to an opposite one. It flapped cheerfully in the wind and made the day feel happy. She came out into Borgo dei Greci, pitching from side to side as she favoured her good leg, swinging the other forward with determination. Her walking stick clicked against the paved stones rhythmically. Finally there was the church. She pulled a sprig of rosemary from a wild bush and inhaled the sweet fragrance as she walked the final path. Her father had told her it was not so long ago that this part of the city was still marshland outside the walls. Luna tried to picture what it would have looked like. It was not so hard to imagine the smell, for the boggy waters still festered.

She slipped inside. After the activity of walking, the church felt as still as the moment a wick is snuffed. She relished the cool. Then a woman shrouded in silk netting brushed past her on the way out and Luna stood aside respectfully, listening to her own laboured breath. She saw that there were a few early worshippers dotted about the tall columns and private chapels. The water in the font glinted as a beam of sunlight shone down from one of the stained-glass windows positioned like paintings along the walls on either side of the central arch. She dipped her finger into the shallow bowl and made the Sign of the Cross before moving through to the south side, past the grand chapels of Florence's wealthy families, which the novices had to keep clean. She stopped briefly at the Peruzzi family chapel to admire the painter Giotto's work. The women and men in the scenes seemed so real; they bowed towards John the Evangelist like she might do towards her father at a family dinner, and the women's expressions of amazement might have been cast from her step-mamma's face. In each of the six panels she could see a whole story. Luna thought him a most excellent painter.

She crossed the dusty flagstones and the reverberation of her footfall hung high in the wooden beams, up with all the secret, whispered prayers she imagined were struggling to escape from within that vaulted cover. She didn't stop long, knowing the painter would be waiting, so she went out into the large cloister, dominated by the Pazzi chapel at one end, and made her way around the open gallery until she found the door that led along a corridor and out into the smaller cloister. Luna breathed in the clean garden smells, leaning against one of the columns. Were the oranges on the tree hanging a little heavier than yesterday?

She saw a group of monks in conversation on the opposite side of the quadrangle and for a moment thought she saw her father amongst them, but she could not be sure. She hastened to the room set aside for the painter and closed the door softly behind her. Friar Bartolomeo was seated at a desk, writing furiously. He looked up sharply.

'Good morrow, friar.'

'Leonarda!'

She laughed. 'I did not mean to startle you.' The painter's easel was not in its usual place. 'I've beaten Master Lippi this morning,' she said with satisfaction.

'Did no one tell you?' He rose and came around from behind his desk. He seemed flustered. 'Master Lippi does not need to see you again. He has only to finish the detail of your skirts and the painting is complete.'

'So I have come all this way for naught?' Luna sighed and took a seat without waiting to be asked.

Friar Bartolomeo turned to his desk again and shuffled the papers, looking for something. He handed Luna a book. 'Take this. At least your visit will not have been in vain. I believe you will enjoy it, though the mathematics might be difficult for a girl.'

Luna took the book and frowned. She didn't like to be criticised, but her expression turned to one of delight when she realised he'd given her the textbook every young student of astronomy began their studies with: the astronomer Sacrobosco's *Tractatus de Sphaera*. 'How did you know this was exactly the book I wanted? Thank you!' She opened the thick cover and scanned the title page. It was a marvellously detailed wood cutting of the author and another man sitting beneath an astrolabe.

'Take it home with you,' Friar Bartolomeo said, and Luna realised he was hovering over her. She closed the book and tucked it under her arm.

'Thank you so very much for this,' she said again.

Friar Bartolomeo went to open the door. He muttered something that she did not hear but she watched him looking left and right.

'Are you expecting someone?'

'What? No, no.' He seemed flustered, though he didn't move from where he stood.

Perhaps, as she'd feared, his mind had begun to go soft. 'Are you well?'

The look he gave her was one of surprise. Then he clasped his hands together and sighed heavily, and there was her friend once more, his eyes crinkling. 'You are my kindest student, dear girl. I thank you for your concern.'

'I don't know what I'd do without your guidance. You cannot get sick, for I would be lost.' She squeezed his shoulder gently.

'Now, no fussing please.' He patted her head as he ushered her through the door and Luna found herself unexpectedly dismissed.

After walking back across the piazza, her leg throbbed. She'd expected to be sitting down for the next hours, not walking again so soon, so she took some rest on one of the stone seats. The sun's warmth encouraged her to linger. She was glad the sessions with the painter had finished but she had to admire his dedication to his craft. Even though she'd tried his patience with her reading and fidgeting, he'd stayed focused. Luna watched a country woman gathering her baskets and the remaining herbs she hadn't sold that morning. Other traders were closing up their market stalls. A final few customers wandered amongst them. A gush of dirty water spread across the dry stone as a serving girl from the tavern emptied her cleaning bucket. The smell wafted all the way across to where Luna sat but it wasn't enough to make her move. Rather, she let herself dwell on the drop of her shoulders and the heaviness in her chest.

The truth was she would miss these visits to the monastery. They'd given her days an order she'd not felt since her regular lessons with Friar Bartolomeo. She wished they had kept going beyond her fourteenth year, but when her womanhood arrived, Mamma Lucrezia had gone to Papa in a blaze of horror and shame for her, and he could not refuse her request that Luna stop her unseemly education. She patted the hard cover of the Sacrobosco sitting in her lap. Her return to learning was about to begin with this book. The friar's commendation of it echoed in her head and she thought of how much purpose his guidance had given her. She missed that.

A lone cloud moved swiftly across the broad expanse of sky. It was shaped like a hand reaching out to another. As Luna watched it she felt a surge of affection for Friar Bartolomeo and his library. The cloud drifted and before long it was just a blur of milky white against the blue but the image stayed with her. Friar Bartolomeo had led her into his world of books and from that first day as a little girl she'd felt a thrill at her own capacity to understand his teachings. She smiled and nodded, and anyone looking at the young woman with the walking stick sitting on the bench would have said she was a simpleton, but Luna was too busy with her thoughts to care. She'd never felt anything as powerful as that sense of her own capability from discovering that she was at last better at something than other children. Learning under the tutelage of the friar had been the first time she'd ever experienced such accomplishment and she craved it still.

More clouds swelled to form an opaque mass that bullied the sun into hiding. She pulled the hood of her cloak forward as she hurried for home, hugging the book. She didn't see the trail of horse droppings until her walking stick skidded through the sludge. The smell of sewer water was rank but she had to stop. She'd nearly fallen. It was close to midday and the street was noisy with men and animals. Peasants pulled their wagons for home, already emptied of produce at the early markets, whilst some sat in a cart drawn by a mule. She muttered under her breath as she leant against a building. Young boys employed by the cloth factories scurried back and forth, delivering consignments of wool or yarn or dyestuffs from one shop to another.

A dog stopped nearby and eyed her with the desperation of a hungry belly. She held out her hand. His nose was damp and cold. 'You're a friendly thing.' She bent down and ran her palm along the ridge of his hard back. 'I don't have anything to give you.' She ruffled his ears. The dog let her pat him and it revived her spirits. 'You are not afeared of me, are you?' she said softly but then he shied suddenly. She reached out to stop him but he scampered away. A group of men in the recognisable white robes sauntered into view, pulling a drunkard from a doorway and kicking him into a puddle of stagnant sewer water. The wretch didn't move but others did as the group passed and even the stray dog skulked into an alley.

'Heh!' one of the young men shouted at the dog and it stopped and turned, its ears pricked. The same man held out his hand and Luna observed something disconcerting in his wide-set eyes. He kept his arm extended as the dog approached. When the stray was within range, the man grabbed it by the scruff. The dog scrabbled to free itself but the man was big and strong and held him fast. His friends bellowed encouragement as he dragged the dog back into the alley from whence it had appeared. To Luna's horror, she heard one sharp, high-pitched yelp then nothing. The man ambled back to his friends, wiping clean the blade of his knife. They continued along the street, past Luna, who had frozen to the spot.

'Those strays have rabies, you know,' the man said to her in passing.

Luna didn't move for quite some time. Her hands shook, so she couldn't hold her stick and easily walk. It was horrible to be so near to where the dead animal lay. Her body grew cold at the thought.

When she did eventually turn for home, she went more carefully; she couldn't afford to lose her concentration, whether it be on something as simple as walking or the more complicated task of keeping out of the path of bullies like those young men.

*

That evening, Luna walked in the garden. She needed to clear her mind. She'd spent the afternoon reading the Sacrobosco when she should have been sewing and now her head was full of mathematical calculations and diagrams of the alignment of eclipses. After she'd returned home, Mamma

Lucrezia had given her a roll of white cloth to begin on the robes that Filippo would wear when he joined the preacher's choir of boys. But all Luna could think about as she'd measured the cloth was how bright the dog's blood had looked on the boy's knife. So she'd set aside her sewing and turned to the Sacrobosco instead. The friar had been right, there was much she did not understand in the text. It was frustrating and disappointing but she wouldn't shy away from the work.

She turned her face to the heavens, closed her eyes and breathed the evening air. Diagrams of planets swirled in her mind beside white robes and a bloodied knife. The dog's dying yelp rang in her ears as though she were in the street beside him. Luna shivered. Better to move about. She walked along the path and stopped by the pond. There was peace in the stars. The night sky blinked. There was Venus, so bright. 'Hello, wandering star,' Luna whispered and wished she were up there, afloat in her own perfect sphere in that more perfect world.

She held to the low wall to steady herself and stared into the pond's inky black surface. It flickered and danced with a film of starry, glistening spots. The true beauty was above, but it was here too, clear in the reflection. We are all God's people, she thought, though some cannot hide their darkness.

CHAPTER SIX

Vincenzio made ready to ride out at first light. He'd been grateful for the softness of his pillow after the brutal attack in the alley but he'd not slept well and now, only several hours later, he'd had to rise, his thudding head a painful reminder of last night's misadventure. The day ahead was already laden with commitments; now he must find time to meet with the Medici agent. All this with a face disfigured by bruising. Luna had surprised and impressed him with her bravery and quick thinking. Thank God it had been his own daughter who'd found him in the alley and brought him back to the sanctuary of their garden—anyone else and he'd have had to come up with a better reason for being outside the gate at that hour.

He ran a hand through his hair and winced at the pain but a few bruises were preferable to a knife in his side. He pressed his fingers against his scalp to ease the ache. He must not panic. Whoever had attacked him might still be watching the house, so he would go about his business as calmly as ever. It was a damnable nuisance that he'd miss the weekly reconciliation of his account book of debits and credits because of this meeting, but that was as it must be. His manager would attend in his stead and prove his worth. In his head, Vincenzio listed the debtors least likely to repay: seventy-four florins owed by Taddeo di Piero, now deceased; sixty-seven florins by Michele Bonichi, bankrupt; the yarn broker Daddo d'Ippolito owed eighty-three florins but he had run away. Then there was the Venetian nobleman Giacomo Dandolo, whose debt of 350 lire Vincenzio considered lost. He cursed their wickedness. His profit margins had been dropping steadily—as low as three or four florins per bolt—with the growing demand for silks. This was not the time to be distracted and he cursed again under his breath as he realised he'd probably miss the daily rounds of his shops too. He'd only recently returned to overseeing the operations. He had no patience for wasting time on the shop floor, but his business demanded attention and there was too much at stake for him to leave it to anyone else, except today he must.

He slapped a glove against his thigh and realised too late how the fast action made his head hurt. The workers pushed harder when he visited, but in his absence the lazy dyers would no doubt slacken off and that would slow down the rest of the production process. He did a quick calculation of how many orders might be late and slapped his thigh again. He could little afford to have dissatisfied customers right now; his trade relied on his exemplary reputation and he needed all the business he could get. At least he'd managed to keep his problems private, though God only knew how much longer he could hide his dismal accounts from his creditors or his wife.

His mind turned briefly to the instructions he'd given Lucrezia to keep Luna home today. He'd spoken plainly enough so that even a woman could understand. He did not need his curious daughter discovering that it was he himself who had commissioned her portrait. Whilst he was at the monastery, he'd make sure the painting was dispatched. By the time Luna found out why she'd been reproduced in paint, the contract would be signed and he'd have no reason to lie to her. The notion gave Vincenzio a moment's relief before his mind turned once more to the business at hand.

The timing of this Medici agent's arrival could not be worse. No doubt he was here to demand funds from loyal supporters such as he to begin to raise the army Piero should have summoned when first his rivals challenged him. Vincenzio shook his head at the thought of losing more coin to the cause of returning the Medici to power. Piero was draining the Fusili coffers faster than Vincenzio could fill them. The new shopfront in Prato was supposed to increase his income, but trade there had been disappointing. At least he'd be able to assess what was causing the slow trade in Prato when he visited the shop himself. He must finalise the date of his forthcoming work travels.

His head still ached monstrously so that he grimaced as he shouted to the stable boy to make haste. He was angry that Roberto had gone first to Friar Bartolomeo rather than directly to him, when it was Vincenzio who had Piero's confidence. The man was unpredictable; who knew where else he might have stopped, a tavern even! If someone had recognised Roberto, then the attack in the alley last night may not have been as random as Vincenzio had led his wife to believe. It could very well have been a warning to him.

Vincenzio remembered the bolts of cloth in production for the mistress Palagio and his wife's unsubtle questioning of the previous evening. He scribbled a note for his manager to push the progress of that order above all others and sent it off with a servant. If the order was late, Lucrezia would never serve him roast pheasant again and he did so love the fatty flesh on the bigger birds.

The dawn was just leaking into the sky as he rode out of the courtyard. He kicked hard against his horse's flank and bent low to the reins. The throbbing in his head increased but he ignored it; he meant to reach the monastery before full daylight brought activity into the streets. They clattered across the piazza and he tilted sharply to the left as they swung into Via dei Neri. Apollonius reared and snorted as if to say give me my head, but Vincenzio held the reins short and hard, knees tight against the beast's flank as their path narrowed and it became impossible to do more than walk. His brow dampened with the effort of keeping his horse in check as they weaved through the alleyways and it was with some relief he saw the road widen as they turned and the gates of the city prison came into view; only a short distance beyond was Piazza Santa Croce. Thankfully, it was still too early for the usual crowd of plaintiffs to have gathered outside the prison or even any dauntless bystanders hoping to see a fresh victim hanging from the rope.

Apollonius walked on unimpeded. A blur of grey and white wings passed overhead as the church bells began to peal, heralding the lauds prayers. The pigeons swooped and then scattered across the sky like a handful of thrown seed. Vincenzio thought of the open skies of the Medici villa at Careggi where he would normally remove with his family through the hottest summer months. The sooner the Medicis were returned to society, the better, but it must be done when they were assured of success. The Medicis were bankers, not soldiers, and till they had the numbers in the Signoria they should stay away. He blamed Piero for the family's fate; Lorenzo's son was weak and lacked his father's tactical mind. Vincenzio cursed his old friend for raising a fool, then thought better and crossed himself in deference to the dead who might yet hear his thoughts. He needed the Medicis back in control of the city; their bank had always lent to him handsomely at attractive rates but only a fool would taunt the dragon that was Savonarola without enough armour to protect himself. Piero must be patient; now was too soon to raise his defence.

Vincenzio shifted in the saddle as they passed the prison's open window, where a body swung on the hanging rope. He could not tell if the lost soul was young or old, for the man's flesh moved with maggots and his eyes were no longer distinguishable in the sink of muscle and cheek. Beneath the window were the portraits of those sentenced for lesser crimes; traitors and sodomites, even debtors were pictured, their names and crimes writ large for all to see. Shame was almost worse than death in this city, now forever under the eye of the preacher Savonarola. Vincenzio crossed himself and spurred his horse into a canter once more.

Apollonius shied skittishly as the first clang of hammer against anvil came from the dark interior of a blacksmith's shop. A figure crossed their path. Vincenzio recognised the familiar lope of a drunkard skulking home the moment the city gates reopened. There were always a few who chose to drink and gamble all night rather than risk a fine for violating the curfew. He'd enjoyed such nights in his youth and felt a stab of longing for the appetite of his younger self. Since Friar Savonarola's preaching ways, he'd been careful to restrict his pleasures to the intimacy of his own private rooms, but he'd been forced to curtail even those evenings with so many of the preacher's marauding boys sticking their long noses into the business of respectable households. Damn the puritanical preacher; Vincenzio sorely missed visiting his favourite brothel girls. He laid a hand on his horse's neck, feeling his own raised heartbeat as he stroked the quivering skin. Keeping only to his wife's bed was bearable if it was but a temporary stay, as would be the demands on his purse if he had not over extended. He'd not the coin to purchase the expensive silks all the ladies requested lately. They were fools for believing it superior to wool. He did not understand the fashion for it.

He pressed his knees more tightly against the horse's flank. First they must free the city from the clutches of Friar Savonarola. He was mightily popular and had the whole city believing the Medicis were Devil-bred and their success a sin; all success a sin, in fact! So many families thought he truly was the mouthpiece of God. Vincenzio would laugh at their gullibility had not the preacher such a strong hold over his beloved city. The recently established Great Council was stacked with the preacher's supporters. Tommaso Palagio, the puritanical fool, did Savonarola's work amongst the gentlemen of the Signoria. Vincenzio had had the misfortune of being in the audience for one of Tommaso's weak-lipped speeches in favour of Savonarola at the Platonic Academy. If that institution fell to the preacher's honeyed ways, then they'd all be lost. For now though, he must appear to support Savonarola; he'd agreed to his own son joining the preacher's fanciulli at Mass. It was distasteful, but he'd take the family and be loud in his praise. No doubt Tommaso Palagio would be there with his son, Guido, too.

A pigeon flew straight towards Vincenzio and he instinctively dipped his head to avoid the bird. He had no intention of accepting the Palagio marriage offer for his most valuable daughter, Maria. The man was a fool to think he had a chance. Vincenzio had his own plan in progress.

The horse whinnied and Vincenzio shifted in his seat and pulled on the reins so his mount slowed to a walk as they turned towards the wide, open square of Santa Croce. He must fix his mind on success; melancholic thinking would only beget failure. A donkey cart rumbled slowly past on its way to the morning market and the peasants doffed their caps. A few devout souls hurried across the square to early Mass but otherwise the space was empty. Vincenzio steered his horse down the broad length of the church and around the wall of the monastery until he came to a wooden door.

'God's blessings, I am relieved to see you.' Friar Bartolomeo stood back to let him pass before shutting the door. 'What happened to your face?' Vincenzio told him of the attack and the friar crossed himself. 'Are we mad to meet with Roberto?'

'The fact is I cannot be certain who attacked me,' Vincenzio answered. 'Come now, show me to this emissary.'

The men hurried along the covered walkway. They spoke sparingly. Friar Bartolomeo's thoughts were on suppressing the fear that quivered in his brow. Vincenzio focused on the meeting ahead; he was determined to be done as soon as possible so he could return to the business of his day.

'I slipped away from lauds,' the friar said in acknowledgement of the sound of chanting as they passed the novices in prayer. 'We can attend early-morning prayers before you depart,' he added as though in compensation.

Vincenzio followed him through a door that led to the novitiates' corridor and brought them out by the Medici private chapel. How excellent is the work of Andrea della Robbia, he thought, as they passed the terracotta altarpiece; Lorenzo's grandfather, Cosimo the Elder, always did have an eye for good art.

They kept to the shadows and passed across the outer edge of the main transept towards the entrance to the crypt. Vincenzio drew the hood of his cloak forward to shield his face though the few worshippers paid no heed to the soft pad of cloaked men.

'Come, come,' Friar Bartolomeo urged as he pulled out a heavy brass key and unlocked the door to the crypt. 'It is better we move quickly. He waits for you below.'

Vincenzio dipped his head through the low doorway and led the way down the stone steps into the catacombs. The dank air stuck in his throat and his coughs echoed through the chamber as they descended. At the bottom, the room opened into a broad and deep space that disappeared into dark corners. The vaulted roof was low and arched in regular waves. It pressed upon those beneath like a weighted plate and the men bent even though they could stand straight. A line of heavy iron doors sealed off the tombs of the oldest Florentine families and a powdery haze of light filtered in through two small windows cut low into the stone. Vincenzio wrinkled his nose as he and the friar moved farther in to where the dankness intensified.

'May God protect you.' Roberto appeared from the shadows.

'May He protect us all from Savonarola's spies,' Friar Bartolomeo greeted him.

Vincenzio stepped forward. 'Why was I not forewarned of your arrival in the city?' He was in no humour to waste time on pleasantries.

The man snorted and bucked his head like a young horse readying to throw its mount. 'I am not beholden to you.'

'Yet whilst Piero is exiled I am his ears and eyes in the city.'

Roberto did not deny the statement.

'So he would have done well to consult me before sending you. I can advise on the risk to his family. That is what we agreed.' Vincenzio ran a hand through his hair before turning away as though he was about to leave. Sending Roberto into the city with no warning was rash and impulsive; if that was how Piero planned on continuing, then they would all likely be exposed and arrested. That boy had none of his father's cleverness, and more the shame of it, for the Medicis needed a strong and wilful leader to retake the city. Vincenzio sighed and turned back. His loyalty was to the family, not the individual. 'Support for your family's return gathers slowly. The preacher Savonarola's criticism doesn't help. We do not have the numbers yet to overturn the decision of the Signoria.'

'Piero could wait no longer.' Roberto did not sound perturbed.

'I cannot protect you if I don't know you are here. Piero has been ill advised. Sending one of his own back into the lion's den this soon is madness. All Medici are exiled, not just he.'

'We cannot be idle whilst Florence suffers under Savonarola's hold.'

Vincenzio snorted. Altruism didn't sit well on Medici shoulders; he'd rather they could all speak plainly about the importance of their banking position and power.

'No one knows of my presence here save you,' Roberto said.

Friar Bartolomeo crossed himself immediately and shared a knowing look with Vincenzio.

'Someone knows,' Vincenzio answered flatly. 'Last night I was set upon in the alley behind my house.'

'And so the fight begins. Stay your course, my friend.' Roberto's voice was charged with energy and there was a glint in his eye.

Vincenzio shook his head, unsure if he was seeing madness or bravura. 'I cannot be sure who attacked me, but I was dispatching a message to Piero telling of your safe arrival.' He rubbed his arms. An uneasiness had settled in his bones after the incident. He'd not acknowledged it till now and did not plan on letting it take root. 'I urge you to return immediately to Siena and wait until I send word. Mayhap the messenger was intercepted by the same man who attacked me. The Great Council may already know of your presence in the city.'

'Piero has not the patience for politics. He chooses force and we will overthrow this city with an army. Yet the Medici do not keep soldiers like other families. That is why I am here.' Roberto shook the pouch that hung from his belt and the men heard the clink of gold within. 'I will buy my family soldiers enough to take back the Signoria.'

'Dominus vobiscum.' Father Bartolomeo's voice was a whisper.

'How much do you need from me?' Vincenzio asked with resignation. His mind turned momentarily to his struggling business as the man thrust a letter with the Medici seal upon it into his hand.

'It is all writ here.'

Vincenzio turned away from the pair to read the parchment.

'How fares the Devil-preacher?' Roberto asked the friar. Vincenzio kept one ear tuned to what was said. He did not trust this man.

'There is to be a great reckoning of our wealth, have you not heard?' Friar Bartolomeo spoke quickly, crossing himself again. 'The preacher calls it God's work but I do not believe the Lord would sanction all he does. Books will burn even faster than flesh. I am moving the church's precious volumes down here for safekeeping. I will of course move the books paid for with Medici gold first.'

'Then the sooner we get rid of him, the better.'

'I pray for the swift return of Piero to end this madness as much as you,' Vincenzio said, turning back. 'But Savonarola's popularity is still strong. Though it wavers in Rome, here he is adored. The people follow him like dogs on the scent of a bitch in heat ever since he prophesied the invasion of the French king, Charles VIII.'

'Piero needs the use of his trading routes if he is to keep the bank from floundering. We will not survive much longer in exile,' said Roberto.

'We are in agreement, and there will be change, you have my word. For now, though, I pray you do not tarry long in Florence.' Vincenzio looked to his friend and the monk nodded in agreement.

'What say you to his letter?' Roberto asked, raising his eyebrows expectantly. 'I am charged to stay within the city walls, but we will need more soldiers than can be procured in Florence, and Piero looks to the families he's supported in the past who live in the country estates between here and Pistoia.'

Vincenzio sighed. 'Yes, yes,' he said, brushing his acquiescence aside with a wave of his hand as though that would diminish the impact of the letter's demand. 'Piero has my commitment, though the amount he demands I give up to his cause will cut a most painful hole in my profits.'

'What does the letter say?' Friar Bartolomeo asked nervously.

'I am to use my own purse to buy Medici support from the country estates Piero has listed.' Vincenzio paused. 'And I am to provide for him a list of men from these families who commit to join the Medici forces when the time comes.'

The friar raised his hands and brought them together as though he were about to pray. 'Please God, this goes well.'

Roberto pulled out a second smaller pouch from his cloak and handed it to Vincenzio. 'This is from Piero, in gratitude for your loyalty.'

Vincenzio took the money, though it was a token amount. 'Any journey must wait until my work travels. At the end of the month I visit my shop in Prato and I will make it known I hope to seek out new customers. I have a need to travel on to Pistoia for family reasons. In that way I can stop at these family estates without suspicion.'

'I have given you safe cover for a night but I am nervous that your presence here puts us all in danger,' Friar Bartolomeo said to Roberto.

'Piero would not put God's house in jeopardy,' Vincenzio answered before Roberto had a chance to speak. 'Tell the good friar he has no need to worry. A soldier does not hide behind monks' robes.' He spoke lightly but there was a steeliness in his voice.

'As you say,' Roberto answered. 'I will not stay another night in the monastery. There are others I can call on.'

'So be it.' Vincenzio made ready to depart. 'We will leave you to make your plans; better we do not know where you sleep tonight.'

He stopped at the bottom of the stone steps and swung round. Roberto stood like a sentinel amongst the tombs. 'A civilised Florence is what has always set us apart and will once again.' Then Vincenzio turned and took the steps two at a time so that Friar Bartolomeo had to hurry to keep up.

When they reappeared in the church, it was littered with monks and good people come to prime prayers. Vincenzio and Friar Bartolomeo joined the worshippers. A pigeon flew above their heads, battering into one of the stone columns as if disoriented by the noise below.

'Is the portrait ready to send?' Vincenzio asked Friar Bartolomeo and was relieved at his nod in reply. 'Take this to send with it.' He handed the friar a sealed letter. 'Go now and have it done, so I may return home at least one worry lighter. I will wait for you here.'

Vincenzio bowed his head and closed his eyes in prayer, though it felt perfunctory and he struggled to hear the Lord's voice. A sense of misgiving needled his mind like the moth larva that burrowed into his bolts of cloth and planted its rot before he even knew it was there. Vincenzio clutched at the bag of Medici coins in his pocket. When would he have money enough of his own to be no man's puppet?

At the end of prayers, he hung back then stood before one of the private chapels. Offerings of candles burned in a simple altar. He did not hear Friar Bartolomeo return, but there he was again, standing beside him.

'Why did you take so long?' Vincenzio held a corner of Piero's letter to a flame and stood patiently as it flared and smouldered.

'Roberto might be a fool and a spy, but he is still my family. I do not know where he will rest his head this night but I can make sure he has bread and wine to keep him company. A candle too.' He shrugged.

'And was he grateful for your kindness?'

'Mainly there was a great deal of self-aggrandising,' Friar Bartolomeo replied. 'He makes ready to leave the monastery shortly. At least we will be rid of him.'

'And the portrait?' As he spoke, Vincenzio dropped the charred remainder of the parchment to the ground and stamped on it till there was nothing left but ash.

'It is dispatched, though Luna was there, too,' he said softly. 'I have just sent her home.'

Vincenzio swung round sharply. 'What say you?'

'She thought she was to sit for the painter this morn and surprised me in my rooms.'

Vincenzio felt a fiery heat rising in him. Only the night before, he'd told his wife to keep her home. He did not want Luna to know of his plan just yet. He saw a tremor of consternation cross the friar's face and it only served to fuel his anger. 'By Christ's body, I shall have to hit you on the head. Did you let slip the real purpose of the portrait?'

'I sent her home with a new text to read. She has no idea.' He crossed himself with trembling hands then clasped them anxiously to his chest.

'Settle your gibbering nerves or we begin to look guilty.' Vincenzio could hear the pad of feet behind them as the congregation splintered. He fell to his knees and bent in prayer. Friar Bartolomeo followed suit. They stayed thus until the sound of movement dropped and a quiet settled on the church. Vincenzio felt his bones pinch as he heaved himself to stand. He would need one of Lucrezia's poultices this night.

The two men walked to the outer doors of the church and stood in the sunlight. The square was busy now, with traders hawking their wares and people bustling into shopfronts. Vincenzio watched the familiar scene and when he spoke it was with a tone set to convince himself as much as Friar Bartolomeo.

'Be assured we are working for the good of our city, and when Piero returns to take his rightful seat in the Signoria his favour will be our reward.'

The sun burned against his forehead. He dreaded the heat, for it brought drought and that would slow production and only add to his woes. He had not reckoned with losing more funds to the Medici cause so soon. He willed the panic broiling in his chest to settle as he looked out into the strangers' faces, hoping not to see Luna's amongst them. He had not the patience to deal with his daughter's curiosity.

The people moved about their business, content as those who'd only ever tasted farro soup. It was his duty to aid in the return of justice and liberty to this great city, even if only a few of its citizens appreciated the value of what he aspired to restore. They were all of them at the mercy of the preacher Savonarola and his prejudice, from the peasants to the intellectuals. He'd heard Savonarola planned on issuing a decree that locked all women in their homes to save them from licentiousness.

'Did you yourself see the portrait into the wagon?' Vincenzio asked.

'Yes, it is already on its way to Pistoia.' Friar Bartolomeo was pleased to talk of something other than the Medicis.

'Excellent,' Vincenzio said. 'I want to be rid of this Medici task as soon as possible, and a work journey gives me an excuse to visit the estates on Piero's list. I will make arrangements for a few weeks hence; let us hope the painting arrives in time.'

'Your decision will be hard on Luna,' the friar said as he turned back to the grandeur of the church, but Vincenzio barely heard the words; he was already striding off down the stone steps.

*

It was near midday by the time Signore Fusili arrived home. He went straight to his studiolo and closed the door firmly but he did not sit idly, for the sounds of his family and household activity told him his task was best done before anyone interrupted. He opened the strong box kept within his desk and withdrew the sum of money he would need to fulfil the demands of Piero de' Medici. It filled three purses and emptied his coffers. As hard as it would be on the household's needs, he knew he must set aside the money now, to secure the amount. Then he dropped the pouch of Medici coin into the box. Though it was a meagre offering compared to what he'd just removed, it would have to do for the month. He had no doubt his wife could manage and he'd take a little extra from the business account to tide them over. Loyalty to the Medicis was counted in coin and he could not break trust with his ally however much it hurt his purse.

He must send word to Signore Spinelli in Pistoia to expect his arrival in the first days of July, and pray to God that he'd received Luna's portrait and thought her marriage worthy for his son. He did not enjoy knowing he'd have to carry bribery money with him and get it to those whom Piero courted, though the sooner it was done the better. The Fusili name was at stake, as was the financial security of Vincenzio's business.

'Bring me wine,' he shouted, pondering how best to convince the families on Piero's list to entrust their sons to a Medici-led force and what tactics to use to negotiate a lucrative marriage contract with the Spinelli family. Why did everyone test him so? He'd saved Luna from being cast out at birth, that was the important thing. He'd stopped her being sent to the convent to live as an orphan. Would any other man have shown such compassion for a motherless crippled baby girl? No one really understood the depths of his grief. He'd not realised Giulia was so close to death and afterwards, he'd had to get as far away as he could from the blood and stench of that room, from the clouded white of his wife's dead eyes, the creep of cold in her flesh. The rest of what he'd done that day was his burden to bear and he would take it to his grave.

Vincenzio stood abruptly and threw his head around the door, shouting to have his wine else the whole damned house be sacked.

'It is here,' Lucrezia said as she hurried in and placed a tray down on his desk. 'Do not shout so, husband. It upsets the children to hear their father angry.'

Vincenzio waited till she poured him a cup, then drank it immediately and demanded another. She had no idea what pressures taunted him. He was the head of a successful and very busy cloth business and he must manage the expectations of the Platonists and keep up with politics and his commitments to the monastery as well as his own readings. Yet he could not even rely on his wife to do his bidding without error. When he'd drained the second cup, he stood and felt the heat of the wine course through his blood.

'You did not keep Luna home as I instructed,' he said.

'Forgive me, but you know how wilful she can be. I did my best.'

'She went to the monastery, did you know? She fair near discovered the painting and that would have ruined all my endeavours. I do all this to ensure our family's future but you thwart me, woman! Why am I the only one who can control the children in this family?'

Lucrezia's hand shook as she filled his goblet again. Wine splashed onto a piece of parchment. The discolouration spread across the sheet.

'You've ruined it!' he shouted and swiped out with his hand, catching his wife on her chin. The noise of it was electrifying.

The force of the blow knocked Lucrezia to the floor. She dropped easily and stayed down. Vincenzio heard her gasping. He sat and poured himself another cup of wine whilst she gathered her wits enough to leave him in peace.

Vincenzio pulled a fresh parchment sheet from the pile stacked to one side of his desk. He dipped his quill into some ink and began to write, drawing up a balance sheet of his assets. A wool cloth business built to an impressive fortune though now reduced—he grunted with displeasure at the sight of the words on the page but continued nevertheless; his own likeness by Botticelli; his luxuriously bound copies of Petrarch and Virgil, and now the newly acquired *Almagest*; his Donatello sculpture; Apollonius, who came at great expense from a horse trader in Venice; a devoted wife. Here he paused, remembering the immense relief and pleasure he'd felt at securing Lucrezia and determining to better control his temper in future, if only she did not test him so. He resumed writing: one beautiful daughter and one talented daughter; a healthy son and heir; his friendship with the Medicis and other prominent families; membership of the Platonic Academy; and a residence that rivalled the Medici villa at Careggi in the finest and most beautiful city not just in Christendom but in the entire world.

When he'd finished he sat back and breathed in deeply; listing these things soothed him.

CHAPTER SEVEN

The next sennight passed as any other as the first month of summer came to an end. The rising temperatures led the family outdoors into the restorative cool of the longer evenings and the intense, unmistakable smell of salted fish became a familiar scent on the clothes they wore. It was an aroma Luna would forever associate with late evenings spent in the garden.

The family usually travelled to the Medici country villa to escape the city through the hottest months, but this year they were to stay home. Luna missed the sense of busy anticipation that normally filled the house before their journey. Mamma Lucrezia was agitated. She faced the prospect of summer in a hot kitchen with no change to her routine. She insisted the windows in the main hall be left open through the night and then closed before the heat of the day set in. Each morning, the family gathered briefly in the dulled light, where the cool of the flagstones allowed each of them to continue more comfortably into the business of their day.

Luna walked into the main hall early one morning. It was the most formal room in the Fusili palazzo, used for important celebrations and to entertain dignitaries. Colourful tapestries draped down the walls on one side, the other offered a view of the piazza through squares of glass. This summer the grand space had become the family's morning retreat. Luna's relief at the feel of the captured night air evaporated immediately. Mamma Lucrezia was standing by the windows, a shawl gathered around her shoulders. Luna worried she might be unwell for it was far too warm for a covering. The shutters had already been closed against the looming sun yet her step-mamma still stood before them. Luna hurried over. Mamma Lucrezia swung round at the sound of her peg-leg and Luna briefly saw the fresh bruising on her neck and upper arm before she pulled the shawl around her.

'Let's sit before your brother comes and takes the best chair.' Mamma Lucrezia said nothing further and Luna asked no questions. The rest of the family began to appear and Mamma Lucrezia kept the shawl wrapped around her. Luna saw bubbles of moisture on her upper lip. She offered to fetch a glass of cold wine but in response, her step-mamma announced that they'd sat idly for long enough and it was time to look to their daily duties. Luna was glad to leave the main hall that morning.

Her father was talking heatedly with a gentleman in the courtyard, someone who had come to cancel an order, or so she thought she heard. It seemed the man feared the colour of cloth his wife had chosen was too garish, though Luna loved the vibrant blue and yellow combination and imagined his wife would be sorely disappointed when her brown wool arrived instead. The gentleman bemoaned the new rules from the Great Council. He said the preacher ordered his bands of children to report to the authorities all examples of unbecoming or ostentatious dress, so he had no choice but to change his wife's order. Papa followed the man out.

He'd taken to spending more time in his shops. Luna asked to accompany him as she used to do but he shook his head and said that, at her age, even a girl such as she could no longer prance around the shop floor amongst the workers. He left early, before the heat of the day set in, and returned with the weariness of a long-distance traveller, rather than someone who had been only as far as the river Arno and back.

That day on his return, Papa disappeared into his studiolo, wiping a hand across his face and shouting for wine. Luna hovered out of sight nearby, watching for Mamma Lucrezia. She listened for shouting and any loud noises after her step-mamma passed by with a tray of wine and some hard cheese. She only retreated to her chamber once she'd seen her step-mamma safely return to the kitchen, calling to one of the girls to help her with the dinner.

A few days later, Luna saw Mamma Lucrezia wearing a new ring and despite the heat that night, the ovens were lit and they dined on Papa's favourite, roast pheasant. Mamma Lucrezia said there was not a wife in all of Florence who suffered less than she, nor received as much in return.

*

Mamma Lucrezia wore her new ring proudly to Mass in the cathedral the following week. Luna watched the gold reflect glints of sunlight across to where she sat beside Maria in the family carriage as her step-mamma tapped her fingers against the seat and surveyed her children. The streets pulsed with the energy of the crowds converging on the cathedral to hear Friar Savonarola lead them in prayer. The Fusili carriage made slow progress. Street sellers and beggars jostled for business amongst those who were walking. Hawkers offered up trinkets and Maria popped her head out of the carriage to see the quality of their wares but Mamma Lucrezia chided her and pulled her back within the cover. Luna had helped to get Maria ready for Mass that morning and surveyed her sister with pride. She wore a modest dress which on many would seem drab, but the simplicity of the style was just right for Maria. Pippo, sitting beside Mamma Lucrezia, had not been so docile. Luna gave him a rueful smile as she noticed the soiled patch of his sleeve, dirty from playing with the pebbles in the courtyard. Papa had left earlier and was somewhere walking ahead. He would meet the carriage when they arrived at the cathedral.

The shouts of hawkers and the rumbling of carts mixed with the hollow clatter of a passing rider on horseback, who sounded so near Luna peered out excitedly, hoping to see the colourful banners of a visiting nobleman. A shriek made her crane her neck up to where a hawk circled high above. It would be cooler up there, and the view so much better.

She saw the rider already far ahead, a lone traveller and not a person of note. A man stood at the corner of one of the smaller alleys, shouting and gesticulating. Luna spied men in the cloth of the preacher moving a group of older boys away from a doorway that had a sign above its entry, which she'd seen a few times in passing. She strained to make it out. It was definitely the one her step-mamma referred to as the mark of disrepute, though the gentleman who slipped out after the boys left appeared respectable enough. Luna knew it had something to do with the women whose powdered faces appeared in the windows on the upper floors. As the boys hurried away, the preacher's men slapped them about the legs with sticks and joked with others of their pack who were going into a home two doors down. Luna felt her cheeks burn with the words they used. A woman cried out from a window as someone threw out a richly worked tapestry. It ballooned a moment as the air caught beneath it before plummeting to the ground with a heavy thump. Like a beautiful gown, Luna thought. The men were throwing objects into the wagon below. Luna saw the broken wood of a painting, a pile of books left where they had fallen, pages open and flapping, and a bronze urn already discarded. The group of older boys slunk past the carriage as they retreated and Luna could see where the sticks had left red welts across their calves.

'Move on,' Mamma Lucrezia ordered the driver and Luna settled once more. Her step-mamma rolled her ring round and round her knuckle. 'I pity the Canturi family. Friar Savonarola and his children now govern Florence.'

'Did you know that house?' Luna asked.

'We were often guests together at the Medici palazzo on Via Larga, but I have not seen the lady for some time.'

Her step-mamma's tone made Luna reach over and take her hand. 'We will send them some chicken soup when we get home. Yes, Mamma?' She squeezed encouragingly.

The family sat in silence after that. Luna could still hear the men shouting but soon the noise faded into the general din of the street. They edged slowly towards the cathedral. As they drew closer, she heard singing and strained her head out to see a group of the preacher's boys chanting hymns with crosses in their hands, calling for alms for the poor. She looked at Pippo, who had pushed closer against Mamma Lucrezia. Soon he would be one of those white-robed boys. She wished their father had refused the suggestion he join. The fanciulli processed through the streets to the cathedral in a big messy group and Pippo was still so little he might get lost, or worse, get bumped and fall. The tolling of the cathedral's single bell began and the familiar sound brought some ease to the group within the carriage.

Papa was waiting on the street and helped Mamma Lucrezia from the carriage. Luna clambered down after her brother and sister, using her walking stick as support. The throng of parishioners was large and crowded through the doors with little order or gentility. As they entered, Papa tried to create some distance from the fray by stretching out his arms. Every corner was packed and the space beneath the magnificent domed arches felt as hot as the kitchen during baking. So many people standing close together made it smell sour too.

Luna followed her father to a space where they could stand. She let her eyes wander across the cobbled collection of strangers' faces; some ladies' heads framed by elegant silk hoods, others wearing simple kerchiefs. She saw men as familiar as the visitors her father welcomed, whilst others reminded her of the factory workers she'd known in her younger years. Close to the pulpit, she noticed the rows of chairs set aside for the most important parishioners. A friendly hum of chatter surrounded them as people moved through and greeted one another. Mamma Lucrezia clasped her hands in prayer and Papa did the same, leaning his head against his wife's, and Luna was momentarily taken aback by their unusual display of intimacy. She turned the other way.

A tier of wooden stands framed each side of the pulpit, erected for the choir boys, but this day they were empty. The noise sank to a low whisper as the congregation settled. This was the time Luna enjoyed the most, just before Mass began, when the communal silence felt like a soothing blanket. She dropped her head and tried to clear her mind so that she might hear the grace of the Lord. Her laced-up boots stood out against the other ladies' shoes. Then a sprinkling of light glittered on her arm. She looked up to where the sun's beams shone through a pane of painted glass and was reminded of Giotto's painting of St John Ascending. She accepted the warmth of the sun's touch as a sign from the Lord that she was as welcome as any of the other ladies in church.

A gentle nudge to her waist made Luna turn. Maria pointed to a line of monks in the dark robes of the Dominican order moving slowly down the aisle, swinging their censers. The way they shuffled made Luna think they must be old and wearied but as they passed she saw smooth-skinned cheeks peeking from beneath their hoods. The incense floated a few moments around them, then disappeared into the air. Luna shifted her weight. A monk separated from the group and climbed the pulpit. He was small and gaunt, which surprised Luna, for she'd expected Friar Savonarola, so full of passion and fire, to be a big man.

At first he spoke calmly, in a loud voice, surveying his audience. His eyes flashed deep green beneath heavy black brows. Luna thought he sounded a little like her father. Spittle flew from his thick, fleshy lips and hit the faces of those standing closest to the pulpit.

'The Lord has placed me here,' he declared, 'and He has said to me: "I have put you here as a watchman in the centre of Italy that you may hear my words and announce them to the people."

'The Lord has driven my ship into the open sea; the wind drives me forward. The Lord forbids my return. I spoke last night with the Lord and said, "Pity me, O Lord. Lead me back to my haven." "It is impossible," said the Lord. "See you not that the wind is contrary?" "I will preach, if so I must, but why need I meddle with the government of Florence?" "If you would make Florence a holy city, you must establish her on firm foundations and give her a government which favours virtue."'

The preacher held aloft a crucifix and the sun caught its gleam and sent a blinding light into the congregation. 'God has called me to reform the city and the Church, and God's will will be done. I urge you to put to death all those who desire the restoration of the Medici. Repent, O Florence, whilst there is still time,' he called. 'Clothe thyself in the white garments of purification. Wait no longer, for there may be no further time for repentance.'

Luna glanced anxiously at Papa but she couldn't tell if the preacher's words worried him. He listened as those around him did, his expression immutable as the marble face of the carved Virgin Mary looking down at the babe in her lap in the private chapel on the far aisle.

'To preserve and strengthen your city now, Florentines, you must love one another. The citizens must drop feuds and forget all past offences. God will reward your benevolence.

Go back, Florentines, to the spare, simple ways of Christ, and show others the way.'

Luna heard tenderness in his entreaties to the congregation and there was a murmur of agreement from the floor. The people swayed and gasped as one as the preacher grew ever more impassioned. Luna swayed just as the strangers around her did, and there was a warm fealty in doing so.

'The Devil uses the great to oppress the poor so the poor can't do good.' The preacher pointed sharply into the crowd and Luna felt as though he was singling her out but then she noticed others' faces in equal measure of rapture and remorse. No one uttered a sound; they were all beholden to the man in the pulpit. His voice rose, high-pitched in its condemnation. 'Remove from amongst yourselves these poems and games and taverns, and the evil fashions of women's clothes.' His voice rose again, this time to a violent squeal, feeding off the congregation's adoration like a sapling to water. 'Throw out everything noxious to the health of the soul. Let everyone live for God and not for the world. Love all in simplicity and charity.'

Luna felt a stirring of rapture in her belly. She turned to her step-mamma and grasped her hand a moment, holding steady to her stick with the other. Then, noticing Friar Bartolomeo beside her, she nodded to him. Her father stood nearby and so, without thinking, she reached across and grasped his palm, warm in her own, before letting go. Luna felt this preacher had found the good in them all. She reached out and took Maria's hand next. They were all here together.

The seated parishioners moved forward for the consecration of the Host. Luna closed her eyes and prayed. She prayed that Papa might find rest from his busy schedule; she gave thanks for Mamma Lucrezia's stew; she prayed for Maria's future as a wife, may she find courage to enjoy it; and she prayed for Pippo to be safe when he joined the preacher's boys. It was good to be heard. She knew it was wrong, but she slipped in a final prayer for the poor dead dog.

The congregation had begun to disperse and, in a happy daze, Luna joined the crowd moving towards the doors. She waved to Maria farther ahead then turned to look for Mamma Lucrezia and Pippo in the sea of faces behind. As she did, she lost her footing and fell. Sawdust pressed against her cheek and one elbow stung painfully. The crowd flowed around her like water around a rock and Luna pushed herself up as quickly as she could and reset her walking stick firmly. She moved on more carefully and managed herself well enough, but her cheeks burned.

Then she heard voices and turned again. Three young women around her own age stood close, though none of them as tall as she. Luna didn't know them but she could tell by their dress they were from good families. Still, they stared. A man drew himself up to stand beside the ladies, older than they and of an age to hold sway, though by the cut of his tight velvet breeches, Luna wondered with what intent. She held to her walking stick, feeling the press of the pearl against her palm as he sidled closer. How many such as him had she encountered through the years, who saw first and foremost an opportunity to court attention when they spied her. She rounded out her shoulders decisively.

'I remember you, cripple legs. I see you are still falling down,' he said, making sure his lady friends had heard. 'I should have dealt with you when I had the chance; the house of God is no more a place for mongrels than the street. You are just as pitiful as that mangy dog.'

Luna felt a surge of disgust at the man's cold indifference. 'And you're a coward who takes pleasure in killing helpless animals,' she replied without hesitation.

Surprise spread across his face. His Adam's apple worked ferociously. 'If you were a man, you would not be able to say those words to me.' The girls sniggered and made Luna even more furious.

'Yet I am a woman, and I will shame you all the same.'

Not until she was out of the church and finally able to swing off to the side did Luna breathe again. Her chest burned and something like elation peppered her breath. She looked around, expecting to be set upon by the stranger, but no one followed. She overheard a lady mention the temperature was expected to rise and her companion complained about the impact on the fruit of her peach trees. Two gentlemen made plans to gather later. Luna's heart pounded fierce and proud.

She saw her step-mamma appear at the cathedral's entrance, Pippo swinging from her arm. Maria must be somewhere in the crowds milling around the piazza. Mamma Lucrezia and Pippo were forced to halt by the tall wooden doors whilst those in front progressed slowly. Luna walked towards them, excusing herself as she weaved through groups of parishioners heading in the opposite direction. When she saw that they'd noticed her, she stopped and waited. She took a step to the side to make way for the passing crowds.

'The crippled daughter of Signore Fusili fell. That's what slowed our exit,' Luna overheard a woman say. 'Thank God my husband would never allow such shame upon his name.'

'Only think how much sin there must have been in her mother's womb to corrupt a baby's body thus,' her companion answered. 'Every good lady of Florence knows it was the Devil got her with child.'

Other ladies near to the pair heard too and crossed themselves hurriedly. How fast they are to judge, Luna thought, who feign a charitable heart. She was about to make a fiendish face but then the first lady spoke again.

'I hear the preacher plans to make her kind attend the lepers' Mass.'

There were muttered approvals all round and it was like the murmurings of the congregation but Luna heard the truth of it. She stumbled away and nearly walked into her step-mamma, so distracted was she. The glower in Mamma Lucrezia's eyes told Luna that she'd overheard too. She took Luna by the arm and steered her back around in the direction of where the carriage waited, towards the ladies. Luna's pulse thrummed loud in her ears. She dropped her head. She did not want to see their judgement. They came upon the group and her step-mamma pushed through, holding firm to Luna's arm and dragging Pippo along with the other.

Luna didn't let go of Mamma Lucrezia's hand as they moved away from the women who had insulted her. She was relieved to see Papa walking towards them, and there was Maria waiting by the carriage. Papa waved the driver forward.

'Get us home,' Mamma Lucrezia said.

Papa helped Luna into the carriage before hauling Filippo into his arms and depositing him beside his mother. Maria followed and sat close to Luna, grasping her hands. Their father directed the driver before turning away.

'You are not coming?' Luna asked.

'Papa will be home later,' Mamma Lucrezia answered, and they watched him stride towards the circle of men.

Luna sat back. She felt her step-mamma's gaze and tried to smile. A fine shard of wood from the rough sawdust had attached to the wool of her skirts and she plucked at it methodically until it was out. She would not be complacent again in Mass, if she was allowed to worship there.

'Do you think the lady was correct in what she said, that I will have to attend the lepers' Mass?' Luna asked.

'I'm not sure, though there is always much gossip straight after Mass.'

Luna nodded. A good crowd still milled about the square. At least that man would most assuredly hesitate before speaking to her again. A smile broke across her face.

'Where is your shame, Leonarda?' Mamma Lucrezia was staring at her. 'I would like one day not to have to scurry away from the judgement I see in all those women's eyes. They are my friends but that can change. Do not tempt such a fate on your family. Be modest and silent. Be the daughter I want and the sister Maria needs to ensure her own future is not tainted by you.' She looked down at Luna's boots and grimaced. 'How I hate those.'

CHAPTER EIGHT

Vincenzio breathed deeply. He'd be gone from the city soon enough. Two more days till he could really give Apollonius his head and feel the power of his gallop across the hills towards Prato. He'd prepared a strong box to hold the bags of his own money. With any luck, Roberto was already back in Siena. In the meantime he'd enjoy this breezy morning as best he could. Lucrezia was taking the carriage to the cathedral and he'd not objected. He preferred to walk to Mass; it gave him time to think away from the constant demands of his family and Lucrezia's badgering about the Palagio offer for Maria. He turned back to admire his home, the bold street frontage as impressive as the Rucellai Palazzo. He'd only need a Palagio union if he became so desperate for coin he had no choice, and he didn't plan on that happening. The Spinelli family in Pistoia needed a bride for one of their sons and, from what he knew of the boy, they'd even pay to secure one. He was sure Luna would suffice.

Still, he could not lay the blame for his mood entirely at his wife's feet; he was monstrously distracted by his business. His studiolo had become like a prison of ledgers and accountability. However long he spent massaging the numbers, he could not make the books come out positive. The truth was that wool cloth no longer commanded the prices he'd budgeted for nor did he have the coin to invest in the more expensive silks. He should sell the property in Prato and probably one of his shopfronts in Florence too, but he refused to be forced back to being just one of the weavers. He'd be rejected from the company of all those gentlemen whose favour he'd fostered, rejected from the Platonic Academy, a failure as a businessman and no better than his father. His pace slowed.

Vincenzio remembered his father as a tired and unhappy man, who never ventured beyond the district of his wool guild, praying at the local church each dawn on his way to the shop from their home in rented rooms in one of the older houses, returning each night as the curfew bells rang out. The sourness of potential failure dampened Vincenzio's tongue. His father had been content as a weaver, but he'd always needed more, and he still did. He determined to return to the days when his business was one of Florence's most successful, when he produced two hundred bolts of highest quality cloth a year at a cost in excess of nine thousand florins. He would not give up the life he'd worked so hard to establish.

Damn Piero for sending Roberto to the city and adding to his stress, and damn the preacher's puritans for clamping down on his easiest form of relief; he could really do with a stop at the whorehouse on Via Maggio. He stood and forced himself to swallow through the tightness in his throat. He must not forget to gather his most valuable books to give to Friar Bartolomeo for safekeeping in the monastery crypt. How had it come to this? Others passed Vincenzio and stared curiously at the well-dressed gentleman tugging on his collar. There'd be no relief this day. The preacher's boys were worse than the old gangs who used to hawk their little backsides to any pot-bellied banker for a few grossi. Friar Savonarola made sure there was drabness where there used to be colour; no poetry safe, no great art, none of the joyful lusts of spring.

He walked on, no time for pleasure even if it had still been acceptable, no time for any entertainment whilst he grappled with his business woes and the Medicis' plot to return, though the delightful Ambrosia would say that was a piss-poor excuse for not visiting her bed. The terce bells rang out, as predictable as the Sun's movement across the sky. These difficult times were sent by God to test his faith. He must not lose sight of what was important. If his plans went well there'd be money soon enough. The thought made Vincenzio step more lightly. He was not beaten yet.

The cathedral bells crescendoed and the sound was uplifting. He set his shoulders squarely and cleared his face into an affable smile. This morning he would turn his attention to the word of God. The Mass would be very busy with all the good families of Florence attending. Who knew what opportunity might present itself?

Ahead he saw groups already gathered in the cathedral square, gentlemen in the tall hats and colours of Florence's oldest families, and he went to greet Bernardo Rucellai and his associates. His mood sank as he observed the grave demeanour of the circle.

'He was severely wounded.'

'Of whom do you speak?' Vincenzio asked Donato Velluti, a successful lawyer who was also a fine storyteller.

'A relative of that vermin Piero de' Medici, discovered on his back in a hovel near the church of San Giorgio,' Donato answered before crossing himself. 'Some say it was an old vendetta come back to claim him, but I say this was a traitor's reward and well deserved.'

Vincenzio felt the blood drain from his face. 'Does he live?'

'Why do you care, Vincenzio? If a Medici man is mad enough to defy our city's laws then he must accept the risk and consequence. No doubt he was here to do some skulduggery set for him by Piero.'

'The man is dead and there will be an investigation. It is better we do not gossip on this matter.' Bernardo spoke for them all.

Vincenzio nodded in agreement, furiously scanning the faces around him for signs of suspicion. It must be Roberto of whom they were speaking.

'We Florentines are tranquil men who seek to maintain peaceful relations with everyone,' Donato said. 'The Medici are arrogant and ever since Lorenzo's death, the family's activities have become frivolous and dishonourable.'

Roberto was a fool, Vincenzio thought. Probably believed himself invincible and paid heed to none of his warnings, choosing rather to enjoy the city's bars till he'd lost his senses in wine and let slip something incriminating:

a boast of his Medici blood or some such pride-filled bombast. Unless, of course, Vincenzio had been right in his conjecture that the same man who'd attacked him had stopped the messenger from delivering his note to Piero and so Roberto's presence in the city had been known. That would mean he was at greater risk of discovery, for surely they'd seek out the author of the letter next. This turn of events was troubling.

A torrent of bells drowned out the men's conversation as the many smaller churches picked up the hour and all across the city the call to Mass went out. The knelling marked the hour of the day for the cloth dyers and wool cleansers as much as for the bankers and lawyers Vincenzio fraternised with on the cathedral steps. The group of men made their way towards the church doors but Vincenzio hung back. His mind was madly hunting through his last conversation with Roberto for anything that might expose his connection to the man.

A small group of worshippers wandered past and Vincenzio heard one of the men talking excitedly. He turned abruptly, convinced he'd been recognised as a Medici traitor and his connection to Roberto was about to be exposed. But the man didn't stop to accost him. What coward's elixir had taken hold of his senses? Vincenzio bent to his knees a moment and gasped. Then he righted himself and watched the party of gentlemen disappear into the darkness of the cathedral's interior. He must quell these nervous reflexes.

Before long, he saw his family's carriage drawing near, so he rearranged his face into as agreeable a smile as he could manage—just broad enough, he hoped, to convey an easy confidence—and went to greet them.

Inside, the cathedral was congested already, and Vincenzio wrinkled his nose at the smell of the unwashed crowds who'd gathered to hear the preacher of the people. It reminded him of standing with his mother and father in the poor church of his childhood. That boy had admired the plain white-washed walls with what Vincenzio now knew was misplaced awe. He waved his arms and pushed back roughly to create some space for his family. He kept alert for any sudden movements towards him, fearing an attack just as Roberto had suffered. He'd not be taken by surprise.

When he was satisfied they were all comfortably positioned and could see the pulpit, he turned his attention back to who was standing nearby. Bernardo had stopped to his right and slightly ahead. Vincenzio felt the tightness in his shoulders ease. No man would be mad enough to attack him so near to where the Gonfalonier of Justice stood. He determined to remind Bernardo that he had a copy of Joannes de Monte Regio's much lauded *Epitome of Ptolemy's Almagest* and would be pleased to bring it to the lecture in late August. Best to continue confident as his usual self.

His wife was trying to attract his attention, so Vincenzio turned back to his family. She pulled him in even closer so that his head was almost touching her own bowed forehead. Such an immodest display made his skin burn but he knew recoiling would only draw further attention.

'I saw trouble at the Palazzo Canturi on our way here,' she said softly.

'Indeed?' He raised his eyebrows with consternation.

'They were being harshly treated and their home disrespected. I saw my dear friend Cosima's precious things discarded into the street like waste. It worries me, husband. If good families such as they are targeted, then we are none of us safe.'

'Calm yourself, mistress, there is nothing to fear. Look, the preacher comes.' He directed her attention to the line of monks processing towards the altar and turned too, any sign of alarm smoothed from his face. There was no need to worry his wife, though Vincenzio's mind raced. Marco Canturi was a friend of Piero's, though he, like Vincenzio and all the other Medici supporters, had publicly disavowed that alliance. Was Roberto's presence in the city the excuse the preacher needed to begin a purge of the last of the Medici supporters?

He saw his client Mistress Letta Sassetti and smiled in greeting as she passed, noticing the tired drop of her cloak; perhaps he could persuade her husband to put in an order. Vincenzio made a note of where she stopped. More than likely Marco Canturi's house had been chosen for his wine-sodden parties and notorious taste for young boys; Vincenzio had warned him to suspend his revelries until it was acceptable once more. Though it did not make it any better, to be sure. The old families of Florence had endured two years of Savonarola's supposed peaceful leadership, when in truth what he did most effectively was to burn their books and mistake their knowledge for evil sin. But Vincenzio would steel himself against another bout of panic; the preacher's methods were unsophisticated and he must surely fall on his sword before long. His day of reckoning would come.

The noise dropped and the people settled as the preacher stepped to the pulpit. This was the time for godly reflection. Vincenzio had to squint to see anything through the stream of sunlight. It was very clever the way the preacher stood in the halo of luminosity, just as he spoke of the divine light the Lord had sent to him. All around, people murmured in agreement with his words and Vincenzio was astounded. Was he the only sane man to hear the brittleness in the hollow-cheeked voice? How could Savonarola speak of a new era of universal peace whilst ransacking the homes of good citizens and banishing others? Discord was growing and word had travelled that Florence was become unstable, yet the people believed the preacher's promise of riches, glory and power.

Luna leant over and grasped his hand; he'd not expected that. Her eyes were bright and he saw straight away she'd been beguiled like all these other fools; the fickle nature of her female emotions was no match for Savonarola.

After what seemed a tediously lengthy wait, Vincenzio finally stepped up to accept the blessed sacrament. One day, his place would be amongst the seats of honour, but for now he must ensure his actions did not raise the Great Council's suspicions. Perhaps it were best he did not travel so soon after a Medici spy was killed in the city. He must think carefully on the risks.

Once back with his family, he dipped his head closer to Lucrezia. 'I may have cause to delay my journey to Pistoia.'

His wife's face dulled. 'You disappoint me. Some good news right now would be most welcome.'

'I do what I must to ensure this family's safety and our future,' he said through gritted teeth.

Finally the Mass concluded and the family began the slow move towards the exit. Vincenzio felt a hand grab his shoulder and jumped like a rooster in a snake pit. But Friar Bartolomeo only indicated he should follow as he slipped through the crowd. Vincenzio joined him behind one of the side pillars.

'God's blessings on you,' Friar Bartolomeo said in greeting.

'And on you,' Vincenzio replied curtly. 'I did not expect you here.'

The friar looked about before leaning in closer. 'I had to speak with you; we had visitors at Santa Croce earlier this morn. They were rooting around for illuminated manuscripts and objects of wealth to confiscate, or so they said.' His voice shook a little.

Vincenzio thought of what his wife had just told him and it seemed that what she'd witnessed in the street was not a random raid but more likely part of the organised approach they'd all been waiting for.

'They have begun confiscating things, then? I will send my books to you for safekeeping in the crypt.'

The friar nodded. 'That is not what I am most concerned about, however. They asked if I knew of any of my family returning to the city.'

'What did you tell them?' Vincenzio kept his face empty of expression as he spoke; who knew where the preacher's spies loitered.

Friar Bartolomeo wrung his hands.

'Take control of yourself,' Vincenzio snapped.

The friar shook his head. 'I did not tell them anything, but I fair thought my tongue would slip from my throat.'

'God's teeth, that is a relief! The news is bad. Roberto is dead. I heard it said before Mass. More than likely there will be an investigation. So we must keep our mouths shut tight.'

'God save his soul,' the friar said and crossed himself. 'What should I do? They will surely come for me next.'

'Try to control yourself. Your face is red as a whore's painted cheek.' Then he spoke more reassuringly. 'If the Great Council believed you'd colluded with Roberto then surely they would have arrested you when they searched the monastery this morn and you'd already be hanging from the prison wall.'

'I may have condemned my brothers.' Friar Bartolomeo spoke more evenly, but there was still an edge to his voice.

His friend could be right. Vincenzio thought quickly. The Medici trail still might lead the soldiers of the Great Council to the monastery as well as his own door. But what could he do? 'Maintain your calm,' was all he said, 'and be careful, for the risk to us now is doubled. I will delay my journey to Pistoia.'

'But what of your pledge to Piero, for the soldiers?' Friar Bartolomeo hissed. 'Would it not be better to get it done whilst attention is on the city and the Medici spy they uncovered?'

'It is too risky right now.'

'I don't know which is worse: the ire of the Medicis or the Great Council? How verily I wish I were not related to that family!'

Vincenzio looked at the trembling hands of the monk. He heard fear in his weakened voice. Was this how he must be too? 'The Great Council's soldiers will indeed focus their discovery within the city's walls and certainly my travels are well justified.' Vincenzio worked through his own doubts as he spoke. 'My business interests do not wait on the Great

Council's permission, nor would the Council expect me to delay an important trip because a Medici spy had been discovered. Indeed that would make me appear more guilty.' The Medicis were not easily riled, so nor would he allow himself to be. In this very church, Lorenzo had lost his own brother, Giuliano, to an assassin's blade and still bravely united the city behind the Medici colours and put an end to his rival Francesco de' Pazzi's plot to kill him and place his own family in the Medicis' stead. 'I will leave for Prato and then on to Pistoia, as originally planned,' he said decisively. The Medici star would rise again, just as it always did, and Vincenzio would be right there beside the family. 'Now I must go. My wife and children will be waiting.'

'So be it.' The friar nodded but his lips quivered. 'We are in God's hands and He alone knows our fate and when it will come to claim us.'

There were still crowds on the steps and in the square. Vincenzio spied Rucellai and went to join the group of gentlemen, but before he had a chance to speak with Bernardo he saw Lucrezia waving to him. She stood with his children at a distance from the other churchgoers. They were a handsome lot, even Luna in the fine dress he'd had made for her portrait. His boy stood firmly, he noted proudly. He lifted his chin and nodded to the gentlemen in farewell, capricious as his wife, the lot of them, but he'd do anything to avoid being banished from their society. They must have no reason to judge him or his family. News of Roberto's death rang in Vincenzio's ears, but he did not feel he was mad to maintain his support for the banished Medici family; Piero's father had helped Vincenzio when he most needed it and he'd always be in their debt. He'd swear allegiance to the

Medici camp thrice before any here; loyalty was still a coveted virtue in Florence, at least the last time he checked.

Vincenzio made his way over to where his family waited and took his wife's hand to help her into the carriage. He stood back to let his daughters enter and then lifted Pippo onto the seat beside Lucrezia. When they were all comfortably seated, he waved the driver off.

This was a most valuable time of day, when he could stop and discuss political events without the pressure of business calling him. He wanted to hear any further fragments of information about Roberto. It would take him much longer than his family to get home, given the number of gentlemen he saw the potential to engage in discussion, but it mattered not. Still standing on the edge of the street, he closed his eyes a second and breathed deeply. When he turned back to where the crowd of men gathered, he was smiling. He mounted the steps two at a time, cursing the precarious state of his fair city as he went. It was to be a challenging time ahead, in more ways than one, but change was coming; he just needed to endure till then.

CHAPTER NINE

Luna hurried to the balcony when she heard her father's step on the flagstones. They'd been home from Mass for more than an hour and Mamma Lucrezia had taken Pippo off to the kitchens to find something to eat whilst Maria had gone upstairs to sit with her sewing. Luna had been listening for his return and her insides churned. Her temper had gotten the better of her; she should never have spoken back to the stranger like that, but hers was not a tongue that could stay silent when insulted and the young man had deserved it. Still, the thought of being relegated to the lepers' Mass filled her with dread. Papa would know if there was any truth in what she'd overheard.

Her father went straight to his studiolo and, after what she felt was time enough for him to have settled, Luna followed. She remembered the hawk she'd seen flying through the city; that was a good omen. She hesitated at the door.

Her father was standing on a small stool, his back to her, reaching up to a shelf of books. It was impossible to tell what mood was upon him; he seemed so lofty and distant up there. This was her favourite room in the palazzo, the smallest and the fullest. The window to the left of where he stood looked out across the piazza in front of their house and from that vantage he could spy every visitor if he wanted to. The midday sun peeped over the ledge and tendrils of light played in the air like insects, dappling the floor then flitting across the desk that Luna saw was a mess of books. One was open with pages crushed by the force of being dropped, she presumed, whilst a second balanced precariously on another's spine and Luna worried that any more additions would simply topple off and smack to the ground. Her father closed the book he held and dropped it to the desk. Sure enough, it landed on the edge and dropped to the floor. She couldn't help herself; without even knocking, she went in and picked it up. Then she saw the one that had its spine almost rent apart. It was the copy of the Isotta Nogarola dialogue that Luna had borrowed so frequently she'd begun to believe it was her book. The sight of it now broken distressed her. She pressed her palm across the crushed page and smoothed the hide cover as best she could to soften the creases.

Her father heard her and stepped down. Luna greeted him with a fast bob. He stretched his back.

'All those can go,' he said, sweeping his arms out with a flourish.

She hesitated. 'Do you wish me to take them somewhere?'

'Why else are you here? You can tell Mamma that I cannot do this any more quietly if that is her complaint.'

'No, Papa. Mamma did not send me.' She turned to the jumble of books again. 'What are you doing with these?'

'Your sister is probably threading a needle to her tapestry as we speak, but you, Luna, still prefer musty old books.'

She nodded.

'Very well, my dear,' he said, stepping onto the stool once more.

Luna listened to the distant sounds of the street, waiting for him to continue.

'I am deciding which of my books to save from the purge of Savonarola's fire. Those on the table will go back onto the shelves.'

Luna decided it was no longer the time to ask about the lepers' Mass. Here was work that needed her attention. When her father stopped throwing books to the desk, he leant across and Luna saw a smaller pile on the shelf beside where he stood.

'These are the precious volumes that I will entrust to Friar Bartolomeo for safekeeping.'

He added one to that stack, then tossed another carelessly down to the table, followed by another and then a fourth. Luna arranged the volumes on the table into neat towers. She recognised a recently published collection of musings from a local Florentine writer, one her father would not allow her to read. Near it was the first in Marsilio Ficino's *Three Books on Life* from which her father gave her step-mamma recipes to aid his headaches. She remembered the man from the few times she'd seen him at her father's gatherings. A most learned and soft-hearted individual, who she'd always thought would have encouraged her to read his works.

'Would you allow me to borrow a book?' she asked.

'If it's one of those on the table, I see no issue. More than likely they will end up in the preacher's bonfire anyway. But these,' he motioned to the smaller pile on the shelf beside him, 'you may not take any from there.' He reached across the shelf for another volume and passed a small text down to her. It landed lightly in her hands. 'It's a shame your Greek is not better; a true scholar must be versed in the ancient languages.'

She read the words of the title, ignoring his comment.

'What will I do without my Aristotle or Plato?' He gestured to the shelf as he reached for another book and lifted it to his nose. Luna loved the smell of a favourite book too. Then he added it to his small selection. 'So much knowledge to be put to the fire in the name of our Lord. Damnation to Savonarola.'

Luna ran her hand across the leather-bound cover. 'I cannot believe they will really burn our books.'

'Only the Lord's word is sacred enough for the preacher.'

'Do you think they will come to us like they did the Canturis?'

'His eye bears in our direction.'

'It is not right they can take from people's homes.'

'I do not intend for them to take my prized volumes. Friar Bartolomeo is hiding his books to save them; we must do the same.' He scratched his head, peering up at the laden shelves. 'We need only gather the most important texts: Pythagoras, Cicero, Pliny the Elder, Plutarch, Philolaus, Heraclides, Ecphantos, Plato. The rest I can afford to lose.'

The book by Isotta Nogarola lay where it had been dropped. Her father didn't value it. Luna sighed. All these books deserved to be saved. She opened the one she held, a translation of a Greek mathematician's work. *The Sand Reckoner* by Archimedes. The illustrated work was very unusual. The small, neat text was dense.

Papa turned and rested a moment on the stool, stretching his arms out.

'This reaching and lifting invigorates my mind but it makes my bones ache.' He noticed the book she held. 'I've not opened that one for many moons. How proud I was to secure that translation of Archimedes from the family of Paolo dal Pozzo Toscanelli. God rest his soul. I took it to the Academy and Marsilio looked at me with new interest; you see he wanted it too, and Paolo was his dear friend, but I got it. That book led to my full acceptance into the Academy.'

'Well done, Papa.'

He nodded. 'They saw what I was capable of and they could not refuse me.' He gestured to her and she handed the book back. 'It served its purpose,' he said and dropped it on the table.

Luna treasured these books as much as he and would have saved them all if she could. She took each one he passed to her as carefully as if it were Venetian cut glass. 'I would choose to save this one, Papa,' she said, holding up the Nogarola.

He inclined his head. 'You've always admired the writings of that woman.' He reviewed the growing collection of books that were to be saved. 'But I have only so much space for my treasured volumes, and Isotta Nogarola doesn't deserve to sit beside Plato.'

He turned back to the shelf and Luna slipped the book into her pocket. 'Where will you hide them?'

'At Santa Croce. Friar Bartolomeo will store them in the crypt where he's already preparing to put the important books from the monastery's collection.'

'What of other things, like the sculpture in the courtyard or the paintings in the main hall? Should we not hide those also?'

'Yes, if I want to keep them from the fire, I should remove them immediately, but I do not want to raise suspicion, and empty walls where yesterday hung painted scenes would be clearly visible. Books I can rearrange.'

'But, Papa, we cannot lose all of our beautiful art.'

'I will do my best, Luna.'

She pressed on with renewed vigour. No one else in the family understood how important were her father's books, and together they would save them. His shape blocked the window as he moved to the lower shelves. Luna lit a candle so they could better read each title.

'There are many books piling up here,' she commented as she began a new tower. 'Perhaps we should begin placing them back onto the shelves?'

'You may leave if the work tires you.'

She shook her head. 'I didn't mean that.'

'Did you mean to shame me at Mass earlier?'

Luna felt her cheeks fire up.

Her father turned, his eyes narrowed. 'I had the displeasure of hearing your name uttered as I stood conversing after Mass.'

So the gossip-mongers had not wasted any time. Luna put down the book she held.

'Signore Palagio made a complaint against you.'

Luna knew it had been too much to hope the incident had passed without any accompanying gossip. Yet of all the men to have overheard the exchange in the cathedral, she felt deeply unlucky that it had been Signore Palagio. Of course he'd take the news to her father; he was considering her sister for his son after all. 'Forgive me, Papa.' She wished he'd get down off the stool. 'In my defence, I was provoked.'

'Beyond the point of common sense it seems. Did you lose your wit?'

Luna stared up at him. 'I did not, sir,' she replied firmly, wondering if Signore Palagio had actually seen the incident or if he'd only heard about it through the talk of others. She had no hope of convincing her father if the gossipers had taken her outburst to their truthless lips and spun it into something much worse than what had actually happened.

'It is a woman's burden to be overrun by her emotions.' His voice had shifted to a more conciliatory tone. 'But I am disappointed, Leonarda, by your irrational antics. You used to be so sensible.' He paused and stepped down from the stool. 'Now I go to rest but you must stay and put all these books that will remain back onto the shelves.'

He raised his eyebrows as he turned back to her, one hand on the door. 'Be careful on the stool.'

Luna listened to her father's heavy step as he walked away. She took in the scene of disarray before her. Books were strewn across the table and some had fallen to the floor again. Her father's selection of volumes to keep were dangerously balanced on the lowest shelf. It would take her until well after nightfall to rearrange it all. She stood in front of the stool as though facing down an opponent in battle rather than a simple wooden step. Her father knew how much harder it was for her to balance and she understood this was her punishment. She would not show weakness; that had been implicit in his warning.

By the time she'd finished replenishing the shelves and then moving his collection ready to be sent to the monastery, Luna's back ached from bending and reaching, but she was pleased with herself. The room looked neater than it had for a long time. Admittedly the top shelf was left empty; she could not reach that high, but she'd managed to spread the books across the remaining shelves so it gave the appearance of being full. Should anyone come seeking books to confiscate, they'd not think to ask if any were missing. It still saddened her that so many might be burned and she'd just stacked them ready for Savonarola's fire. She'd taken a moment to open the small book by the Greek mathematician. Her father had inked his name on the title page, and he'd drawn the 'F' of their surname with a flourish that was unusually ornate. It was like a cipher to a younger, freer version of her father. She decided to keep it along with the Nogarola, already safe in her pocket.

*

Papa arrived home late the following night, having delivered his books and precious belongings safely to be hidden in the church's crypt. He explained he'd made slow progress on the return journey because a huge bonfire had already been lit and had brought crowds into the streets. He described the enormous scaffold in the shape of a pyramid that had been erected opposite the Palazzo della Signoria and the pile of personal belongings, high as the first set of windows in the tower, spread round its base: looking glasses, velvet caps, scent bottles and pomade pots, jars of rouge, beads, fans, necklaces and trinkets of every kind. On top of these were piled books and drawings, chessboards, busts and portraits of celebrated beauties as well as sensual paintings by Lorenzo di Credi and Botticelli sacrificed by the now-reformed artists themselves. All dangerous items that might engender lascivious thoughts, according to Savonarola's men. At the very summit was an effigy of a Venetian merchant who had offered 20,000 scudi for the works of art now about to be consigned to the flames. The huge pile was surrounded by guards and was set alight whilst members of the Signoria watched from a balcony. A choir chanted and trumpets blared as the flames rose. The church bells of Florence rang and the smoke fanned out across the city as a warning to any who thought to challenge the preacher.

Luna watched as Mamma Lucrezia gave Papa a goblet of wine and he told them how looters, or the preacher's men—he couldn't tell them apart, so indiscriminate was their appetite for destruction—ransacked house after house to add to the growing pile on the bonfire. Luna sat with Maria and listened with a growing sense of unease. Mamma Lucrezia gave them some wine too and Luna was glad of its fortifying effect, for she did not like the fires. Nothing distinguished the swirl of a bonfire's thick smoke from the pyres that burned the dead. Fires had been used to burn the bodies of those infected by the plague and, as a child, Luna had lived through three such terrifying times when the orange haze over the city had lasted days and the thud of bodies dropped into the pyres had been indistinguishable from the logs collapsing into ash. There was no pleasure in feeling the heat on her cheek when the crackle and spit of flame was so close.

Her papa described the plumes that reached as high as the cathedral spire. 'Friar Savonarola's loyal flock continue to fill the cathedral. He is a law unto himself.' He gulped down the wine. 'He has split the city into angels and demons. Apollonius didn't like the huge pyres of belongings; they spooked him. At least I am reassured by visiting the monastery. All our most precious things are now safely stored within its crypt.'

'I know you suffer, my husband, but do so here; stay home in the private bosom of your family.'

'I must still travel to Prato in two morns' time but now the fires are lit, the worst is over. This will satisfy the preacher's thirst for penance for a time at least.'

'I despair amidst so much chaos.'

'The city will be calmer after this night. There is nothing further to fear, my wife.'

Later, when Luna lay in bed, she thought of the two books she'd taken from her father's collection. Both would have burned easily, the old paper already crinkled and dry as kindling. Hers was a small gesture of defiance but she was glad to have saved them. She hoped her father's collection was not discovered by the marauding looters. She still had the friar's copy of the Sacrobosco and she took it up from where it lay on the small stand beside the bed. Reading would distract her from the frightening discord in the streets.

Luna read again about each of the planets in their individual spheres, circling in epicycles and constantly moving towards the centre of their orbit and closer to Earth, and then out again, each following a distinct pattern within their immutable sphere. All these planets and stars coexisted in perfect patterns within the ethereal, the fifth essence. That was a true miracle of God's making to inspire mankind, not this preacher's fire.

She thought about the Moon, always there in the night sky, far from the reach of earthly men, unchanged by shadows cast upon it. She thought of her mother up there with the Moon, guarding over her. It was a fancy but, with the smell of burning books in the air and the frightening sounds of cheers and whoops from the preacher's men in the streets, Luna wanted to believe in her mother's protection now more than ever. Her mind went back to the Mass when the preacher had demanded that Medici allies be killed. She prayed to her mother in the Moon to protect Papa too. Then she took up the Sacrobosco again and read on. She turned the information over in her mind, slowing at the section that detailed how one could use calculations from observing the Moon in eclipse to fix the position of other planets. This was challenging; though she could absorb a philosophical argument from one reading of a text, she found mathematical-based processes less easy. The sphere of heavens was beyond what any person could touch and see with clarity and she wondered how Sacrobosco so confidently determined what moved and what was fixed, when it was all so far above. Even though she understood the process of mapping the positions of planets as a way of showing movement, it seemed an arrogance of man. How could they really understand the sphere of perfect patterns that was the fifth essence?

She looked at the explanatory drawing of an eclipse, running her finger across the lines that linked the image of the Moon and the Sun and Earth in a conical frame on the page. One night she might be blessed with witnessing a lunar eclipse; they were uncommon and infrequent, but that only made the possibility more exciting. She read on. Sacrobosco's measurements were accurate to a degree. It was a fool's wish to think she could ever replicate anything like this level of accuracy but it would help her understanding if she could put the science into practice. She pictured standing with Papa in the courtyard at night, the book open on the wall of the pond, the Moon above moving slowly, relentlessly, into shadow and darkening before their eyes. They would take their time, carefully marking the positions and time of alignment of the Moon with the Sun and Earth, working together.

Another night of star gazing would allow her to show Papa how much she'd already learnt. She must find out when the next lunar eclipse was due. She prayed he'd be as excited as she was to watch it together, father and daughter, teacher and student, in perfect companionship.

CHAPTER TEN

July 1496

Luna was sitting in the garden with her step-mamma. Papa had been gone for three days. He'd journey first to his shopfront in Prato, ten miles northwest of Florence, then on to Pistoia and the prospect of new customers, Mamma Lucrezia explained, and would be back in time for the Mass at which Pippo was to sing, which was only a month away.

'Take heart, my girl. Anyone would think he'd gone to fight in the Milanese wars from your downcast eyes.' Mamma Lucrezia's voice was bright as the morning sun glaring down on them, though when she stood to go back into the house, she didn't reach down and kiss Luna on the top of her head or remind her of her tasks—she turned and disappeared without any further word. When Papa was absent she lost her sense of purpose.

Luna plucked at the grass, pulling up weeds as she found them and smoothing over the soil where they left a hole. Any hope of observing an eclipse with her father would have to wait. Instead, she'd use this time to finish reading the Sacrobosco. Then she'd have more to contribute when Papa took her star gazing again. Her mind turned to the night of the attack on her father. What if he decided it was too dangerous to take her out at night at all? Despite the way it had ended, that evening had reminded Luna how sweet and warm it felt to be favoured by Papa. She watched mites scrabbling around, unhappy to be exposed, and sprinkled dirt on top of them. Watching an eclipse with her father would be very special indeed. Luna eased herself up off the grass and went inside. She could find out easily enough from his book of astronomical predictions when the next lunar eclipse would take place. She'd seen the book when they were sorting through his collection and she'd put it back onto the shelf herself.

Luna hesitated at the door to her father's studiolo. He was not there to give her permission to enter but nor could he stop her, she told herself as she went in. Even though so many of the books had already been sent to the monastery, the room still had the distinctive smell of parchment mixed with the herbs from his poultices. The state of the desk made Luna frown. She didn't know what made Papa so quick to anger of late, but if this mess was any indication, he had much on his mind. Quills had been dropped and ink spilt, and her father's business ledgers were piled atop one another in a ramshackle heap. A dirty wine goblet still sat where last he'd drunk, leaking a stale, sharp smell. Used poultices grew stiff and discoloured. Luna brushed her hand against the string of glass beads hooked over one of the shelves and took some pleasure in the familiar sound. At least that was crisp and clean. Footsteps reminded her she'd entered uninvited and moments later, Mamma Lucrezia appeared in the doorway.

'What business do you have in your father's private room?' she said impatiently. She had a cloth draped over one shoulder and bent to put down the basket of salad greens she carried so she could fold her arms firmly across her chest.

'I disturb no one whilst Papa is away. I am being very careful.'

'That may be so but he will be annoyed if he returns to find anything amiss in his studiolo.'

'He won't, I promise.'

A crashing of pots followed by shouts sounded from the kitchen. Mamma Lucrezia looked towards the staircase. 'The lady Margherita Palagio visits later and I am most nervous. I have not hosted her since my days in Bologna, and with your father absent I must manage alone. It is important that she leave this house impressed, for her opinion will influence the course of the marriage negotiations between our two families. I must make sure everything is perfect.' She frowned at Luna. 'I have asked Friar Bartolomeo also. His presence will be a comfort.'

Luna stayed where she was. Her heart sank at the mention of wedding plans for Maria again. She no longer felt any sympathy for her step-mamma's sagging shoulders when the cause was impressing the family who might steal away her sister. She sighed, for she must still help, however she felt about their guest. 'I will join you shortly, Mamma. Please just let me review one page and then I will be with you for the rest of the day.'

'Very well, Leonarda, but mind I don't have to come looking for you.' Mamma Lucrezia picked up the basket. 'We all miss dear Papa,' she said.

Luna pulled a book from a pile on one of the shelves. She recognised it from its slender spine. It was a tall, thin text and the pages stiff; it had not been read often. This was the list of astronomical predictions that her father had had prepared for him using the detailed data in the Alfonsine Tables. The book's perfect condition made her wonder how long it had been since Papa had indulged his enthusiasm for the science—another reason for her to remind him of its pleasures. She was disappointed not to find an eclipse listed until February of the next calendar year.

She tidied the room with vigour, replacing the dirty poultices into the bowl, rearranging the ledgers neatly and gathering the quills to be sharpened. Even without an eclipse, she hoped Papa would be impressed by her understanding of the Sacrobosco. She might also learn from the other book by the Greek mathematician that she'd kept—the Greeks offered much knowledge of mathematics, which was the basis for predictions in astronomy. *The Sand Reckoner* might offer her an insight into her papa's views as a younger man, as it had helped her father's rise from cloth maker to member of the Platonic Academy. Perhaps it could help change how men of import viewed her too.

*

It was late in the day when Margherita Palagio arrived. Luna and Maria sat in the main hall as they'd been told to do and listened to the voices of their mother and her guest grow loud as they approached from the staircase. Luna looked up at the ceiling high above painted with a scene of angels and clouds surrounding the baby Jesus held within his mother's embrace and silently prayed to Mother Mary for self-composure. Any who stood beneath the fresco understood its import; the Fusili family were within reach of the heavens. An arrangement of chairs had been placed near the windows that looked out across the piazza so that the shaft of sunlight might offer a pleasant backdrop to the conversation. A table laid with plates of sweets and fruits sat in the centre of the chairs.

Luna smoothed her skirts and stood so their guest would not see how she hung on her crutch for support. Maria jumped up when she saw her sister rise. They dropped into a curtsey when the door opened and Mamma Lucrezia led a tall and slender woman through. Mistress Palagio was older than her step-mamma but the sag in her cheek was covered with a powder of an unnatural colour that gave the effect of brightness. She nodded in acknowledgement of the two girls, then sat, and Mamma Lucrezia called for refreshments.

'I am so glad that you found the time to visit with us. I have missed your company.'

Luna heard the unsubtle flattery in her step-mamma's tone. Their guest smiled and nodded, then sipped her wine.

'Do you leave for your country villa soon?' Mamma Lucrezia asked.

'My husband insists we remain in our city home for at least another month, though I am keen to remove to cooler surrounds. The dirt is so much worse when it's hot, on my skin and on my clothes, and the smells.' Her mouth turned down as she spoke.

'We usually retire to Careggi, but not this summer.'

The lady raised her eyebrows. 'It must be worrying to be so closely aligned to that family in exile. I'm surprised you still speak of the Medici and their palaces.'

Mamma Lucrezia turned to a servant and Luna saw how her cheeks flushed. 'More wine,' she ordered.

Luna and Maria still stood awkwardly, for they had not been asked to sit. Luna gave her step-mamma a pointed stare but got no reaction.

'The Medicis were your benefactors, I believe? Disappointing to lose that support. I hear the Fusili shop on Via Tuargo has little stock these days. A sign of difficult times? How are you managing?'

'I'm sure we do not listen to gossip.'

'Lucrezia.' Mistress Palagio touched her step-mamma's arm as a close friend would do. 'We have known each other many years. There's no shame.'

'I assure you, I am quite content. We want for nothing.' Here she turned to Luna and Maria. 'Sit, my daughters, and let us share some delicacies.'

'Perhaps the gossip I hear is wrong,' the lady answered. She reached out her hand again to Mamma Lucrezia, who took it willingly.

Margherita Palagio then turned her attention to Luna and Maria. Mamma Lucrezia beckoned to Maria and Luna watched her move closer to the ladies. Their guest lifted Maria's chin so she could better inspect her face.

'Your daughter is a pretty thing.' Signora Palagio nodded to Luna next. No one spoke so that the click and clack of Luna's crutch sounded loud.

'This is your other daughter?' she asked Mamma Lucrezia, although she already knew the answer. Luna's face grew hot under the scrutiny.

'This is Leonarda Lunetta, my husband's firstborn.'

'Yes, of course; I recall the story of the cripple.' Her eyes lingered on Luna's leg. 'You are a good woman, Lucrezia, I remember that of you, but I caution against allowing her out in public. The sign of the Devil is upon this one.'

Luna's fingers closed tight around her crutch. She would not give this horrible woman the satisfaction of seeing her wobble.

There was a knock at the door and Friar Bartolomeo appeared. He was welcomed by them all, mostly by Luna, who deemed his timely arrival a sign from God. Mistress Palagio seemed pleased to have him join them. She clearly enjoyed parlaying with a gentleman; her voice dripped with honey. At least her attention had turned away from Luna, who was trying to hide the colour she felt rising along her neck. She'd not been insulted so directly since the boy at Mass had spat words of hate her way. She'd lost her temper then but she would not do so now. She turned and walked to a settle that sat against the wall. No one commented.

Mamma Lucrezia patted a spot beside her guest for Maria and the conversation turned to the Mass when Filippo would join the preacher's boys.

'The fanciulli will sing a new lauda as Friar Savonarola enters. No one has yet heard it, except for the families of the choir boys of course,' Friar Bartolomeo told the ladies. Luna saw how much he enjoyed being the bearer of news.

'Such an honour,' Mamma Lucrezia murmured.

Their guest listened with middling interest. Luna watched Signora Palagio drink the wine her step-mamma offered and eat the sweetmeats put in front of her without compliment.

The woman's eyes roamed from Mamma Lucrezia to Maria and frequently to the portrait of a young Vincenzio hanging on the wall.

'It is an excellent likeness, is it not?' Mamma Lucrezia commented.

'I know the master painter, Sandro Botticelli; he was supposed to come to paint me next. Now, though, he tells us he will not paint again for fear of God's wrath. I've told my husband to insist on it. I suppose this one was done a few years ago?'

Mamma Lucrezia nodded. 'Indeed, before he was everybody's favourite. My husband has an eye for a good painter.'

Friar Bartolomeo wandered over and sat beside Luna atop the upholstered cushions decorated with flowers and hares and prancing unicorns. Luna thought they must look out of place, a grey-robed monk and a plain cripple on so much glorious colour, but the friar nodded to her casually.

'How are you faring, my student?' he asked.

'I am trying not to make it so plain how much I hate this, but from your question, I think I am failing,' she replied.

He chuckled and nodded. 'To someone who knows you as well as I, indeed you are! Though I do not think the lady can tell or cares if you are uncomfortable. She seems more interested in the sweetmeats.'

Sure enough, their guest was putting one more into her mouth as Friar Bartolomeo spoke. Luna had to stop from laughing.

'Have you been reading the text I gave you?' he asked.

Luna glanced at her step-mamma, but all her attention was on her friend. She told him she was hoping to learn as much as she could from the Sacrobosco in the weeks until her father returned. It was good to speak freely. She smiled at the friar and continued enthusiastically.

'It is an impressive text, to be sure. I'm not ashamed to confess I find the technical detail challenging,' she said.

'It takes years of study to master astronomy.'

Luna sighed. 'I long for such a luxury.'

'It is hard work to be a student! Boys must display immense focus and commitment to study astronomy. Your father has a friend, Professor di Novara, who teaches at the university in Bologna. Perhaps one day he will introduce you. His students are highly regarded.'

'I do not doubt it. I would certainly choose to study under him if I was ever given the chance.'

Father Bartolomeo grunted. 'The Earth may move around the Sun afore we witness such a day!'

'Yes, I know,' Luna said. 'Though I can dream.'

'You would make a most excellent student,' Father Bartolomeo answered sympathetically. 'Your father has arranged for Professor di Novara to speak at the Platonic Academy next month, on the other text you covet: the *Epitome of the Almagest*.'

'My father's copy was sent to you for safekeeping, was it not?'

The friar nodded.

'I beseech you, could you show it to me?'

This time the friar shook his head, but there was a lift in his smile that made Luna hope.

She took his hand and squeezed gently. 'It could be something we do together whilst my father is absent, like old times when I was your student. I do miss those days so keenly.'

She waited for him to reply. The afternoon light moved more deeply into the room. Maria was speaking with Margherita Palagio and Mamma Lucrezia was engrossed in whatever was being said.

'You were always an eager student, and a worthy one, Luna.'

'Well, then?'

Her step-mamma motioned to them. 'Signora Palagio takes her leave of us.'

Friar Bartolomeo rose stiffly and went to where the ladies waited.

'It has been a pleasure to see you, friar. I bid you a good afternoon.' Signora Palagio dipped her head in farewell.

Luna curtseyed and then hung back as Mamma Lucrezia and Maria followed their guest from the room. There was just enough time for Friar Bartolomeo to speak to her.

'Come and see me in the monastery library when you are able,' he said and inclined his head with a wink.

*

As the summer intensified, Mamma Lucrezia decreed that the oven not be lit, so hot was the temperature outside. Bread was bought from the bakery rather than made and the flour store lay idle. They ate salted fish and fruit and cured meats, sometimes even taking their food outdoors in the garden where Mamma Lucrezia felt more comfortable, because she could see the sky and smell the rose-scented air and pretend for a little that they were in the hills of Careggi.

The girls slept long in the morn. Mamma Lucrezia had a new complacency. Many of her friends had already left for the cool and space of their summer retreats so there were few social gatherings for her to plan. Luna noticed how she no longer walked with the nervous energy of one who has a never-ending list of things to do. She let them stay abed and allowed them more freedoms within the house. She spoke of Maria's match with Guido Palagio as though it had already been finalised.

'Margherita was most impressed by you,' Mamma Lucrezia told Maria. 'She will relay as much to her husband, and I will speak to Papa on his return. You see, we women have a plan; we may yet have a betrothal to celebrate.'

Mamma Lucrezia went so far as to insist Maria begin to learn the arts of her kitchen in preparation for running her own household. Luna thought this ridiculous—Maria was still only a child—but it occupied her sister's time. She took Maria into the garden and showed her which fruit to pick for stewing and which for pickling, and which herbs to add to her tonics. The girls helped their mamma gather rosemary for treating nausea and the yellow flowers of the rue plant for adding to Papa's wine to help ease his headaches.

Once the household was abed, Luna took herself into the garden to watch the night sky, resting a lighted taper on the low wall of the pond beside her small pigskin notebook into which she'd copied parts of the tables from the Sacrobosco. She began to feel a degree of competency with the calculations required to predict the movement of the planets. A pot of ink and a quill lay at the ready so she could write her own notes based on what she observed. It was the best that she could do as she didn't have a specialised instrument to use for measuring the distance of planets or stars and did not know how to use one anyway.

Luna felt the hard earth beneath her boots as she turned her eyes to the heavens. It was God's hand that established the fifth essence in the finest order and painted the universe into life. His divine ruling directed the course of the stars. Luna felt her mind settle. It was calming to contemplate such certainty. She peered into the dark, listening to her own breath and the click of her neck as she strained. She sought out the young maiden Virgo and the star Spica—the ear of wheat in her hand—before turning to make a note of its intensity in her book, and that she'd seen it during the second sleep of the night. She went on to map other stars as she found them.

After some hours of observation, Luna's eyes stung from so much staring and she decided to retire to bed. The house appeared dark and solid as she took up the candle and walked along the garden path in the circle of its light.

Perhaps, when she'd convinced Papa of her acuity for astronomy, he'd inquire if any of his circle of friends owned a triquetrum and take the instrument with them one night, to track the position of a planet against the background of the stars. He'd balance the long, hinged bar on his shoulder and slide it until its peephole framed the planet, then show her how to read the elevation from the calibrated lower scale. For now, though, Luna must be content to observe the night sky with her eyes. She fell asleep, dreaming of star gazing with her father.

The lack of any breeze in the confines of their chamber woke Luna earlier than usual the following morning. She left Maria sleeping, donned her cloak and went to find Friar Bartolomeo in the monastery at Santa Croce, just as he'd suggested. As she laced up her boots, she thought about the monastery library. It had always been a sanctuary where the friar had encouraged her to explore ideas through books. How excited she'd been the first time he'd shown her an illuminated manuscript. Together they'd turned the long, heavy pages in wonder at the detailed illustrations that glimmered in gold and vibrant blue. He'd explained to Luna how the lapis lazuli was brought over from Constantinople at great expense to be used in the story of St Thomas Aquinas, the first Dominican to be sainted not so long ago. The images of fantastical creatures, half-man, half-animal, had intrigued Luna. She remembered how she'd traced the line of ink carefully with her finger, pretending to be the accomplished artist. The book had been a great gift to the order; she prayed it had not been destroyed by Savonarola's zealots. She couldn't understand how such beauty presented a threat.

Friar Bartolomeo was pleased to see Luna when she knocked on the door of his cell in the monastery. They walked in silence to the library and Luna felt a familiar sense of anticipation and wonder brewing inside her. She was his young student once again. She took his hand as she used to do.

'Thank you,' she said.

'Who am I to refuse entry to the house of our Lord?'

'The Lord is thy keeper, the Lord is thy shade,' she recited. 'Psalm 120; your father's favourite.'

Luna held her stick firmly as they entered the library. She nodded to a young novice who passed them carrying books.

'The crypt is too full so we must now divide our collection by those we will move into the other catacombs,' Friar

Bartolomeo explained as they walked down one of the long aisles of shelves. 'Some of your father's collection will be moved too. Come, I will show you to a table where you can read whichever texts you choose from those still on the shelves. You will find the volume I know you are most keen to read, the *Epitome of Ptolemy's Almagest*, on the table where some of your father's collection is stacked. It is at the end of the aisle. I must leave you now to attend to church matters, but I shall not be gone long.'

Luna nodded. 'Thank you.'

She heard the door close behind him as she took in the high ceiling and expanse of shelves that spread in either direction from the small table where he'd seated her. Luna laid out the copy of the Sacrobosco she'd brought and then the Archimedes. She opened *The Sand Reckoner* first. She decided Archimedes was either a man of unflinching faith or grandest self-belief to undertake such a task as to calculate the number of grains of sand required to fill the universe. Yet he'd done it, and part of the process was estimating the biggest potential size of the universe. She read on with amazement at the enormity of his undertaking. The detailed account of how he'd gone about it was complicated beyond belief and she reviewed the mathematical calculations slowly to try and understand them. He'd used the theory of Aristarchus of Samos, the Pythagorean, in his methodology and this caught Luna's attention because she didn't recognise anything of basic astronomy in it. Here was a totally preposterous notion of the universe that said the fixed stars and the Sun remained unmoved and that the Earth revolved around the Sun!

She sat back and shook her head, then bent to the page to read the sentence again. She'd been correct: the Earth revolved around the Sun in the circumference of a circle whilst the Moon orbited the Earth, which in turn spun on its axis. She looked about, expecting someone to grab the book away, or at least condemn her for reading it, but the aisles were clear and only distant footsteps broke the peace and quiet. Archimedes must have agreed with Aristarchus of Samos if he'd used the Pythagorean's theory to furnish his own calculations, which meant that the Greeks thought the Earth turned. The idea was as ridiculous as a talking dog, Luna thought, as she closed the book and rested it atop the Sacrobosco.

She took up her stick and headed down the aisle to where her father's books sat on a table, curious to see which of her father's collection were to be moved.

She felt protected in the shadow of the tall bookshelves. Despite what Friar Bartolomeo had told her, there were still many books ranged across them. Luna breathed in the clean, distinct smell of ink on paper. She used to enjoy watching the monks bent over manuscripts at these tables and was encouraged by their craft to spend time on her own lettering skills. The slow, deliberate movement of their hands as they copied the words was easy to replicate but these monks made every word perfectly uniform. Their skilled artistry and precision extended to drawing the tiniest details of facial expressions and mythical beasts entwined in branches of ivy and acanthus on graceful curved stems in ink and liquid gold. It was satisfying to see the coloured ink mark the page and bleed out to fill the body of a letter, the brilliant blue of lapis lazuli, the red crystals of cinnabar.

Today the desks were piled with books, the jars of ink removed. No one sat bent over a parchment script. Another novice passed her, his arms full of books, and went to the table nearest the door, where he stacked them. Luna followed and watched as he took up a large sheet and added the titles to the list. These were the precious volumes waiting to be removed to their new location for safekeeping. A tingle of goosebumps ran across her arms. She watched how carefully the books were handled as two other novices approached and were each given a heavy stack that they carried away through the outer doors in the direction of the main church. The novice then unrolled a clean sheet of parchment and turned to a different table, also stacked with books. He began recording the titles. Luna saw her family name written at the top of the page and surmised these were the volumes from her father's collection. She moved closer, making sure she didn't disturb him. The young man worked in companionable silence as Luna rummaged through the stack he had yet to begin on. She ran her fingers down the pile of hard spines: the set of volumes of the *Epitome of the Almagest* of Joannes de Monte Regio. Very gently she pulled the first volume out, letting it fall into her hands. She rested her palm on the hard leather cover as though it were made of gold.

'I will return this shortly,' she said to the novice, and she lugged it back to her desk.

She sat and laid the heavy volume on the desk. It was as long as the length of the tabletop and when she lifted the front cover it fell back with a soft smack. On the opening page there was a detailed printed image: the author sitting beside his teacher, Ptolemy. Luna hoped it would reveal signs of their great intelligence but though it was a fine likeness, her eyes were drawn to the astrolabe above them. Gold paint shimmered on the rings representing the celestial circles and there were brilliantly coloured hoops for the equator and the tropics. She had heard of these globes that spun when pushed but had not seen one in person. The pages were crisp and she turned them slowly, holding her breath at each fold for fear of damaging her father's precious volume.

Her progress down the page was slow as she read through the technical and mathematical detail beside drawings of epicycles and circles within circles. There was her father's scribbled handwriting in the margins of the text, the ink smudged slightly where he'd rested his wrist and reached over to write on the opposite page. These were his notes, with numbers too, sums he had done to perhaps test the author's theory. This is what she'd planned on doing; testing her own calculations of the position of the planets against the degrees listed here. Her papa's inked letters and numbers were scrawled in his small, messy script and on some pages numbers had been scratched out, on others he'd scribbled exclamations of frustration. He'd even drawn a small, perfectly proportioned hand with outstretched finger to mark an important point in the text. She moved from the text to the drawings, trying to make sense of the explanations, but after rereading the first few pages, Luna had to acknowledge she lacked the expertise to fully grasp the concepts. She must go back to the Sacrobosco first. She closed the book and moved it to the side so she could open Sacrobosco's text.

This was the introductory text for students of astronomy and she'd gotten ahead of herself, thinking to understand

Joannes de Monte Regio's exploration of Ptolemaic theory so soon. She thought of the stories Papa had told about her grandfather's ability to read the night sky and wondered at his natural talent. He'd not had the luxury of texts from which to learn, nor could he afford any of the instruments used by modern astronomers; he'd only had his eyes, but that hadn't stopped him. Luna knew she was fortunate to be born in an age when science had developed to the point where men could rely on a hand-held quadrant to measure the height of a celestial body.

She brought her mind back to the topic in front of her again but could not find a focus till the page turned to an illustration of an eclipse. The Sun shimmered on the page in fine gold leaf, its features so realistic she almost expected to feel the pointy edge of the Sun's nose as she ran her hand across the lifelike nostrils that flared in challenge to steadfast Earth during a solar eclipse. That the naked eye could see such a mystical event was in itself a miracle, for so much space separated them from the heavens. Luna was drawn to the image of the Moon, in its dripping crescent shape.

She was still contemplating what she'd read when Friar Bartolomeo returned. She was deep in thought and did not hear him approach until he was standing beside her. He noted the books she had on the desk, smiling in acknowledgement of the *Almagest*, before lifting the Archimedes up curiously.

'Which is this text?'

'One of my father's that he planned on leaving to the preacher's bonfire, so I saved it. I brought it with me today thinking I might find something of interest within its covers.'

She tried to sound nonchalant though her voice quivered as she spoke. Why had she brought a book of blasphemy to a monastery? She hoped the friar would move on to consider the Sacrobosco and pushed it towards him but he'd already taken up *The Sand Reckoner* and opened it.

'I know this book,' he said. 'I'm surprised to see it in your hands. I did not realise you would go back to the early astronomers and mathematicians; your education in the subject will take years if this is your approach.'

Luna shook her head. 'I was drawn to this book because of Papa. It felt different to the others in his collection, more personal to him, so I thought to keep it. I am sorry if it was wrong.'

'I did not say it was wrong; all reading is knowledge. Archimedes was a brilliant mathematician, but constrained by his times.'

'What do you mean?'

'You must remember, back then, learned men were ignorant of much we now understand; even the very great amongst us make mistakes. Archimedes used a theory of the Pythagorean Aristarchus's making, but nothing survives in Aristarchus's own hand, so we cannot be sure of the veracity of what is written in *The Sand Reckoner*.'

'Yes.' Luna knew this. She hesitated. 'Still, he suggests something I find hard to even voice, for it sounds so wrong, but it is intriguing and I trust you will not judge me, so I will raise it with you.'

He crossed his arms in a familiar manner and nodded. 'Continue,' he murmured. Then he pressed his hands to his chin. Luna recognised this contemplative stance and it eased her nerves enough to keep speaking.

'That the Earth revolves around the Sun. What do you make of this?'

The friar laughed in such a way that Luna found herself laughing too, else she be counted a fool.

'This book was written a long time ago,' he said simply.

'Indeed, and yet the same author, in the same book, also used the Pythagorean's concept to calculate the width of the universe using the diameter of the orbit of the Earth around the Sun. That was the basis of working out how many grains of sand would fill the universe, and we don't dispute Archimedes on this, do we?'

'Dear Lord, you've been sat here too long with only books for company. Do you fall and tumble about as you walk?'

Luna frowned at this and the friar coughed with embarrassment. 'I beg your forgiveness, Luna, for my unfortunate analogy, but common sense tells us that if the Earth was spinning right now, then surely we would feel it.' He shrugged, but Luna found this frustrating.

'It seems logical but still, how can we admire Archimedes's theory whilst discrediting one of the concepts that underpins it?'

'The strongest argument comes straight from the word of God in the Book of Joshua, wherein the Sun is ordered to stop its movement and stand still.' Friar Bartolomeo's voice had changed, it was firmer, deeper, as if he was speaking from the pulpit. 'Stand still, O Sun at Gabhaon, O Moon, in the valley of Aialon! And the Sun stood still, and the Moon stayed, whilst the nation took vengeance on its foe. Thus said Joshua in the presence of Israel.' He paused, as if for effect. 'The Holy Scriptures show us the truth.' His voice shifted once more into the melody of recitation.

'O Lord, my God, Thou art great indeed. Thou fixed the Earth upon its foundations, not to be moved for ever.' Then he reverted to his normal voice. 'It could not be more explicit—Psalm 103.'

Luna repeated the words 'O Sun at Gabhaon, O Moon, in the valley of Aialon', for they sounded wild and prophetic on her lips, and Friar Bartolomeo nodded approvingly.

'This is a matter of faith, and so it would be heretical to say that Abraham did not have two children and Jacob twelve, as well as to say that Christ was not born of a virgin, because both are said by the Holy Spirit through the mouths of prophets and apostles.'

Luna nodded, even though the friar had not really answered her question.

The idea that the Earth moved through space was surely madness, but it was rooted in her mind, perhaps because it was so extraordinary. Luna looked up at the tall bookshelves. The friar was right of course; if the Earth moved then all these books would slide one way and then the other.

'Now more than ever you must not stray from the word of God.' He spoke firmly and Luna nodded. 'We must all tread carefully in the gaze of the preacher Savonarola and I say to you again, Leonarda, your voice puts you in danger.'

She mulled over what she'd read as she followed Friar Bartolomeo from the library, first returning the volume from the *Almagest*. The Sun-centred theory was a madness, but it had been printed and accepted as useful to a degree, at least by the Greeks, and Luna knew her father's contemporaries at the Academy held Archimedes in the highest regard. Her curiosity was not about to let go of the idea.

*

As the day of her father's homecoming drew near, Luna returned his copy of *The Sand Reckoner* to its place on the shelf in his studiolo, not wanting to raise his ire. Her curiosity about the Greek mathematician's theory of a moving Earth and a stationary Sun did not abate, but it had been disproved by modern astronomy. She found it nowhere in the newer texts. But she kept the Sacrobosco under her pillow, checking on its safe presence before she slept. It had come to represent all the knowledge and joy of learning and the pleasure of star gazing with her father she planned in the future. During the day she moved it under her bed, so it was hidden.

The week that Papa was due home, Mamma Lucrezia watched from the top-floor windows frequently in case he'd made faster progress than expected. 'No sign of him today,' she'd tell her daughters, and they shared her impatience. Luna watched from her bedroom window each morning, too, for the sight of Papa's silhouette on horseback crossing the distant hills. Some mornings she could see all the way to the spiked cypress trees that stood out green against the dry hills of Fiesole as she scoured the hilltops, and she pictured a life in the countryside, with lettuces to tend and broadbeans even, instead of her books. A happy life away from the city and the eyes that judged her every day for being a cripple. She'd lie in an expanse of open grass, just the soft ground beneath and sky above, as wide as the fields. She'd watch the stars like her grandfather had. Yet when she thought of a country life, it didn't include studying, and as much as she longed for acceptance, she could never give up her books. The future she envisioned for herself of a purposeful life was very different. It did not include managing a country estate or even a city palazzo for a husband, nor the alternative of joining a convent. Luna's future was one of books and further learning within the walls of Palazzo Fusili, caring for her father as he aged, with his blessing. She was ready to begin the discussion of her studies with Papa again, as soon as he returned.

CHAPTER ELEVEN

August 1496

Luna sat on her bench outside her father's rooms, taking off her boots as noisily as she could, for she hoped he would hear and call her in. Papa had been home for two whole days, though they were yet to sit as a family and share a meal. He ate late and alone, after he returned from business, and then retreated to his studiolo. She placed the Sacrobosco beside her and waited. Her lips moved as she silently repeated what she'd already memorised. Here was purpose and distraction and she was ready to impress Papa with her knowledge. A servant passed her with a pitcher of wine and she sat a little straighter. Shortly after, he returned again with the empty pitcher and disappeared up the stairs towards the kitchen.

Luna got up and walked quietly to the door the servant had left ajar. She could see a cup sat on the desk, half full. There was a bottle of tincture too, the label crinkled and flaking, the poultice in a bowl beside it like a dried mushroom. Her father's headaches had increased and he demanded more of Mamma Lucrezia's homemade poultices and tonics. The desk was strewn with pages of accounts and the oversized ledgers that Luna recognised from when she used to help her father in the shopfronts. She was surprised to find him poring over his business accounts, for usually he liked to end the day with a book of poetry.

She stood inside the door and saw that he was asleep. He looked exhausted, or perhaps it was just that when he was asleep his mouth slackened and his head dropped back against the chair, so that he seemed older. His Adam's apple pulsed with each slow breath. A page fluttered to the floor. Luna crept into the room and picked up the fallen sheet. She noticed the seal of the Great Council and read with alarm. The Great Council had decreed that all those who advocated the restoration of the Medicis be put to death. All the households in Florence would have received this, she knew, but still, her heart beat swift for her papa. She secured the proclamation in the pile under a weighted stone as an image of the preacher's fiery stare flashed before her. Her father did not stir and she felt a swell of pity for all he must contend with. She saw his cloak abandoned in a corner and laid it gently across his knees. His eyelids quivered like a moth's wings; she liked the idea that her papa dreamt. She left him sleeping quietly, collected her book from her bench and retreated to her bedchamber.

*

Through the month of August, each night became a repeat of the same relentless oven-hot discomfort. Luna longed for the cooler autumn temperatures to sweep through the city on the winds from the hills but they were still weeks away. Maria was awake and tossing in the bed covers. Luna took her hand and the girls walked down the stairs and through the corridor to the garden, nightdresses hanging listlessly against their hot skin.

They lay in the grass, sprawled like lizards baking. Luna hoped the change would settle Maria. Their conversation was peppered by the noise of the night carts rumbling in the streets beyond the garden wall. The girls covered their noses against the smell of heated sewer water, despite the roses. The wealthy families of Florence might have left for their country villas but most of the city still sweated through each day and night.

'When will Papa tell us about his trip?' Luna asked to the sky above. There was something freeing to talk so, without scrutiny nor care for who heard when there was only Maria beside her. The silence that followed was welcome. She expected no answer and so the question did not beg for one.

Luna felt rather than saw Maria sit up. She was reluctant to move from where she lay with the cool feel of the grass, damp with night dew, against her back and the view of the stars above. She was looking for the Virgo maiden again, but she heard Maria digging and stamping her feet into the earth.

'Stop that! You'll ruin the grass,' Luna said without looking over.

'What do you care?' Maria grunted from the effort as she dug up clods of grass. A lump of soil flew across the garden and crumpled into specks of dirt as it thudded against the low wall of the pond.

Luna sat up. Maria was hunched over and rigid with a bursting energy that she was directing through her feet. She began to rip at the grass with her hands.

'Are you tired?' Luna asked, speaking softly and gently, as she'd learnt this helped Maria's melancholia. She'd told herself to never be surprised at the fickleness of the dark bile when it rose in Maria, but this time it had taken her unawares. She curled her arm around her sister's shoulder. 'Let's go back to bed,' she suggested, but Maria pulled away and shook herself as though she'd a mouse caught in her nightdress. She shuffled on the grass so there was a distance between them and wrapped her arms around her knees bent to her chest. Then she dropped her chin to rest upon her knees.

'What else is going to happen?' she said angrily.

'I don't know what you mean,' Luna replied, wary of the rawness in Maria's tone.

'After Mamma has finished teaching me how to cook.' Maria pulled out a handful of grass and threw it on herself. 'After I leave home and all of you.' Her voice rose and she threw more grass. 'After I am wed.' Maria lifted her head then and glared at Luna, who wanted to cry too at the sight of so much fear and anguish on her sister's childish face. 'What then?' Maria cried.

'Well, I expect you will have children, my love, many sons to make your husband proud and they will love you and, in time, they will care for you.' Luna tried to keep her voice calm. How could she possibly know what the future held for Maria? The enormity of her sister's question struck her.

Maria had stopped digging but now was pinching at the skin of her arm. Luna was used to seeing her sister hurt herself like this. She wished she could feel the pain instead of Maria but all she could do was lay her hand over Maria's arm.

'I saw a basket of eggs as we passed the kitchen. Shall we take some and pattern them tomorrow?' She didn't move, and after a few minutes, felt Maria soften beneath her hold. A teardrop splashed on her nightdress and she knew that the melancholia had broken.

The sisters sat. A cat mewled in the alley and Luna listened to another hiss in reply. Maria was crying. How could a child comprehend her future, Luna thought with bitterness, but it would be so, as it was for all girls. At least, nearly all.

After a while, Maria's sobbing eased and Luna moved closer but didn't reach out to her sister, not yet. She waited, gazing around the shadowy garden. The dark shape of a cat tripped daintily along the lip of the back wall and over the gate, its tail pointed skyward and swaying. The new bolt on the garden gate was shiny, even in the dark.

'Leave it to Papa; he'll take care of everything. He always does,' Maria said.

'Yes, he always does.' Luna repeated Maria's words, hoping it would make her believe the sentiment a little more. She took her sister's hand and held it tightly as they turned back to the house and their shared bedchamber.

*

Luna didn't see her father again until the family gathered in readiness to depart for Mass at the cathedral. She was tired, having stayed up late the night prior finishing the white robes she was sewing for Filippo. But even when her head was on the pillow she'd not slept. The same alarming thought kept circling: her papa had always been loyal to the Medicis and the proclamation she'd seen in his room made any connection to the family a crime punishable by death. Surely he no longer kept favour with the exiles? She'd not been able to stop her mind from worrying so she was tired when she stepped into the carriage and took her seat beside Maria. She'd offered to accompany Filippo and walk through the streets with him in the throng of boys but Papa reminded her that no girls were allowed and laughed at the notion that she thought she could keep up and hold the red cross they were all given whilst she walked. Luna had smiled but there was a harshness to her father's voice that was strange and unlike him. Ever since he'd returned from his business travels, she heard him shouting for bread in the mornings and complaining of the heat. One time he'd cursed so loudly and so viciously they'd all stopped their tasks in the kitchen, the servant girls included, and crossed themselves. Mamma Lucrezia had hurried off to his studiolo, but she'd not explained the outburst. Luna thought again of the Great Council's proclamation about Medici loyalists.

She turned her mind to little Filippo. This day was his to shine, with his hair freshly cut around his ears to meet the Great Council's strict new codes. She reminded herself to press upon her brother the importance of staying close to the other boys. They would make an unforgiving crowd as they filed through the streets and any who fell would not be helped. Luna fretted about his safety; best Pippo kept to the centre of the group. At least they would all meet up again in the cathedral and, as Maria liked to say, Papa always took care of them. He wouldn't let anything happen to his only son and heir.

*

Luna kept close to her family as they pushed their way through the crowded nave. Her step-mamma had insisted they leave as soon as Papa had returned from delivering Filippo to the piazza where the boys gathered under the guidance of Friar Silvestro Maruffi, but it still seemed they were late to arrive. It was impossible to use her stick so Luna tucked it under her arm and grabbed Maria's hand for support.

'How on Earth am I going see my son from here?' Mamma Lucrezia moaned.

'Is this close enough?' Luna's father had managed to get them a spot beside one of the high wooden stands, erected as balconies so that the friar's fanciulli could be seen as they sang a lauda to greet his entrance. Luna thought his unkind tone was out of sorts, though her step-mamma did not seem to notice.

'Thank you, my love,' she replied. 'Please, everyone, keep watching for Filippo; he'll be in one of those balconies.'

Luna looked up to where the boys all waited quietly, like a sea of angels in their dove-white shrouds. She scoured the faces but could not see her brother. One little boy was crying but he made no noise and Luna's heart contracted at the sight of his silent tears. She turned her attention to the stand on their other side, though it was farther away and harder to make out the individuals. There was an air of excitement amongst the throng of worshippers.

This was the first time the Fusilis had returned to the cathedral for Mass since that uncomfortable morning in June. Luna pushed the memory from her mind and determined to only think compassionately whilst in God's house this day. She lifted her right boot to momentarily relieve the pressure on her stub.

'We'll be able to see the preacher easily from here,' Maria said excitedly.

'It's Pippo we must find first,' Luna responded. Their view was blocked by so many heads. She turned to her stepmamma, who was herself trying to get past a man standing directly in front of them. 'Do you see him yet, Mamma?'

'Sire, would you kindly let me pass?' Mamma Lucrezia asked the tall stranger in the hope he would shuffle slightly to the left but he turned around, a lungful of hot breath hitting Luna in the face as he opened his mouth to speak.

'Get, dog-worm friends of the Medici! I don't want you anywhere near me,' he growled and bared his filthy gums before swinging back to face the altar.

Mamma Lucrezia grabbed Luna's and Maria's hands and dragged her daughters to where their father stood. Luna's heart pounded loudly in her chest. She moved closer to her father and saw Friar Bartolomeo standing on his other side.

'Good morrow, friar.' She went around to where he stood and bobbed a curtsey, only noticing his ghostly pallor as she lifted her gaze. 'Is everything all right?'

The friar did not speak, only shook his head. It was such a pitiable motion, Luna felt compelled to reach out and hold his hand. It was cold as stone. 'What on Earth has happened?'

'My apologies, Leonarda. You need not fret. I am suffering a bout of fatigue and should have stayed away today.' He attempted a smile that only made her more concerned.

She moved closer to her father. 'Papa, something is not right with the friar.' Her father's expression was like a mirror of the friar's. He was ashen-faced, his eyes wide and white and searching over the heads of the congregation. His neck strained and pulsed with the effort. 'I should not have let Filippo go,' he managed to say, the words torn from his throat. Luna felt her legs go heavy.

'The preacher is coming,' Mamma Lucrezia hissed excitedly, and Luna felt her father stiffen beside her, but she had no choice except to turn and watch the silent procession of black-robed monks move slowly towards them. She was as alert as her father now, for what danger, she did not know.

The crowds stood back as the procession advanced and the voices of the boys rose in a sweet crescendo of Latin that echoed around the white-washed walls of the dome. Luna watched the preacher with a steeled heart; she'd learnt her lesson about giving in to momentary passion.

With a thunderous voice, Savonarola addressed the congregation. 'Go back, Florentines, to the spare, simple ways of Christ, and show others the way. You think wealthy people help pull up the poor with alms and charity? Think again. The ambitious projects of the rich impoverish the poor even more. Your great men buy land and shops from the poor at a low price, taking advantage of others' poverty to aggrandise themselves in vain shows of extravagance.'

Many around her nodded.

'You merchants, you bankers, you ladies weighted down by jewels and gold. You think you can buy everything with money. You pay master painters to depict your beloved selves, your sons and daughters as saints. Do you really believe the Virgin Mary went dressed as you paint her? Efface these figures that are painted so unchastely. You do better to risk your lives for Christ instead of amassing riches or building your great palaces.'

There was a scuffle in the stand near where the Fusilis stood. The sea of faces watched. A monk had a boy by the collar and was manhandling him to the front. The boy cried out and fought against the man as he was pushed towards the edge of the balcony that looked out across the gathered worshippers. He kicked and scrabbled to free himself but the hooded figure was too big and had him by the scruff of the neck. People murmured and shifted uncomfortably at the sight of the boy dangling like a goose at market from the hand of the black-robed monk.

The monk thrust the small boy out over the congregation. People moved, some making to catch him in case he was dropped, but most curious to see what would happen if he did, and in that moment Luna saw who it was.

'It's Pippo, he has Filippo!' she cried out in horror.

Her father, too, had seen and rushed forward. 'Let me through! That is my son! Let me through,' he shouted angrily and Luna saw him leap upon the stairs to where Pippo hung precariously, taking them three at a time in his haste to reach his son.

'Hold him! Do not let him fall,' she called.

Friar Savonarola did not change his tone, but Luna saw how he followed her father's progress and a smile of gratification crossed his face. There was utter silence in the church; the gathered many stood in fear and dread of God's judgement turning on any of their families next. The preacher was all-powerful, a small fury of a man in the pulpit, and his wrath kept them mute whilst his eyes stayed locked on Papa. His words seemed directed at her father alone.

'Everyone has to die: that great master, that youth, the rich, the handsome, the strong. They are all stink and ashes. And whose lives will leave behind the worst stench? Those who pretend to live by holy orders: those priests who, for a handful of ducats, absolve the rich from the darkest of sins and threaten the poor with hellfire unless they hand over a week's living for indulgences. And you, Rome! Rome! The entire Holy City reeks of perdition.'

The man let go of Filippo. Her brother fell silently, his white shroud flapping and curling. Her father watched helplessly, stuck halfway up the stairs. Luna heard her mother cry out beside her, but she could not take her eyes off Filippo. Shocked disbelief flashed across his face and then he was gone, lost in the sea of worshippers.

An eerie silence fell upon the packed church. Her father leapt from the stairs and hurtled towards the pulpit, his face red, but monks moved quickly and held him back.

'You go too far, Savonarola. Damn you to Hell.'

Luna watched him fight against the monks with the same hopeless energy as Filippo had the monk who held him.

Savonarola looked at her father and the scuffle unfolding, and spoke with the same calmness that had captivated Luna only weeks earlier.

'When you see me holding the Sacrament in my hand at Communion, pray, every one of you, make a fervid plea to the Lord that if this work does not come from Him, He will send a fire to consume me in Hell.'

The people listened intently and Luna felt the crowd join in a willing fellowship with their preacher. The silent complicity of the congregation frightened her.

'Believe me, Florence. You have heard with your ears, not me, but God. You think I am crazy? But you ought to believe.'

Then he pointed to the spot where Filippo had fallen and there, in the midst of a dumbstruck crowd, was their Pippo, held aloft by one of the preacher's men. His face was as white as his smock but he was alive.

Luna stretched her arms high and waved madly to her father. 'He lives, Papa, he's safe!'

The congregation gasped as one, and Luna heard cries of 'miracle' and 'God save us, preacher'. The monk put Pippo down and patted him on the back, smiling as though it had all been a game. Mamma Lucrezia crossed herself and fell to the floor in supplication, weeping and murmuring, 'Thank you, Mother Mary,' at the sight of her son alive. Pippo ran to where the family stood and crumpled into his mother's arms.

Then Papa appeared. He dropped to his knees beside Pippo and took his son's face in his hands, searching it intently as though he could see any injury to his very soul. The boy stared back with large, shock-ridden eyes and began to whimper. Mamma Lucrezia cradled him and refused to move at the sound of the bells that preceded the consecration of the Host so that only Papa stepped forward.

Once the final prayers were done and Luna and her family could leave, she saw a group of worshippers huddled close around where Pippo had been dropped, as though expecting more miracles from the shadow of her brother's near death. She shrank from the sight; it was God they ought to be supplicating before, not this preacher's cruel trickery.

The crowd was flowing easily towards the doors and Luna saw her parents just ahead. She felt unsteady and moved carefully, using her walking stick despite the closeness of others. Then she heard a voice that made her shiver.

'They let the vermin back in after all,' the young man said, leaning in so that his heat was on her back.

Luna ignored him though the hairs on her neck prickled. It was the same lout who had taunted her in this very spot the last time they had come to Mass in the cathedral, the same one who had killed the dog in the street.

'They did not tell us to watch out for maggots and rotten peg-legs.'

'Yet here you are,' Luna said under her breath then swallowed hard. Her legs felt more unstable than usual and she was still trembling, but she would not be drawn into another ugly exchange. She'd be out of the church doors soon enough. She just had to keep her tongue silent for a few more minutes. She leant on her stick.

The man pointed to it. 'I hope Signore Fusili beat you with that.'

She shook her head; what madness this vile man spoke. Still, they were out now and the fresh air took her away from his spite. Luna breathed deeply as she scanned the square for her family. She saw them not far off, standing with Signore Palagio and his wife. Pippo was holding tightly to Mamma Lucrezia's hand and Luna waved to him as she made her way down the stone steps.

When she reached the last step she was annoyed to see the young man beside her still. 'I thought you had tired of insulting me,' she said, without even giving him her full attention. She was so thrilled to see Pippo running towards her that she cared not, indeed she pitied him.

'I have not forgotten the way you shamed me last time—a crippled Devil-girl talking to a gentleman like that.'

Luna laughed and spoke without thinking. 'You are no gentleman.'

The words were barely out before she realised her mistake; he was stood so close she felt the puce of his face might burn her with its intensity. He thrust his hand behind her and grabbed her buttocks, pressing his fingers into her in an ugly and unholy way. Luna stiffened and felt the blood drain from her face. Her mind blurred and for a moment she lost sight of the daylight in her shame. She lifted her walking stick and struck him across the shoulder as hard as she could. He stumbled backwards.

Then Pippo was there and Luna grabbed hold of his hand and steered him away. She heard voices but did not look back. Her face was flushed and she was in danger of crying out but she breathed deeply to calm herself before reaching her parents.

As she drew closer she saw her father talking rapidly and remonstrating with Signore Palagio. Please God, she silently prayed, let them not have seen.

*

The rest of the day, Luna moved about the house with the burn of the boy's vulgar fingers on her flesh. The shock of the assault was still in her body. She shook at every sound and her head throbbed mercilessly. She was too ashamed to go to her step-mamma, and Papa had not returned home with them in the carriage. Luna sat on her bench and let her hands rest on the marks of the wood, but she shivered uncontrollably and, after only a short while, had to rise and find a woollen cloak to wrap about her shoulders. As she walked, she felt a shameful twinge. There was no one behind her as she climbed the stairs yet she turned suddenly at the creak of a board and again only moments later.

She lay on her bed and willed the hours to pass so that she could disappear into sleep, but when she closed her eyes she saw Pippo's white robes floating out like the wings of an angel as he fell. On the way home, Mamma Lucrezia had decried the incident as a foul way to scare the family into obedience, but she'd shut her mouth when she'd heard shouting and they'd all sat nervously for fear of being stopped by the preacher's boys. A servant had carried Pippo into the main hall and laid him on a settle whilst they waited for the doctor to arrive. Mamma Lucrezia had insisted on making a special drink to ease the pain of his bruising and calm his nerves. Poor little Filippo shook uncontrollably and had to be pried from his mamma's lap. Luna's ordeal seemed minor next to her brother's torment.

When she was very little, one of her favourite days involved helping her father procure and deliver supplies to the monastery. They would gather up a bundle of cloth for the monks to use for robes, then spend time in the tannery where Papa would select leather skins to use to cover the manuscripts copied out by the monks. The items would be loaded into a small wagon with Luna snuggled into one corner and then her father would manoeuvre it across the cobblestone streets. He'd pause often to talk to this merchant or that gentleman, inquiring after a shipment of cloth or the quality of beans that season. Luna would listen to the mellow tones of his conversation from her safe little spot and doze when the talk dragged on, with her head resting against the pillowy weight of the sacks of cloth. When they arrived at the monastery, her father would lift her out along with the sacks and she thought him the strongest man in the world. He'd have killed Savonarola if the monks had not held him back. He would die for his son. What would he do when he found out she'd been attacked in church too?

*

Luna woke with a throbbing pain down one side and realised she'd fallen asleep curled up against the wall with her arm pressed beneath her. She stood and stretched, and reckoned by the way the light fell on her dresser that it was now late in the afternoon. Her body no longer shook but when she breathed, it felt like a torrent of shame and relief flooded from her all at once and it was as much as she could do to stop from crying out. She pulled her hair back and up into a knot, then she fixed the buttons on her skirt and reviewed her reflection in the pane of glass. There was nothing different about the girl who stared back. She saw no mark of the shame that rankled within.

Filippo's voice carried upstairs and Luna went to see him. He was in the main hall, lying on a settle beneath a thick cover, though from the looks of it, he was ready to get up and play. Luna slipped into the room quietly, making sure to close the door behind her so that they did not hear the men talking in the courtyard below. The afternoon activity of business negotiations and discussions of politics stopped for nothing. She bobbed a curtsey to her step-mamma then bent to kiss Pippo on the smooth, broad forehead she'd washed so many times. Her lips pinched at the memory of the monk's treatment of him but when she rose it was with clear eyes and a smile.

'How do you feel, my brave little warrior?'

'A bit sore,' he answered, 'and bored.'

'You'll soon be up and running around again, thanks be to God.' She crossed herself and had to smile at her brother's scowl. It was good to see his spirits revived. She took the chair beside her step-mamma and sat. How still and alert Mamma Lucrezia was, like a mother bird watching her nest for danger.

After a lengthy silence, Mamma Lucrezia rose, took Luna's arm and walked with her across to the windows that overlooked the piazza. 'You shamed us all again,' she said when they were out of earshot of Pippo. 'Scrapping like an alley cat. What were you thinking, Leonarda? To insult so important a family!'

Luna didn't reply at first. She should have guessed her step-mamma would have heard about the incident in the cathedral; gossip in Florence never stopped. Still, she'd not expected her to speak of it here, sat with Pippo as they were. 'I don't know, Mamma. Forgive me,' she said eventually.

'Your father will be fearfully angry when he gets home.'

'I will go to him and apologise, but the man was …' She couldn't finish the sentence. Her words felt loose and inadequate.

'I expected better of you, especially after the last time you got into trouble at Mass. It does not seem you're able to control your own wilfulness and now your father must deal with Signore Palagio.'

Luna stared at Mamma Lucrezia. 'I don't understand. I wasn't rude to Signore Palagio?'

'What do you expect, child? He is shocked by your indecorum, so shocked he is not sure that Maria is a good match for his son.'

'Why would Signore Palagio care so much about my behaviour?' Luna said. 'Truly, Mamma, I am sorry for my actions, but Signore Palagio's reaction seems excessive.' A rising heat flared in Luna's chest. It threatened to burn her shame to charred anger. 'If he judges Maria by my actions, then it is better she doesn't marry his son.'

Her step-mamma looked at her with cold eyes and her chin lifted in judgement.

Luna steadied her voice as best she could. 'I will go to Papa and apologise.'

Mamma Lucrezia shook her head vigorously. 'Do you not see that it is your independent spirit that causes us such shame?'

Luna breathed heavily and repeated herself more firmly. 'I will go to Papa and make amends.'

'He will have words to say when we sup together. You can wait until then to learn of your punishment.'

*

Luna was tired when she sat beside Maria at the table, but anticipating her father's anger made her pulse quicken. She reached for her cup and drank, hoping the wine would settle her belly. The girls waited in silence for the rest of the family to join them. Luna's innards had not stopped their horrible churning since Mamma Lucrezia had warned her of her father's ire. She put down her cup and rubbed her hands, wondering what was keeping the others.

Pippo appeared and ran towards them, and Luna saw Livia disappear before anyone else had seen. He was not at all disarmed by the morning's events and Luna was so pleased to see him unscathed that for a brief moment she forgot about her own travails and watched him swinging his little legs back and forth on the chair. Papa followed, and he was watching Filippo so intently it made Luna hopeful that his mood had shifted. Mamma Lucrezia walked behind them both.

Papa drank deeply from his cup of wine, leaving a thin trail of moisture on his upper lip. He sat back abruptly and wiped it clean. Luna noticed the way his hand dragged; he was weary, and that meant short patience for any of them. The thudding in her chest picked up again and she took another mouthful of her wine.

'Come, come, settle yourself.' Mamma Lucrezia fussed about Pippo, at the same time cautiously watching her husband. 'Eat, master; you deserve a good meal after such a day.' She piled her husband's plate with a large portion of chicken pie then refilled his glass.

Papa nodded. He ate quickly and with little care. Luna imagined he'd barely be able to taste the flavours, yet she supposed he'd had a long day and was hungry. Mamma Lucrezia was fastidious with her ingredients and Papa's disregard for the food would disappoint her.

'Give Filippo some food. He's been through enough already this day.' Papa waved his hand towards his son and Luna watched as her step-mamma took some meat for Pippo.

Her own plate and Maria's remained empty, and it felt like Papa was making them wait as a punishment. Luna saw her step-mamma fiddle with the citron sweets before moving the plate to within Papa's reach. She made soft tutting sounds as he ate.

'You will feel much restored soon enough,' she said.

Luna swallowed hard; Mamma Lucrezia's over attentiveness did not bode well. She coddled Papa thus when she knew he was close to anger. Eventually Papa nodded to Mamma Lucrezia and she pushed the platter their way with an encouraging nod. Luna filled her plate and Maria did the same.

'Thank you, Papa,' they said in unison.

Luna drank her wine and saw that her father finished three cups to her one.

'I am indeed restored,' he said eventually, burping loudly and pulling a chunk of bread from the round to sop up the leftover juices. Grease dripped down his chin.

Luna took another draught of wine for its encouraging burn. 'Papa, I would apologise.'

He stopped eating and sat back in his chair, wiping his hands clean and taking up his cup. He frowned at her and sighed, then looked at Mamma Lucrezia, who nodded as though encouraging him, an odd sight indeed. Luna feared what was afoot.

'No,' he answered. 'You will listen to me. I do not like to hear of your disrespect, daughter.'

Luna opened her mouth to object, but shut it before speaking.

'Once again, I must make amends for your behaviour. You have shamed this family at church twice now and it is enough, Leonarda. I will not protect you a third time.'

Mamma Lucrezia laid a hand on Papa's arm. It reminded Luna of the way the Palagio lady had reached across to her step-mamma. 'Thank you, husband. This is the wilfulness of which I told you, the very same that disarmed your best intentions. She needs a father's firm reminder of her place and it gladdens me to hear you give it.' She turned to Luna. 'Leonarda, mark this, child.'

Luna nodded. An uncomfortable feeling started in her belly.

'I forbid you from leaving your chamber. I forbid you from visiting Friar Bartolomeo and I especially forbid you from joining us at Mass. Do you understand?'

Luna stared at her father. She was used to being reprimanded, but this was different: his tone was hurtful. She swallowed, building courage enough to reply, but her tongue sat limp and fat in her mouth and her voice would not sound.

'Answer me, girl!' Papa shouted.

She nodded.

'Is that all the respect you can muster? You, who best of my children knows how to thread words into silken sentences? Do you find insults more poetic now than apologies?'

Luna was silent. It fired her papa's anger more.

'After my business finished in Prato, I travelled all the way to Pistoia, an extra week of difficult journeying, to the home of Signore Spinelli, who seeks a wife for his son, Francesco. The negotiations for you had begun before I left.'

Luna gaped but still she could not rally her voice to speak. Papa's words had choked the air from her lungs.

'My intent was to finalise a marriage contract in your name, so good a father am I to you. But I underestimated how far the winds of Florence gossip travel and I could not convince Signore Spinelli of your suitability. He refused to sign the contract and I returned empty handed.'

'Why do you think I've always chided you so harshly, Leonarda, if not for your own reward? But I relinquish that responsibility now, for I see that you will never change.' Mamma Lucrezia spat the words at Luna.

'Yet still, I thought, someone will have my clever Leonarda Lunetta.' Papa slammed his hand on to the table and laughed. 'Foolish hopes! I'll have my work cut out for me to find a family willing to take you now.'

'This may be so for Leonarda,' Mamma Lucrezia said, 'but for Maria we must rejoice!'

Luna listened, astonished.

'I will not rejoice,' Papa said grumpily. 'My hand was forced. I take no pleasure in accepting Signore Palagio's offer for Maria's hand.'

'Come now, husband, your youngest daughter's future fixed to a wealthy and connected Florentine family. Allow me a little jubilation.'

'Do as you wish, but don't expect me to join in.'

Mamma Lucrezia clapped her hands and filled her own and Papa's cups. 'There, now I am content. My family seated around the table, my most beloved husband in good health and my daughter's future secured. I am truly blessed.'

'The Lord graces us,' Papa added flatly.

Luna slid down in her chair; she could barely keep herself upright. One moment she was being punished, the next they were celebrating Maria's betrothal. Her step-mamma was angry and now excited. Her papa was … She dared not glance at him. Luna drank a full wash of wine. He intended to marry her off to whoever would take her. The wine slaked her throat and fed the sourness of her disappointment. The tinder in her belly ignited and she felt a flame of hot injustice. She met her father's gaze steadily.

'You lied to me, Papa.'

'Do not speak rudely; it does your pretty eyes no kindness.' His compliment confused Luna. He continued, even more gently, 'These are circumstances you do not understand.'

'Only because you did not share them with me.' She didn't mean to whine but his gentler tone lured her back to him. 'I thought you enjoyed my conversation and debate. Why give me books and tutors if you did not want me to form ideas? More so, what good are ideas if we cannot debate them? I am mightily confused, Papa. I have only ever wanted to make you proud. Have I failed?'

'Why must you always want for more? More books, more answers, more approbation? Your curiosity has become tedious.'

Luna sat back in surprise; she'd not expected such criticism.

'I chose to spend my nights teaching you how to find the stars, my bed cold, my eyes wearied, yet it gave me pleasure to do so, daughter. Could those nights of star gazing not have been enough for you? No, indeed, you must beg to understand the science of it too! I see no inkling of my humble, kind-hearted little girl in the grown woman haranguing me at my table.'

'You see?' Mamma Lucrezia interrupted. 'This is your own doing, Leonarda. That wilful tongue of yours—'

Luna laughed only the sound was harsh as a dog's bark. She felt ablaze with the injustice of her father's words. She turned to him, and only him. 'Why speak to me like this now?'

'For goodness' sake! Do you think Papa has a choice?' Mamma Lucrezia shouted in outrage. 'The whole of Florence gossips about the Fusilis' crippled daughter who goes about in public mimicking the manner of a boy—pretentious and vulgar behaviour, to be sure. Your brazen thinking is an insult to good society; it has been so since you reached womanhood, but your father would indulge you. You demand to learn astronomy, bold as any man, but you are not a man, Leonarda, you are only a woman.' Her step-mamma was pointing at her with a long, slim finger as though she could cut Luna's insolence from her breast. 'An impudent and indecorous unmarried woman.' She thrust her finger at Luna with each insult. 'You will not shame this family any longer!'

Luna addressed her father. 'If I have transgressed those rules of silence especially imposed on women, as you say, then better you'd cut out my tongue when I spoke my first word, for I will not stop now.'

'Enough!' Papa's hand slammed on the tabletop. 'I am the master of this family. I alone may take such a tone.'

'You taught me this skill!' Luna twisted towards him. 'Now I beg you to indulge me with an explanation.'

'You have my determination, that's certain.' He sighed. 'There are matters at play that are too complicated for your female wit. In any case it is all immaterial, as Signore Spinelli had made up his mind to reject you even before the painting arrived at Pistoia. I could not convince him otherwise.'

'The painting?' Luna asked.

'Bring it to me,' her father shouted to a servant and Luna could only watch in surprise as a small wooden painting was handed to him. She recognised it immediately.

'But that was to be a gift for you,' she blurted, then saw from the knowing look that passed between her parents that she'd been misled. 'I don't understand. Mamma, did you know about this all along?'

'Signore Spinelli requested a likeness,' Mamma Lucrezia answered, taking the small portrait from her husband. 'You have such a pretty face; how could we not send one?' She sighed with obvious frustration and turned it around so Luna could see.

It was very odd to gaze upon herself. The painter had caught something of Luna in the flatness. She sat in her finery, the tiny, delicate strokes making the lace edges quiver where her arm rested, a book in one hand, her hair richly coloured and silken, her skin perfectly pale. Her painted eyes gazed out with astonishing familiarity. Luna hadn't expected to see herself so completely. Then she noticed two dainty pointed shoes peeking out from the hem of her gown.

'Why am I painted in ladies' shoes?'

'You appear very pleasing to the eye,' Maria murmured and Luna exchanged a grateful smile with her sister.

Pippo giggled. 'Luna can't wear girls' shoes!'

'No, I cannot,' Luna added in a dour tone.

'Enough, Leonarda!' Mamma Lucrezia shot her a warning glance, but Luna was too angry to heed it.

She turned to her father once more. 'Papa, you have not answered me.' But Luna knew the answer: no one wanted a cripple for a wife, and that was why he'd had her painted so perfectly. 'Do I shame you so unbearably?' she cried.

'Remember your place,' he said.

Her eyes stung. 'What place?' she shouted. 'Please tell me, as I do not know where my place is in this family any more.'

'You test me, Luna. You speak as my equal but you are not.'

'This is how you taught me to be, Papa!'

'Chastity, piety and, most importantly, modesty; these are the virtues I had hoped to instil in you, not arrogance, though it appears that is what you are known for. Signore Spinelli had heard whispers about your temperament even before your latest tirade at the cathedral. He did not want to bring a wilful bride into his household, and how could I disagree, especially as their son is a simpleton. I could not convince him otherwise.'

'You would wed me to a simpleton?' Luna could hardly believe it.

'Signore Spinelli promised me compensation for his son's deficiencies, and the boy would have been an easy husband to manage—and kind enough.'

'At least now you must see the harm of your indulgence of Leonarda,' Mamma Lucrezia said to her husband whilst frowning at Luna. 'Perhaps you will listen to my advice, for there is still more that could be damaged by her outspoken pride.' She turned and looked at Maria.

'Enough fawning, woman.' He scowled. 'She'll not invite further gossip from the confines of her chamber.'

Luna sat silent and still. She felt hollow as a worked deer carcass ready to be mounted on the wall. Did everyone know of the painting's true purpose, even Friar Bartolomeo? Was she so lowly esteemed? Yes. Even a simpleton would not have her as his wife. She felt Maria take her hand under the table and squeeze it. Luna shook her head. This was not the way it was supposed to be; she was the one to comfort Maria.

Mamma Lucrezia filled Papa's glass yet again. 'Best she knows the truth of where her future lies.'

'I had hoped to enjoy this meal with my wife and children, but I am fair disappointed,' he said as he rose from the table. 'There is no marriage now so the rest of it matters not.' He stopped by Mamma Lucrezia's chair. 'Make sure Maria is handsomely decorated when I see her future father-in-law again at Mass. If I must endure a Palagio betrothal, at least let it be with a father's pride.' Then he turned to Luna. 'This was always your destiny, child,' he said.

Luna watched him leave the room. The boards creaked where he stepped and the heavy plod of his familiar footfall continued even after he was out of sight. She heard the outer doors downstairs open and then a loud thump as they closed; Papa had gone out. There'd be no further conversation, though she knew now, with crushing certainty, that her value was no different to that of any other girl: it lay in the price she could raise as a bride, and in that she'd let him down. Even a simpleton didn't want her for a wife. Who next would her father approach?

Luna excused herself and stumbled to her room. She took out the Sacrobosco and stared at it. Was she a fool to believe herself worthy of learning? The injustice of her lot sat firmly in the leather-bound text, which she would never be allowed to read once she became someone's wife. How cruel a fate. She flung the book across the room and heard it smack sharply against the far wall. Damn this world that elevated men above all others.

CHAPTER TWELVE

If he could go back and change the way this morning had begun, Vincenzio would surely have left Luna at home when the family gathered to depart for the cathedral. But he'd been distracted by his little boy, who needed his attention ahead of joining the preacher's fanciulli and, in faith, he'd no comprehension of how utterly his daughter had befriended her own vulgarity. Lately Luna did everything she could to vex him and prove his wife right. How was it that someone with intelligence could be so foolish? Because she was a girl, of course, and despite all his teachings, the weak nature of her sex would always overwhelm his attempts at nurturing her mind.

Vincenzio slapped his gloves against his thigh. He did it again and again and the sharp sound made him feel a little better. He'd bundled them all into the carriage at the conclusion of the Mass and sent it home. God's teeth, how he'd wanted to join them so he could be there when the doctor arrived to assess Filippo, but he'd had to leave that to his wife's good work. He trusted she'd waste no time in calling the doctor.

At least Guido Palagio had not been hurt by Luna, though Vincenzio anticipated with rueful distaste another bill of reparation forthwith, a cost he could little afford. He'd assumed Luna would have recognised Guido, surely the womenfolk gossiped? The man was to marry Maria after all! Vincenzio shook his head. Luna had no interest in such talk and so the man who was to become her brother remained a stranger.

Signore Palagio waited for him already in the tavern on Via San Gallo but Vincenzio needed a moment to think and found a stone seat to rest upon. Tommaso had been outraged when he saw how Luna comported herself and they'd exchanged heated words, which Vincenzio now regretted. The man's reaction was understandable; Luna had struck his son, and he'd be lucky to only receive a fine. She'd become unmanageable and because of her behaviour, he must claw back the good reputation of his name yet again. What was worse, now he could not afford to lose the Palagio marriage contract. His hands formed tight fists against his thighs; without the Palagio name to underwrite his new loan, he'd be forced to leave the shipment of wool at the docks for another month. It would mean reprioritising the orders. He shook his head. Would God's benevolence desert him forever? The Palagio fabric was still not finished and Vincenzio would not countenance disappointment from his wife. The thought of her reaction filled him with resentment. He'd have to delay paying the fullers and the dyers, then there were the contract weavers in the contado. Damn it, if any of them refused to work without getting paid it would affect all the orders. He'd already been forced to shut his shop in Prato and planned on keeping that quiet for as long as he could. The Medici coin had all gone to the household expenses. He peered about cautiously. Friar Bartolomeo had warned him there was gossip afoot about coins stamped with the Medici crest in circulation. A shopkeeper had received one as payment only last week. Vincenzio closed his eyes to settle his racing pulse. He must be more careful from now on.

The most sensible course of action was to plead his daughter's case to Signore Palagio and ensure the marriage contract remained secure. That loathsome man would no doubt take great pleasure in Vincenzio's fawning, but he would do it. Once the contract was signed, he anticipated the usual early wedding presents from Guido for Maria—gems and luxurious clothes—and fully expected them to be extravagant, as Tommaso Palagio's pride demanded. His son's status would be reflected in their grandeur after all. Vincenzio would pawn the items and use the funds to discharge his debts. There would be ample time for him to purchase them back, albeit at a vastly inflated rate, before Maria would be expected to wear them at the wedding festivities.

He sighed and stood up, stretching his neck from side to side till he heard it crack. The Lord sent him challenges and he would meet them with faith and courage. At least he'd get wine in the tavern and his family would be home by now and Filippo safely recovering. He must be thankful to God for saving his son.

Vincenzio turned out of the square towards the tavern. He walked with an assured swagger, making a point of nodding politely when he passed a familiar face. The streets were busy and a number of the preacher's followers roamed from house to house. He had no desire to fall under their scrutiny and quickened his pace. If Savonarola had evidence to prove he'd been in league with Roberto and was working to return Piero to his seat in the Signoria, then surely he'd have been arrested by now. So that meant the preacher's antics during Mass were a warning and that was the best that he could do. Vincenzio felt a rapid flush of hot blood inflame his chest at the memory of Filippo falling, but the preacher's provocation had not borne fruit. Thank God he hadn't said anything to condemn himself. Still, he would forever feel guilty about exposing Filippo to such danger. Roberto's death should have been a warning. Certainly the note that accompanied Vincenzio's copy of the Great Council's proclamation was a direct threat. Yet he'd delivered his son to the viper's nest. What nonsensical lunacy. What mad bravado.

He held his hand to his chest, feeling for the beat of his heart. It thudded deep within its hollow chamber. Vincenzio breathed slowly, letting the notion sink into his bones. He was not going to be arrested. The Great Council did not know of his efforts to buy soldiers for a Medici army. If he dealt with this Palagio problem swiftly, he'd be home in time to join his family to sup. He had a strong desire to sit at the head of his table, with Lucrezia to his right and his children spread around him, and most of all to see his son revived and back to his usual mischievous self.

*

It was well past curfew when Vincenzio slipped through the doors of his home for the second time that night. Any man would have chosen the quiet of a tavern after the disrespect he'd endured around his own table. After Mass, he'd convinced Tommaso Palagio with a honeyed tongue to sign the marriage contract, accepting the conditions Tommaso had added. Then, when all he had wanted was to eat in peace surrounded by his family, he'd been rudely challenged by Leonarda. It was a delicate and exhausting dance, this parlaying of his daughters' futures to keep his own and that of his business alive, as well as holding faith in the Medici exiles whilst showing loyalty to his city. He'd needed to escape after enduring such an unpleasant meal, just for a few hours' relief from the constant pressure of being the head of this family. This day had very nearly undone him.

He'd not meant to stay out past the ringing of the bells, but he'd drunk too much to care and, in truth, he'd enjoyed skulking home in the shadows. It made him feel like a young buck again. Only now he needed his bed. He trod lightly as he could across the courtyard and made his way upstairs, conscious he was late and a little over-indulged. The stone was slippery, though, and he stumbled on the steps. The noise it made felt like Apollonius's hooves were pummelling his head. That brought Lucrezia out.

'Don't judge me, woman.' Even to his own ears, his words sounded slurred.

'Indeed I do not. I know what a challenging day you've had and I forgive you the libation.' She took his arm and helped him up the stairs.

'How is my son?'

'Well enough. He sleeps now quite calmly and I hope he will wake in the morn no less active from his mishap today.'

Vincenzio grumbled at the uncomfortable pinch of her fingers as his wife guided him to his chamber and began to undo the buttons on his vest.

'It was no mishap,' he said. 'That was a direct warning to me.'

'What say you?' Lucrezia stared at him in confusion.

'Stop shaking, woman, or it will never be done.' He was tired and wanted to be out of all these clothes.

'I need you to be strong, husband.' Lucrezia dropped her voice. 'If what you say is true, then we are in real danger. Filippo was nearly killed at Mass. The preacher is a law unto himself; he could so easily do worse. I see it happening to our friends every day and it scares me.' She applied a cold compress to his forehead as she spoke but he pushed her hand away.

'Yet Filippo is recovered. I saw him eat heartily at the table. Sleep easy, wife, and leave the politicking to me.'

'Sleep!' Lucrezia hissed the word. 'How do you think a mother sleeps at all knowing her son nearly died? If, as you say, the eye of God's chosen preacher is upon us, I doubt I'm ever to sleep easily again.'

Vincenzio swayed as Lucrezia undressed him. He coughed great exhalations of sour breath and she took him by the shoulders and shook him till he revived. She was not to be silenced this night. The horror she'd felt at seeing her son dropped from so dangerous a height to the cold stone ground festered within her and the disbelief in her darling Pippo's eyes as he fell would not fade. He may have recovered but Lucrezia's hands would not stop shaking.

'Our daughter is near betrothed, Vincenzio, and with the Lord's blessing, there will be much to celebrate in the coming months. Your loyalty to the Medicis must end.'

'Be quiet in your mouth!' Vincenzio shouted, then paused as he remembered something. 'They will join us next week to sup, the Palagios. I invited them to celebrate the betrothal.'

'Thank you, my love, for being gracious even as you suffer.'

He nodded; it was too much effort to speak and Lucrezia's voice was like a sword thrusting in his ear.

She kissed him. 'I will tell Maria the good news in the morning. Thank you, husband. Now, I beg you to spare me more florins so I may begin to fill her marriage chest with those pieces every wife needs.'

Vincenzio grabbed his wife's arm. 'What?' His brain was addled by the wine, he knew that, but still, mention of the coin brought him momentary clarity. 'I must have that money back.'

'What money? I have all but spent this month's allowance and I still need more to help pay for Maria's things.'

'Don't coddle me, mistress.' He pushed her away. 'Those coins are not yours to spend.'

'Then why did you give them to me?' she asked.

He sat on the bed heavily. The room moved, fast as a circling hawk. 'I had no choice.'

Vincenzio waved his hand erratically, the alcohol having loosened his limbs as well as his mind. 'I had no choice but to use those coins.'

'I do not wish to know of what fool's errand you speak. Please, husband, hear me. I have always supported you but I fear for myself and our children. If the preacher's men rout you out, what will become of us?'

The cold compress was working poorly, or perhaps it was his wife's badgering that kept him ill. Vincenzio felt his head might split.

'Something so simple as to cease your involvement with the Academy would be a boon. Signore Palagio says the humanists are not to be trusted.' Lucrezia moved to stand by the window.

'The Platonic Academy is well respected.'

'It is still a Medici institution. Do you not see how you allow danger into our chamber like the kiss of Judas?'

He grumbled at such hysteria. Women, especially his wife, were incapable of understanding nuance and had no stomach for politics. His head hurt and he needed to close his eyes; he could not even muster more anger.

'Cease these hysterics and let your poor husband rest, for I am sore wearied by this day and it gets no easier in my own chamber.' He lay back and closed his eyes. 'Away with you before I hit you on the head.'

He did not hear his wife leave the room; he was already asleep.

*

Vincenzio woke with a crushing pain across his forehead. He sat on the edge of the bed, waiting for the room to stop swimming. Then he called for a restorative tonic as he dressed slowly. He'd need a cup of wine with which to wash it down and stumbled to his studiolo, where he dropped into his chair and let his arms fall slackly to either side. His back still ached from his undignified scrambling up into the choir stand and nothing he did seemed to ease the discomfort.

Sitting in the stark light of morning, he remembered his wife's rebukes and, still groggy, wondered if there might yet be some truth in what she said. A servant interrupted his musings with the tonic and he drank it quickly, gagging at the intensity of flavour, then flushed it down with a cup of wine. By the time he'd finished the jug and eaten the bread that came with it, he felt restored, and any stirrings of self-awareness had been drowned out along with the alcohol.

He called for a new quill, turning over the one on his desk with its blunt tip, and prepared a fresh balance sheet of his assets. Still a dwindling mercantile fortune, soon to be boosted by the financial benefits of a marriage. Extensive possessions, though he made note of a reduction in his collection of books, having sent so many away. A devoted wife; here Vincenzio's quill hovered, remembering Lucrezia's temper of the previous night, but he decided to be gracious and carried on to the next item. Talented children; another moment of hesitation, lifted by the certainty of his son's robust constitution in the face of danger. He did not include the Medicis on his list of friendships but added the Palagios to bolster his respectability and to keep his numbers up. At the conclusion of his writings, once again, he felt the burdens of his mind abate.

A servant knocked and brought in a large jug of wine and some of the citrons left over from dinner. Vincenzio allowed himself to eat them all. For these delicious sweets he might yet forgive Lucrezia her arrogance. She was an excellent housekeeper. He supposed she'd also not been entirely wrong when she'd brought up Luna's reputation; his pride had been bruised by Signore Spinelli's rejection of his daughter. Christ's blood! The man's son was a simpleton and still he'd turned her down. At least confining Leonarda to her chamber would curtail any further disobedience. He thought of his daughter's pained frown and those pretty eyes turned dark. She looked more like Giulia each day.

Vincenzio stood abruptly and paced the small room. She'd shamed the Fusili name at Mass again, and yet he couldn't help snorting at the image of Guido Palagio toppling over. She had her father's strength, but even he could see she'd become too much like a man and that did not serve anyone. Dabbling in public forums of debate was acceptable when she was under his authority, but since she'd reached the age of womanhood, it had become socially dangerous. He'd made a mistake and began to understand the critics who'd told him she was an aberration of female nature. If he could find no family willing to take her then he would have to approach a convent. He made a note to speak to Friar Bartolomeo about it. He pitied his little moon, with her grand ideas of learning astronomy. At least in a convent she'd have time for her books and he'd make sure to send her one new volume each year. He struck out at the beads that hung from the bookshelf and they flung up with such force the string snapped and broke. The small glass baubles scattered across the floor like frightened beetles. It didn't matter how old Luna grew or what he did with her, his dead wife would always be staring back at him from those eyes.

Vincenzio poured another cup and sat quietly drinking. This was man's medicine and he deserved a reward. He sighed heavily, thinking about his recent expedition to Prato and Pistoia. The marriage negotiations for Leonarda might not have gone to plan, but the journey had not been a failure. He'd visited the country families at their estates and already sent the list of names to Piero. No one had uncovered his actions and that gave him huge relief. Despite the increased risk to his person after Roberto's murder, he'd done everything Piero demanded. Vincenzio straightened in his chair, pressed his shoulders back and felt the thrust of his chest. Even in the face of the death of a Medici supporter, he'd still done his duty as a loyal friend. Piero would reward him.

His eyes flicked briefly to the Great Council's proclamation still sitting on his desk in a pile of paperwork. Friar Savonarola was now the most powerful man in all of Florence. The preacher had used his innocent son to threaten him and Vincenzio clenched his teeth at the memory of his own pitiful attempt to save Filippo. He'd not fail his son again. The pleasure in the preacher's eyes had been like a madness to see. He was dangerous. Vincenzio set his mind anew to plotting Savonarola's downfall. His only son and heir had nearly died at the preacher's hands. He'd make the man suffer.

CHAPTER THIRTEEN

Luna listened to the smack of mallet against meat as the kitchen girls got to work preparing dishes for dinner. The noises of the household had become her lullaby since she'd been confined to her chamber. The first full day she'd railed against the injustice of her lot, but that had soon turned to resignation and then finally to clarity. She slept longer and felt her head clearer as a result.

Isotta Nogarola had not let her emotions eclipse her thinking mind and so Luna made a promise to herself that she would find a solution to her problem. With her own hard work and knowledge, she would defend herself against a future she didn't want. She turned to practical reasoning; at least she wasn't getting married to Signore Spinelli's son. She must be thankful, for if it came to it, she would have to do as her father commanded. Therefore, she must make sure she would never be considered a worthy bride, then she'd live in this house forever. She'd picked up the Sacrobosco from where it had landed on the floor and smoothed its bent cover. Throwing it had been a rash moment and she was glad it hadn't been damaged. Books were essential; they would offer her a solution.

Luna heard Maria's voice from her step-mamma's chamber. She was listing which shops they were to visit and Luna was relieved to be confined to her chamber and unable to join them on their expedition.

She kept the image of an unmarried Isotta Nogarola burning in her mind as she finished reading the Sacrobosco. She had nearly memorised all the important sections. She slipped it under her pillow when a servant brought food or when her step-mamma came to her room. It wouldn't be wise to let Mamma Lucrezia discover the book of astronomy in her hands. Yet books were not dangerous; it was what the reader did with the learnings that could cause damage. She thought about the ideas within the small book written by Aristarchus. There was an example of how a written concept could be ignored or embraced; for one reader it was blasphemy, for another, inspiration. Luna sat up and looked out the window, her mind ticking. If she wanted to make an indelible impression of unsuitability as a wife, then writing an exploration of Aristarchus of Samos's Sun-centred model was her answer. She'd need to retrieve the book from her father's studiolo, which simply meant picking a time when she knew he wouldn't be there. Just like Isotta Nogarola, she would write an astonishing treatise, something to shock the very core of Florence society. If she did a good enough job, her father might even be pleased with her homage to his own rise.

She got up and leant out over the window frame, breathing in the morning air. The garden spread out below and from so high its patterned pathways looked like a mathematical diagram. At its centre was the walled pond where all the paths collided. She'd best get started if she was going to write an argument so astonishing as to put an end to Leonarda Lunetta Fusili becoming any man's wife.

*

The Palagios would soon be arriving to celebrate the signing of the marriage contract. Papa would not be home till his guests were due. He'd left early, as he so often did these days. Luna had heard him on the landing by her chamber, shouting to a stable boy to get Apollonius ready. Then she heard him tell Mamma Lucrezia that all of his children must be present for the Palagios' visit; anything less would be disrespectful. Luna would be expected to sit at the table and eat but not to speak. Her inclusion in the celebration was only a pretence of family unity and seemed cruel indeed. Till she was summonsed, she'd fix her thoughts on the book she was reading and how she was going to use astronomy to free herself.

Luna prayed for patience and forbearance as she dressed; she'd endure the gathering for Maria's sake. Signore Palagio and his wife and son would hardly view her any more kindly, since her step-mamma had made it very clear that all of Florence had now heard about her brazen attack on the man on the steps of the cathedral who, not surprisingly, had been deemed the wronged party. She fastened the belt at her waist and took one last look at her reflection in the pane of glass. Her skirts fell cleanly over her peg-leg and the stump that so offended all of Florence society and condemned her as nothing more than a cripple. She shook her skirts to add lightness and volume and liked the way she now appeared bigger. All of her was hidden.

Luna stood with Maria behind her parents and waited for their guests to arrive. Filippo hung off Livia's arm, impatient with being made to stand still. Luna watched the easy freedom with which he scuffed the flagstones with his boots. Then footsteps sounded and Signore Palagio and his wife appeared. Up close the man was short and he carried himself angrily. Luna remembered Signora Palagio's arrogance and composure and saw that she was taller than her husband. Tonight she held back and waited behind him, her head dipped in dutiful politeness. Their son followed next. He cast around the company and his wide-set eyes settled on Luna. She gasped uncontrollably and had to press a hand against the wall to steady herself; here was her tormentor. How could she not have thought to ask her step-mamma anything about Signore Palagio's son before now? His reaction to her behaviour at Mass made sense; it was his son she'd insulted.

'My daughters, come forward.' Her father held out his hand and beckoned them to him. His voice was calm and his eyes spoke only of the pride of introducing his children. Luna forced herself to move with Maria, though she remained a step behind her younger sister.

'This is Maria Benedetta, who will fulfil her duties as a wife and mother in the house of Palagio.'

Signore Palagio nodded formally as Maria made a curtsey.

'Guido Michelangelo.' Signore Palagio spoke and his son stepped forward and took Maria's hand. Her little fingers clung to his. Luna wanted to rip them away and pull Maria back to her. He was so much bigger than her sister.

'Hello.'

Luna heard Maria's politest attempt at a greeting and her jaw clenched at her sister's childish desire to please this wretch of a man.

Guido nodded as he dropped his forehead to touch the back of her hand. He remained bowed in silence. Luna saw Maria's skirts quiver as she smiled and waited. Her own legs threatened to give way. After a respectable few seconds, Maria's suitor let go of her hand and stepped back in line with his father. Luna took a deep breath, readying herself.

'And my eldest child, Leonarda Lunetta.'

Luna heard her name like the echo of a stone Pippo might drop into the well just to hear the novelty of its splash. She stepped forward. The ease with which she moved was surprising, for she'd thought perhaps her legs might betray her. She curtseyed as best she could and was rewarded by a nod from Signore Palagio. Thankfully that was all the acknowledgement it appeared she'd get, and she moved into the background once more. After acknowledging Filippo, the two gentlemen led the way through to the main hall where the table was laid with a feast of dishes. As they moved off, Luna felt the eyes of Guido Palagio upon her.

Before they sat to eat, Signore Palagio gave Papa the first of his family's wedding gifts for Maria, carried in a decorated wooden jewellery box. Maria would wear the jewels and clothes during the wedding celebrations and thereafter Guido would take back possession of the treasures. Mamma Lucrezia came closer to see. From within the box, Papa pulled out first a headdress bedecked with peacock feathers, silver pearls, enamelled flowers and gilded spangles. He handed it to Mamma Lucrezia, who inspected it most keenly before showing it to Maria. Then he held up a garland of plumes and pearls, and then two more strands of luminous pearls. Mamma Lucrezia made a noise of delight and Maria smiled broadly. Papa carefully replaced the items into the box.

'These are indeed beautiful and of great value,' he said to Signore Palagio. 'We are honoured by your generosity.'

'I will expect the first payment towards Maria's dowry within the day. The rest you may pay in coin and gifts at the time of the wedding,' Signore Palagio replied.

When the formalities were done, the party sat and Mamma Lucrezia called to the servants to pour the wine. The meal began well enough. Signore Palagio, sitting at the head of the table to the right of Papa, described the countryside outside of Prato where the Palagio villa was located; they hunted deer and rabbits, and had well-established groves of pear trees and olive trees. He talked of Friar Savonarola's greatness and Papa did not challenge him. Mamma Lucrezia fussed about the table, ensuring the wine was replenished before any glasses were empty and insisting Guido try her specialty dishes. Luna sat beside Maria and ate in silence. Every now and then she pressed her hand against her sister's and in that way felt safe.

'I understand you still attend gatherings of the Platonic Academy,' Tommaso Palagio said to their father.

'Indeed,' Papa answered. 'Though of course these days there is only the occasional lecture or conversation.'

'More the better too,' Guido interjected. 'It is wrong for men of different standing to come together thus.'

'My son prefers private, more sophisticated forms of reflection,' Signore Palagio explained.

'The Academy is a respected place of debate; its members may not all be as fortunate as us but even bakers and weavers can be thinkers. You may be surprised to hear that one of the University of Bologna's professors will address us, on the publication of Joannes de Monte Regio's last work, the *Epitome of Ptolemy's Almagest*.'

Signore Palagio raised his eyebrows. 'A worthy guest to be sure.'

'We are curious men who search for harmony and perfection in the subjects we explore.'

'Sounds like heresy to me,' Guido said.

Luna hadn't noticed his brows before. They hung across the wide space between his eyes most ungraciously.

'There you are wrong; it is the ultimate contemplation of God.'

Luna listened to her father with pride.

'Church is the only true place to convene with the Lord,' Guido responded hotly.

Papa nodded. 'Lord, in thy hands are all things.'

'Indeed,' Signore Palagio added. 'And are we not fortunate to have a man of such passion as Friar Savonarola directing the soul of our city?'

'Will you be attending the lecture?' Papa asked.

Signore Palagio nodded. 'I have received an invitation from Bernardo Rucellai, as have most of the Council. I do not hold with the tenets of the Platonists, but I cannot refuse our Gonfalonier of Justice.'

'He has been very generous in allowing the Academy to use his villa. Joannes's work has been highly anticipated and the printer in Vienna only made a few copies, so many will come to hear Professor di Novara.' Papa turned to the younger Palagio with a polite inclination of his head. 'I hope you will accompany your father?'

'I find books tedious and talking about them even more so.'

'Indeed,' Luna said, noting how Guido Palagio slouched over his plate, like a boy who'd always had to protect his food. She did not want him as her brother-in-law.

A look of warning crossed her step-mamma's face. Luna cursed her disobedient tongue.

Guido laughed and addressed her father. 'Do you always allow your daughters to interject so rudely, Signore Fusili?' Then he turned to Luna and in those eyes that deceived everyone with their wide-set, childlike innocence, she saw malice. 'I doubt you even wash your father's collars without an investigation of whence the dirt came.'

Luna felt her cheeks burn. 'Curiosity, sire, has no limit. It is not wrong to wish to understand as much as I can, for God gave us all the same opportunity.'

'Arrogance and perversity!' Tommaso Palagio cut in. 'Is it because she is a cripple that the rules of society do not apply to this one?'

Signore Fusili frowned but didn't reply.

'Your daughter shames you at your own table, Vincenzio, and I cannot commend this behaviour when our two houses will soon be matched through marriage. I must insist the girl does not speak her mind again. Indeed, I would be more comfortable knowing she were hidden.' He eyed everyone around the table and Luna felt her cheeks burn as she saw his wife nod in agreement and Guido smile.

'Luna is harmless,' her papa replied. A pitiful response.

'You cannot deny her reputation, Vincenzio! She is known for her unseemly rhetoric.'

Luna stared at her plate. It was positioned a little too far to the left of her place and the imbalance of it rankled. There were streaks of grease amidst her unfinished stew and the juice around the edges had begun to congeal.

'I do not, but she is a good girl.'

Signore Palagio laughed at that. It was weighted with derision. 'If a woman throws her arms around whilst speaking, or if she increases the volume of her speech with greater forcefulness, she will appear threateningly insane and requiring restraint.' He looked at Luna as though he'd just defined her.

'You quote Leonardo Bruni d'Arezzo,' her father commented.

Luna felt the eyes of everyone around the table on her and hated it. Worst was Guido, who sat between his mother and her dear Maria. Papa was still speaking but she couldn't make out what he said for the pounding that had started in her head. She could quote Leonardo Bruni just as well if that's what she had to do to quiet this arrogant little man.

'Proficiency in any form'—she adapted the quote for in fact Bruni spoke of literature—'when not accompanied by broad acquaintance with facts and truths, is a barren attainment; Leonardo Bruni could just as well have been speaking to you, sir.' The fierceness of her voice surprised Luna and she saw from the others' faces that they were taken aback.

'Be quiet, Leonarda.' There was thunder in her father's eyes. He flicked a glance at Signore Palagio then across to Mamma Lucrezia. 'You must be silent and dutiful. That is all the world can know of my daughter.' Her father's voice was resolute.

'Of course she is,' Mamma Lucrezia echoed her husband with a cheeriness that belied her fury. 'My girls are good daughters of Florence.'

For the rest of the dinner, Luna sat as she'd been instructed, silent and dutiful, but her mind rushed furiously through her plan. She would write the treatise on a Sun-centred universe forthwith. She pictured Signore Palagio hearing of it; that ignorant man would instantly dismiss her as a madwoman. He'd waste no time in circulating the news amongst the good families of Florence; he'd not be able to keep it to himself. When Signore Palagio realised the parchment was writ by her, he'd make sure that all of Florence society knew of her impudence. Her papa would assuredly have to curtail any notion of her marriageability after that. Luna was relying on it.

'There are excellent dishes still to come out,' Mamma Lucrezia spoke hurriedly as she picked up a plate of roast woodcock and walked round to where the gentlemen sat. She served Signore Palagio. 'We are most excited about our children's betrothal.'

He nodded in acknowledgement and then again to encourage her to drop another bird onto his bread.

'May God bless their union.' Signore Palagio turned his attention to Papa. 'Though it did take much convincing for me to overlook the faults of the sister.'

Papa nodded and took a slug of wine.

'We are forever in your debt,' Mamma Lucrezia said.

Luna watched Signore Palagio slowly chew; she wanted to smash that bird's leg into his mouth and see how well he spoke then. Her step-mamma stopped behind her chair and she felt a warning pinch to her shoulder.

'It is late in the hunting season to bag wild game.' Signore Palagio held up a clean bone appreciatively.

'You can still find them, if you know where to search,' Mamma Lucrezia answered in her most gracious voice.

'And where would that be?'

'Across the river; there are acres still rich with game.'

'Well I thank you for your generosity in sharing both this meal and its source.' He threw another bone into the basket and drank deeply from the goblet of wine set before him. 'I am relieved that fine food and good wine are still to be found in Florence.'

'We do our best.' Her father refilled his guest's empty goblet as he spoke.

'You will find excellent apothecaries and, of course, cloth merchants, in Florence also,' Mamma added. 'I have been most impressed by the quality of offerings in Matteo Palmieri's shop compared to those I used to favour in Bologna.'

'Indeed,' Margherita Palagio replied, with a nod of excitement. 'I have been meaning to visit the apothecary and replenish my perfumes.'

'I do not advise you to buy from Palmieri, wife,' Signore Palagio said. 'I hear he accepts Medici coin. The shop must be a hotbed of traitors.'

His wife gasped.

'I visited Master Palmieri only days ago with my daughter. I can assure you it is safe. Nothing untoward was happening there.' Mamma Lucrezia had clearly only meant to reassure the lady but the glare that Papa gave her made Luna think she'd said something terribly wrong. She waited for her father's rebuke, but instead he mentioned the order of cloth that was ready for Signora Palagio. Her step-mamma hurried out of the room.

Mamma Lucrezia returned and presented Signora Palagio with a paper package drawn up with string.

'This is the crimson-coloured wool, as you requested. I am pleased to have it finally ready.'

'Thank you, though I'm not sure I have any use for it. When I first placed the order, the colour was in fashion, but since then Friar Savonarola has opened my eyes to the decadence of such attire.' Signora Palagio waved to a servant and handed the parcel over without bothering to open it.

'We have another shipment of the finest plain wool arriving soon, do we not, husband?' Mamma Lucrezia said. 'I would be happy to set aside a quantity for you.'

The lady Palagio looked to her husband with surprise.

Papa coughed awkwardly. 'Forgive my wife's impertinence,' he said. 'Offer our guests more wine, Lucrezia.'

'No need to apologise. I know your business woes and admire your wife's determination and optimism.'

'You are misinformed,' Papa said. 'Business is strong and when I take delivery of the latest shipment it will be the largest yet received in Florence.'

'I sympathise with your predicament,' Signore Palagio said, 'but do not lie to me. No one buys wool any more when there is fine silk to be had. Word is that shipment of yours arrived last month and still sits in the docks gathering dust. The Signoria has catalogued your debts in the public register put out yestereve, and it is no secret your shop in Prato closed recently. What else are we to deduce?'

Luna watched Guido Palagio smirk at his father's words.

'Whatever you damn well like! I will not discuss business at my table,' her father answered hotly.

'As you wish, though after dinner I would talk with you privately on this matter.' Signore Palagio turned to Mamma Lucrezia. 'Forgive me, madam,' he said.

There was no flicker of concern in her step-mamma's smile but she rose soon after and Signora Palagio rose too, signalling an end to the dinner. Luna and Maria followed the ladies through to Mamma Lucrezia's chamber where they took more wine and sweetmeats. Luna listened to the conversation about fabrics and cooking techniques. Her cheeks ached from the effort of maintaining her smile and her head had begun to throb. She wished she could escape back to her bedchamber. No one would miss her. She heard the muffled voices of the men talking in the main hall. When Signora Palagio commended her step-mamma on her sweetmeats, Luna took the chance.

'I will fetch some more,' she offered, and was at the door before her step-mamma could object. She hurried along the balcony, looking down to see that no servants were watching her scurry away. She'd sat through the dinner as was commanded of her and now felt sure that her absence from the women's company would go unnoticed. Mamma Lucrezia would be happily discussing wedding plans with the Palagio lady whilst Papa and his gentlemen guests drank wine in the dining hall. She passed her father's studiolo and remembered she needed the copy of *The Sand Reckoner*. She slipped through the half-open door and closed it gently, resting her forehead against the cold wood in relief at this moment of privacy. She held her skirt up a little so she could more easily lift her peg-leg to relieve the pressure on her knee. It was sweet pleasure, such relief, and she let out an easy sigh as she resumed standing and dropped her skirts. Then she turned around to the bookshelf and stopped short. She was not alone.

Guido Palagio sat at her father's desk with his feet resting on the beautiful wood.

Luna fell back against the door in shock. 'What are you doing in here?'

'Your father suggested I might enjoy perusing his shelves, though I'm not sure why when I told him how I dislike reading. Perhaps his hearing fails? In any case, I am more comfortable here than at the table listening to the gentlemen's dull conversation.' His eyes travelled up Luna's body. 'You have a crutch hidden under those skirts?'

She ignored his vulgarity, though she could not stop the tremors that shook her whole body. 'Please take your feet off the desk.' As she spoke, she fumbled behind her for the door handle.

He raised his eyebrows and snorted. 'Provocative she-Devil. I believe I will get to know my future sister-in-law properly this evening. Much more entertaining than books.' He came towards her.

Luna's chest hurt, she was breathing so fast. She did not take her eyes off Guido as she fumbled blindly for the door handle. Up close she saw that the flesh of his cheek was pinpricked with small cavities from scarring of the pox. She thought of calling out but knew that her cries would be heard only as evidence of her impropriety, her shame. Guido grabbed her arm and pulled her roughly. Luna could not stop herself from falling against him. She turned away from the smell of his breath and so she did not have to see his eyes. Her heart beat furiously. She was mightily afeared. His hands grappled with her skirts and she fought him, losing her balance. As she struggled, the ties that secured her knee to the peg-leg broke and the contraption fell off, smacking loudly to the stone floor. Guido reared back in shock at the sight of Luna's stump and she took the chance to escape, wrenching open the door. Then she was out into the hallway and glad to see a servant stare in shock as she stumbled past, insensible to the pain in her leg, towards her chamber. At least Guido would not follow.

*

Signore Palagio and his wife and son left the Fusili palazzo uneventfully in the dusk hour of that night. Luna watched from a discreet position on the balcony above, intent on knowing when she might feel safe in her house again. Her father bid Signore Palagio good health before seeing the family to their carriage and the two mothers parted with newfound familiarity as soon-to-be matriarchs united by their children's marriage.

Luna disappeared back to her bedchamber, tugging at the formal dress to get it off her skin. It was the same gown in which she'd sat for her portrait and Mamma Lucrezia had insisted she put it on for the Palagio dinner. Now she threw the beaded skirts to the floor. One of the small pearls broke free and skittered away. Her mind burned with shame and dismay.

Outside, a late summer Moon rose and its ethereal light illuminated the bedchamber. Luna clambered into bed and when Maria slipped through the door she pretended to be asleep. She listened to her sister disrobe, humming a tune softly, happily, to herself, but it burned in Luna's ears. When she climbed into bed, she rolled against the wall. Even when her sister's arms reached round her she didn't stir but felt the pull of that embrace like a silken rope tethering her to this life.

CHAPTER FOURTEEN

Vincenzio opened the flask of wine and poured two glasses, passing one across to Friar Bartolomeo and drinking his own swiftly, then refilling it before the friar had even put his lips to the cup. The chair in the friar's cell afforded him a view of the cloister garden. He watched a bird nesting in the orange tree and marvelled at how tall and broad the tree had grown.

'We need this, my friend; it's been a fearsome summer.' Vincenzio raised his glass, thinking of Roberto's fated end and Filippo's fortunate escape. He'd delivered the proceeds from the sale of Signore Palagio's wedding gifts to his bank, and even after he'd deducted the reparation fee for Luna's misdemeanour, it had still amounted to two hundred florins. That had been a sweet moment indeed. He had ample time to replace the headdress and strands of pearls before the marriage took place. At least the gossip would now be centred on the future pairing of the Fusili and Palagio families and not on his wayward daughter. He'd soon enough be in a position to pay off his warehouse debt and collect the bolts of wool that sat gathering dust. Now, he just needed to move the shop stock, though there was a drought of customers of late. He regretted closing his shop in Prato—no bonfires there to impact sales—but he was not a soothsayer. He must be resolute and acquit himself in public with equanimity, and feed the gossip-mongers whom his wife listened to with a new story, one of the resurrection of his fortunes.

'God bless you,' Friar Bartolomeo said, savouring the drink. He pulled a letter from the pocket of his habit. 'This is from the Mother Abbess at the Convent of San Matteo in Arcetri. She is pleased to welcome Leonarda as a sister of St Clare. She suggests the child join them in the autumn, before the stark cold of winter sets in.'

Vincenzio sat back and let out a long, slow hiss. Here was news indeed. 'So it is settled.' He raised his glass again in salute; the wine went down smoothly. He'd expected to feel some relief at Luna's future being secured, but blast it if he didn't want to rip the letter into pieces.

Leonarda Lunetta, his little moon. He'd still harboured some doubt at the notion of sending her to a convent, even after the incident at Mass with the younger Palagio, but any prospect of a different future had been well and truly destroyed by her behaviour at the dinner. Ever since she'd come of age, he'd been told by all and sundry that she must marry or enter a convent. He'd left it longer than was prudent, in truth, hoping neither husband nor God would prove a better future than staying home with him, but Florence was a city that did not suffer rule-breakers and he'd not counted on his daughter developing quite so independent a voice. She'd become wilful, speaking her mind whenever it pleased her and asking for the freedoms of a man. He'd tried to find a husband, a fool's errand he now realised, and so the convent must be her salvation and his family's resurrection. Guilt coursed through his veins as heady as the wine. He would support her, naturally, and she could write to him and he would visit when it was possible. In part, Luna's future had been taken out of his hands: Tommaso Palagio had forced his decision. He'd insisted it be written in the marriage contract: the cripple sister must enter a convent. Vincenzio had to admire the man's tenacity. Luna was a good daughter; she would accept his decision dutifully, even if she didn't like it.

Friar Bartolomeo leant across the table. 'Do you wish me to find an escort for her?'

Vincenzio swung his attention back to the conversation. 'What do you ask?'

'I say do you want me to arrange an escort to take Luna to the convent, or would you prefer it were you or me who delivered her to the sisters?'

He stared at the friar whilst the image of his daughter turning her back on him and disappearing through the convent doors filled his head. 'Arrange it, if you would. I cannot spare the time.'

Friar Bartolomeo sighed. 'As you wish.' He knew what really lay beneath Signore Fusili's stern exterior and he would pray for the man's tormented soul.

Vincenzio thought once again of the Medici coin he'd given to his wife. He'd wanted to shout at Lucrezia to shut her mouth at the dinner when she'd mentioned shopping at Matteo Palmieri's, where the coin had been discovered. She'd no idea what she'd said and he'd sat there grinding his teeth in frustration as she prattled on. Still, no one had come asking questions, so he reasoned the authorities had not traced it back to him.

The terce bells sounded and Friar Bartolomeo rose slowly, wincing. Vincenzio didn't like to see him struggle; ageing was something he planned on ignoring for as long as he could.

'Walk with me to prayers,' Friar Bartolomeo said, and Vincenzio fell into step beside him. The rich tolling was as familiar as his own heartbeat and the story it told hadn't changed since he was a child. Yet Vincenzio hardly remembered the boy who stood watching for his father's return each evening when the vespers bells rang out. He remembered the damp smell of their small home, the dull light, the muffled thwack of his father's fists on his mother's cheek. These memories he allowed to fester like a weeping sore; he needed them. But the nervous boy waiting for his father's tired eyes to see him, that boy had all but vanished.

The pair passed through the larger cloister and into the main church, where others were gathered for prayer. Vincenzio dropped his head and closed his eyes; he needed God's touch this day. Noblemen stepped forward to take the eucharist. Vincenzio hung back and waited. One day he would be first to drink of God's blood and eat of his flesh. For now, he spoke the prayer and waited his turn. A shimmer of white and grey flew in the air behind the altar. It was a bird, so frequently seen amongst the rafters of the church, but the sight made Vincenzio stop still. The flash of white dropped downwards suddenly, just as Filippo had fallen. God's teeth, he'd never forget that sight. There'd be no peace till the preacher Savonarola was gone, no peace for him or for any other father of Florence. He clenched his fists. There was still much to do.

Vincenzio rode home slowly and brought Apollonius into the courtyard with a firm rein. The horse still had energy to lose and pulled against the strain of his hold. The hollow clop of his pawing hoof echoed on the stones and Lucrezia's face appeared over the balcony above.

'Husband, I would speak with you.' She followed him into his studiolo. 'How fare you?'

'Well enough, my dear,' he answered and sat whilst she eased off each of his boots. Something was amiss but he had not the concentration for his wife's hysterics.

'Some wine.' Lucrezia poured a cup and gave it to her husband. She stood by the window watching him. He was still a handsome man, despite the years. His curls would always be thick and luxuriant and that gave him a youthful air that many of his peers no longer boasted. 'I wish to speak to you of something Signore Palagio said over dinner last week.'

Vincenzio drank the wine and held out his cup for more, ruing the fact he'd not tackled this conversation earlier. She didn't wait for him to drink the second cup of wine before speaking.

'Is your business in trouble? Must I stop purchasing almonds or the pheasant you so love? What am I to cook if I cannot have my preferred ingredients? Will the girls get new dresses this winter? How will we host a wedding celebration?'

Vincenzio jumped up. 'Enough, Lucrezia!' He took her by the shoulders and pressed firmly. She flinched a little at the pressure of his fingers. 'You have nothing to worry about, I assure you.'

'Then can you explain to me why Signore Palagio spoke otherwise? Am I to be gossiped about in town now?'

'He is a frivolous man who listens to every little peep without the mind for context or discernment. Do you understand?'

'I suppose you mean he believes everything he hears, much as all of Florence does, husband, which is why I am distressed.'

Vincenzio sat down. 'I will not justify my business to my wife.'

'I ask no such thing, only tell me if the wool shipment is in your warehouse or in the docks still.'

'Damn it! These things are delicate and complicated and I do not expect you to understand.'

'Will we still have friends left to grace us with their society when Maria's wedding day arrives?'

'Why ever wouldn't we?'

'Because if you lose your business we lose our position and the society of good people with it. Mark me, husband, for I have lived the life of a poor widow before, with only a small stipend left me after my husband's debts were paid, relegated to renting rooms, fearful of losing even that level of security. Were it not for you, I'd be there still and I have no wish to return.'

'Nor shall you. Now give me peace, woman, and find me something to eat.'

Vincenzio made sure Lucrezia did not stay a moment longer. He'd had enough of her badgering. He glowered at the window where she'd stood and brayed rudely into the emptiness of her shadow. She got inside his mind like none other with her needling comments. Just when he'd found some modicum of peace too.

He turned to the lion statue beside his desk and kicked it. It resisted, so he kicked it again and again till the tip of the lion's nose broke off. He stomped it to dust. Then he shook out his leg and refilled his cup before sitting again. It took longer than usual to control his breathing. He focused on the unlit candle taper. The women in his life were causing him more pain than pleasure these days; only young Maria gave him solace. It was when a girl grew to a woman that her spirit changed.

He thought of Luna, his dark-haired, curious child, who would have become an orphan the day she was born if he'd not arrived when he did. He'd lost his wife, but he'd saved his baby. He was sending her to a convent now though, so was there any difference between his decision and the fate Giulia had chosen for their crippled firstborn? He drank more wine. Luna had brought this upon herself, he reasoned, and he must think of the rest of his family and their future. There was naught else he could do. He would send books to sustain Luna and Lucrezia would undoubtedly send sweets.

He raised his glass to his little moon and swallowed the final drops. He'd make sure they shared a few more evenings reading together before she left; he'd miss her delivery of Petrarch's *Canzoniere*, nuanced to perfection. He'd not further her interest in astronomy; that would only serve to make her more disaffected and it would go more easily for her if she entered the order with a calm mind.

Perhaps he could afford her one last intellectual pleasure. The discussion of Ptolemy's *Almagest* was only days away.

Vincenzio sat up straighter as an idea formed: he'd take her with him. If he disguised her as a boy she'd be able to accompany him without fear of judgement. He slapped his thigh and laughed. The sound felt good in his throat and he chuckled again. What fun it would be to sneak her in and what delight to hear her rhetoric in public one last time. Then he could unveil his companion as not a boy but in fact his daughter. Ha! That would shock and impress his fellow humanists—and without the sting of judgement, for she was sworn to the convent now. He thought back to those years when the revered gentlemen scholars of Florence crowded into his hall to hear the Fusili child prodigy's public orations. Those gatherings had been of his making, as was Luna's intellect. She was an illustration of his talents, after all. It was disappointing that she'd become arrogant and impudent in her womanhood, but it would not hurt to remind the members of the Academy that he remained the same dedicated scholar the Academy had first admitted.

CHAPTER FIFTEEN

From somewhere within the house, Luna heard her step-mamma talking about an invitation for the family to pay a visit to the Palagios' city villa. The excitement in her voice was sickening. Luna felt the imprint of Maria's shape still there in the dip in the mattress. She knew she must speak to her step-mamma about what had happened between her and Guido Palagio before her sister was allowed to see him again. She looked at her peg-leg balanced against the wall. She'd done a poor job of re-attaching the ties that had broken, but they held. She didn't look forward to having to explain to Papa why he must pay for its proper repair.

'I would welcome the excursion,' Mamma Lucrezia said. 'The streets have been more settled these past weeks but we will take the carriage nonetheless.'

'Very well, you may go, though I cannot attend as the lecture at the Academy is later this afternoon and before then I must visit the shops,' Papa grumbled. 'In any case, Tommaso Palagio won't be home as he said he'll be at the lecture too.'

'Why would I know such details of your gentlemen's affairs, my dear?' Mamma Lucrezia said, exasperated.

'Well, I'm sure Signora Palagio does not expect my presence,' he answered.

'Yes, you are most certainly correct. I don't expect to be home till vespers, so do not worry.'

Luna heard his easy laugh. 'I will do my best, my love.'

Footsteps grew louder and Luna went and sat on her bed and waited. Mamma Lucrezia appeared. 'I will need your help in getting Filippo ready and whilst we are out, Luna, I trust you to a quiet day.'

'Mamma, I must tell you something,' Luna said.

'What is it?'

'When I left you after dinner, I went into Papa's studiolo to find a book, only Guido Palagio was in there too.' She spoke slowly, as the words were not easily said. Her neck felt hot and uncomfortable. She remembered the tang of his breath and the stain of wine on his teeth.

'You should not have been in there,' her step-mamma chided. 'I must get ready, Leonarda. Is there something important you wish to say?'

Luna felt tears begin to well in her eyes. 'You do not know what sort of man he is.' She took a deep breath and tried again. 'He was foul. He attacked me obscenely.'

Mamma Lucrezia turned sharply. Luna wanted to add that she was unhurt, only ashamed and angry, but her step-mamma's hardened eyes told her that would not be wise.

'Do you accuse him?' Mamma Lucrezia asked. She didn't sound angry; Luna had expected her step-mamma to be horror-struck.

'I do,' Luna answered.

'This is the boy your sister will wed, Leonarda.'

'Well, not now, of course, now that you know what he is like. Maria can't marry him now.' The words spilt from Luna's mouth in an indignant rush.

'Maria will most certainly marry Guido Palagio; there is a signed contract. Which is why I ask you if you accuse him, for that would mean I must take this to your father.' Mamma Lucrezia sounded as though she was explaining a dilemma of practicalities. She came to stand in front of Luna. It was a simple thing, her open palms implied, a problem easily solved. 'Are you hurt?'

Luna frowned then shook her head.

Her step-mamma smiled and brought her palms together as though in prayer. 'My dear girl, then you are still whole. No harm was done.' She drew Luna into a hug. Her shoulder was warm and Luna closed her eyes and dropped into the hold. 'You are lucky,' she said softly, 'else you would have ruined this whole family.' She kissed the top of Luna's head. 'Now, we need never speak of this again.'

Luna kept her head against Mamma Lucrezia's shoulder, working her step-mamma's words round in her mind like a hard sweet she must soften in her mouth. She was lucky? She felt Mamma Lucrezia's hand rubbing her back and she wanted so badly for the gentle touch to do its job and soothe her.

Papa left for his shopfronts shortly after the carriage took Mamma Lucrezia with Maria and Filippo to Palazzo

Palagio. Once she was alone, Luna went to the main hall. It did not matter where she spent the rest of her day, she could roam the house freely, though she did not feel any of her usual delight in having time to fill with her own desires. She stood in the centre of the hall where her father greeted important visitors and where she'd entertained them with her rhetoric. Today, it was empty of most furniture, save for serving tables set back against the walls. It was a room always waiting to be filled with people. She turned full circle, remembering the thrill of the audience's applause and her father's pride. This would be where the family feasted to celebrate Maria's wedding to the man who had attacked Luna and she knew she must be there as Maria's loving sister. She saw, with a jolt, that her portrait was mounted on one of the walls, the painted shoes on view, as was her dutiful smile. She stopped and let out a long anguished sigh and with it all the breath she felt she'd been holding in since her step-mamma pressed her into her embrace. She looked up to the fresco far above. There was adoration and strength in the painted Mother Mary's love of her baby. Luna thought of the mother she'd never known. She would have spoken in her daughter's defence. Her true mother would have protected her from Guido Palagio. She sighed again, forcing her breath out to the point of choking and it became a loud, ragged sound. She bent over with the exertion, but then she lifted her head and the sound came again. It was guttural and base, and she could not stop its power escaping, weaving around the muscles of her tongue at the back of her throat, and from deeper still it came, from the dark spaces amongst her organs that worked the life into her woman's form and where her pain lived. She howled.

Papa thought she was worth only as much as the price he could bargain in a marriage contract. How cruel his endowment of education now seemed when he had never planned on allowing her to fulfil its calling. She dropped her head to the rose flowers resting in a large glass bowl on one of the side tables. Papa had called her impudent and indecorous, said she was without humility. Just a girl. As though there was nothing worse that she could be. The smell of the roses was pungent and almost rotten, the flowers close to dropping. In a few days, her step-mamma would collect the petals and steep them in water to use in one of her tonics, a salve to ease her father's headaches through the autumn months. Luna would prove her father wrong. She'd show him that her female sex did not lessen her mind's alacrity or her right to his acceptance. That if he opened his books and his goodwill to her once more, she'd repay him with a cleverness beyond what anyone believed her capable of, something to salve his brain. Just like the rose bush.

Luna left the hall and went to her father's studiolo. It would be at least four hours before his return, a good amount of time for writing. Guido Palagio's irksome face flashed before her and she felt her scalp prickle with the memory, but she'd not be deterred. She closed the door before turning to assess the state of the room. There was a dirty cup on the desk, stained red round the rim from wine, and near it a few discarded poultices. She recognised the faint smell of lavender as she placed the poultices into the bowl and pushed the cup to the farthest corner of the desk. She reached out to run her hand down the length of beads but the cotton thread was empty.

Luna hovered for a moment then went and sat in her papa's chair. The frame was strong and big, the arms wide. She shuffled to seek better comfort from the hard wood and to dispel the guilt of trespassing. She pulled herself in to the desk and placed her hands firmly upon its cool wood, just as she'd seen her father do. The oak was smooth and marked with thin streaks of the darkest brown. She ran her finger along the seams. The pattern flowed like molten rock through the wood and her mind burned with a similar fierceness. She would feel no more guilt; it was time she listened to her own voice.

The goose quill her father used lay to the left and beside it were clean parchment sheets. Luna took up the quill and rolled it in her fingers, testing its weight. The feather swivelled. She unrolled a precious parchment. The sheet was roughly finished, unlike the calfskin vellum of the books her father cherished, but she did not mind. She moved the pot of ink closer and positioned the blotting rag beside it and sat back, stilled by the weight of what she was about to do. Then, just as once before when she'd sat for the painter, an overwhelming sense of clarity came across her and she breathed through the rise and fall of her chest and felt the current of blood through her veins as her mind centred on her task.

She smoothed out the page and whispered a prayer. Closing her eyes, she thought about the power of words and the art of writing; her scholarship was indeed a precious gift. She drew the curve of a y slowly down the page. Her hand was unsteady at first. How she would have loved to watch Isotta Nogarola write. She imagined the silence of her concentration as she put to parchment her arguments in those beautiful words, like choosing a very large head of raw wool and condensing it to thread. Luna wrote slowly and carefully.

You, who wish to study great and wonderful things, who wonder about the movement of the stars, must read the theory of Archimedes, the Greek mathematician of great renown. Knowing the ideas in his work, The Sand Reckoner, *will open the door to all of astronomy. We must follow in the footsteps of the master mathematicians and hold fast to their observations, bequeathed to us like an inheritance.*

Archimedes set out to determine an upper bound for the number of grains of sand that fit into the Universe. In order to do this, he had to estimate the size of the Universe and for this he used the hypotheses of the Pythagorean, Aristarchus of Samos.

Aristarchus of Samos proffered an alternate Sun-centred model of the Universe, namely that the fixed stars and the Sun remain unmoved and that the Earth revolves about the Sun on the circumference of a circle, the Sun lying in the middle of the orbit.

Here, I ask you, most learned reader, to suspend all that we know to be true, for God gave man the gift of intelligence to use in glorious expression of His Faith, the path of which is revealed through persistent investigation and moral duty. I hear you argue that the closer stars do not shift position relative to more distant stars as they would most assuredly do if the Earth were moving around the Sun. To this I answer: is it man's arrogance that refuses further investigation? Let us not run back to Holy ground at the first sign of a challenge, but rather, let us use our Faith to push farther into the unknown. Could it be that the stars are very distant and, thus, display parallaxes that are too small to be seen with the eye?

Therefore, with the utmost earnestness I entreat you, most learned reader, my honoured F–

Luna's hand paused, her quill hovering over the unfinished acknowledgement to her father. She bent her head, listening to the unmistakable sound of Papa's heavy footsteps in the courtyard below. She thought she'd be finished before he returned from the shopfront. An impatient excitement curled her fingers—she had so much more to write, but there was no time now. She hurriedly rolled the parchment and reached up to retrieve the pigskin volume of *The Sand Reckoner* from the shelf. She placed her own page against the inside cover. Then she closed the book and laid it on top of the three others on the shelf. She would return to finish writing as soon as she was able.

Luna retreated to her chamber and went to the window. Her pulse had thrummed fast as she hurried along the corridor but it settled as she stood and watched the empty garden. A creak in the corridor made her turn. Her door opened a crack and her father's face appeared. He beckoned to her.

'I have not left my chamber the whole time of your absence,' she said and her voice quivered with the lie, but he didn't chastise her, only handed her a set of clothes and gestured that she should put them on.

'These are boys' clothes. What do you want me to do with them?'

'Put them on, Luna. Hurry, hurry.'

'Am I to leave my room?' She stared at him and he nodded. Her stomach did a little flip and her eyes widened. She was unsure what to say. Then she looked again at the doublet and tights with an indignant frown. 'If you allow me a few minutes I will find my own dress and cloak.' She raised her eyebrows at him as she held out the bundle but he shook his head and would not take it from her.

'I have purposely brought you boys' clothes.'

She eyed them sceptically.

'I think you will be quite content to wear them when you learn why,' he said impatiently, then turned and disappeared before she could ask anything more. Luna stood for a few minutes, confounded by his sudden change of heart. Dressing as a boy implied they were going somewhere girls could not. As much as she felt uncomfortable, she hopped and shimmied into the tights and doublet and shrugged on the overshirt as quickly as she could before following him. Her curiosity had gotten the better of her.

He was already down the stairs and in the courtyard by the time Luna caught up to him by the heavy doors that led out into the piazza. His cloak was wrapped around him, his cap pressed firmly into his springy grey curls and a flash of excitement wrinkled his eyes. Luna grabbed her boots and sat on the bench to put them on. Once she'd laced them, she stood again and hurriedly did up the buttons and tied the belt across the jerkin. Her father was waiting in the street. The sound of hawkers' activity was loud.

She held her arms wide to each side. 'You see what a fool I look?'

'I'm surprised how well the clothes fit. The stable boy is about your height but still his frame is so much stronger than yours. I feared they would be too big and loose. Luck is with us, it seems.'

Luna realised the musty smell in the shirt was dung and hay from the stables. She wrinkled her nose with distaste.

'Just one more finishing touch.' He pulled a boy's cap from his pocket and tucked her thick hair under it as best he could. 'Better. We might just get away with it now.'

'Get away with what?'

In answer, he held up a large invitation card. She read the details of the Platonic Academy's discussion of Joannes de Monte Regio's *Epitome of Ptolemy's Almagest* and suddenly understood the need for her disguise; no women were allowed into the Academy. She grasped her father's hand with pure delight and kissed it. He was taking her with him.

'Won't I be terribly obvious?' she asked.

He looked her up and down and then gave a self-congratulatory nod. 'No one will be interested in a young student.'

Then he took her arm and led her out into the street. A passing man hastily slid sideways to avoid bumping into them. They halted and Luna breathed through her racing pulse. Ahead there were potholes in the road and she made a note of where to step.

'Stay close,' Papa said.

Then she remembered her walking stick, propped against the hallway bench and muttered crossly to herself as she pulled on her father's arm.

'I've left my stick at home.'

'Better not to have it. We can manage.'

It wasn't a question but she nodded, to convince herself more than anything.

They followed Via Condolotti and turned right, crossing over the small square that led towards the city's main piazza. Her father paused a moment to admire a new statue of milk-white marble. 'Leonardo certainly has a way with the knife. How I love the smooth curve of his back.'

'It shines like the real flesh,' Luna added. They stood together admiring the tall, lean man of marble, his hand on a dog's upturned head.

After that, they turned off the major thoroughfare and walked down the smaller laneways, making for Via Rucellai and the Palazzo Venturi Ginori of Bernardo Rucellai. Their footsteps echoed along the narrow streets. Luna was forced to slow down when a jarring spike of pain flashed up her leg.

'Luna!' Her papa stopped and took her by the shoulders. 'This is an exceptional opportunity and I demand only a little pain from you for it to succeed. I know you are capable of playing the part, including walking as normally as you can. We don't want to miss Domenico—am I right?'

'Yes, of course, Papa. I won't let you down.' Luna tugged the cap more tightly onto her head.

'There now, that's my girl. Onwards.'

Luna walked faster after that, even though with each spike of pain her limp became more exaggerated. She kept her head down, expecting to hear gibes and insults, but all that broke her thoughts was her father's fast and noisy step; no one was staring. At one point they were so near the river, Luna could hear the sluice of a barge as it passed. Farther away, she saw one of the fulling mills that her father used to cleanse the wool cloth of oils and dirt. She straightened her back a little. A peddler with a cart of apricots held out a bag expectantly. Luna shook her head as they hurried past and the peddler gave her a disappointed wave of dismissal before turning his attention to the next potential customer. Luna turned back and caught his eye; she wanted one more moment of being seen as just another boy in the street.

After that, she quickened her pace even more, with only Papa's hand as support. In the distance loomed the white and dark green marble face of the Basilica of Santa Maria Novella. Her father strode confidently, all the time talking to Luna about the event. She listened, full of delight at her papa's attention. He was her teacher again.

'Now, you know of Peuerbach's contribution? He was the first to prepare a summary and commentary on Ptolemy's *Almagest*, but he died after completing only six books. So Joannes de Monte Regio continued the task. Very few of us have yet read the completed work, it being published only recently, so this gathering is a very popular event. I hope you realise how fortunate you are.'

Luna nodded. 'Have you read all of the volumes, Papa?'

'Yes. I have no doubt in my mind that his *Epitome of the Almagest* is the most accurate portrayal of astronomy yet.'

'How many will be there?'

'Not as many as usual. These times are difficult and I expect some will stay home.'

Luna stepped sideways just in time to avoid a large group of the preacher's men. They passed a flagon between them as they walked. One of their number stopped outside a bottega and the others joined him. There were rich pickings of jams and fruits on the table on the street front. A shop assistant hurried out to serve them. She fumbled in the pocket of her apron as she waited and watched the men pick up an orange, a peach, some grapes, then drop them back upon the counter. They sidled off without purchasing anything, and the poor girl was left to rearrange the bruised fruit as best she could.

Luna stopped. The sight made her uneasy.

'What's the matter?' her father asked.

She didn't answer. Her stomach had begun to twist. She couldn't tell him that she feared crossing paths with Guido Palagio again, and if not him, then any other of the myriad young men who would be at the talk; they were all the same. She pushed her curls back under the boy's cap.

'These are friends and colleagues, not the preacher's men,' Papa was saying. 'Bernardo Rucellai offers us a place where we may yet meet. The Academy may very well be forced to close soon, and who knows how long we will be allowed to publicly discuss books of science and philosophy? We must seize this chance.'

'Very well, Papa,' she said.

A rush of nerves flared again in Luna when they arrived at the Oricellari gardens in Bernardo Rucellai's estate. A group of Friar Savonarola's followers loitered near the gates.

'All are welcome here,' someone was calling out. 'We have nothing to hide.'

But Luna noticed that some did hesitate and even turned and hurried off. She pulled her cap down and moved closer to her father. The villa was at the end of a pathway that wound through trees and ponds. Groups of men stood around the entrance, dressed in richly coloured robes and wide hats. Luna was surprised by how unimposing the flat-fronted building seemed. As she came closer, she saw the

Medici crest mounted above the entrance but that was the only sign of the Academy's original benefactor.

'Do we go straight in?'

Her father raised his eyebrows at her. 'You are as impatient as I! Follow me, my student, but only speak if you must.' Then he cuffed her round the chin just like she'd seen him do to Filippo. 'Once we are inside there will be so many about, you will go unnoticed.'

They walked through an arched entrance into a room adorned with noble figures of marble. Luna had underestimated the grandeur of the building from its exterior and she would have happily stayed in that first apartment if Papa had stopped, but they went through to a rotunda that echoed with the buzz of men's voices. Luna kept close to her father. The walls curved like the bend of the river Arno encircling the city and imposing columns branched from floor to ceiling at regular intervals. In the centre of the room was a raised podium with a low lectern. Gentlemen of the city's illustrious families and their sons sat or stood on travelling boxes and chairs. Luna felt the hot air about her as they weaved between the groups. It was stifling with a strong tang of brackish water. She breathed in and, looking up, saw the ceiling was carved with flowers and cherubs playing on trumpets. Her papa had moved on and she put her head down again and made her way over to the pillar he now stood alongside.

'See how much excitement there is? No one is paying you any attention,' he whispered conspiratorially. Indeed, he was right. A group beside where they stood was deep in debate. One man was arguing a point with gusto, his thick-set brow moving furiously as he spoke, and then tilted around his companion to remonstrate with a third fellow at the other end of the box upon which they were jostling for space. Another group stood nearby with vexed expressions and arms crossed whilst someone Luna thought must be most important spoke from one of the few wooden armchairs in the centre of the group.

'That is Niccolò Machiavelli, a young thinker getting much attention, as you can see,' her father said softly in her ear. The noise of so many different conversations echoed off the rotunda. There was a momentary hush as Savonarola's men entered but even their presence could not quell the enthusiastic debate that erupted again once the silent group had positioned themselves towards one side. They did not engage in conversation or show any curiosity at who stood near them. Rather they stared ahead with expressions as cold as the statues Luna had just admired.

A man stepped onto the podium. He shuffled some papers without acknowledging the crowd, but that was enough for the volume in the room to drop. Professor di Novara had a stout frame and a long face. His smooth black hair hung below the dramatic cappuccio that surrounded his head like a bulbous growth. He wore a red gown and black cloak and his small eyes moved about the room with an intensity that pulled them all into his focus. Eventually he nodded at a group of students standing on the opposite side of the room to Luna and her father. They responded with enthusiastic shouts. His gaze moved on and circled slowly so that everyone felt acknowledged. When he spotted Vincenzio Fusili he raised his hand in welcome and Luna's father responded with a flourish. Luna instinctively moved to hide herself and heard the chuckles of those standing nearest to them.

'Your student need not be afeared.'

'Indeed,' her father replied to the friendly gibe. 'But do not we all feel intimidated by the attention of such a bright star as Novara?' There was a chorus of cheers and Luna felt her father's push. She stood beside him even as her stomach lurched. But just as he had predicted, no one paid any further attention to her. Luna craned her neck to get a better view.

'Now you will hear one of Joannes de Monte Regio's own students discuss his work. Do you know, before he went off to Bologna, Professor di Novara—Domenico—was first educated here in Florence?' Papa spoke excitedly. 'We don't do too badly, do we? His position at the university has kept him away from Florence for too long.'

'But he is here now.'

'Yes, indeed, and now I must stop talking. I wonder if those fanciulli plan on engaging in the debate? I'd like to see them try.'

She looked to where the young men watched the assembled crowd, like hawks with prey. Their bland countenances scoured the room, seeking potential traitors to the preacher, she thought.

'It is a shame Domenico returns when Savonarola has us fixed in an age of ignorance. I fear he will find our beloved city much changed and not for the better,' her father said. Around the room there were only a few hushed conversations still in play; most men were now waiting for the speaker to begin. Luna realised that her father would probably be standing with his peers and friends if she wasn't with him.

'I'm sorry that you can't talk to your friends.'

'I chose to bring you,' he said pointedly. 'I'll get the chance to speak with them later.'

She found her father's changed attitude invigorating, though very confusing. It had not been so long ago he'd told her to be silent and dutiful and had quashed any hope of her continued studies. Yet here she was. If there was a more fickle man in all of the city state then she'd like to meet him.

He held a slim finger up to silence them both and she nodded, suddenly wishing she'd brought a notebook and quill. Surely her being here was a sign that he'd reconsidered his decision about her studies? Luna took a step forward so she would be able to see the speaker as well as hear him.

'Most learned friends, we are indeed fortunate to be alive in a time when such men as Peuerbach and Monte Regio have lived. Sadly both have gone to God, but not before giving us the *Epitome of Ptolemy's Almagest*, begun by one—the mathematician and astronomer George von Peuerbach—and completed by the other—his student and my teacher, Joannes de Monte Regio. I have here a full set of volumes of the work fresh from the printer in Venice.'

There were murmurs of appreciation from the assembly as Domenico held up a large hard-covered book, opened to a page that Luna recognised. It was the detailed woodcut illustration of the two authors sitting beneath the astrolabe. This was the same volume Papa kept. On the lectern were more of the books that made up the completed work. The man patted them as he laid the one in his hand back on top of the pile. It thudded softly.

'With this remarkable work we gain a knowledge of astronomy that has not been possible since the time of the early Greeks. As we know, Joannes de Monte Regio used the Greek original of Ptolemy, so for the first time we have an explanation not just for scholars, but for everyone.'

Cheers and shouts broke the silence. Novara held up his hands and the room fell quiet once more. He began an account of how the work had finally come to be printed in Venice, twenty years after the author's death. Luna focused on the stack of thick books, wondering at the wealth of knowledge contained within those pages. She'd sat with one of the volumes open before her. It seemed tragic that neither of the authors was alive to see their hard work applauded by this group of peers. She saw the grand old bearded men of import and their eager students jostling to impress and learn.

There was a loud banging. Luna saw it was coming from the group whom the professor had first acknowledged when he took to the podium. A young man, tall and with hair fashionably cut to chin level, was stamping his foot dramatically. His hose were red on one leg and white on the other.

The speaker stopped, looking at the man with a frown. 'Do you have a point to make, my friend?' Novara called to the heckler. Luna heard bemusement in his voice rather than anger.

'Is this a discussion of astronomy or the printing presses?'

There was an uproar of shouts at such disrespect, though some of the younger amongst the audience laughed and hooted.

The speaker seemed unperturbed. 'Young Nicolaus, patience is the companion of wisdom.' He paused, shuffling his papers. 'Yet I hear what you ask. Learned men, let us turn our attention to Book Five of the *Almagest*.'

The room fell silent again. Luna watched the man who had interrupted Novara, expecting another entertaining outburst, but he only stared with intense focus. He scowled at his friends when they tried to heckle the speaker a second time, glints of hazel flashing from beneath wide brows that swept outwards from a prominent nose. He was clean-shaven yet with a young man's smudge of hair upon his top lip, which Luna found unexpectedly charming. He pressed his round-brimmed cap down firmly.

'You may think I point you to a minor detail,' the professor continued, 'but I do so to show the depth of analysis of the author. As we know, Joannes de Monte Regio read Ptolemy in the original Greek, unlike most of us.' He shook his head as though it was too hard to conceive of such a mistake. 'Until now, we have confined ourselves to the Latin version, itself translated from an Arabic copy, but the author shows us what virtue there is in using the original text. According to his reading, Ptolemy is wrong in his calculations of the Moon's motions.'

There was a gasp from the listeners, then the room erupted.

'Friends, settle and hear what I tell you. It is all laid out in Monte Regio's detailed work.'

'I did not come to hear Ptolemy mocked!' someone shouted.

'Let me explain. Settle, friends, let me speak. I do no such thing. By Ptolemy's calculations the diameter of the Moon varies in length as its distance from Earth varies, and we have had no reason to question this. Yet Monte Regio carried out his own observations, and his computations revealed that the Moon's diameter does not vary. The Moon's distance from Earth does not change every month. It does not grow by a factor of two then shrink again as we have always believed. My friends, this may only be a small miscalculation, within a volume of extraordinary work, but is it significant?' The professor was forced to shout to be heard. 'I put it to you, learned friends.'

Luna was transfixed by the scene, watching her father and the men around him talking furiously.

'You go too far, Novara. Ptolemy is the father of astronomy, not its wayward son!' someone called, then others shouted their questions and surprise but all were in vain as none could be heard above the din.

The professor attempted to answer his detractors. 'I do not suggest this warrants throwing away a whole history of theory.'

Softly at first, Luna once again heard the sound of banging. It came from the group on the opposite side of the room and she saw that the same man was stamping his foot. Slowly the volume in the room dropped until the only sound was the repetitive pounding of one man's boot. The group parted and gave him space to be seen and heard. He was taller than Luna had first seen, slim and lean like her father, though much younger. His expression was furiously demanding. Luna thought he seemed a bit mad. His intensity was captivating.

'May I speak?'

The professor nodded and the young man stepped onto a box. Luna realised it was passion in his eyes.

'I applaud Monte Regio's contribution to the betterment of the sciences. He has made Ptolemy accessible for the common man.' There were shouts of agreement, which the man stood silently through until the gathered gentlemen hushed once more. 'The detail which the learned Professor di Novara brings to our attention, however, leaves me in a most vexatious quandary. If we believe Monte Regio, and I see no reason not to, then it follows that the very father of modern astronomy, as we all rightly name Ptolemy, made mistakes.'

The room erupted yet again with shouting and booing. Men stamped their feet and railed against the speaker.

He raised his voice. 'If we must accept now that there are errors in his calculations, then I call for a complete reassessment of Ptolemaic theory.'

Luna was drawn to this young man's fervour. He spoke honestly; there were no dramatics in his delivery. His arms stayed still and he did not cheer to his compatriots like the others who were keen on making noise as much as sense.

Someone in the audience cried out, 'Still your tongue, fool! Ptolemy's mathematical treatise is the most important book of our generation. You do well to show more respect.'

'It may be that I am a fool but I ask you, as indeed I ask myself: what else of this science must we now question? Should we be reconsidering the very basis of our astronomy?'

His words took Luna back to her own musings on paper; she thought he might be the only man in Florence who would not dismiss her as a madwoman. The room erupted in roars of outrage again, men shouting down the speaker, and there was a bustle of activity about him.

Luna turned to her father. 'What's happening?'

'A debate, that's what's happening!' His eyes narrowed. 'I didn't expect it to be this contentious.'

'Who holds up the illustrious Professor di Novara? Are we so base in Florence a man cannot even finish his sentence without rebuke?' a stranger's gruff voice shouted from a far corner of the room.

'I cannot help my mind from ruminating,' the man who'd set the room into this maelstrom replied, 'it is a constant burden and yet I would have it no other way. I always seek the truth, my friends, with both eyes open.'

'As do we all, though with humility in God's name, which you'd do well to remember.'

Luna was startled when her father called out next.

'Domenico, Professor di Novara, take back the floor!' His cry was echoed by others in the room, rising in volume until it silenced all else.

The professor spoke again, his voice loud and strong as he addressed the young man who had challenged him. 'Nicolaus, my student, do you question the veracity of Ptolemy himself?'

'I do not know, I do not know,' came the reply. 'I hoped to honour this forum of learned gentlemen by contributing my ideas to this debate.' The doubt in the young man's voice seemed to calm the room.

'Ptolemy has compiled the most comprehensive presentation of mathematical astronomy ever known,' the professor said, 'and without doubt it is the godly truth. You'd best have an alternative that stands up to the scrutiny of this forum if you wish to challenge him.'

The man in the group who had spoken stayed silent. Whereas before he had been focused and attentively listening, he was now distracted. Luna noticed that this man, Nicolaus, held his head at one point and didn't even look at the professor when he addressed him. Shortly after that he pushed through the crowds and she lost sight of him.

She felt someone bump against her. Her father pulled her close to steady her.

'Forgive my friend.' An older man stepped around them and behind him was Nicolaus, the professor's vocal student with the fiery eyes.

'I've been humiliated enough this day,' Luna overheard him say as he passed by. She caught sight of the flash of a red cap covering dark locks before he disappeared again into the throng.

'Who was that?' she whispered to her father but before he could answer another voice shouted, 'Nicolaus has no respect; he criticises the very nature of the heavens when he criticises Ptolemy. I say he blasphemes most dangerously.'

The mood in the room shifted as the speaker revealed himself and everyone saw his colours. It was Tommaso Palagio. Luna saw Guido amongst the men who rallied around him.

She shrank behind the pillar and stood quite still. Her heart boomed loud as a church bell in her head. The charge shouted by Signore Palagio was enough to stifle the enthusiasm for debate. They were a confident pack bunched together, stronger like that. The professor stood tall at the lectern and glared furiously as others turned and left. No one wanted to challenge the preacher's men, they were each as insecure as the next whilst his authority still ruled. Not even the learned Professor di Novara's reputation was enough reason to remain at a forum where the word blasphemy had been decried against the gathered many. Friar Savonarola's punishments came swift and unmeasured, upon not just the individual but on all others close enough to catch the eye of his men.

Luna rubbed her hands down her tights and did not move.

Eventually, Professor di Novara stepped down and left the lecture room and its audience.

'Come, we will find the professor outside.' Papa took her by the arm and they left the rotunda. In the first room, she looked about; some brave men stood in groups talking, but others made their way to the outer doors. Luna felt her heart begin to slow. She followed her father to a large group who welcomed them into their circle. Bernardo Rucellai was talking and Luna noticed a few other familiar faces. The professor was amongst them. There was a deceptive lightness in the conversation that centred on his forthcoming journey back to Bologna. Luna listened without paying too much attention. She was fascinated by the freedom of the boys' clothes. How easily she moved without the weight of tight bodices or that feeling of catching a foot in the length of her skirt as she walked. It was liberating.

'An interesting point,' her father said, reaching out to greet Professor di Novara.

'My friend, Vincenzio, it is good to see you.' The professor turned to Luna next and nodded formally in greeting. She bowed as judiciously as she could though she chose not to speak. The professor's gaze lingered; any longer and he'd surely realise she was no boy.

'May I introduce a most unusual young student,' Papa said by way of introduction. His voice dipped smoothly.

'I am always pleased to see the youth of today amongst my audience. What did you make of the debate?'

Luna felt her father's subtle prod. She could hear his heavy breathing though her own had stopped.

'Speak, boy.'

The circle of gentlemen waited.

'Vincenzio, we need students who are unafraid to voice their opinions. So many have been stifled by the preacher whom your city adores; at least here I had expected to find the bold and disobedient, like young Nicolaus Copernicus.' The professor's voice didn't hold any malice. He spoke genially enough, assuming his words would encourage Luna to speak.

'We don't need the sort of attention Nicolaus's outburst will bring upon the Academy. The preacher's men will most assuredly relay the whole exchange back to Savonarola.' Luna heard the frustration and impatience in her father's voice.

'I admire the young man's spirit,' she said.

'Speak up,' her father demanded.

Luna begged him with a stare to stop but he took her arm and led her into the middle of the circle of gentlemen. She knew this attention would not end until she'd addressed them.

'Though he was rude to interrupt you, professor,' she said.

'He is a Pole; we cannot expect the same refinement as a Florentine,' the professor replied with good-natured humility.

Luna raised her head and steadied her gaze on her father before speaking again. 'If Joannes de Monte Regio found errors in Ptolemy's model then is this not worth further investigation?' she said.

'So you agree with the Pole?' Novara asked.

'I side with curiosity in the pursuit of knowledge.'

'Well said.'

Luna stood straight-backed and resolute whilst all eyes were on her. Her chest burned and her head grew hot under the foolish cap.

Her father stepped towards her, reached up and pulled the cap off. Her thick curls fell easily past her shoulders. 'Gentlemen, may I introduce to you my daughter, Leonarda Lunetta.'

She heard them gasp and guffaw.

'What game is this?' Professor di Novara asked.

'Is she not a marvel?' her father answered.

Luna remained still, staring straight ahead.

'Take the poor girl home,' the professor said more forcefully. 'She is out of place here.' He gave Luna a kindly smile. 'You do yourself no favour with this dupery, Vincenzio.' Then Novara turned his back to them and pointedly, it seemed to Luna, began talking to another gentleman.

Luna grabbed the cap from her father and did the best she could to tuck her curls back into it. A rush of heat consumed her with the force of a burning pyre. She'd not be gawped at by these boys and men who had begun to stare and laugh.

Her father took her by the arm and dragged her from the room. The sting of Papa's tight hold forced her on, past other men stood in conversation, through groups descending from the palazzo till the low babbling of voices was a distant murmur and they came to a stop at the end of the path leading away from the building. Her father was panting and muttering under his breath. He dropped his hold and walked on till a length of garden and grass separated them. She could still hear his cursing as he paced back towards her and then away again, as though he could not decide whether to acknowledge her as his own.

Others passed them and Luna waited uncomfortably. Two gentlemen stopped nearby and when they turned to speak to Papa she recognised Signore Palagio. Luna prayed they'd move on. She stole another glance and in that moment saw it was Guido Palagio standing with his father, looking back at her. Then he turned and the pair walked off. Luna wondered if he'd recognised her.

Shortly after, her father beckoned and she went and stood by him. He didn't speak for a while, only looked past her to where the last of the gentlemen were departing.

'Damnation!' he cursed and slapped his thigh. Then he turned to Luna and she saw the humiliation she thought was hers alone reflected in his eyes.

CHAPTER SIXTEEN

In the week that followed, through the final days of summer, Luna's routine returned to the limited activity of reading in her chamber and watching the antics of her family from her bedroom's view of the garden. Each morning, she lay in bed till it was fully prime and the sun had pierced her eyelids with its brightness. She kept her eyes shut against the shameful memory of her father pulling the boy's cap off her curls, still too close to set aside, and hugged herself beneath the covers, waiting till Maria was dressed and gone before she rose. She moved about the room with a sluggish step, all thought of the freedom of boys' breeches long gone. Each afternoon, she watched Pippo in the garden, scampering between the rose bushes chasing insects and lizards, and remembered his pleasure at pulling off their tails. Livia was always nearby, sitting on the bench beside the pond. Pippo stamped his feet in frustration at what she imagined was one of the slippery creatures escaping from his fingers. She didn't know what changed an innocent boy into a man like Guido but she felt a new mistrust of her brother's childish cruelty. She didn't see her papa but heard his footfall as he descended the staircase and, at other hours of the day, his voice shouting for wine and bread.

Friar Bartolomeo visited and Mamma Lucrezia allowed him to sit with Luna. He spoke of the state of the city and she was patient and didn't interrupt with the questions she wanted to ask: if he'd seen her papa and heard talk of the lecture at the Academy, and then, more intimately, about the portrait and what he knew. He spoke to her of the preacher's boys who walked the streets with the confidence of the mob and acted with force before principle, of the noise of their escapades loud as an invading army, without melody, of goodly people enfeebled and degraded, and of the crypt of his church and the catacombs too, full now with books and the precious belongings of her family. He spoke passionately and Luna listened like she used to when just a child. When he began to talk of the professor's lecture without mentioning her or her papa, she wondered if he was just being kind, but she didn't have the energy to press him and chose instead to change the subject.

'Friar, did you know the true purpose of the portrait I sat for in your rooms?'

He looked at her with guilt and pity and it stoked Luna's outrage so she lifted her chin and said, 'I did not expect you to lie to me. I put my faith in you.'

'I am sorry, Leonarda. Keeping the truth from you did not sit well with me. I did not agree with your father's decision to court the Spinelli family, but I could not refuse him.'

Luna's anger evaporated as quickly as it had flared. She understood her father's wrath. 'Thank you for answering honestly.'

They turned to the open shutters at the sound of Pippo laughing outdoors. 'I do not know how long Papa intends on keeping me confined to this room. I gulp in the breeze when it wafts up from the garden.'

'You've been kept from your family and your church for a lengthy time,' the friar agreed.

'His punishment is unjust, for all I have done is defend my honour and speak on subjects as he taught me.' Luna paused, thinking that her father kept her hidden to avoid the reminder of his humiliation at the Academy.

The friar nodded as though he were listening to her confession and indeed, Luna felt some relief at speaking the words out loud.

'He would rather I had been born a boy,' she said bitterly.

Friar Bartolomeo shrugged his shoulders. 'That may be so, and nothing can diminish the need of a father for sons to ensure a family's legacy, but men and women die the same, and you should take comfort in knowing, Luna, that in the afterlife, when we become angels, your sex will lose all significance. For all God's children are born with a divinely created soul. I say this to you as your priest and friend, but will deny it should you think to repeat my words.'

'I fear I will never be allowed to speak with my own true voice again.' She thought of the unfinished treatise in her father's studiolo with frustration.

'Do not despair, child,' he answered, 'but rather try to understand your father's actions, even if you're unable to control them. You can still live a worthy life if you are governed by your God.'

He made the Sign of the Cross and Luna did the same and it felt as though he were talking solely to her future.

*

It was not many morns after the friar's visit when Luna woke to be told by her step-mamma that she could leave her chamber and re-join the family. Relief and pleasure showed in her smile as she followed Mamma Lucrezia downstairs. It seemed the friar had told Papa he'd found Luna contrite and humbled by her confinement and her father had relented.

The servants were preparing the house for the colder months. Young men carried heavy tapestries outside to air before they would be laid upon the stone floors. The kitchen girls were busy making room in the dry store for additional flour and grain. Luna stood back against the wall as Alessandro passed her with a heavy sack thrown over his shoulder. She waited till he'd disappeared into the kitchen. She couldn't hear her papa so, with cautious steps, she made her way to his studiolo, hopeful of finding it empty so she could retrieve the parchment and take it back to her chamber to finish writing her defence of the Sun-centred argument. The friar might have found her humbled but she still planned on changing her papa's mind and the course of her future.

She paused in the hallway, listening outside the studiolo, and was disappointed to hear her father's raised voice within. She turned away, already wondering what she would do with her afternoon, when she heard her step-mamma mention

Professor di Novara. They were discussing the lecture. Quietly, Luna moved closer so that she could eavesdrop.

Mamma Lucrezia was in a fury. 'What madness came over you to take your daughter?'

'This is why I keep things from you, mistress. If you do not lower your shrieking, I will say no more.'

'Did you think about Leonarda when you put her in that ridiculous disguise?'

'Do not make this about Luna.'

'Then, pray tell me, husband, what is it about, if not your misguided fascination with her talents? For I predict further trouble to come from your tomfoolery. Maria's betrothal is not so secure as to be beyond disaster.' Luna heard the exasperation in her tone. 'You say Signore Palagio was at Palazzo Venturi Ginori. Did he witness Leonarda's unveiling?'

'Do not speak to your master with such contempt.'

A chair scraped back and Luna heard a slap and a thud. Silence. Her father's anger was never easy to predict. She crossed herself. Next she heard the ting of glass against glass; Mamma Lucrezia must be pouring wine. Luna pictured her father downing the wine and more than likely demanding another. She waited to hear him loosed by the drink but her step-mamma's voice came again.

'Listen to me, Vincenzio. No man seeks out a clever girl to wife and we cannot afford to keep Luna nor can we afford to let her damage Maria's future. Her only place is as a wife and mother in some other home. I want her gone.'

Luna's heart throbbed loud in her ears. She knew her step-mamma's first loves were Filippo and Maria, but she'd thought she had a small place in her heart too.

Then her papa spoke.

'I have made arrangements for Luna to join the Sisters of St Clare in Arcetri.'

Had her father gone mad? Luna swayed dangerously and leant into the wall for support.

There was a brief silence, broken by her step-mamma's exclamations of delight and relief. 'Why did you not tell me sooner? This will put an end to any gossip. A most welcome outcome.'

'Let this be a lesson to you, mistress.'

'Most assuredly, my husband, you do solve the worries of this family. When does Leonarda leave us?'

'After the feast of St Francis.'

'It will be fortuitous to have a nun in the family. God bless you, Vincenzio.'

Luna's head swam. Days earlier, Papa had made her dress as a boy; today he'd have her a nun! Five weeks, that was all the time she had left with her family. She felt her heart tearing apart and all her papa's love draining out, yet still the blood burned hot within her veins. This home was where she belonged. She would not be silenced.

There was shocked surprise on both their faces when she swung open the door and stormed through to interrupt her parents' conversation. She steadied her peg-leg and took a deep breath.

'I would speak with you both.'

'Good morrow to you too, Leonarda! Where are your manners?' Mamma Lucrezia said.

Luna bowed but would not be abashed. 'I overheard you discussing my future and I cannot remain silent.'

A darkness crossed her father's face and Luna thought for a moment he was going to strike her as well. She went and curtseyed to him. Let him turn away from the truth in her eyes, if he dared.

'I have no more the makings of a nun than I do a man, and equal revulsion for pretending I am either.'

'Tell me what you would have me do differently?' he asked. Mamma Lucrezia scoffed, but Luna answered eagerly. She didn't see the indifferent curiosity in his eyes.

'Let me stay here with you, as I believed was always our plan … your plan.'

'What will you do each day once Maria is wed and Pippo grown?'

'I will read and spend my hours cultivating ideas on paper when not in discussion with you.'

'You are a woman now and the more I hear such talk, the more I am assured the convent is the best and only place for you.'

'Then why take me to the lecture?'

He slowly shook his head and laughed. 'Why indeed. It was a misjudgement on my part. I thought to indulge you one more time before sending you to the convent. Professor di Novara's concern for your wellbeing made me realise the public theatre of ideas is no place for a woman.'

'What of all my years of study? My mind will go to waste.'

'A woman's mind is made for the contemplation of God and family; anything greater will fester into darkness. I've learnt my lesson. You were my beguiling prodigy and I will sorely miss that charming child, but I too must sacrifice.'

'I pose no threat, Papa. Truly you must know this.'

'The good reputation of this family is at stake.'

The more he spoke, and the longer they parleyed, the more profoundly did her heart burn till there was naught but despair and fire inside her head.

'Please let me stay with you, Papa. I beg of you, do not send me to a nun's cell.' She dropped her crutch and clasped her hands together as though in prayer. She could not look at him for fear of what she'd see. She kept her eyes lowered and listened to the loud beat of blood in her ears.

'A Fusili never begs.' His voice was tensely charged as a sky of lightning and thunder. 'Leave me. The decision is made.'

Luna stumbled from the room and hurried along the corridor. Men's voices sounded in the loggia and she recognised one as belonging to Bernardo Rucellai, whom she'd spoken to at the Academy. She climbed the stairs with haste to avoid meeting the visitors, tears blurring her vision. At the top she lost her footing and crashed to her knees. The fall knocked the breath out of her and she stayed against the cold wood as the mark of her tears darkened the boards. The echo of little girls' taunts from all those years ago played in her ear but even through those memories, she could hear her step-mamma's raised voice addressing the visitors.

'Bernardo, what a surprise to see you, though welcome of course.'

'Where is Vincenzio?' the man commanded.

Luna sat up and listened more intently; there was an abruptness in his tone that made her nervous. Next she heard her papa's footsteps and she went to the balcony and peered over cautiously. Her father was bowing to Signore

Rucellai, who wore the crimson coat of his office as the Gonfalonier of Justice. He was flanked by two officials of the Signoria. Papa stood aside then followed the three men into his studiolo.

Luna could see her step-mamma standing rigid as a statue, then Mamma Lucrezia rushed to the closed door and pressed her ear against the wood. Luna moved to the top of the staircase from where she could see along the hallway to Papa's studiolo.

The gentlemen reappeared soon after and Mamma Lucrezia went to stand by Papa.

'Yes, that book belongs to me.' Her father frowned as he answered Signore Rucellai, and Luna recognised the annoyance in his clipped tone. She strained to see what book they were discussing. Rucellai was holding *The Sand Reckoner*. In the courtyard below, the hollow clop of Apollonius sounded as he was led across the cobblestones into his stable. He struck the stable door impatiently. Papa had not taken him out yet today.

Luna watched the Gonfalonier open the book. He unrolled a sheet of parchment. 'Did you write this?'

An explosion like fireworks went off inside her head.

'What is that?' her father asked, his eyes narrowing as he took the page.

'Do you not recognise your own handwriting?' Rucellai stepped towards him and spoke again. 'What were you thinking, Vincenzio, writing such heresy?' This last was said with a friend's familiarity.

When he stepped back again it was with an official air. He straightened his shoulders and spoke formally. 'What say you, Vincenzio Fusili?'

Luna held her breath and stared with horror at the parchment she herself had written and slipped into the pages, unfinished.

'Answer me, Signore Fusili!'

Her father was reading. Luna couldn't see his face but she knew the words so well; how much care she'd taken writing them.

'It is mine.' His voice was steady and resolute. There was a note of finality in it. He rolled the parchment and handed it back.

The officers stood on either side of him, like bookends keeping him in place. They were big men who did not need to speak and their silence made them fearsome.

'Vincenzio Fusili, I arrest you on suspicion of heresy. You will have the chance to defend yourself in front of the Great Council,' Signore Rucellai said. Then he turned to Mamma Lucrezia and spoke in a gentler tone. 'I will do my best to defend him, mistress.'

'Do not fret, wife, I will be home soon,' Papa said lightly.

The soldiers marched Papa down the stairs.

Mamma Lucrezia was weeping when Luna hurried to where she stood. She led her to the kitchen and made hot drinks of lemon and spice. They cupped the glasses to their cheeks, as though the heat would soothe their fears. Her step-mamma bit her lip and rocked in anguish.

'Let me go to the monastery,' Luna pleaded. 'I will ask Friar Bartolomeo to help.'

'Yes, you must go straight away, Leonarda, and tell him we demand his assistance.' She did not rise when Luna gathered her cloak about her, only crossed herself in prayer.

Luna did the same, beseeching the Virgin Mary to protect her father, before slipping through the courtyard and into the street via the small side door.

*

Luna took the long way to the monastery. She turned left at the end of their road and hurried as best she could down the alleyway that led to the path that hugged the river bank. She was afraid, of what exactly she didn't know, but the path by the river was more secluded than the main streets. Her stick clicked against the roughly hewn stone. She wrapped her cloak more tightly about her as she passed a team of dyers carrying cloth and then the miller's factory, and a fresh determination caught her. She kept close to the line of trees.

Before long the path turned to a grassy track and wound its way up the hill towards the monastery. Luna had to force herself to go carefully, watching where she set each boot down and holding firmly to her walking stick, when really she wanted to rush on.

The monastery was already busy with midday prayers. Luna heard the rich, deep chanting as she made her way around to the small sacristy door. She pushed against it with her shoulder but was surprised when the door didn't give way; she'd never found it locked before. The wind gusted past her down the laneway. She dipped her head into the warmth of her collar and followed the path that ran the length of the church. At the point where the church met the high stone wall of the monastery, Luna stopped. Another gust sent her cloak flapping like the wings of a hunter's hawk keen to take flight. She knocked loudly and someone slid back the spy hole. Then she heard the bolts lifting on the other side.

'Leonarda, child, come inside.'

'Friar Bartolomeo.' His name caught in her throat.

'Yes, I know; word has already reached me.' The friar ushered her through, the door creaking shut behind her. 'Come, follow me.'

The sounds of chanting rose and fell as they passed the canticle room. A monk nodded as he hurried off in the opposite direction. Friar Bartolomeo stood in a doorway and gestured for her to enter. It was his private cell, dimly lit, with only a pallet and mattress stuffed with straw and a simple table that served as his writing desk. Luna noticed a bronze ring of fat keys, tarnished with age and use, hanging on a hook by the door. A wooden cross was mounted on the opposite wall. It was very similar to the room where she'd spent all those months sitting for the painter. That seemed a lifetime ago now.

Luna accepted the chair Friar Bartolomeo offered though her heart raced. She wanted them to rush to her father's aid immediately.

'Tell me, when did they take your father?'

'Not more than two hours ago—the Gonfalonier came to the house.'

'Bernardo,' the friar muttered. 'It is good it was him.'

'We do not know what will happen. Mamma Lucrezia is desperate and pleads for your help.' Luna rubbed the spot on her arm where her father last had touched her. She knew why they'd taken Papa, and she must tell the friar. 'There is something more.'

'Speak, Luna. Now is no time for secrets,' he said, clasping his hands together.

'It is my fault, friar. I should be the one in prison, not him. They found a parchment I wrote, an argument I thought would impress Papa, full of fanciful notions against God's law—I see that now, Heaven forgive me!'

'My dear child.' Friar Bartolomeo spoke with a weary sigh. 'Calm yourself. Your father's arrest is most assuredly the work of the preacher, who wants to intimidate those of us who plot against him. This may not ease your fears, but it is the truth, Luna, and you are intelligent enough to understand. Your father never gave up his support of the Medicis and has been working secretly to aid my family's return to Florence. This parchment you speak of may be reason enough for them to have taken Vincenzio, though it is not the cause of his scrutiny. He will go before the Great Council, and even though that forum is weighted with Savonarola's men, your father is sharp and he will ably defend himself to the assembled officials and more than likely return home by day's end.'

'Please God, it must be so,' Luna said softly.

Friar Bartolomeo poured her a small glass of the monastery's wine. 'Your colour is returning,' he said as she sipped it. Then he gave her a curious look. 'What did you write that could upset Rucellai so?'

Luna spoke plainly; there was no need to hide from her friend, though the moment she opened her mouth she felt the colour rise in her neck. 'I wrote in defence of the Pythagorean Aristarchus's theory that the Sun is stationary at the centre of the universe and Earth moves.' How monstrous the notion sounded.

The friar pressed his lips together firmly. 'This is heresy, to be sure.' He paced the walls of his small cell. 'How many moons ago did I warn you that your vanity would be your undoing? Well, perhaps that day has come, only it is your father who must bear the consequences.'

'What can we do?'

'First, I will take you home then I will go to Bernardo and find out exactly what Vincenzio is charged with. I will ask for Piero's support if needs be; your father has been loyal to the Medicis so if there is a fine to be paid, then Medici coin can pay it.'

'I want to help,' Luna said with determination.

'Your place is with your mother. She'll need you.'

Friar Bartolomeo ordered the library's wagon to be brought around when he saw how agitated she was. Luna sat beside him and clung to the sides as they bumped through the rutted laneways, thinking how relieved Mamma Lucrezia would be once she saw Friar Bartolomeo, even hoping that Papa might already be home.

They made slow progress through the city centre. Merchants loitered across the path through the main square where the fortress tower of the town hall cast its afternoon shadow over them. They travelled down the narrower lanes and were forced to stop more than once whilst carts, empty after a day at market, passed by. Finally they turned into Via Fusili. There was much commotion in the piazza ahead. Luna saw an extraordinary halo of deep orange and red around her home. She felt the heat before she saw any flames.

The wagon was forced to stop a distance from the house. The noise of stone cracking and wooden beams crashing was thunderously loud. It stilled Luna's heart. Her home burned as easily as a bonfire of paper.

She fell from the wagon in her haste to get to her family. Friar Bartolomeo helped her up and forced a path through the crowd that had gathered to watch the spectacle. The building rumbled under the pressure of the heat. Flames flew from the windows and licked the already scorched corners where the gargoyles' mouths sat open to guide the rainwater. A group of the preacher's fanciulli threw sticks at the house, swarming ever closer to the heat in excited skips of daring. A cold dread flushed through Luna so that she called out like a madwoman to her step-mamma and Maria. For a dreadful moment she couldn't remember little Pippo's name, instead calling out, 'Brother, my brother, where are you?' She stared up at the windows and prayed Livia would protect Pippo and Maria.

People had begun to gawk. Luna felt them turning towards where she stood with the friar. Her heart pounded. 'Find them, friar; they must be about here somewhere.'

Friar Bartolomeo disappeared into the crowd. Bright sparks of red and cinder shot up. Luna looked around frantically at the faces mesmerised by the dancing flames, some even shouting encouragement, but they were all strangers. She stared into the blaze engulfing her house till the heat burned her cheek and stung her eyes and she was forced to turn away.

Friar Bartolomeo returned soon after, his face mired in ash and gleaming with sweat. 'I could not get close enough to go inside; the fire is too hot. But I found this.'

He handed her a dirty parchment and opened his mouth to speak, but no further sound came. The authority of the Great Council and the Signoria was stamped upon the proclamation and below it the judgement against Vincenzio Fusili.

'I don't understand,' Luna managed to say. She sobbed as a thick beam of wood crashed noisily into the burning core of the fire. It was the courtyard, where she'd sat with her step-mamma and watched Pippo play, where the sunlight had warmed the stone.

Friar Bartolomeo grabbed Luna by the shoulders and turned her forcefully to face him. 'We must go. If any of the preacher's men recognise you, then most certainly you will die here.'

'Let me!' she wailed. 'I want to die!'

'No, we must go!' The light of the fire flickered on Friar Bartolomeo's panicked face.

A monstrous heat pressed on them. Luna found it hard to breathe. She cried out once more, for her sister, her brother, her step-mamma, for Livia. The fire crackled in response.

CHAPTER SEVENTEEN

Vincenzio took in his surroundings. There were worse rooms in the Palazzo della Signoria and this was nothing like he'd heard prison cells described; indeed there was a bed and a woollen blanket, a writing desk with quill and ink, even a small pitcher for washing on the desk. There was little here to give him cause for concern. A cup also, he noted, relieved to think he'd get some wine. The window was small but it opened when pushed. The door was held shut with a bolt that would not shift under even Goliath's strength, but Bernardo would return soon enough and the bolt loosed and he home by day's end. At least he wasn't up in the tower.

What an extraordinary turn of events had overtaken his morning. Never before had so much attention been paid to him, and by so many illustrious gentlemen. Even now he thought he could hear the senior members of the Signoria gathering below. Everyone of import would be there. Most of them had been at the lecture yesterday afternoon too. The thought fired him and he turned for the cup, forgetting for a moment he was not at home and the wine yet to appear. Bernardo would defend him; together they'd make a formidable voice.

He turned his attention to the parchment page thrust upon him by Bernardo from within his own studiolo. What a duplicitous cat he'd spawned in Luna. To think she went behind his back and wrote that! Her hand was never as confident as his own; her letters were obvious, to him at least. If it came out she'd written that nonsense, his reputation would be permanently damaged. He'd believed her mind, adorned with knowledge, was excellent, and trusted that her soul was manly, but now she seemed so abject and so truly a woman that he saw none of the estimable qualities he'd thought she possessed. He paced the room and decided October was too long a wait to be rid of her; he'd send her to the nuns forthwith.

A wretched feeling swamped him and Vincenzio was forced to hold the table for support. Once he'd managed to control himself, he looked to the heavens and made the Sign of the Cross. Giulia had been right all along, God bless her soul: there was a part of Luna that was the Devil's work. He would no longer trouble himself about where she lived out the remainder of her days. It was God's will she be sent away.

The bolt creaked loud as it was swung aside and Vincenzio was glad to see Bernardo appear through the doorway.

'What news?' he asked his friend without waiting on pleasantries. 'When do we address the Signoria?'

Bernardo had a pitcher of wine and he filled the cup and handed it to Vincenzio.

'Why did you have Medici florins?' he asked, and sat heavily. 'Speak openly, my friend.'

Vincenzio slapped his thigh. 'By Christ's body, will that family never give me peace? How did they discover the coin was mine?'

'Master Palmieri told the magistracy that it was your wife who paid him with Medici florins.'

Vincenzio shook his head. 'Will this go badly for me?'

'I will do my best, but they raise an argument you plot to return Piero de' Medici and his brothers to Florence.' He got up and refilled Vincenzio's cup. 'The blasphemous parchment gave me evidence enough to arrest you on a charge of heresy. Now they want me to add another—the charge of a crime against the state—for good measure and to secure your fate.'

'I am neither. I love my city and my God.' Vincenzio spread his arms wide then saw the way his hands shook like an old man's, like his father's used to do. He clutched them together and made as though to pray.

'The evidence points otherwise. They mean to condemn you. Savonarola's men still dominate.'

'They lie in their throats. I do not agree with the preacher, but I would not have him dead, for sure.' The words tumbled out as easily as grain from a sack, so fast any guise of honesty loosened and was lost like chaff.

'You damned him to Hell at Mass only two sennights ago, by your own tongue, Vincenzio.'

'Words, only words. You know me; I am hot to anger, that is all. His men were threatening my son.' He closed his eyes from the vision of Pippo's body that flashed into his mind.

'As I say, I will do my best, but I am the Justice and I must be seen to do my duty for the people.'

The men finished the rest of the wine in silence and Bernardo left Vincenzio alone. He tried to settle his thoughts in preparation for the trial to come. The preacher's supporters would be there in numbers. He wondered if Tommaso Palagio would stand with him or against him. Bernardo would defend him as much as he could but his role as Gonfalonier kept him out of the thick of it. Vincenzio tried to remember the detail of the paper Luna had written but his attention had been distracted by the guards standing over him. That the Sun is the centre of the universe and immovable and that the Earth is not the centre and moves; that was it. He held his hands to his face and shook his head. Dear God, his daughter was a she-Devil, but he'd not let those guards or Bernardo or any man of Florence believe his daughter wrote such heretical nonsense. He'd rather defend himself against the charge, painful as it was, than suffer the ignominy of a daughter so corrupted, so beyond his control.

The door opened again and Vincenzio gathered his cloak before being led by a guard down to the court. He wrinkled his nose at the smell. This was not the Signoria; it wasn't even the hall of the Great Council. This was a lowly courtroom. Surely a man of his standing deserved more respect than this? Vincenzio was livid and refused to speak. Despite his silence, discussion of his crimes and charges lasted from morning till the sext bells rang. The court broke for midday prayers and Vincenzio was returned to his room, where he demanded to see Bernardo.

'You must get me in front of the Signoria,' he urged his friend. 'This pedestrian court is no place for one such as

I. They discuss men who've drunk a season's worth of my vineyard's finest.' Vincenzio breathed deeply. He would not panic. 'Do you know they want to condemn me to death?'

'I will form a meeting of the Great Council.'

Vincenzio sat back but his friend's words gave him little relief. 'We both know the Council is a collection of the flawed beings that make up most of the city's motley citizens, not the men you and I know and admire. This is the preacher's council, and I will not receive a fair hearing before it.'

'Still, it is the way.'

So Vincenzio descended once more, to stand before a meeting of some two hundred citizens formed to discuss his case. He stood proud and tall but in truth his throat was parched and he'd not eaten since a piece of bread that morn. His spirits were raised, though, at the sight of Professor di Novara, who appeared to speak on his behalf. Vincenzio inclined his head enthusiastically at his friend.

'Let us remember,' the professor urged, 'that in Florence you have a law of appeal. It states that any citizen condemned to death for political reasons should have the right to appeal to the Great Council. This law was originally proposed and pushed through by Friar Girolamo Savonarola himself.'

Indeed, thought Vincenzio, how can they refuse an appeal according to their friar's own law? He stamped his foot in approval but stopped at the sight of Tommaso Palagio moving through the crowd towards the speaker's podium. Vincenzio raised his hand; surely Tommaso would defend the father of his son's future wife?

'So,' began Tommaso, 'now friends of the traitor invoke the same law of appeal they called outrageous when we proposed it, saying it was madness to submit matters of treason to an assembly of ignorant donkeys! Go back to Bologna, professor, and teach on a subject you understand.' He bowed in acknowledgement of the cheers his words elicited as he stepped down.

Vincenzio followed Tommaso's progress from the room with eyes that would cut his perfidious tongue from his mouth.

It seemed he was not alone in judging the proceedings poor; Bernardo moved the debate to the Signoria. Vincenzio viewed this as a good sign; finally he would be amongst his peers. Tommaso appeared beside him as they walked to the main hall of the Signoria. Vincenzio gave him no courtesy but the degenerate ass spoke regardless.

'Look where we are come, my friend.' Tommaso's voice was giddy with power. 'And how our association ends. I hardly knew how close my good name was to ruin. No son of mine will marry a Fusili. If I can rid this earth of all your imperfect offspring, I will, and may the Lord have mercy on your soul.' He walked away.

Vincenzio did not react, even though his throat burned with insults ready to shout. He walked on to the final forum of his trial. So Maria would not marry Guido Palagio; ill health to them. He would build his name again. He cast his eyes about the room at all the good and noble gentlemen of Florence who sat in judgement on him. Unlike these patricians, he knew how to rise from insignificance; he'd done it before. There was real value in loyalty, hard as it was to find, and he'd proved his fealty to the Medici family. They'd not abandon him.

The discussion in the assembly degenerated into a brawl. Vincenzio rallied at the sight of fists thrown in his name. Tommaso stood between two snarling men and held out his arms as though he could control their anger. 'Either the convicted man dies, or I do!' he shouted but no one took any notice. Vincenzio saw another Savonarola supporter shove Professor di Novara towards a window and come close to hurling him out but the professor was taller and stronger and pushed his assailant to the ground. It seemed all men were fighters when it came to it. This is where we fail, Vincenzio thought in a moment of clarity as the hall descended into tavern brawling. We are all inclined to behave badly, to take more than our fair share of power or wealth, to profit from other people's weaknesses, to cheat, to betray promises.

The assembly managed to reclaim enough order for the final vote. It unanimously condemned Vincenzio Fusili to death for heresy and treason. He scanned the room for those he knew best—the professor, Bernardo Rucellai, even Tommaso Palagio—and held each of their gazes with a smile he hoped conveyed his disbelief and strength to demand a challenge. This was some trickery aimed at shaming him. No one spoke, and Vincenzio knew this was the protocol of the Signoria: once a sentence was decreed it was final. Yet still he held that smile rigid on his lips.

He was returned to the prison, only this time the room was bare and the bed a straw pallet on the ground. Vincenzio longed for a cup of wine, a taste of his wife's sugared citrons. He pictured his family enjoying the evening meal, sitting around the table, talking and laughing about Filippo's antics or Maria's sewing; even Lucrezia's complaints of not enough coin in the household account became suddenly a sound to cherish. Yet he was not there to hear and his mind had never been so quiet as in this cell. That same evening he was given confession. Even as the executioner sharpened his blade, Vincenzio looked hopefully towards the quarter where his family awaited his return. A bright spark of fire shot up towards the heavens and he took this as an omen of great things still to come for the Fusili name.

CHAPTER EIGHTEEN

September 1496

For the next month Luna did not leave the monastery. She slept in one of the novices' cells, on a bed that Friar Bartolomeo tried to make more comfortable by adding blankets on top of the straw mattress that rested on the wood pallet. She kept to the bed, and when she could not sleep she hid beneath the cover that was musty with damp and smelt of years of burnt candle wax. After early-morning prayers, Friar Bartolomeo brought her food and stayed a while. She drank the draught he gave her because it made her sleep and for those hours she did not think. He returned again after vespers each evening and the candle he lit told Luna another day was ending. She thought his voice was a dream though she did not care to open her eyes and find out.

Outside the monastery walls, the burning colours of autumn flourished and the streets were noisy with families enjoying the cooler evenings. Luna heard their laughter as she lay, eyes closed. What reason had she to see the day? Her family, branded as heretics, was gone: her step-mamma and siblings burnt to death, her father executed. He came to her one night, as a ghost in a room full of strangers and only she recognised him, complete again though his features were dim. She shouted to the party that a ghost was amongst them, but no one took heed of her words and she alone said hello before he disappeared.

Friar Bartolomeo brought news of an emissary arrived from Rome. He described the pomp and ceremony of the riders and carriage as they passed on the way to the Signoria. There was confusion and excitement at what this might portend. She heard his rosary beads click feverishly as he padded about the room, debating with himself how the errant preacher might react and even through the fog of her own grief she could sense his hope. Luna cared not what happened.

Then, just as quickly, the visitors departed back to Rome with the preacher amongst them for an audience with the Pope. Florence was left without its religious leader. Friar Bartolomeo moved about the monastery with a spritely step after that. The people of Florence bundled themselves against the cooler weather, staying close to the protection of the buildings as they walked the streets, caught in the swirling tide that had turned against their favoured preacher. None of this moved Luna.

The orange tree in the cloister had lost its leaves by the time Friar Bartolomeo led the monks in a Requiem Mass for Signore Fusili and his family. The Great Council deemed it sufficient time since the heretics' deaths. Luna sat in a chair placed discreetly in a side altar but she did not pray.

She didn't feel anything. Her heart was numb. There were no bodies to bless and bury, nothing of Mamma Lucrezia, of her beloved Maria or Filippo. Her father too, had gone, when she did not know, only that he'd been put to death. What God would leave her breathing whilst all the people she loved were gone to Him? She remained after the monks had padded off quietly to their duties.

When she heard a muffled cough, Luna realised someone was hovering nearby. She caught her breath at the sight of the thin, hesitant figure.

'Mother Mary, save me. Livia, it *is* you!' Luna exclaimed and didn't resist when her loyal maid pulled her up and into a hug that was so unexpectedly loving she closed her eyes and gave in to the need that it touched. Luna sobbed until it felt that all her heart and innards had been leached. Then she felt her face lifted gently.

'It is God's mercy that you survived. He protects the lamb.' Livia kissed Luna's forehead and crossed herself.

'How did you survive?' Luna said when her breath had steadied.

'I'd taken Pippo off to rest that morning and when I woke, the house was in disorder; the kitchen girls unsure what to start on, their gossip fuelled by the absence of Mistress Lucrezia, who was closeted in her room. Pippo was with me and he held my hand tightly; we both felt the fear. I went to the mistress and found her standing by the window in her chamber, though there was nothing to see. She swayed as she told me what had happened. I offered to go in search of you since she was so worried. So it was that I left the house before …' She crossed herself again. Luna did the same.

It was Livia who drew Luna out of her grief-ridden stupor. She visited daily and her conversation and company was like a thread to Luna's old life. With each visit, it was as if that thread twined round Luna, holding her together until it bound her so firmly she could lift herself once more. She saw her father again in a dream, this time hale and hearty, chuckling at her with eyes atwinkle as she remembered when he'd surprise her with a night-time excursion to observe the stars. Luna knew it meant he was with God. She rose after that night's sleep and, reaching for her stick, walked out into the cloister. Around her nothing had changed; the garden was just as it had been when last she'd stood in this spot. It was she who was different; her shame flared like an ugly bruise that would never fade. The sun was so bright she had to shield her eyes. God was thrusting light upon her and she dropped her hand and let it burn red behind her lids.

Friar Bartolomeo was in conversation with a novice on the stone pathway. He held a book open and was pointing at something on the page. Their heads dipped together, and a memory flooded over Luna. She was back in Mass at the cathedral watching her step-mamma and papa. They felt so close; she leant towards the memory.

The friar saw her and hurried over.

'Praise God! It is good to see you up.'

She nodded but did not move. The normalcy of so much light and air was paralysing.

'Do you wish to walk?' he asked.

Luna looked around; she knew this place so well. Since she'd first played beneath its shade, the orange tree had grown and now its branches spread out stark and empty after bearing fruit throughout the summer. There was her bench.

She went and sat. Friar Bartolomeo followed. His stoop was more pronounced and she didn't wonder at the sight, for who could not have been bowed by the past month, poor man. A season of emptiness was upon them.

'I cannot burden you forever.' As she spoke, Luna felt the words give her strength. She must consider practical steps. That would be her father's way. She turned to the friar and pressed her hands into his. He was surprised. 'I am still a Fusili,' she said.

'Indeed you are,' he replied.

'I must make a plan.'

He shook his head. 'No one is expecting you to do that.'

'No one?' she asked. 'Who is this no one you speak of? I have no one and that is my challenge.'

'You have me, Luna. I will help you. Don't think so much on the future.'

Luna grew hot sitting in the sunshine. She felt the wooden bench burning against the cloth of her skirts. Her forehead burned too and her chest throbbed. 'What else would you have me do, friar—think on the past?' She turned away from his watery eyes.

He sighed. 'How can you control your future? You are but a girl.'

'But I must and I will.'

Friar Bartolomeo rose and walked about the garden in the way he always did, his fingers pressed to his chin in contemplation. Eventually he came back and stood before her. His footprints in the grass marked a circle around the bench.

'I know your father had a place set aside for you at the Convent of San Matteo in Arcetri,' he told her.

'We spoke of this,' Luna said, ignoring the memory of her angry words.

'Yours would be a secure future as a sister of St Clare, though you would live frugally and dedicate your life to Christ.'

'You speak as though there is any other choice open to me.'

The friar didn't respond.

'Very well,' she said a little too quickly. 'Let it be so.'

'I thought I would need to convince you of this life, but it seems you are closer to the light of our Saviour's forgiveness than I'd realised.' He pressed a small bottle of holy water into her hands, then made the Sign of the Cross upon her forehead. His fingers moved as if upon another.

Is this what Isotta Nogarola felt when she chose the convent as her home?

CHAPTER NINETEEN

Estate of Professor Domenico di Novara
October 1496

The carriage travelled slowly through the Tuscan countryside. It had begun to rain on the day that Luna left Florence and now great sheets of water fell unremittingly and so hard they created dangerous potholes in the road. The sky was grey and there was no hope of finding even a corner of blue, smothered as it was by so much bulging cloud. Luna braced herself against the jolts. There did not seem to be any end to the drenching, but she peeled off her cloak, for the rain brought with it a humidity that clung to her skin uncomfortably. The insistent pounding was like a Greek chorus singing her gone.

Luna looked back one last time upon the rainy blur of her home as they passed beneath the Porta San Gallo. She kept the shape of the cathedral's dome in her sights as the carriage trundled on and with each turn, that symbol of the city's ingenuity grew smaller. Cloud hung right against the top of the rounded arc. God had pressed His hand upon the sky so that where the cathedral ended and His world began diminished. The days would soon be short as the winter's sky was low.

They moved along a road beside the river. The water levels had already begun to rise and the tides swelled along the banks. The river passage was busy; soap-makers lined the stretch of shore nearby and Luna saw the familiar view as like a painting. She was glad to be leaving Florence. The city had turned on her family with the ferocity of the lions that guarded it and she would never return.

The travellers left behind the stink of marsh before the sun had passed across the midday mark and the view became an open stretch of undulating hills. The road was lined with chestnut trees, the leaves already dappled by autumn's hand. A fresh downpour pummelled against the roof and when the rain eased, Luna put her head out for some air. She saw a trail of leaves beaten free by the rain, the fallen mix of crisp copper red and deep yellow bruised and sodden as the leaves underfoot in the piazza outside her home. Her mind bumped from one thought to the next and she wondered if her father had had a similar sense of foggy disconnection after her mother's death. The farther she travelled, the thinner stretched the thread that bound her to her old life. Eventually it would break altogether.

Livia sat opposite, clutching the seat nervously, and her fretting woke Luna from her daydream. The friar had suggested Livia accompany Luna on this journey and Livia, who had never thought to outlive Pippo and Maria as well as her own children, went willingly. Still, she did not enjoy the physical impact of the rolling wheels on her body and her mouth clenched into a nervous smile as she shuffled back on the seat.

They travelled on until the sun was low in the sky once more, and the shadows leapt about the distant hills like rabbits. Luna dozed despite the discomfort. Livia moved closer and pressed her gently till she woke.

'We will soon be arriving,' she said. 'I will not stay, so you best make friends with the mistress of the house if you want to be well cared for.'

The distance to the convent was not more than a day's journey but Friar Bartolomeo had arranged for Luna to stop and rest at one of the country estates that dotted the hills. The friar had been very pleased to tell her how he'd written to Professor Domenico di Novara about her circumstances, knowing he was a friend of her father's, one of the few still brave enough to call himself thus, and how the kind professor and his wife had taken pity on the Fusili orphan. The professor had suggested she stay with them for an extended period, the friar had explained as he encouraged Luna to agree to the generous offer. She'd not answered; making any plans for herself beyond taking vows at the convent seemed a privilege she no longer deserved.

'I'm sure it will be comfortable enough. Where do you go?' she asked Livia.

'To visit my sister until we continue on to the convent. She lives in a village not far from here.'

Luna felt a sudden panic. That thread had not yet broken, she realised. 'When will I see you again?'

'When you are ready to travel on to the convent, I will come. This family is generous to offer you a bed so take the chance to rest. You've been through so much, my child, but you only have to send word and I will return.'

'Thank you, Livia. I'll be glad to get out of this carriage.' She did her best to smile and poked her head out from the covers, hoping to catch a glimpse of the estate as it came into view. A low stone wall stretched away from the road through the fields towards a grand villa in the distance. Her stomach churned; she didn't know this family, but Professor di Novara had seen her utterly disarmed, dressed as a boy and lost for words. That had only been a week before the end of everything; she steeled herself against the memory.

'You will be well cared for; do not fret.' Livia patted Luna's knee. 'I remember how your father and the professor worked together when you were still just a child, discussing ideas late into the night. I would often have to extricate you from under the desk, where you'd gone to listen in hiding. The menfolk indulged you so. The Novaras will be kindly hosts.'

Luna felt the carriage begin to slow. A line of cypress trees marked out the last section of road as they rounded a bend and the imposing facade of the Novara estate came into view. She paled at the memory of the professor's judgement when last she'd seen him.

'Do you feel ill?' Livia asked.

'It is the constant movement,' Luna lied.

It was late in the day when they finally turned into the entrance yard and the sound of men's voices grew loud. Luna saw that a harvest was being delivered. Carts heavy with baskets rumbled past and the horses' hooves clattered loudly across the cobblestones. The ground was stained with dark purple splashes where some of the grapes had fallen.

It was dusk and the light would be gone soon. She thrust her arms into her cloak again, with its musty reminder of Friar Bartolomeo, before taking the hand Livia offered and stepping from the carriage. The sturdiness of her walking stick strengthened Luna. It was the only possession she still had from her former life and she held it tightly as she made her way to the steps, skirting around men shouting to one another as the overseers assessed the quality of the grapes. It must have been a good day; everyone seemed pleased with the pickings.

A woman stood at the top of the stone steps that fronted the villa's main entrance. Her height was dwarfed by the broad building behind her and a bell tower that rose dramatically into the sky. The tower was squared at the edges and built to an open balcony at the top. The woman was following the movement of the carts eagerly. She held herself confidently and shouted to the workmen.

'Branco, make sure you get all the grapes into the store! We cannot risk leaving them out tonight, for I feel a frosty bite in the air.'

The overseer doffed his broad hat and turned back to the task, heaving a basket of grapes out of one of the carts and trudging towards the storage barn on the opposite side of the courtyard.

Livia stood close to Luna's side. 'Go, go, Leonarda,' she whispered urgently. 'Greet your hostess.'

Luna took a deep breath, steadying her step as she went up the stairs; she was still a Fusili. The lady wore a woollen dress, unadorned and plain. Her hair was the colour and thickness of a barn owl's winter feathers and was tied back with a simple length of twine. She was framed by the broad stone archway of the entrance doors and the ochre tiles on the roof set a painter's touch to the image. Luna came to a standstill in front of her.

'Good morrow, Signorina Fusili.' The woman smiled and as she did, Luna saw delicate lines wrinkling from the edges of her eyes. 'Forgive our activity.' She jerked her head in the direction of the courtyard and as if in answer, a rowdy cheer broke out as the last basket was unloaded. 'We'd hoped to get the harvest in before you arrived, though I'm sure you're used to bedlam, coming from the city.'

She spoke with an easy familiarity that Luna was not used to. In Florence there'd always been a sense of fear around stepping outside the strict order of social manners; her parents worried about the judgement of others. But even in this small exchange, Luna sensed this lady had no such qualms. Her eyes creased again when Luna suddenly remembered to curtsey.

'We don't stand on such ceremony here,' she said, and Luna viewed her surroundings with a fresh curiosity. 'Only the Pope deserves a curtsey; perhaps my husband does, when he's shown me a particular kindness, but even then …' she frowned and a light smile crossed her lips, 'I think, even then, he does not deserve to be treated like God's chosen one. Here, we are all Toscani together.' She spread her arms wide as Luna righted herself and, as if she'd commanded it, the sun began to drop behind the building and the light about them bloomed into luminous shades of orange and dusty pink. Everything was mellowed and bathed in a warm glow. Here, there was no press of winter just yet. The air was easy to breathe. Luna saw the mark of the Tuscan sun on the lady of the house too, in the honest lines round her eyes and in her warm welcome. She waited patiently to follow her hostess inside but the lady sighed and did not move.

'This is my favourite time of day,' Signora di Novara said.

Luna turned to watch the dusk draw in and it was indeed marvellous, but she didn't want to stand there in sight of so many servants and this stranger's unknown expectations of her. She wanted to be taken to her chamber to withdraw in private. Already Signora di Novara's kind welcome was more than Luna could return.

The men wandered out of the entrance yard, their work finished for the day. Luna searched for Livia amongst them but the carriage had already left. Soon the yard was silent save for the scrape of horses' hooves, and the lady ordered a boy to retire the horses to the stables before it was too dark.

'Come, Signorina Leonarda; the temperature drops swiftly once the sun disappears.'

'Please call me Luna, if that is acceptable?' Luna said, glad to be finally leaving the yard as she followed Signora di Novara up the steps with as little hobbling as she could manage and into the entrance hall.

'Indeed, it would be my pleasure to address you as one of our family. You must call me Elisabetta.' She pulled Luna into a hug. 'May God give you strength, child.'

The embrace caught Luna unawares and a flush of longing coursed through her so violently that she pulled back. 'Thank you,' she mumbled.

A man appeared behind Elisabetta and Luna recognised his stout frame and the long face but he was not the same as the imposing professor she'd listened to at the Academy. Here his clothes were simple; the doublet was finely made but it was a plain grey and his head was bare so his hair hung freely to his shoulders. The drama and colour of Florence did not extend to his life in the countryside, though the sight of him brought back shameful memories of her papa whipping the cap from her head. Luna stood uneasy as she had then.

'Hello again, Signorina Fusili,' he said.

Luna curtseyed then righted herself on remembering what the lady had just told her and felt the firm press of his hand as he took her own in his. The gesture was unexpected.

'You are welcome in my home,' he continued, 'though I cannot join you to sup this evening as I must meet with my overseers.'

She was wary of this man and held herself tightly. He turned to gather his cloak and whistled, and Luna watched with surprise as two giant hounds barrelled through from a nearby doorway towards their master. He bent down and ruffled their ears, letting the dogs jump up and around him with skittish excitement. 'They are impatient to be outdoors.'

'Cannot you postpone the overseers till the morn?' his wife asked.

'And disrespect the men? Tell me you know how that would make me look, my love.' He spoke with good humour but Luna recognised the patrician tone. They were not so different to her parents after all.

The lady shook her head, pushing back the dogs that panted around her as she went to gather her husband's cloak and see him off.

Luna was relieved to stand back whilst the couple fussed. It gave her a chance to take in her new surroundings; she'd already noted the airy space of this reception room. The beamed wood of the ceiling hung so far above it seemed to meet the sky. The floor of brick was laid out in a herringbone pattern and a shimmering glow of light showed where candelabras burned at the other end of the reception room. A long table flanked one wall with a set of oversized ceramic pots elegantly arranged in the centre. Through the door she saw an equally broad central hall where a staircase wound to upper levels and a corridor cut a wide path to the rear of the house.

The dogs pushed through the outer doors and ran off down the steps into the entrance yard, the professor following. Elisabetta turned back and Luna couldn't help herself, scanning the lady's cheek and arms for signs of bruising. She expected to see the same marks of wedded discord as on her step-mamma but Elisabetta's skin was burnished brown only by the strength of the sun. Perhaps the play of a husband's power was different in this household. Luna followed Elisabetta to where she stopped at the base of the staircase. A bench seat lined the wall opposite the stairs and when she put her foot on the first step, she saw a thick tapestry hung against the stairwell's drop, from the top floor down to where the stairs first turned. It was a magnificently detailed scene of men and boys hunting on horseback. Below them, servants carried bows and arrows, flagons of wine and books; above them ranged deer and boar, hawks and pigeons. Luna imagined it to be the family's lineage.

'You must be tired,' Elisabetta said and Luna nodded. 'A quiet evening in your room would be best. I will arrange for supper to be brought up to you.'

Luna found her hostess's directness a relief and she accepted willingly. On the first floor, she was shown into a small but comfortable bedchamber. A fire had been lit in the hearth and Luna went to warm her hands. A desk sat beneath the window, which looked onto a courtyard garden and beyond to the estate's working fields and farther still to hillocks that rose like watchmen against some distant enemy.

'You should find this room quite comfortable.'

'It is a great reprieve to stop here,' Luna replied. 'Thank you for taking me in.'

Her hostess nodded. 'We will talk properly in the morning but I hope you will stay a goodly time. I'm looking forward to having another woman in the house.' Then she left, closing the door gently behind her.

Luna hung her hands in front of the fire again, taking some comfort from the warmth. She looked around the room; shadows leapt about the walls and across a portrait that hung above the bed of Mother Mary wearing a soft expression and cradling baby Jesus in her lap, one hand firmly balanced on his chubby stomach, the other holding his fingers. Around her head an aura of gold leaf shimmered. The paint had cracked in one corner. Luna's memory went straight to the fresco of Mary with the baby Jesus in the main hall of her family home. That mother had always felt strong and protective.

She walked away from the image to stand by the window. There was a swoop of wings and an owl hooted close by but it was too dark to see anything more. As she stared, the emptiness seeped in behind her eyes and spread with a terrible keening ache. She turned away from the dark and clambered onto the bed, high and plumped with a tapestry coverlet, and reached up to briefly touch the Virgin before creeping under the covers without bothering with her victuals or ablutions.

*

When the dawn finally came, Luna sat up with relief, for she'd lain awake in the unfamiliar bed through the darkness of a night she felt would never end. So it was she descended as early as the first cock's crow. She listened for the sound of voices as she slowly walked the corridor in the hope of hearing only silence, but the master of the house was already sitting in a chair by the monumental fireplace in the main hall. Luna greeted him and took the chair opposite.

He raised his eyebrows when he saw her. 'A fellow early riser! I hope you slept well?'

'Yes, thank you.' She tried to sound refreshed but her voice was ragged and he frowned.

'Faith, you cannot hide the tiredness; I could never settle in another's home as well as my own. You will be restored in a few days.'

'I have no home, so that is no longer a problem for me.'

He grunted in response, then stood and, to Luna's surprise, came to where she sat and dropped to his knees before her. She shuffled back with as polite a smile as she could manage but he was so close she felt unbearably self-conscious.

'You have suffered enormous loss.'

She could not meet his gaze and dropped her eyes; these country folk were flushed with emotion.

'I would gladly offer you a home here, if it suits you?'

'You would take in a crippled orphan?' The words slipped out.

He peered at her intently and Luna sat up a little straighter. She had no need of his pity.

He pressed his lips together. 'I see you are a plain speaker, just like your father. There will be no judgement here, only help, if you choose it.'

'That is certainly a relief to hear, sire.' Luna raised her chin. 'But I will not burden you long as I travel on to the Convent of San Matteo, where I will take my vows as a sister of St Clare.'

He nodded then and rose unsteadily on knees that cracked with age. The effort made him hiss. 'So I am told by Friar Bartolomeo in the letter which accompanied your arrival.' He paused and rested both hands against her chair. 'Do not rush to the convent; stay with us a while. I would be honoured to have Vincenzio's daughter join my household.'

She frowned, confused and a little taken aback. 'That is very kind, but I have no place here.'

'Let my wife be the judge of that. And in due time, I would find a suitable match for you.' He walked a short distance away, turning back to observe her with hands on his hips.

Luna's insides shrank but she held her voice firm. 'Even my father understood that marriage was not in my future, and that was when he was alive and our family still respected. I do not expect miracles.'

He remained silent.

'Nor could I accept,' she added wearily, 'even if you did find a madman willing to have me. I am expected by the abbess.'

'I beg you to consider what you lose by entering the convent. I know your father had you educated.'

'He did, sire, and now I have a head full of knowledge which, in the end, even my papa found too confronting.'

'Indeed, I do not mean to offend, but an educated mind is a wonderful gift; I'm sure Vincenzio would want more than a convent for your future.'

She laughed then. 'Even before my family perished, I was to become a nun by my father's choosing. The truth is, he wanted to hide me away because my wilfulness brought shame upon the family.' Luna tried to keep the bitterness from her voice but this gentleman she hardly knew went too far. She rubbed a hand across her eyes. When next she spoke her voice was quiet. 'Forgive me, I am still tired from my journey.'

The professor sat again. He tilted back in his chair so that the front legs left the floor and he rocked with a rhythm that made Luna think the whole thing would up-end him.

'This could be your chance to make a different future. You are young and pretty, and being educated strengthens your character in the eyes of a future husband.' He spoke encouragingly and Luna was shocked by his compliments, but she'd no patience for his misplaced sympathy.

'Be that as it may, I have a place secured at the convent and so there I will end my journey.' Despite the fact she had no money and no family, so in truth she had no choice, Luna did not lie; she went willingly to the sisters of St Clare.

'Then that is that,' the professor said after a long pause and with a tired finality. 'We are happy to entertain you until such time as you choose to leave us for the convent.' He rose slowly, languid as the gracious host he was, whistling to his dogs as he turned to the doors.

Luna did not linger either, for she had no desire to find herself in conversation with any other member of the household. She shook out her arms before reaching for her walking stick; the professor had avoided any mention of her deformed stump of a foot in his consideration of her marriageability. At the other end of the house she went through long doors that led out into a courtyard garden. She could see the window of her room from here, the shutters pressed back against the stone.

The sun was just beginning to hit the low wall at the southern end of the garden and farther off, the morning light dusted hills that rolled away to the horizon. From somewhere beyond the gate she heard hens. Luna wandered amongst potted plum trees and decorative roses positioned around a central well. It was not dissimilar to the pattern of the garden at her home and that soothed her. Small birds flitted between the bushes and flew off skittishly into the olive trees that sloped away down the gentle hill. These were aged trees, long since left to spread their low, gnarled branches freely. They curved towards one another like old friends, no longer pruned or plucked; a different generation's harvest. Luna viewed them appreciatively and then went out through the low gate, standing a moment to take in the view. A light breeze played in her hair and the air was fresh and peppery.

She carefully picked her way down the hillside, leaning against the ancient trunks for support with one hand whilst firmly placing her stick down with the other. Below, the flat fields were neatly dissected into rows of grapevines. The earth broke easily beneath her feet and the mud dirtied her boots. The trees were grey from years of harsh weather yet thickly sprung with evergreen leaves and small, hard olives. Sunlight spotted the ground through the gaps in the branches and leaves. Luna skidded at one point where the recent rains had made the earth slippery. Still, she continued determinedly, for the focus of where she must step next was a refreshing distraction.

As she walked, the olive trees grew sparser and she saw where the land flattened out into the vines. Beyond that, squares of deep green lined up beside bone-dry summer browns, the patchwork pattern spreading as far as her eye could see. Luna stopped and sat a while to rest her foot, listening to the click of birds moving amongst the branches. On the ground beside her she saw a snake's skin pressed flat against the earth, its owner long since gone. She picked it up but it was so delicate the tail end broke away and flew off in the breeze. She laid the remainder of the papery skin back into the thick of leaves and closed her eyes, leaning into a knobbly trunk. It wasn't uncomfortable. Every now and then she heard distant voices on the breeze and was glad she had no part to play in this household. She just wanted to be left alone.

She must have dozed, for when she woke, her back was stiff and her left leg numb. A prickling burst forth in her foot and she cursed the intense tingling that made her wince as she walked back to the house.

That evening she ate in her room again. Elisabetta brought food to her door and Luna could tell that her concern was genuine, but she didn't press Luna to join them at the table. There was much that was different in this household, Luna thought as she fell into bed so tired she knew she'd have a sounder night's sleep. Sometime through her slumber she was woken by dull noises of activity. She lay and listened in a half-awake state to thuds and footfall, wondering who was busy in the room at the top of the tower whilst all the household slept. But the noise was not enough to keep her from her dreams, and soon enough she drifted off again.

*

With the dying colours of autumn came colder weather. The workers hurried through the yard hunched over against the tramontana that blew from the north and dropped the temperature to an icy chill. The Novara household began the busy activity of the season's change. Luna watched the maids pull squirrel-lined cloaks from the storage trunks and shake them out to air. She watched the wooden shutters being attached to the outer windows and thereafter the rooms were bathed in a duller shade. Tapestries were hung against the cold stone walls in the reception rooms and in the professor's chamber. The clatter of firewood being delivered became as regular a noise as the stores behind the kitchen being stocked.

Each day, Elisabetta supervised the household's preparations for winter diligently. Luna saw her disappear to the kitchens then out to the grain stores or to where the flour was being weighed. She was equally involved in swapping out the summer linens for winter wools, which involved much cleaning before the lighter garments could be stored. She spent time each day in her kitchen garden where she tended to her vegetables and herbs, and Luna often saw her appear from a different path with a basket of fresh eggs on one arm. When they came upon each other, the lady would stop and engage in brief talk of the weather or the task at hand before letting Luna continue on her way.

'I see you have a fine bounty of eggs this day,' Luna commented on seeing Elisabetta's basket.

'My hens have been busy, which will make the cook as happy as I. For a while they stopped laying till one of the workmen found a viper inside the hen house. Poor things had been too afeared to sit, as indeed would I in the presence of such a thief!'

'I've discovered skins on my walks,' Luna offered.

'As the weather cools, the snakes are disappearing, so you shouldn't see any. It's one good thing about winter. Be careful, though; they like to sleep in the warm hollows of tree trunks or burrows within the earth. If you do not bother them, they will leave you be.'

Luna nodded and continued towards the hills. The professor and his wife left her to her wanderings and though it was strange to have no one calling her to chores or waiting on her return, she soon became used to the freedom. Each day she returned to the hillside of uneven olive trees, where she found that the challenge of not falling stilled her mind. The sun still flickered through the leaves but it had lost the clarity of its hot summer brilliance. As autumn came to an end, the big blue skies shifted and lightened to dusty greys and some days she couldn't distinguish sky from cloud. It was quiet except for her footfall. Through the trees she could see the endless rolling shape of hills and valleys, tightly packed together and extending to the distant horizon. She knew that Florence lay somewhere in one of those unseen dips of hill, and wondered if Friar Savonarola still preached; much could change unexpectedly in less than the two sennights it had been since she left the city. She set her mind to the path she walked and stopped to rest then walked some more, content to repeat what was becoming her regular excursion.

She found the chicken coop in a tumbledown hut whilst walking one day beyond the manicured gardens behind the north side of the house. She followed the sound of hens past the main house, behind the pig pens and through an unkempt vegetable garden that had been left fallow so long the rosemary bushes were wild willowy things and the broadbean vines grew tall as the rusted pitchforks forgotten against the rocky wall. Luna picked her way over a clump of wind-dropped persimmons rotting in a cushion of mud and bracken, flicking at the grasses with her stick, and a sadness came over her for this neglected garden. The warble of a cock sounded and repeated unremittingly. Luna walked over to where the grass was beaten and crushed by regular use, then to where the chickens scattered at the sight of her. The wind pushed the hens into one another with force and sent the dust swirling. She opened the gate and stepped into the small yard, listening to the soft noises of the hens inside the hutch. It calmed her. The rooster was strutting atop a beam. He crowed rudely when he saw her and flew down into the afternoon light. This was his home and she an intruder. Luna looked through to where most of the hens were roosting out of the weather. There were only three still sitting; the rest flapped madly around the enclosed space. Luna waved her arms to shoo them off. One hen would not shift and her instinct to stay on the nest made Luna pause. She crouched down. The hen eyed her then flew over her head so close she felt the wind off its feathers brush her cheek. It made Luna step away nervously, for fear of a snake, but when she bent slowly towards the nest there was only an egg in the straw where the hen had sat. Luna rolled it around in her palm. The warmth of it was comforting. She thought of the many times she'd watched Maria scratch patterns in an egg. Why had her sister never been allowed to rage and shout? Pippo was praised for being boisterous but Maria's passion was a curse. What good had come from pushing down her emotions? The egg sat neatly in her palm. She'd taken care of Maria as her step-mamma had desired when really she'd colluded in turning her sister into a meeker version of herself, a marriage-worthy Maria.

She placed the egg carefully back into the nest then walked out into a mistral that carried the bite of winter in its touch. The hens scattered. It was later than she'd realised and she turned to the path back to the house. She burrowed her head into the collar of her cloak, Maria's spirit so close she felt her neck prickle.

She'd expected something of her step-mamma's control from Elisabetta but her hostess didn't seem concerned that her guest kept so much to herself and preferred to walk outdoors than join in the household tasks. Not having the weight of another's expectations on her made Luna loiter a little longer each time their paths crossed, and before long she always took the path that led past the kitchen garden just so she could begin or end her day with a chat with Elisabetta. Luna came to enjoy listening to her talk of the fattening lettuces or how well her seeds had taken. Sometimes hers was the only voice to break a day of walking.

At night, Luna slept with a tiredness that kept her dreams at bay. The mornings were broken by cocks crowing and then the scratching and clucking of the chickens would begin. Noise started early in the yard too, for even though the grapes were in, there were many jobs to be done to prepare the estate ahead of winter. She occasionally came across the workers on her walks and they would make the sign of the horned hand when they saw her, but after the first time when they'd passed one another and a worker had run back to the villa to warn the master that the cripple had escaped, they did not bother her again. They seemed to begrudgingly accept she was not in need of containment, even though the Devil's touch had been upon her.

Luna walked to exhaust her body so her mind had not the energy to think. The boundless paths across open hills, the focus of where she placed her walking stick, the cries of birds of prey, all acted as diversions from her memories. Her guilt was as powerful as the circling hawk, her grief as desolate as the mice scrabbling for cover. She walked because it was all that she could do. She knew her future loomed and the few days of rest at the Novara estate had become weeks of walking and sleeping, yet still she let the convent wait.

CHAPTER TWENTY

November 1496

By the time winter had closed in on the Tuscan hills, Luna knew the pathways of the estate close to the house as intimately as her bedchamber. She knew where the olive trees grew thickly so she could use them to balance her descent when she trudged down the hill. She marked the path to the herb garden by the copse of younger trees planted closer to the house. The pain that walking brought on did not deter her. She bore it willingly and at night she soaked her stump in rosewater. Her hostess noticed Luna's curiosity with the land and offered to join her but Luna didn't want company.

On All Saints' Day she stayed indoors, at prayer in the Novaras' chapel. That week she did not go out walking or enjoy the kitchen's delicacies. She lit candles for each of her family and only ate after vespers. The hours of daylight she spent in the chapel. Friar Bartolomeo would be honouring her family in his prayers also. It had been two months since the fire and yet she saw each of them still as they were on that last morning: Pippo's small hand holding to Livia's; Maria walking off happily to the kitchen; Mamma weeping. But she could not think of Papa. She could not.

She wrote to Friar Bartholomeo and told him of her acceptance within the Novara household and how welcoming they'd been. She spoke of the peace of the countryside and her newfound passion for walking. She asked him to write back with news of Florence and the preacher, all the while aware the one thing she avoided discussing was what the friar would want to hear: news of her departure for the sanctuary of the convent. Luna signed off, *Your Most Devoted Student, Leonarda Lunetta*, and waited for his reply.

When the professor was home, the table would be laid for a midday meal. Luna joined the Novaras; it was the right thing to do, especially since they allowed her to take her meals in her room so often. Since she'd begun to seek out Elisabetta's kitchen-garden conversations, she found she sat at their table more easily each time. One day, as she mopped up the juice of a chicken pie, Luna heard the professor mention his workroom.

'It is only three moons till the eclipse. I hope I will have everything ready by then.'

'Of course you will, Domenico. I do not know a more dedicated astronomer than you.'

'How many astronomers do you know, my dear?'

'As many as I may invite to my bed,' she answered with a smile that made Luna return to mopping her plate. 'There is ample time. And don't you have your assistant arriving soon?'

'Yes, you are right, of course.'

'For a professor you worry more than most.'

'There will not be another lunar eclipse till after the next grape harvest and I mean to collect as many measurements as I can. If it is cloudy and the event obscured, or if I am inefficient in my tasks, then we will lose at least six months' worth of research time.'

'Can I help, my love?'

'Get the wood stock replenished, for my tower becomes mightily cold when winter sets in, and have some more covers laid against the stone.'

Luna realised the tower that looked like a great spike driven into the roof housed the professor's astronomy room at its top and the noises she'd heard from her bedchamber were the sounds of his night-time work.

'How much can you see, professor?' she asked.

'The Lord offers me a view of the heavens I believe few others are fortunate enough to witness. When it is a clear night, I can see the planets and stars as easily as the seeds embedded in this loaf of bread.' He reached for the warm loaf and pulled off a chunk. Luna saw the dark spots of seeds baked into the crust. She thought the view from her city garden had been splendid but star gazing here must be extraordinary. A sensation she hadn't felt for months tugged at her.

'You must join me one night,' the professor offered.

Luna shook her head. Of course she had expected she may be confronted with talk of star gazing at some time during her stay with the Novaras, but his offer still took her by surprise. She didn't speak until she was sure she could do so evenly.

'I have no more interest in the stars,' she answered and rose shortly thereafter to avoid any further discussion of the subject. First the professor had wanted to find her a husband, now he invited her to watch the stars; it was too familiar, too close to home, and yet there was also something different—kinder—about the way the professor asked. He gave Luna a choice and accepted her decision even when it went against his request.

When she passed the stairwell to the tower she stopped a moment and listened to the wind whistling down, wondering at what glory there must be in witnessing the breadth of view from so high. The professor had talked of the lunar eclipse three months hence. The same she'd hoped to convince her father to watch. She had no intention of watching it now and her refusal had been solidly expressed, so why did it feel like a betrayal of her very essence? She hurried away to her chamber, closing the door behind her and then closing the shutters across the window too. She sat by the fire in the dwindling light. Despite everything, her curiosity was still dangerously alive.

At least she no longer had the dull beat of tiredness behind her eyes, she thought as she woke one morning soon after to the drip of melting frost on the window ledge. She stood and looked out at a fantastical mist hanging heavy over the land, trees emerging like islands from the billowy mass. Luna watched until the sun began to bear down upon the scene and the mist cleared. It was going to be one of those unexpectedly sunny winter days. These were Pippo's favourite, when he'd rush outside and Mamma Lucrezia would chide him for forgetting the cloak that kept a winter sickness at bay. Luna could picture her little brother so clearly, tumbling down the grassy slope of one of those distant hills, over and over, dirty-kneed and laughing. She held onto his laughter as she dressed, looking out to those hills, hoping to hear him again.

When she set out that morning, Luna didn't turn towards the kitchen garden and the chicken coop, but rather went out through the entrance yard with the intention of exploring a section of the estate she'd yet to walk. A group of labourers were already trudging towards the fields. They carried scythes over their shoulders and the sharp edges cut crescent shapes against the sky. The trees were motionless in the cold air and the sun shone crisply. She wore a warmer cloak she'd borrowed from Elisabetta and her cheeks stung in the brisk air.

A walking track led away from the road and she set off with a shiver of determination. She could almost hear Pippo in the wind, calling to her. The band of farmhands in their loose-fitting leather smocks were on a distant hill, a smudge of shifting shapes against the horizon. Their singing carried to her on the fresh breeze. Her skirts flapped playfully and she thought again of how much Pippo would love the freedom of these hills. Her dress was more suited to a convent than to hill walking, but she no longer owned a full wardrobe and took little interest in her clothes. She regretted not tying up her hair as the wind tossed it with relentless abandon. The knots would take her all evening to brush out.

A cluster of woolly clouds drifted high above and she pushed her stick into the firm earth and strode out. When the hills grew steeper she bent her knees into the effort and set her pace against the thrum of her heartbeat in her ears. She'd added extra linen to the lining of her boot, and it helped to keep her stump from rubbing. She raised her face to the Sun and, with tears of longing that caught in her throat, to the memory of her brother and sister. She called out to Pippo to run and play in the clouds of his new home in Heaven, just as she'd watched him do in their garden. She spoke to Maria, telling her sister of her journey to this place, of her freedom to walk and explore, how much she would enjoy the chickens and their perfect eggs. She told her that her passion made her strong and she never should have quieted her or made her feel small.

She stopped walking as the last words slipped from her lips and a great swell of tenderness stung sharply in her throat and rushed to her eyes. Tears streaked her cheeks. 'Forgive me,' she said as loudly as she could muster.

She came to a field where the rain had done its job and the grass was green and long and tufted with seeds that stuck to her skirts as she pushed her way through. It was very different to the naked dirt beneath the olive trees' shade and Luna had to tread more carefully. She grunted at a sudden twinge in her ankle and slowed her pace, untying the rope that belted her walking smock and threading it behind her neck and beneath her hair so that she could pull the two ends up atop her head. Her smock fluttered but her hair no longer caught in her eyes.

After walking on for a while she stopped to rest. The morning light made everything seem a little brighter and clearer to distinguish. She noticed a smaller goat's path that veered off to the left. Keen to avoid bumping into the labourers, she followed it, treading more carefully as she followed it down a slight hill and over another, through a copse of low, broad fruit trees. She saw an empty basket at the base of a tree and looked about, expecting to hear the sounds of farm workers, but there was only the rustle of a rabbit in the fallen leaves. When she picked up the basket the woven handle broke apart and she realised it had probably been there since last season's fruit picking.

When she turned again to the path two figures were walking towards her over the next hill. They were not so far away that she could pretend she hadn't seen them and so she leant against her stick and waited. Her pulse raced. There was not a soul else on these hills. Her hosts were goodly people, but these fields were far from the house and it could be anyone approaching. She steadied herself and saw that it was two men with leather satchels slung across their chests. Her heart thumped as a familiar dread flooded her chest. She drew herself up to stand tall and firm but her racing heart slowed when she recognised Professor di Novara striding into view. His companion walked energetically, though was bent somewhat awkwardly. Wooden rods stuck out from the satchel he carried.

'Good morrow, signorina.' The professor bowed. 'It is unusual for you to be this far from the villa.'

'I came out walking and the goat's path led me here.' Her skirts billowed freely in the wind and she tried to hold them down, aware of how indecorous she must look.

'It is a peaceful place, is it not?'

Luna turned to the professor's companion. He was of the age she coupled with ignorance and spite in young men, about the same as that odious Guido Palagio. He was flushed with the exertion of walking and his cap had skewed sideways but he did not bother to right it.

'May I introduce my student, Nicolaus Copernicus,' Professor di Novara said as the young man bowed formally. She saw he had a job keeping the satchel from falling and rose with a determined swing of his shoulder. Luna stiffened though he did not seem to notice. Rather, he gave Luna a smile that drew her in despite her instincts.

'I see you were not expecting company.'

The tilt of the young man's brow made Luna blush. She felt him looking at her and stole a glance. 'Good morrow to you, sire,' she said then turned and hastily walked a few paces. She remembered that face. This was the man who had spoken out with such passion at the Academy. She untied the rope from around her hair and knotted it back round her waist. At least her skirts no longer lifted with the wind.

'We will rest here.' The professor doffed his cap to Luna before walking to a spot on the edge of the sparse orchard that faced his home. He dropped happily into the grass and pulled out a flagon of wine.

The young man, Nicolaus, sat by a tree and rested his back against the trunk. He pulled off his cap and scratched his head. Professor di Novara threw him the flagon.

'What do you do out so early?' Luna asked.

'We have been abroad since yestereve, observing the night sky from that spot yonder.' The professor pointed towards the next hill. Luna didn't turn to look. Yearning tugged at her insides again.

Then Nicolaus spoke. 'When I arrived last night it was already much clouded over so I could see very little.'

Luna inclined her head politely, furiously thinking through that afternoon in Palazzo Rucellai; had he been part of the circle who witnessed her unveiling?

'Do you have nothing of more interest than the weather with which to entertain the young lady?' the professor called from his grassy knoll, laughing through his words. 'I'm pleased we came upon you, Leonarda. Introductions on a hill-side like this are much more entertaining, don't you agree?' Then he replaced his flagon in the satchel and rose, staggering a moment before walking over to the young man. 'We best walk on before my wife calls us to eat, and you, young man, need time to wash.' He wrinkled his nose with a cheeky wink to Luna, then strode off without waiting for either of them.

To be left alone with a young man was totally unexpected and for a brief moment Luna was riveted to the spot, but she couldn't ignore the courtesy Nicolaus afforded her, standing patiently till she was ready to walk with him. She nodded and they began towards the villa.

'If I'm not mistaken, those clouds hold more rain,' Nicolaus said after they'd walked in silence for so long Luna thought he must be able to hear her heartbeat. She turned her head to the heavens and had to agree.

'Does it bother you much?' he asked, looking to her boots.

'I've never known any different.'

'Your father liked to challenge you, did he not?'

'And I, him,' she answered, offended by his familiar tone yet also curious as to how this young man knew anything of her papa.

'So I heard from the talk amongst his cohort.'

Luna wasn't sure if he meant to insult or praise her but she decided very quickly not to encourage further conversation.

His comments were surely a veiled reference to that ignominious afternoon. She cast a furtive glance his way before picking up her pace and striding out, planting her stick firmly into the divots on the goat's path and trudging through the pain in her boot.

High above them a hawk circled. Luna watched it swoop and dip elegantly then drop suddenly with the precision of the hunter. Its cry was high-pitched and plaintive and carried in the air like a siren's call. Ahead of them, the professor made fast progress across the hills. His assistant had not left her side but by her dipped head and determined pace, Luna let him know she did not want to converse. Before too long she saw the villa rise in the distance and the way became flatter so that she walked even faster through the first drops of rain. She was keen to get back to the house and the privacy of her chamber.

By the time they hurried through the doors, they were wet through. Elisabetta chastised her husband and fretted over what such a drenching would do to her guests' health. She sent Luna immediately to her room and ordered up hot soup and warm water for her to wash. Luna went gladly and after cleaning her hands and face, she climbed into bed to rest for the afternoon. Had it not been for the appearance of the professor and his assistant, she would never have walked so quickly and now her whole body ached. She fell asleep to the sounds of muffled voices in the rooms below and dreamt of a secret room down a hidden corridor where she watched two people deep in conversation, though she didn't know who they were or of what they spoke and she could not join them.

Luna woke as late as the lighting of the candles. It was dark and the dream lingered. She lay and listened to the household's evening activity: pots clanging in the kitchen, footsteps hurrying through the corridors, and farther away, horses' hooves stamping as they settled in their stables for the night. She didn't want to rise, still tired from the morning's walk, but she dragged herself up and put on her one dress, which had dried whilst she slept and now smelt faintly of the fire. Meeting the professor's student had reminded her how easily men judged her sex and with that came memories she didn't want. As she prepared to go downstairs for dinner, Luna set her mind to planning her departure. The professor had already warned her against travelling the roads during the worst of winter and her hosts expected her to join them for the Christmas celebrations. She would resume her journey after the feast of the Epiphany and arrive at the convent with the new year. She wrote a brief note to Livia, requesting that she join her at the Novara estate once the season's festivities were over. She gave it to one of the servants to send before joining her hosts at the table with Nicolaus, where they were already enjoying the evening meal.

'I have slept long,' she said as she sat.

'There is no need for apologies.' Elisabetta smiled and offered her a cup of wine. 'I only hope that your time with us is a relief from the path you have already travelled and due preparation for the journey ahead.'

'Thank you, signora.' The wine warmed her throat and settled in her belly. She felt her composure return and the remnants of her dream dilute. 'I have taken much pleasure in walking through your estate and watching the winter settle over the fields. I didn't imagine I would gain such relief from physical exercise but my whole person has benefited.' She pulled at a piece of bread.

'I would have thought you'd be more conscious of the benefits,' said the professor. 'Anyone who's familiar with Hippocrates knows that the body in harmony makes us healthy. Exercise draws on the body's materials whilst food and drink restore them.'

'I apologise for my professor. Domenico tends to assume everyone is as well read as he,' Nicolaus interjected good-humouredly.

Luna smiled but didn't reply.

'This young woman's education could match your own, Nicolaus,' the professor said.

The table fell silent. Luna knew the professor expected her to join in their discussion but she did not want the attention that expressing her opinion invited. The presence of the professor's student had turned the table into a forum of debate. Why did men harbour such a need to impress each other? The thought reminded Luna of her papa's humanist circles when it had been she who stood and argued prosaically. It was good she'd sent the note to Livia.

The professor broke the silence. 'Nicolaus lost his own father when he was just a boy. His uncle has been his guardian ever since.' He spoke matter-of-factly. Again, Luna sensed a kinder approach in his words. 'He too is an orphan.'

'I am sorry to hear that.' Luna busied herself with choosing a fig. The professor might be kindly but this was too familiar and she wouldn't be drawn into conversation of her family.

Nicolaus shrugged his shoulders. 'It has been many years since I thought about my past. I choose to live for the future. What say you?'

Luna looked up with surprise. 'I have not thought on this question,' she answered honestly. 'I will soon be joining the Sisters of St Clare, so my future is set.'

'Whereas I am a student at the University of Bologna.' He held his wine glass up as though in salute. 'Though my studies often bring me here,' he added and smiled at the professor.

'Do you not like the university?' Luna asked.

'Indeed I do! I confess I prefer the lectures of Filippo Beroaldo and Alessandro Achillini to the dry legal discussions, but I most enjoy the benefits of practical learning in the field with Domenico.'

Luna took a sip of wine and didn't remark on what he'd said. His was a sensible choice; she'd choose the benefits of practical learning too.

'You are drawn to the humanities, my student. It is no crime, except your uncle will be disappointed,' Professor di Novara said.

'My uncle need not find out. There is still much to learn from you, professor. I'm not ready to go back to Warmia.'

'Well, I cannot deny that you make an excellent assistant! Do you not see, Luna, the possibilities when you seize your own future?'

'For any young man with the use of his tongue, and money enough to buy a degree, yes, but for me there is no such possibility—seize my future?' Luna found it hard to speak; her throat felt sticky and clogged. 'I could no more take the role of advisor to the King of Naples than take control of my own destiny. Excuse me, I will retire early tonight.' She could not speak further and rose hurriedly. The professor's enthusiasm only served to remind her how powerless she was. She'd no right to want for any sort of future.

CHAPTER TWENTY-ONE

The following morning there was a storm accompanied by such violent wind that for the whole day it was impossible to open the doors and windows. Luna listened to the crash of logs dropping and the howl of the wind about the building like a wolf prowling the walls for gaps to sneak through. She wandered the house, stopping at the doors leading to the garden. Splashes of rain fell against the glass and sounded like someone begging to be let in. A small flood had seeped through the door and begun to spread. Servants hurried past her with cloths to mop it up.

The lady of the house was in the kitchen, gathering the things they would need to make Advent decorations. Baskets of oranges and lemons lined the benches.

'How did you sleep?' her hostess asked.

'Well enough, thank you.'

Elisabetta nodded but she did not inquire further. 'We have a busy morning ahead. How are you at stringing lemons?'

'My step-mamma would always decorate our house in Florence like this, so I know what to do.' She held a waxy lemon to her nose. The tangy smell cut through her tiredness. 'Mamma Lucrezia would make us stay up late to pray each night of the Novena and she had oranges ready as a treat. After prayers we were allowed to share one, and the rest we threaded and strung about the rooms. She preferred oranges to lemons. Mamma Lucrezia was good with traditions.'

'I like to use both fruits,' Elisabetta said. 'Come join me by the fire.'

Luna followed her to the reception room. A servant placed a basket of each fruit on the table. The oranges were glossy and some knobbly with bumps. Luna concentrated on threading the string through the eye of the long, thick needle and then into the flesh of the orange and out the other side. Juice dripped down her arm and onto the flagstones. She picked up another orange. The lady sat beside her with lemons in her lap.

'I am sorry for last night. I fear my husband's enthusiasm was not welcomed by you.'

Luna shook her head, embarrassed that Elisabetta felt she needed to apologise. 'I should not have reacted as I did but sometimes my grief overwhelms me. It's hard to talk about my family.' Her needle sliced through the flesh of the orange. Luna was grateful for the distraction of the work at hand. The log in the fire hissed and cracked.

Elisabetta shuffled in her seat and described the celebration on the Epiphany for the estate workers and household staff. Luna remembered how Mamma Lucrezia would give them sweets and fruits entwined on spruce twigs at this time of year. She listened to her hostess talk enthusiastically about the dishes her kitchen always prepared, and that too reminded Luna of Mamma Lucrezia. A rush of emotion threatened to undo her. Tears prickled at her eyes. She put down the orange, confused and embarrassed. She missed Mamma Lucrezia but she was angry with her too, angry at her passive reaction when Luna had told her of Guido Palagio's attack and angry because, in the end, she'd wanted Luna gone. Yet still Luna grieved. Her hands were sticky with juice. She wiped her eyes discreetly and the citrus smell shamed her with its sweetness.

What right did she have to sit comfortably preparing for Advent festivities when the rest of her family was dead? She excused herself and hurried out, pulling on her cloak. The rain had stopped though the sky was cloudy and dark. She strode out, only thinking to put some distance between herself and the comforts of the house.

She followed the path to the chicken yard. The cock's call grew louder as she approached. She dipped her head beneath the hutch's doorway and stood in the dimly lit interior amongst the dust and feed. The weather-beaten walls had crumbled on one side and been replaced with planks of wood shunted firmly against each end. The chickens bobbed and scooted about. Her nose wrinkled at the sloppy smell of wet earth and chicken droppings. She listened to them coo and liked the way their feathers puffed up when they shook. Luna pictured Elisabetta talking to them like children as she collected eggs. One hen rose, shivering out her feathers as she hopped to the ground and scuttled past.

Two alabaster eggs were snuggled close together in her nest. They were perfectly rounded and almost equal in size. Luna should take them now and use them as her sister did, etching a pattern in the shell, for she was the one who needed to be silenced. Maria's passion would have blossomed like the orange flowers had she been allowed to express herself, whilst Luna's passion had brought on a season of death and emptiness. How ridiculous an exercise in feminine control it was to etch patterns in the shells of eggs. It would take a roomful of eggs to suppress all that Luna felt. A gust of wind made the gate swing wide and shriek loud as the rooster.

She hurried into the yard. The sky was darkening to the south; another storm was on the way yet to be out in the elements felt freeing and Luna didn't rush back to the house. The storm kneaded and rolled the dark clouds to its doing. She pulled out the ivory comb that held the bulk of her thick hair in place so that her curls fell free. They whipped and tossed wildly as she turned towards the gate once more and walked into the weight of the wind.

The smell of wood smoke from inside the house met Luna as she drew close. The storm clouds spread across the sky and the darkness closed in so that all of a sudden it felt later than it was. Dollops of rain splashed on her forehead and nose and the cold water trickled down her neck and slid still farther against her skin beneath the cotton slip. She lifted her head and closed her eyes, welcoming its freezing touch. By the time she reached the house she was drenched and shivering, but no longer angry with herself. She wished Maria could have embraced all that was wild and wonderful in herself, wished it with a passion that filled her eyes to the brim with watery love for her precious sister. It was wrong that women were damned and silenced for expressing any of the glorious and complicated emotions they felt. Yet it was the way of society and she must live within it.

Luna stopped just inside the doors and shook out her arms. Water dripped from her fingertips and splashed to the stone tiles. She felt the trickle of rain cross her neck, slide down the crease of her back and over the curve of her bottom. She began to shake again from the cold. Her hair hung dark against her face and bosom, even longer in its wet state. She jumped up and down to loose the water from her hair so she could retire to her room and warm up again by the fire. She couldn't feel where the material of her dress ended and her body started. The cloth was heavy with water so she squeezed out her skirts, tighter and tighter, until a rivulet ran across the slope of the floor.

She looked up at the sound of footsteps. A rush of heat flared in her chest; there was Nicolaus. As soon as she saw him, she let go of her skirts but not fast enough to hide her legs from his gaze.

'What are you doing here?' she asked abruptly.

He stumbled over his words and she had to ask again, all the time keeping her jaw in a lock that made her feel at least a modicum of propriety.

'I came to watch the wild storm. I didn't expect to find you here.'

Still he did not turn away. Water from her hair dripped into her bosom and a trickle ran down her forehead. She stood as boldly as she could, but a droplet of water hung off the very tip of her nose and she couldn't help herself—she flicked her hand across her face and dropped it back to her side.

He laughed. 'Clearly you did not expect to be found either!'

Luna breathed deeply. 'Excuse me,' she managed to say, pushing past him.

She hurried along the corridor and up the stairs to her chamber without looking back, shutting the door with a firmness that made it bang. One final droplet of rainwater slid down the dip in her back and Luna shivered. She moved to stand in front of the fireplace, watching the flames curl and flick their fingers of heat around the logs. Slowly she stepped out of her dress and her undergarments, also wet, and knelt before the flames, stretching her hands towards the heat. Nicolaus hadn't moved when she'd pushed past him. It should have been shocking but wasn't. She rubbed her arms as the fire's heat stung, then turned and sat so that her back was now to the flames. The warmth crept round her hips and up the line of her backbone till she throbbed.

CHAPTER TWENTY-TWO

The Turning of the Year

Luna joined the Novaras in the estate chapel for the daily prayers of the Novena through the days leading up to Christmas Eve. They ate only in the evening, dining on fish and rice with almond milk, and fasted through the day with the rest of the household. Nicolaus had left them and returned to his uncle's home for the festivities.

This time of year reminded Luna of her family's traditions. How she'd loved attending the prayers in Santa Croce with her family and Friar Bartolomeo. Mamma Lucrezia would dress them plainly but neatly to express their pious observance and show her family to best effect. The streets were bedecked with garlands as they walked to the church each morn. Luna remembered how much she and Maria loved to see the colours of the wreaths and what new decorations were chosen each year. The church was at its most beautiful, candles lit in every chapel and along the main aisles, the hush of awe alive amongst the congregation. Papa always joined them in their promenade and then the family also journeyed home together to spend the day threading decorations like the oranges she'd prepared with Elisabetta. Her papa would read to them, a fire blazing in the main hall and the children seated on mats on the floor at his feet.

Luna never wanted to forget those times, yet how could she endure the celebrations without her family? She closed her eyes and prayed, shocked by the familiar thrill that caught in her throat at the sound of the Novena prayers being read.

On Christmas Day, a massive oak branch was dragged into the hall and garnished with juniper and laurel. The professor set the branch aflame in the main hearth and sparks flitted up. There was cheering from the household servants at this good omen for the new year's spring harvest. Luna clapped and smiled along with the rest, though in her head she heard the whispered thread of Pippo's delighted shouts from the year when her papa had brought home a branch for them to decorate.

The Novara estate became quiet through Christmas week. Most of the workers spent time with their families and the professor and Elisabetta entertained themselves with reading or games. Luna was happy to join in when they asked, and otherwise was content to read from the professor's collection of books. She sat with Elisabetta and helped her plan which dishes they would serve for the feast of the Epiphany.

A rich woodiness drifted along the corridor from the kitchen on the morning of the sixth of January. Luna found Elisabetta already at work preparing the celebration meal.

'Have you added salt to this?' Luna heard Elisabetta ask the serving girl as she stuck her finger into a bowl of creamed leeks. 'It is tasteless on my tongue.' The girl hurried over to the pantry to find the salt.

'You sound like my step-mamma.' Luna mused at how the notion soothed her. She smelt the faint reminder of Mamma Lucrezia's favourite pheasant dish.

It was warm in the kitchen despite the icicles on the window ledge. Partridges roasted in the oven alongside a dish of mutton stewing in wines and spices—a tight fit, but there were many estate workers to be fed. Eels broiled on hot coals and pikes roasted on the spits. The fish still had to be ground into the meatballs that were one of the professor's favourites and the eels would be added to the creamed leeks. Luna watched the dish of leeks turn golden as Elisabetta added a pinch of saffron. There was bread aplenty and enough wine to send them all away happy. Bowls of candied nuts and spices were ready to offer alongside the pigeon crostata.

The estate workers were invited into the main hall and Luna sat with the hosts as the room filled with people merry and free from chores. They ate and drank and celebrated the Novaras' generosity. Luna thought Nicolaus would fit in well with these revellers. She wondered if he'd have asked her to dance.

The feast lasted till dawn but Luna retired early, lulled to sleep by the warm memory of her papa's deep voice as he recited the Novena to his children.

*

The January days following Epiphany brought with them an enveloping cosiness of rugs and fires, and the household slowed to a relaxed pace. Professor di Novara was distracted by the business of the estate. It was planning time for the coming spring and he disappeared early each morning to inspect the fields with his estate manager, checking the vines and discussing what seeds they would sow first.

Luna watched the activity of the yard one afternoon whilst she sat at a desk by the windows and read a letter from Friar Bartolomeo. He wrote of the endless pleasure he took in hearing how favourably she found conditions at the Novara estate and her hosts, and spoke of how quiet his days had become without her curiosity to distract him. Luna smiled at that because it told her that he missed her. Her friend wrote that Friar Savonarola had returned from his audience with Pope Alexander VI in Rome and was preaching again, in defiance of the Pope's orders. His devotees were dwindling though, in fear of excommunication, and the city was rallying. A festive group calling themselves Compagnacci—the bad comrades—were challenging Savonarola's ban of Carnival celebrations and hoped to have the season resurrected. Luna read with shock about a gang of these Compagnacci who had pelted the preacher's fanciulli with stones, grabbing crosses from the young boys and smashing them, screaming, 'Take their crosses!' and 'Throw the false prophet in the Arno!' She shivered at the memory of Filippo wearing the white robes of these angel children. The friar spoke of the orange citrons he'd enjoyed, made using the fruit from her tree in the monastery's quadrangle. He had kept some to send on to Luna at the convent. He inquired as to her departure date though reminded her she must take the time she needed for respite. He begged her for another letter and signed off *May the Lord bless you*. She traced the line of his name with her finger, pleased to have had word from her friend. She felt reassured he was safe.

Luna folded the sheet and slipped the letter into her pocket. She would think on her reply and write back to the friar later. Firewood was being cut and she listened to the repetitive whack of the axe. Men hidden beneath sheepskin cloaks trudged across the yard carrying sacks to the kitchen doors. Some wore mittens to protect against the cold. Luna heard the door open and turned, expecting to see Elisabetta returned from inspecting her chickens in their winter coop, but it was Nicolaus. His smiling welcome was such a surprise she felt a jolt that flushed blithely through her. She smiled back and rose to greet him. They stood by the mantel and Luna warmed her hands in front of the fire.

'It is cold as ice out there. Thank goodness for this fire,' he said.

'You look to have been walking?' A path of mud flakes followed him.

He turned with his back to the fireplace and frowned at the sight. 'I'll be in trouble for bringing dirt into the hall. I've been out all morn plotting the most favourable position in the estate to view the lunar eclipse that is predicted for five weeks hence. The professor has me straight back into work.'

'That's why I have not seen you yet. You quite surprised me!'

He looked pleased at that and pressed his cap down cheerfully. Then he bent to warm his hands, shuffling in to the space beside Luna. Never had a man stood this close, save for Guido Palagio. She remained quite still. Her scalp prickled but Nicolaus didn't move further. He hung over the flames, supple as a young olive tree, so the heat could reach his outstretched palms. His torso was broad at the shoulder. She heard him sigh with pleasure and imagined the feel of the heat on his fingertips and through his wrists. She felt it too, like a warm breath against her skin. Then he took a step back and dropped into one of the armchairs facing the fireplace.

'I feel restored already. Did you enjoy the December festivities here?' he asked.

'I did, thank you,' Luna replied as she sat in the other chair, hoping her voice sounded calmer than she felt. This man had a bewildering effect on her.

They weren't able to talk further, as the professor appeared.

'Where have you been, young man? I expected you to join me upstairs the moment you returned. We must be ready for the eclipse.'

'Forgive me, professor. I stopped to greet Leonarda and would have been on my way to you sooner had not her company been such a distraction. I've found what I think will be the optimum location to watch the eclipse. We'll have a fine, clean view and there's a flat area to erect your triquetrum.'

Luna shuffled in her seat, a warm glow rising in her cheeks.

'It will be exceedingly useful to get some new measurements.' The professor turned to Luna. 'Did you know that the Earth's shadow will become visible on the Moon's surface? Quite extraordinary! And as we know that the Sun's position is one hundred and eighty degrees opposite the centre of that shadow in celestial longitude, we can pinpoint the exact coordinates of the Moon. Once we have those we can use them to check the distances of stars or planets to the Moon or Sun.'

She nodded. 'No astronomer would let such an opportunity pass.'

The professor chuckled. 'You are right, indeed. Would you like to join us, Leonarda?'

This was unexpected; she'd already said no when he'd asked her to watch the night sky from his tower. A second invitation seemed generous indeed. Her father most certainly would never have asked again. She was beginning to see how differently the Novaras treated her. Yet she had to say no, lest those dangerous aspirations start to rise in her again.

'Thank you, professor, but I relinquished my right to study the stars when I left Florence.' She rose from her seat and curtseyed to the gentlemen, then left them to finish their discussion.

Luna laced up her boots and left the house to walk. She hoped the cold air would help clear her head. She was confused by the frustration and felicity that jostled within her after the professor's invitation. The wind wailed louder the farther from the house she went. She paused at a gnarled and ancient tree and lay her hand upon its trunk, then she pressed her cheek against the hard wood. 'Forgive me,' she whispered, a phrase she uttered often these days when alone. Then she heard a loud yelp of pain. Luna paused, listening and looking around, and heard a groan. She turned towards the sound and trudged through the trees.

She didn't have far to go before coming across Elisabetta beneath an olive tree, hugging her leg. A basket lay beside her, one broken egg oozing yolk into the woven rope. Her face was pinched with pain.

'I've been bitten,' she said through clenched teeth.

Luna dropped to her knees beside her. She could see the puncture marks of a snake and where the skin was already beginning to mottle and redden. She gently touched the spot. What on Earth was a snake doing out in the cold of a winter's day? Elisabetta groaned again. Luna searched the base of the tree and saw where the snake had probably been asleep. There was an indent in the roots where the wood had bowed and formed a cavity that would be warmed by the winter sun, a perfect spot for a viper. Elisabetta must have stepped right on it but it was nowhere to be seen.

'It hurts.'

'I know it does but I'm going to get help.' Luna pulled the comb from her hair. 'First I must do something. Look at me, Elisabetta, don't look down. Keep looking into my eyes.' As she spoke, Luna dug the sharp ivory teeth of the comb into the flesh of the bite mark and then set her mouth to the bleeding wound. Elisabetta cried out and Luna grunted at the sting of Elisabetta's clawing fingers but she sucked on the wound and spat the metallic tang of blood into the dirt. Then she wrapped her scarf around the wound.

'I will be as quick as I can.' She knew snake venom worked rapidly and a single bite could be deadly. 'Help, I need help!' she called out frantically as she pushed through the doors of the house. Luna looked into the main hall but the professor and Nicolaus were no longer there. Her mind raced; Luna knew she had to get Elisabetta home but she could not do it by herself. She opened the doors to the studiolo but it was empty. She shouted again.

Footsteps sounded and then Nicolaus was there.

She took his arm without even thinking. 'Elisabetta has been bitten by a snake. We must help her back to the house.'

By the time Nicolaus had carried Elisabetta back to the house and laid her on her bed, she was much weakened. She stirred as he let her go, then whimpered, and Luna saw her eyes grow wide. 'Find my husband,' she said through shivering teeth.

Luna stroked her brow. 'We have sent for the doctor. He'll be here soon.'

'I need Domenico—where is he?'

'Hush, Elisabetta, do not speak.' Luna raised her eyes to Nicolaus.

'The professor went out to inspect the site I had suggested for watching the eclipse. I will send one of the servants to find him.'

Elisabetta moaned and her eyelids drooped. Luna turned to Nicolaus. The leg was discoloured from the ankle to the knee and a bulbous lump had erupted upon the stretched skin. Where earlier the wound had seemed small and contained, now it was impossible to distinguish where the viper had bitten. Nicolaus gently touched Elisabetta's leg and the lady did not even flinch.

'She is fading,' he said softly. 'I have some knowledge that might help.'

Luna nodded. 'Then do not hesitate. Please, we cannot lose her.'

'I must tie the spot above the wound as tightly as possible to prevent the poison from spreading.'

Luna handed him the belt from round her waist and watched as he tugged it so tight the skin of Elisabetta's leg bulged furiously.

'Do you know if they have any emetics in the household?'

'I can make one up.' Luna hurried to the kitchen, glad of a task to busy herself. She found the housekeeper and together they filled a bottle with the mixture Mamma Lucrezia had taught her for snake bites. She returned to the room. 'We must get her to swallow this.'

Nicolaus lifted the patient whilst Luna pressed the bottle to her lips. Much of it spilt down her front, but at least a portion was imbibed. Then they waited.

'You are shivering,' he said to Luna.

Luna had not even realised and shrugged helplessly. Nicolaus drew a chair close to the bed for her and tucked a throw around her shoulders. She sat heavily, for in her rush to find help she'd moved far more hastily than was wise and the pain in her stump was unremitting.

'Please God, the doctor arrives before long,' Nicolaus said and crossed himself.

'You seem to know something of medicine?' she said, trying to keep her voice steady.

'I dip my head into as many lectures as there is time for at the university. I hope it may help us now.'

After a few moments there was a moaning from the bed and Luna just managed to position the bucket before Elisabetta let loose the contents of her stomach. The poor woman groaned and fell back after only a few moments. Luna gave the bucket to Nicolaus. 'That is good; there is at least some yellow bile gotten out.'

There was a noise from downstairs and then the doctor appeared. He was a thin man with a long face and extended chin that made it seem as if his jowls had been dragged down and hooked around it. He was a local practitioner, used to treating snake bites, and he went straight to where the patient lay. Luna noticed his hands were large and marked with scars as he lifted Elisabetta's leg and peered at the wound.

Professor di Novara came rushing into the chamber. The men surrounded the bed and spoke so softly Luna couldn't hear. The fire in the hearth had dwindled and she went in search of a servant to stoke it with more wood. When she returned, the doctor was applying a liniment to the wounded area. The smell was powerfully foul.

'It's a traditional remedy,' Nicolaus told her quietly. 'You did well to get the hearth seen to—the fire will warm her body temperature and any sweating will aid the expulsion of the poison.'

'It smells like meat left out too long, gone green and rancid.'

'Fresh sheep-droppings cooked in wine. This is a strong potion.' He sounded hopeful.

'How bad is she?'

'If she survives the night, then she will live, God willing, though the doctor says he may yet have to amputate her leg.'

Luna made the Sign of the Cross. Nicolaus was standing very close.

'If you had not sucked out some of the poison she would be dead already,' he said. 'I'm surprised you know of Avicenna's treatment. I thought the Mussulman's medical text was only ever read by university students.'

'I came to it through reading his philosophical work. He was an Aristotelian. My education was as thorough as any university student's,' Luna answered and her voice was more abrupt than she'd meant it to sound but her mind was elsewhere. She went to the chair beside the sick bed from where she planned to keep vigil and pray for her friend. She felt Nicolaus's eyes follow her but she had not the focus to engage in any more conversation. A terrible keening had taken hold within her, the ache of grief she knew only too well. She could not lose Elisabetta as well.

CHAPTER TWENTY-THREE

February 1497

When dawn broke the following morning and Elisabetta still breathed, however weakly, Luna went with the professor and Nicolaus to the family chapel and knelt in the dusty first light and made prayers of gratitude. Luna used a padded square to take her weight and was glad of the thin layer between her and the hard cold stone. Her breath hung in the air as she whispered the rosary and passed the string of gemstone beads through her fingers. Professor di Novara lit a candle at the altar and then returned to kneel beside her.

'Praise God you and Nicolaus were there to help,' he said, his words carrying up to the beams above them. A dove fluttered out and then back in to hide amongst the shadows. Nicolaus's head was bowed. 'I would be lost without Elisabetta,' he continued. 'She has kept me whole these long years. I'm too often distracted by my books and astronomy.'

'You are fortunate to have each other,' Luna said softly.

'It might be different if our children had lived.'

She'd long wondered on this subject, but did not say anything.

'Our two boys died in the last outbreak of il segno.' He rubbed a hand across his brow. 'Their darling sister was taken only a year later; all now with God.' His eyes were clouded and Luna saw how he shook. 'My wife's companionship is the reason I can still laugh in the face of such grim realities. I would not be able to live if my Elisabetta was taken from me too.'

Nicolaus lifted his head then and caught her eye. Luna looked away. She'd never heard a man speak with such candour about the love between a husband and wife. The professor's honesty was astounding to her and she felt an urge to comfort him. Instead she stood slowly and crossed herself, then went to the side altar where a row of thin candles flickered and smoked. She took a new taper and held it against another's flame till it sparked and flared, then placed it into one of the slots. Luna understood the depth of loss of which the professor spoke. She carried the heaviness of grief within her too.

*

More rain fell later that day and continued for the rest of the week. The cobblestones of the courtyard were reduced to silt-filled rivulets and the sky was a constant blur of slate grey. Luna stayed by Elisabetta's bedside and looked on the older woman's sleeping face with a new tenderness, seeing the sun-worn lines as markers of a suffering she understood. Nicolaus visited the sick room each day and Luna was pleased to see him. The doctor had left an amulet that Luna laid on the wounded leg at the hour of the Moon's first rising. It was embedded with a bezoar stone from the belly of a snake-eating goat. The doctor said the bezoar contained a small remnant of toxin that served as an antidote to the poison. Luna prayed as she pressed the amulet against her friend's cold flesh.

Elisabetta lay in a sunken state of delirium, sometimes mumbling and at other times so still that Luna held her fingers under the lady's nose to make sure she still breathed. Luna kept her rosary beads linked across her wrists and read from her friend's Book of Hours. In her pocket she carried the bottle of holy water that Friar Bartolomeo had given her before she left the monastery. She would use it if the patient worsened.

At the rise of the full Moon three days after the accident, the doctor decreed that Elisabetta was so ill as to be anointed with the holy oil. The professor sat beside her bed through the night, insisting that Luna go to her own chamber and leave him with his wife.

Luna didn't sleep. She saw the Moon rise whole and prayed that her mother was watching over them and would turn her light upon Elisabetta. She snuck back to Elisabetta's room. When she saw that the professor was asleep, she sprinkled holy water upon the bed covers, knowing that Friar Bartolomeo would be glad she'd used it thus.

The next morning Elisabetta was so revived that they all believed she would live to see the new Moon. She drank some wine and even took a bite of bread.

'You coddle me, Luna. Thank you, my dear,' she whispered, before slipping back into a troubled slumber. Luna mopped her brow and kissed the hot skin tenderly. When the menfolk left them alone, she stroked Elisabetta's forehead and thanked God for His mercy.

When next the doctor visited he brought leeches to suck out the bad humours from within Elisabetta's blood. Luna had never minded the feel of the wet creatures on her skin but Maria had hated the treatment and so she was not surprised to hear Elisabetta react with similar horror. Despite the doctor's insistence on the good a leeching would do, Elisabetta refused and so Professor di Novara had no choice but to send him away. Luna suggested another tonic of Mamma Lucrezia's and Nicolaus offered to procure the ingredients from a local apothecary. He returned with viper's flesh and opium, which Luna added to a jar already filled with a mixture of honey, wine and cinnamon. The opium and viper's flesh had cost three gold florins and Luna prayed fervently that the tonic would help. She motioned for Nicolaus to place the jar on the table nearest the bed. Elisabetta drank the tonic slowly, and Luna encouraged her to finish it all as she knew the opium would soothe the throbbing ache of the wound and help her to sleep. Nicolaus took the empty glass from Luna and went to stand at a discreet distance as she helped the lady lie down again.

'Thank you for helping,' she said.

'I am learning from you.'

She scoffed quietly at that, but couldn't help smiling. 'I am merely remembering what my step-mamma showed me.' She paused. 'Though I am most gladdened by your company.'

After that he did not leave as she'd expected, but instead took the chair on the opposite side of the bed. Luna sat close by Elisabetta and placed a cloth upon her brow, then she picked up the Book of Hours and brought the candle closer. The afternoon light was fading.

'Would you allow me to read?'

She nodded, surprised at his request. Nicolaus took the book and settled back into the curved seat with his head bent to the page. Luna studied him as he read aloud; he could not be more than five and twenty yet the timbre of his voice lent such a depth of feeling to the words he spoke. He wasn't a fool like most of the young men in Florence, and certainly not vicious like Guido Palagio, nor did he seem to have the arrogance of the learned men Luna knew from her father's company. She sat back and let the richness of his voice wash over her.

She must have dozed, because the next she felt was his gentle press upon her shoulder.

'I must go to find the professor.'

Luna jolted awake. She felt her cheeks burn hot.

'You did well to stay awake as long as you did,' he said. 'I am a better thinker than I am speaker.' He smiled ruefully and Luna blushed again.

*

Another week passed easily in this pattern and Luna was ashamed to say she enjoyed her time in the sick chamber. There were increasing moments when Elisabetta opened her eyes and smiled at Luna, or waved her hand for a glass to be put to her lips. It lifted Luna's spirits to be needed so and the emptiness that had sat in her belly since losing her sister and brother and parents grew smaller. She wrote to Livia telling her about the accident and suggesting she remain with her sister until Signora di Novara was fully recovered. Luna explained that she was needed at the lady's sick bed and would not leave until she was assured of her returned health.

Elisabetta asked Luna to pray with her each day, for she felt distanced from her faith whilst abed. From then on, Luna said her prayers with Elisabetta rather than in the chapel and the time felt precious and intimate, something a mother and daughter might do. Sometimes they were quiet and hung their heads piously as she read. If they had been close in conversation, Luna would open the book and with a knowing nod climb onto the bed and together they would follow the line of the prayer on the page. Mamma Lucrezia had never shown Luna such closeness and trust. Other times it came upon them to watch the sunlight cross the floor and Luna matched the rhythm of her voice to the twinkling flashes. She liked doing this for it stirred their spirits and Luna felt something different in herself, a sense of comfort.

*

The last days of February brought a burst of warmer weather and the first signs of spring. The servants opened the outer shutters and they creaked from months of rain and ice-locked hinges. The winter tapestries were pulled down and packed away, the hearths were swept clean of ash and dust. Each morning the curtains were drawn a little earlier as the daylight hours grew longer. The changing season was another reminder that it had become time for Luna to move on.

Beyond the yard, the fields were washed in a freshness that challenged the last of winter's cold with signs of new life. A verdant green now filled the canvas entirely. Tight buds clung steadfastly to the branches of the fruit trees and tiny spiked horns of green thrust from the soil in glorious, massed disorder. Soon the ground would be thawed enough for ploughing. A few times, Luna spied Nicolaus trudging across the distant hills in the late afternoon and heard him return before the cock had crowed the following morn. She supposed he was doing final preparations for the lunar eclipse.

'I see that lately I am graced with two visitors,' Elisabetta commented one afternoon upon waking as she looked from Luna to Nicolaus and back again. Nicolaus had brought a book of his own and when Luna finished reading from the prayer book, he opened the small volume.

'May I read?'

She could hear the gentle breath of sleep coming from the bed. 'If it pleases you.'

Luna settled herself comfortably. She'd come to accept his presence and had to admit that she enjoyed the melody of his voice.

Nicolaus placed his hand upon the page and furrowed his brow. 'I know that I am mortal and living but a day. But when I search for the numerous turning spirals of the stars, I no longer have my feet on the Earth but am beside Zeus himself, filling myself with god-nurturing ambrosia.'

Luna had expected poetry, or philosophy even, not these words from the *Almagest*. Even from her limited reading, she remembered the allegorical introduction.

'Do you know the *Epitome of Ptolemy's Almagest*?' he asked her, resting the book open in his lap.

Luna shifted in her seat.

When she didn't speak, he pushed a little further. 'Most students of astronomy know this work of Joannes de Monte

Regio—or Regiomontanus, as he likes to be known. I myself have read it twice, at least. I thought perhaps you'd studied it?'

'What makes you think that?'

'You told me you were at the professor's talk, at Villa Rucellai.' He flashed her a tentative smile. 'Then I remembered what your father did to you. Don't be ashamed; it was a very difficult situation for a girl to be put in, tricking everyone like that. Your father should have known better.'

Luna raised her chin. 'Are you interested in discussing Ptolemy with me or the gossip of my attendance?'

He flinched at her angry tone.

'Forgive me,' she said. 'I am still so ashamed …'

Silence fell between them. It was impossible to fully explain how deeply her shame ran, but then she saw the way he looked at her, without judgement or blame but rather with the same offer of comfort that Elisabetta's friendship had given her, and she wanted him to understand.

'My father would prime me with a pointed comment then sit back with his friends and watch as I performed. His daughter, the curiosity. Oh, I spoke eloquently and at length and I did so willingly because I enjoyed the attention—nay, I revelled in it. I thought I was special.' She reached across to tuck the coverlet more tightly about the sleeping lady's shoulders. 'I was arrogant and needy as they all said I was.'

'You speak truthfully and that is a strength; if you were that person you describe then know that she is not who you are today.'

Nicolaus got up and stretched his back. 'I would stay longer but the professor insists on my attendance in his rooms each night as we prepare for the lunar eclipse tomorrow eve.'

He hesitated. 'I would welcome your company to view the eclipse.'

She saw acceptance in his chestnut eyes. Still she could not say yes and stayed in the chair as he bowed and then left. Luna listened to the sound of his footsteps retreating down the stairs. She sat and watched Elisabetta sleep. Her face had a healthy colour and her breath was slow and easy. She'd be fully recovered soon enough.

Elisabetta stirred and Luna helped her to sit up.

'I'm thirsty.'

Luna passed her a mug of wine. 'I am glad to see a healthy colour has returned to your cheeks, mistress.'

'Thank you, Luna. You are so kind. It was our good fortune God sent you to us when He did.' Elisabetta took hold of her hands and Luna felt her strengthened grasp as she clasped them to her breast. 'You have been like a daughter these last months.'

'I have felt it too,' she answered honestly. 'Friendship is the least I may offer as you have been so gracious and kind, welcoming a stranger into your home.'

Elisabetta raised herself to sit. 'There is something I must tell you, which I've kept a secret for many years, and should have shared with you when first you arrived.'

'What can it be?' Luna asked, bemused at the lady's sudden change in tone. 'You are alarmed. Remember, your nerves are still recovering. How can there be secrets between us when we only met months ago?'

'You do not remember me, that is understandable. You were a baby.'

Luna shook her head. 'I am sorry, mistress. What do you speak of?'

'Your father, Vincenzio, compelled me to remain silent.'

'My father?'

'Your mother was my dear friend.' She took Luna's hands again. Her grasp was firm and her eyes glistened. 'And now I am blessed to have her daughter with me.' Elisabetta stroked Luna's cheek. 'You were a newborn babe.' She sighed. 'I was at your mother's side when she gave birth to you.'

Luna pulled her hands away gently.

'My family sent me to the Medici estate at the same time as Giulia. Your mother and I had been friends since childhood; she was strong-willed, Leonarda. Even at her young age, she carried you with such pride to be giving Vincenzio his firstborn.'

'Tell me about her,' Luna whispered.

'No one realised …' Elisabetta shook her head. 'You came early; keen to see the Sun, we all thought when Giulia's pains first began, but then that day ended and the next too, and still you stayed in the shrouded world of the womb.'

Elisabetta gestured to Luna to pass her the cup of wine again. She drank deeply. 'I stayed with you for as long as I was able after Giulia passed into eternal sleep.'

Luna leant forward. 'But I was three years old when my mother died. She succumbed to the Naples flu.'

Elisabetta frowned. 'Your mother died giving birth to you, Leonarda.'

'No, you are wrong. I remember the feel of my mother's arms around me.'

'That would have been Livia, your wet nurse,' Elisabetta said gently.

'But Papa told me the story of my birth often: my mother holding me in the moonlight and every moment after that till she died.' Even as she said the words, Luna remembered how the details of her birth story had changed with each retelling.

'Your father left the morning after you were born, on business he said was unavoidable. You settled well. Why would you not, an innocent babe? Your father delayed returning to claim you, again and again, so Lorenzo and his son Piero agreed that you could stay on at the Careggi villa. Your wet nurse, Livia, stayed too, and became your carer. Yet it seems God has sent you to me again, Leonarda.'

Luna rose swiftly and went to stand by the window. The light was fading. She couldn't turn around. 'But my father came back.' She pushed wide the shutters to let some air into the room.

'He did, after three years, but I do not know why. By then I was married to Domenico and had begun my wedded life here.'

'Do you remember much of that time at the Villa Careggi?'

'I was only there long enough to see you suckling well at Livia's bosom and to settle the arrangements. Then I accompanied your mother's body to her family's estate, where she was buried.'

'Papa left me for three years?' Luna whispered, sucking in the ice-cold air.

'You were happy and healthy. The Medici family took good care of you.'

'He abandoned me,' Luna repeated. 'No mother even to love me.' With each word it felt like she inhaled horns of ice that spiked her throat.

'I think that is why he kept you always close afterwards,' Elisabetta said.

Luna turned then. 'To prevent me from discovering the truth?'

'To protect you, my dear.' She sighed. 'The dead cannot defend themselves. He tried to make amends by reclaiming you. Try not to judge him harshly.'

The shutters rattled and Luna caught sight of the dark edge of a wing swoop close. 'I don't know what to think.' It felt like everyone she'd ever loved was dying anew, only this time every memory she held dear died with them. 'Now he's left me again, just as my mother did.'

'You know that is unfair.'

'Forgive me.' Luna pressed her fingers hard into her temple. She felt as though she were balanced on a lake of ice that had begun to crack. Elisabetta placed a gentle hand upon her knee and the tender gesture laid bare all of Luna's grief. She sobbed freely.

*

The next morning, Luna lingered over her victuals. Her father had appeared again in her dream, this time fleetingly yet still vivid enough, and she'd woken with a start. A few coals still glowed in the fireplace but the bedroom was as cold as the frozen Arno. The embers hissed softly as she lodged a handful more amongst the dying heat and watched them flare briefly. Outside, the day's activity had just begun in the yard. It would be easy to accept the professor's offer to stay on indefinitely and part of her ached for that sense of belonging, but this morn was different from all the others and she did not trust herself to know what was best or right. Her eyelids were heavy and ached from crying. She must face the day knowing the truth of her birth and early years. Never again would she think on her father's star-gazing adventures with pleasure, for those memories were now tainted by his lies. She'd clung to Elisabetta after she'd told her the truth, crying openly. The lady's good heart was strong, even as her body still recovered from the snake bite. Luna hoped she would not want to talk about her mother again and she lingered on her way to sit with Elisabetta.

The sound of raised voices from the kitchen caught her attention so she stopped to see what all the noise was about. There was Livia arguing with the cook! She must have arrived late the previous night. When she saw her maid's familiar face, Luna let out a cry of pleasure and fell into her arms. It had been months since Luna had seen her and yet she was still surprised by the goodness of the woman's embrace. She did not want to let go.

'Fie, you have a strength about you! The country air has done you good,' Livia said cheerily, pushing Luna back so she could examine her.

'What is the matter here?' Luna asked, turning to the other servants, who stood with arms crossed, frowning at Livia.

'I only wished to make your step-mamma's stew as a surprise, but it seems there's not a pot for me to use. I would have brought one from my sister if I'd known they were so poor here in Tuscany.'

'Hush now, Livia. I lack for nothing and you'd do well to apologise if you want to eat more than bread and sops whilst you are here.' She motioned towards the kitchen girls, who stood beside their cook like guards.

'Very well.' Livia went and made good with the cook and after that Luna took her up to her chamber. She would sit in with Elisabetta later.

When they were in the privacy of her room, Luna hugged Livia again with a fierceness she hoped expressed her gratitude; Livia had been the only constant companion throughout her life. There was a healthy ruddiness in Livia's cheeks. A winter in her sister's small holding had suited her.

'Has your stay here been restorative?' Livia asked.

Luna nodded and sat on her bed. 'I have been exceedingly well cared for.'

'You deserved some fussing before the convent.' She lifted her heavy bottom onto the bed beside Luna. 'Are you ready?'

The question was an easy one but Luna found it difficult to answer. 'I've become used to the comforts of this home.'

Livia patted her knee reassuringly. 'Then it is a good thing I am here. These people are not your family and it is wrong to burden them indefinitely. The days will begin to warm soon enough and you will see in the glory of spring at the convent.' Livia went to the drawers and began sorting through Luna's few pieces of clothing. 'It will not take long to pack you up. Let us set a date for your departure in two sennights' time.'

Luna was no longer listening. She'd not anticipated what peace she'd gained from this place so far from Florence, watching the passing of the seasons from harvest time through to the beginning of another ploughing, rather than the politics of the city with its bigotry and hypocrisy. The Novaras were not like her father and step-mamma; each listened to the other's opinions and they worked together and loved openly. They'd shown Luna the same respect. No one demanded she be silent and dutiful, no one stared at her as an abomination.

'I must confess, this is a well-ordered house.' Livia's voice broke Luna's reverie. 'I see how easily you'd settle here, but let us attend to preparations for when you take the veil. It will help you to have a few fine things to use as barter as you no longer have your father's patronage to pay for a cell to yourself, nor even coin enough to buy a softer woollen blanket than the coarse ones handed out to novices. It's going to be a very different life to the one you have enjoyed. You must rely on your own wits.'

'I have very little.'

'Have you done no embroidery or needlework whilst here?'

Luna shook her head.

'What on Earth have you been up to then? What about candied fruits—could you take a box?'

'I would not like to ask the lady of the house. She has been so generous already.'

'Then we will hope for a kindly mother abbess.' She shook her head at Luna's worried expression. 'You can scribe a letter; that is a skill the abbess will pay you for,' she said pointedly.

'What do you know of the Poor Clares?' Luna asked.

Livia sat on the bed. 'They grow a few fruits and vegetables to feed themselves, so you will likely work in the garden. In the summertime they sell herbal medicines and bread when it is too hot for anyone else to bake. I suggest you offer your services for cooking. To be sure, it will be a different life, but hardship is what brings us closer to God. They have accepted you without a family and such good fortune is a sign of your calling.' She bent to lift the pail of water set aside for Luna to wash. 'This is the last time I will serve a Fusili.'

Luna rose to take the pail from her and Livia took the chance to grasp her hand.

'You will be safe at the monastery, do not forget that.' There was intent in the pressure of her hold. 'For that reason I am content to leave you there, though it will not be easy. I had hoped to see you with a husband and babes of your own before we parted ways.'

'I'm sorry I can't give you that.'

'God's set a path for you and we must accept it willingly.'

'Livia …' She struggled to control her voice. 'What do you know of the day I was born, the real story?'

The maid shrank a little. There were creases where her mouth pressed into a firm line. 'I suppose Mistress Elisabetta could not keep it to herself. She was always very opinionated. I told the friar it was a mistake to send you here of all places, but he did not understand why, and unlike these gentry, I can keep a promise.' She paused and crossed herself, whispering, 'God rest his soul.' Then she raised her voice and said, 'Why would you want to know any more? I'm sure she told you what happened.'

'But you did not tell me what happened. In all our years together you did not think that I deserved to know the truth?' Luna put down the bucket and waited with crossed arms.

'Nothing I could have said to you would have changed anything.'

'Yet I would still have preferred the truth.'

'I promised the master, and I kept that promise to his dying day.'

Luna's shoulders dropped. 'I understand. My father demanded loyalty.'

'What did you think you'd gain by digging into the past like this?' Livia's voice was less indignant now. 'Your father was a fine gentleman of Florence. Did Signora di Novara tell you how on the day of your birth, still damp from the flush of your mother's waters, Giulia ordered me to take you to the convent and leave you there as an orphan? Her own baby! She was afeared your father would blame her for your deformity and cast her out. He saved you from that fate at least, Leonarda.'

So Luna knew the truth now. Her mother had not wanted her either.

'But your father came back for you,' Livia continued. 'Most would never have reclaimed such a baby as their blood. He did the best he could, and didn't he indulge you?'

Luna listened to her own breath and her heart's beat behind each exhale, the one never without the other. Livia was right that her father had indulged her, but that had been a burden as well as a gift. She walked to the window and surveyed the view of the hills she'd come to know so well. The afternoon light lingered. Soon it would be dark and tonight the Moon in eclipse. Would she ever be free of her father's influence? It coloured how she loved and who she was, right to her very core: in the way she'd copied his curved letters and in her passion for books; in the way she'd either chased after him or tried to please him, never succeeding at either; in the silent suffering of his brutish temper; and in never, ever being enough for him. She would carry all that in her heart forever, and now, this new discovery that he'd not even bothered with her for the first three years of her life and yet he'd stopped her from becoming an orphan!

Luna watched Livia fuss around her few belongings as she decided what would go with her to the convent. But she had never wanted to become a nun. That had been her father's choice, and then the friar's and she'd agreed, because what other choice had she?

'Do you want to take this chemise that Signora di Novara lent you?' Livia asked.

'No, leave it here,' Luna answered. Then she breathed deeply, felt her heartbeat and breathed again. This was her precious life. *Hers*. 'No!' she said again.

Livia chortled. 'All right, it's only a cotton thing.'

Luna laughed too with a deep belly full of her own sound. She felt a weight lift. She could choose. She'd always hold dear the many moments of love and laughter that enriched her life as Vincenzio Fusili's daughter. Everything else, she'd let go.

As a child, Luna's joy of star gazing had been always yoked to the story of her birth: of her father's dedication to his daughter and her mother's love, which in death she passed to the Moon, to Luna's protector. When her father explained how to track the red eye of Taurus from the three stars on Orion's belt, it felt like he'd given Luna a precious secret no one else would ever hear. Now that was all gone. But the Moon would still rise tonight and send the Sun to sleep. The stars in their fixed flickering spots would tell the same stories of Greek gods they'd told every night when the dark awakened them. The planets would circle in their perfect spheres, rolling ever closer and ever farther from the pull of their centre, and there would always be astronomers standing below, observing and hoping to understand this grandeur. There was to be a lunar eclipse that night, and if she hurried, Luna might still be able to join Nicolaus and the professor.

CHAPTER TWENTY-FOUR

Luna found Nicolaus in the entrance hall, removing his cloak after another expedition across the hills. The winter sun had left warm spots on his cheeks and his hair was skewed to one side. He was breathing heavily. Here you are, she thought. He saw her then and smiled as she walked towards him.

'The weather is in our favour,' he said excitedly. 'Tonight will be perfect conditions for viewing the eclipse.'

'Would you still afford me the opportunity to watch it? For if so, then I would like to accompany you.' She spoke loudly to cover the tremor in her voice. It had been a very long time since she'd felt confident enough to speak so boldly.

He nodded. 'The professor will be glad of another set of eyes.' Nicolaus spoke quickly and Luna saw how he tried to hide his delight.

She laughed. 'I wonder if he will be glad when he knows it is me.'

'You could dress as a man if that would make you feel more comfortable.' She heard the humour in his voice and a flush of colour warmed her neck.

'You joke at my expense.'

'I was the only fool that day.' He turned and hung his cloak on a hook on the wall.

'Why do you say that?'

'You heard what I said about the veracity of Monte Regio's contention that Ptolemy miscalculated. You saw the reaction of the room.'

'I remember,' she said simply. 'You were passionate and honest.'

'My peers did not think so.'

Luna had no desire to shame him further; she knew what that felt like. But she'd learnt that there was power in having the courage to speak your mind.

'I think you still believe there is merit and more to investigate in what Monte Regio found: that the Moon's distance from Earth does not change every month.'

He arched his eyebrows in astonishment and she held her breath. Then his expression dropped into a look of such appreciation that she felt its warmth against her heart like a hug. She smiled and shrugged her shoulders to lighten the intensity of his stare. 'Don't let the reaction of others thwart your focus.'

'I believe we are equally intrigued by the motions of the planets,' he said, sitting to remove the outer cover of his boots. 'For what could be more beautiful than the heavens, which contain all beautiful things?'

Luna enjoyed his turn of phrase. 'How does your private work progress?'

'I have more crazy ideas than I care to reveal, all jostling for space within my head, but there's been little time to consider my assumptions. The professor keeps me busy, though I plan on taking rooms for myself in town for a while so I can pursue my own investigations and study here at the villa under Domenico's guidance.'

'I hope you don't shy away from your investigations.'

'Sometimes I think it is a madness to question the great and wondrous Ptolemy, but in one area his technique violates the principles of perfect circular motions. It just does not hold true when scrutinised.'

'Yet Ptolemy's model is accepted.'

'Of course! He is the most outstanding of astronomers and using his tables allows us to approximate the position of any planet at any time. So we choose to overlook the mishap, but how can any sphere rotate uniformly about an off-centre axis?' He shook his head. 'My peers ridicule me.'

'You must ignore the critics.'

'And risk the scorn to which I would expose myself on account of the novelty and incomprehensibility of my ideas?' He jumped up and paced to the doors, running his hands through his hair in frustration, then returned and sat beside Luna again. 'We have both seen the devastating consequences of putting forward ideas that might be considered heretical. I do not know that I am strong enough.'

'You must be,' she said passionately, reaching for his hands. 'For no one else will speak for you. It seems to me that nature sets us these challenges to astound and disrupt our thinking. You are justified in your statement and cannot stop there. What of Aristarchus's work? What if he was right and the errors in the predictions about the heavens could be attributed to a displacement of the Earth from its central position?' Luna stopped to breathe. She was still holding Nicolaus's hands and dropped them. The burning in her belly started again. It fired her heart as well as her mind. 'I see the logic in investigating this and I know you do too, so fortify yourself against the judgement of your critics. That is the only way you can free your mind to consider all the possibilities.'

'You astonish me!' He laughed and grasped her hand. 'As I returned this afternoon, I stopped to rest beneath the same fruit trees where we first met and thought how wild you seemed that day, with your skirts billowing and hair loose. How beautiful …' Then he reached out and stroked her cheek, and it was Luna's turn to be surprised but she lifted her face towards him, pulled by the same inexorable force as the motion of a heavenly sphere. She rested her hand upon his that held her face, and felt in that moment more connected to this man than any other person in her life.

*

When the daylight began to ebb, the professor, Nicolaus and Luna set off on the same goat trail where the three had first met. In the distance, the lilac sunset deepened. A rabbit skittered across their path and then another. Luna walked more carefully, though she was keen to keep up. The air smelt damp and earthy. Nicolaus was a few steps ahead, carrying wooden rods in the pack on his back. He turned to her and, as on that first day's meeting, broke into a smile that drew her to him.

An owl swooped over them, leaving the touch of its winged soaring upon Luna's cheek. It was near dark.

'We will stop here.' The professor dropped his satchel and started unpacking.

Luna turned her face upwards. 'It's extraordinary to think what is about to happen.'

'A brilliant view, isn't it?' Nicolaus came and stood beside her.

'It's amazing. I can still see the red eye of Taurus; that much is the same.'

'It's all the same, just where you're standing has changed.'

Turning full circle, Luna saw the Milky Way spread east in a shimmering mist. She followed Nicolaus to a spot where they sat upon a thin rug.

'We still have some time to wait,' he said and handed her a flagon of wine. She drank.

The professor was setting up his instruments. Nicolaus left Luna and went over to assist him and she watched him lug the tall wooden rod to the demarcated space on the grass and drop it into the shallow hole he'd dug on one of his earlier expeditions. He made it firm and secure before pulling down the hinged bar at the top and attaching it to the third arm now extended at an angle from halfway up the wooden rod, so that there formed a large triangle shape. Then he carefully laid out a quill and ink pot on a wooden board he'd carried in his satchel. He placed a small book on the board too. When he'd finished, he ambled slowly back and flopped down beside Luna again.

'It's all ready. And now we wait.'

They watched as the professor, deep in concentration, choose a rocky outcrop at a distance from them on which to sit and wait.

'How long before it begins?' she asked.

'It has already, though till the Moon is high it is difficult to see the entirety. There's a lot of patience in astronomy.'

Luna sat comfortably. The evening had darkened and there were shadows now where earlier had been trees and hills. Something rustled in the grass.

'Did you hear that? My ears have taken over when my eyes can no longer see.' Luna pushed herself farther onto the rug.

'It's only a mouse, I imagine. You get used to curious visitors in the hours of waiting.' Nicolaus took off his cloak and wrapped it round Luna's shoulders as he spoke. He offered her another swig of the flagon. The wine warmed her throat.

'You told the professor you didn't want to look at the stars. What made you change your mind?'

Luna was glad of the cover of dark. 'Time, curiosity …' she began, then her voice died out.

'I'm pleased you did, whatever the reason.'

An urge to stay with him here beneath the stars took hold of Luna. She felt it dangerously strong. He didn't move either and when she felt able, Luna flicked her eyes his way. Nicolaus was watching her too.

'I wanted to study astronomy, back when I was still a hopeful student in Florence, but that was before everything changed.' Her voice sounded like another's in the dark. 'After I heard you speak at the professor's lecture, I went away thinking your notion that one flaw could justify reviewing the rest of Ptolemy was not unreasonable.'

She felt him shift in the grass beside her.

'I've been working on my ideas, you know, even though I tell everyone I'm not.'

'But you are telling me.' Luna smiled even though she knew he couldn't see her.

'It seems easier out here and I feel comfortable talking to you.'

Luna dug her chin into the sweet warmth of the cloak, realising that it was him she could smell in its muskiness. They sat in silence, listening to the sounds of small animals scurrying from nocturnal hunters and the tick of insects in the grass. The ground was cold and Luna's boots were already damp.

She wondered how long they'd sat there when an owl hooted. Nicolaus stood then and craned his neck. He turned and helped her up.

'There, it is begun.'

Luna stood beside him. She couldn't see the professor at all. As the minutes passed, the fullness of the Moon ebbed. Luna's scalp prickled at the shifting hues. She took her eyes from the sight for only a moment. Nicolaus was looking at her.

'Watch now,' he whispered and she turned back to the view before them. Slowly, steadily, the Moon crossed into the Earth's shadow. That was the science of it, but there was so much more to be felt in the living of this moment. The Moon dimmed and its fullness ebbed with steady progress. Even the animals had quieted. There was only the Moon and her body anchored to this hill, whilst so far above, deep into the fifth essence that was the Lord's house, the Moon shifted farther into shadow. Luna swayed, mesmerised, and reached out a hand, which Nicolaus took. They watched for the moment when the Moon would disappear into darkness. But something else happened that left Luna gasping.

'It is as if it's sprinkled with a bonfire's burning embers.' Her voice was hushed. Nicolaus squeezed her hand.

'A Moon of blood red,' the professor intoned, as he came closer in the dark. 'A full lunar eclipse. Rare indeed.'

Nicolaus dropped her hand at the sound of the professor's voice and went to stand with him. Luna couldn't feel her feet, so cold was she, and her cheeks stung, but she didn't want to move. Even breathing seemed an intrusion on nature at that moment. She stayed where she was, staring up in wonder at the Moon, no longer pale but daubed with a rosy hue she'd not thought possible.

Nearby the men were writing down measurements. Ptolemy had tracked the Moon through three eclipses. It was written in the *Almagest*. That's how he'd determined its motion and size; the Moon appeared larger when it was closest to Earth and smaller at its most distant point. She thought this would be a good exercise for Nicolaus to replicate, to test his suspicions of error, if he could be assured of another two eclipses of similar duration and geometry.

'Let's start back to the house and a warm fire,' the professor said after some time, his voice as stark a sound in the dead of night as the snap of a twig underfoot. It brought Luna back to her senses and she turned to see that the pair had their satchels ready and were waiting to depart.

The walk back was slower and Luna was numbed with cold but she didn't notice her discomfort. A burning need had started in her stomach.

The next morning her walking stick was propped against the wall with mud still stuck to it. Luna lay in bed and thought about the night-time expedition and the extraordinary sight they'd witnessed. Her neck flushed hot as she remembered Nicolaus sitting so close. She pressed her palms into her eyes until bright spots flashed behind her closed lids. Then the image of the blood-red Moon appeared, so wondrous, and she felt Nicolaus reaching for her hand. Her mind had fired too, just as the Moon turned red; she'd not been able to stop it.

When she was dressed, she took a cup of wine and sat by the fireplace in the main hall, thinking about the idea that had come to her last night about replicating Ptolemy's method of studying three eclipses. The moment she thought of suggesting it to Nicolaus, her whole body flushed hot. She listened to the crackle of the logs, calming herself, lost in a reverie.

Nicolaus found her there before much time had passed. 'Did you enjoy watching your first eclipse?' he asked.

She nodded, thinking how well the smile on his lips matched the glint of pleasure in his eyes.

'In another few weeks we will observe the Moon passing in front of the star Aldebaran. When it is a star in the Moon's shadow, we call it an occult. This one will be intriguing.'

'How so?' Luna asked.

'Watch it with me and you will see,' he answered. 'From the top of the professor's tower.'

This time when she felt the fire in her belly, Luna didn't hesitate. 'I would very much like that.'

CHAPTER TWENTY-FIVE

March 1497

Luna would look back on that first night when she'd witnessed a lunar eclipse with Nicolaus as the most precious of all her star-gazing encounters. As the Moon reappeared whole from behind the Earth's shadow, in the hushed silence of the night's last hours, she'd determined never again to turn away from her own passion for the science of what she'd seen and resolved to be brave and outspoken.

In the week that followed, she sought out a quiet moment with Elisabetta and spoke to her about declining her place in the convent and staying on at the estate instead. To her delight, Elisabetta pulled her into a hug as fierce as her accompanying exclamation of approval. Luna leant against her shoulder for far too long, breathing in her friend's loving acceptance. Next she spoke to Livia, who initially frowned with suspicion at such unprovoked generosity from their hosts, till Luna led her to see Elisabetta. Luna had become like a daughter to her, the lady explained, before asking Livia to join their household as Luna's maid.

And so it was that Leonarda Lunetta found a new home.

Luna lay in bed, playing over in her mind the shock and then delight on Livia's face when Elisabetta had offered her a place in their household. There was a soft knock at her bedchamber door. Luna let out a gentle exclamation, no louder than the puff of air escaping from the pillow she pressed against. Then she rose hurriedly and dressed. Nicolaus had come to collect her. It was just past the fourth hour of the night. The occult of Aldebaran would soon begin. He was wearing a deep green cloak and she put on her walking cloak, for the tower was cold at night. No fire would be lit and only the one candle was allowed for note taking, else their vision of the stars be spoilt.

She hovered at the base of the stairs then set her foot firmly on the lowest step and followed Nicolaus up, breathing heavily with the climb and expectation of what lay ahead. Excitement tingled in her fingertips.

As she rounded the final bend, slowing from the exertion, she saw the black night across one side of the room and gasped, for it seemed there was no shield between the room and the elements. Where normally a wall would block much of the view, there was an opening so large it let in the sky. Heavy doors framed either side and a long, slim balcony ran its length.

The professor was already preparing for the lunar event. The room was dimly lit and instruments and papers cluttered the desk and lay spread across the floor. He set down his quill and pushed back his chair, beckoning them in. On a smaller round table beside where he worked was a bronze astrolabe. It looked exactly like the one in the illustration in the *Almagest*, only dulled with use. Luna wanted to touch the rings and investigate the detailed wording on each thick band, but she stood politely and waited. Books were neatly ranged upon a set of shelves built into the far wall.

'I'm glad that you decided to join us this evening.' The professor smiled warmly at Luna.

'I'm honoured to be here.'

'Come, stand by me.' Nicolaus motioned to her to join him and together they gazed out across the expanse of night. A cold wind cut into Luna's eyes. She was glad of the heavy cloak. The distant hills were mounds in the dark and the line between land and sky was blurred. Nicolaus stood behind her and she knew with one small step backwards she'd be resting against him. He stretched an arm past her shoulder and even though there was a good inch of air between them, she felt the heat of his skin on her cheek. She looked to where he pointed.

'Do you see the burning spot in the first quarter of the sky, the brilliant star of the Hyades, Palilicium?'

She nodded. 'That is Aldebaran, renamed such by the Arabs. How long before it begins?'

'The Moon is higher up,' the professor said, pointing. 'I predict before the midnight hour, though it is an inexact science.'

'Let us pray the night stays clear and we get no misty vapours,' Nicolaus said.

Luna dug her hands into her pockets whilst she waited. Her breath hung like a taper's smoke; she blew again and watched it disappear. There was a tension in the air that caught each of them alike. The Moon's dark edge crept towards the star as the night progressed. Presently Nicolaus went to stand by a round table that was placed in front of the expansive view of the sky.

'This is an exciting night. We do not often see the brightest star in the Taurus constellation obscured,' the professor said.

Luna stood back respectfully when he placed his parallactic instrument on the round table where Nicolaus waited. It was similar to the triquetrum they'd used in the field, but much smaller. The professor rotated the sighting rod in preparation and peered through the eyepiece.

'Fie, it happens!' he proclaimed. 'See where Aldebaran applies to the tenebrous part of the lunar body?'

The sky was dark and there were many spots of light in the distant night, but Luna kept her eyes on the brightest one. She steadied herself with a hand on the table where Nicolaus stood and watched as Aldebaran seemed to disappear behind the Moon. She heard his breathing and felt her own match his.

'It is already hiding in the Moon's horns,' Luna said.

'It is closer certainly to the western horn, by a third of its width,' Nicolaus added.

Then miraculously it reappeared, and was gone again a moment later. It was as if the bull blinked at them.

The professor put his eye to the instrument again and called out the timed positions to Nicolaus, who wrote them down swiftly. Luna didn't move; her face was turned to the sky, mesmerised by the magic of the flashing spot of light, so far away. She swayed again and felt that other girl in a different life come forward. In the moment of connection, she spoke before even realising the words had flown from her mouth.

'We can test Ptolemy's mathematical model of the Moon's motion with the observations you are recording.'

Nicolaus looked up at Luna, his eyes wide and his brow furrowed. He nodded, but did not speak, turning back to the page and scribbling notes upon it. Luna waited for the professor to censure her. Instead he gestured for her to join him and stood back so that she could put her eye to the instrument.

'Leonarda, if you are staying on here at the villa, I would also like it to be as a student of mine, alongside Nicolaus.'

Luna stared at the professor. 'What is that you say?'

'I am offering you a place here as my student.'

Luna felt a surge of energy course through her. Snippets of what she'd written in the fateful parchment came back to her and she hurried over to Nicolaus.

'I have an idea of something to contribute,' she said, reaching for a quill. Nicolaus stood back so she could add her notes to his paper. His hand rested on her shoulder and he read whilst her hand flew across the page. When she'd finished, Luna stood and stretched her back and together they turned once more to the view of the heavens. She had much to read to catch up to Nicolaus and she planned on doing just that, and more. She must write to Friar Bartholomeo and tell him that she'd accepted the Novaras' invitation to live with them and that she would be studying astronomy under the professor. He'd be gladdened to know she was to become a student once again. She would write that she was happy here and had no need of a nun's habit to feel the warmth of the Lord's light.

The wind had dropped so that all was silent. The sky beyond the window was dark as the winter's soil, spotted with a million stars, and the full Moon hung high above them. Luna stepped forward so she could better see Aldebaran reappear from its hiding spot, bright as before, to lead the Moon across the sky.

ACKNOWLEDGEMENTS

Thank you to my family and friends and to everyone who encouraged and supported me while I wrote this book. We are living in strange times, through years that none of us will forget, which makes creating art in any form harder to realise, and more essential than ever. I'm so grateful that I am part of this creative community, that I get to write and be published; it's a 'pinch me' moment every day.

I am ever grateful to my publisher, Jo Mackay, for your faith in me and patience. Huge thanks to the dedicated, wonderful team at HQ and HarperCollins for your ongoing support and for turning my story into such a beautiful book. Jo Butler, editor extraordinaire, I loved working with you.

Enormous gratitude to my agent Pippa Masson at Curtis Brown. Your wise counsel and positivity keep me going.

Thanks to the rest of the most excellent team at Curtis Brown Australia.

Thank you to astronomer Associate Professor John O'Byrne from Sydney University, who was generous with his time and expertise. It was utterly fascinating to be able to look at a view of the night sky over Florence from 1496.

To my early readers, thank you to Kevin Ralphs for your honest, critical eye and ongoing friendship and support from afar. Thank you to my mother, Karen Harcourt, who reads with the eye of a copyeditor and the heart of a super fan.

Thank you to the booksellers and independent bookshops who do such an amazing job of keeping books and the joy of reading alive. Someone is reading my book because of what you do and that's priceless. A special wave to my favourite little corner of the world, Gertrude & Alice Bookstore in Bondi. To be asked about how my manuscript is going when I buy a coffee each morning is just the best boost—small acts of kindness from some of the biggest hearts in the business.

I have a group of funny, gorgeous, loyal friends, and it is because of their company that I am not entirely a hermit. Thank you, dear friends, for reminding me to laugh.

My family is the bedrock of my world. Love and gratitude to Phoebe, Sean, Alex, Faith, Lily, Harry, and to Rebecca, Ed, Louise and William and to my mum, you are amazing.

I have three gloriously unique children; Oliver, Clare and Zoe, thank you for respecting my work, giving me peace and quiet when I ask, and for believing in me. I love you.

Finally, to my readers, thank you to everyone who read my first book and I hope you enjoy reading this one.

talk about it

Let's talk about books.

Join the conversation:

facebook.com/harlequinaustralia

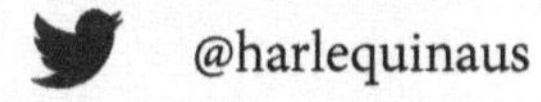
@harlequinaus

@harlequinaus

harpercollins.com.au/hq

If you love reading and want to know about our authors and titles, then let's talk about it.